Mandragon

Mandragon

R. M. KOSTER

W·W·NORTON & COMPANY
New York   London

Library of Congress Cataloging in Publication Data
Koster, R. M., 1934–
    Mandragon / by R. M. Koster.
      p.   cm.
  –T.p. verso.
    ISBN 0-393-30649-6
    I. Title.
  PS3561.084M36   1989
  813'.54—dc20   89–9304

ISBN 0-393-30649-6

W. W. Norton & Company, Inc., 500 Fifth Avenue, New York, N.Y. 10110
W. W. Norton & Company Ltd., 37 Great Russell Street, London WC1B 3NU

1 2 3 4 5 6 7 8 9 0

For Otilita, Ricky, and Lily

Preface

This is the third book of a trilogy. Like *The Prince* and *The Dissertation*, its setting is (mainly) the imaginary Central American Republic of Tinieblas, its subject is (largely) politics, its chief character is a particular sort of leader. Certain characters are shared among the three books. There are, besides, thematic and structural linkages. Each book, however, tells its own story and may be read independently of the others.

Mandragon is the shortest of the three, the simplest in design, and the least populous in characters, but it gave me the most trouble—perhaps, because I didn't give it proper respect, knowing at the start how it would end (which wasn't the case with *The Prince* or *The Dissertation*) and that it would be relatively short. Whatever the case, the book taught me a lesson: it fought me every page, for a long time was winning, and proved a canny, tough, and ruthless foe.

What I like best in *Mandragon* are the Rotunda of Astounding Miracles in Amichevole's circus and the two Ticamalan customs men in Chapter 24. The drought, also, is well realized. What I find most interesting, however, are the visions it extracted from me, at once clear and skewed. I found myself writing about the holy man as political leader. I also found myself writing about a billionnaire who finds refuge in my Central American Republic of Tinieblas, a refuge he gets because they want to shake him down for money. I had no idea why I was doing that, except that it helped me get a more important character back to Tinieblas and that it was fun. I made him a kind of Howard Hughes figure. One of the things I had him do was set up a modern dress version of the Garden of the Assassins as described by Marco Polo when he touches on the Nizari Shiites in thirteenth-century Persia. Okay, I finished the book in September 1978, and during 1979 I discovered what I was really doing. First Khomeini takes over, the holy man as political leader, and finally the Shah takes refuge in Panama where they try to shake him down. I had a vision, at once clear and skewed, that previewed events in Iran. I have no way at all to account for it, but I find it interesting.

Which brings me to the relationship between my trilogy and what God, history, fate, or sadistic happenstance has been doing with the Republic of Panama where I live. I didn't understand the relationship until recently. When I wrote the books, I wasn't writing consciously about Panama. I was making up a country that was a *bouillabaisse* of Central America and the Caribbean, a soup with bits of different things in it of the sort that's called *sancocho* in Panama. Tinieblas, my imaginary country, had little bits of Panama but it wasn't Panama as Panama was during 1969–1978 when I was writing the books. Now I know that what I was really doing, without knowing it, was describing a vision I had of Panama's future, the dictatorship that currently exists here and has since, say, September 1985, when a certain person was murdered in a particularly nasty way.

I wasn't seeking topicality, however. A few years ago an interviewer from the Rio paper *O Globo* asked me if I'd written my trilogy to take advantage of the noteworthiness that Central America was (and still is) experiencing. I told her no, nothing of the sort. When I wrote my Tinieblas books, no one cared about Central America, and my great hope was (and still is) that—to paraphrase Galbraith on Southeast Asia—that Central America may somehow soon recapture the obscurity it deserves.

I didn't go to Panama looking for trouble, but Panama is where I met the twentieth century and learned there's a Chinese curse that goes, "May you live in an interesting period of history."

Anything you live intimately with for a long time—a dog, a car, a book—gets to be like a person. I feel gratitude toward *The Prince*. It didn't baby me, but it was on my side; it gave me confidence while I was writing it and, later on, my first success. I love *The Dissertation*: it gave me every pleasure generously. *Mandragon* I respect. A canny, tough, and thoroughly ruthless foe, it gave me scars. With its publication in this Norton edition, the trilogy is available in a uniform, paperback format.

A word on covers. They were done by Guillermo Trujillo, the best (to my mind) of Panama's many fine painters. Seventeen years ago he and I had workshops on the second floor of a decaying tenement off Plaza Catedral in the old quarter of Panama City—he dabbing with exemplary vigor at a dozen canvases simultaneously, painting a little on one, then moving along, I pecking languidly at yet another unpublishable novel, both of us arting away next door to each other like Marcello and Rodolfo in *La Bohème*, except that we were tormented by heat, not cold, and never (alas!) interrupted by pretty ladies. I made him promise that if I ever had a book published, he would do the cover. At the time it seemed most unlikely he would ever be called upon, but he has now fulfilled that promise not once but three times.

Gracias, Guillermo! If the wise purchaser of this elegant edition finds my words as good as your pictures, I shall be quite satisfied.

Panama, April 1989   *R.M.K.*

Note

The artist's business, akin to Mandragon's, is to put people in touch with things not readily accessible in the ordinary course of reality. The artist's method may be called controlled dreaming.

This book is the third in a series of three—the right-hand panel, as it were, of a triptych—depicting imaginary people and imaginary events in the imaginary Republic of Tinieblas. How fine my frenzy was, how well I've turned these unknown things to shapes, the reader may judge for himself—favorably, I hope—but I dreamed them up.

R.M.K.

El quinto angel derramó su copa sobre el trono de la bestia; y su reino se cubrió de tinieblas, y mordian de dolor sus lenguas.

—Apocalipsis 16:10

Mandragon

1

One day Mandragon toured a personal future. One day I
had a vision of myself:

*A street slopes between three-story buildings hung with
balconies. It is crowded with brown-faced people. Young
men in undershirts, in T-shirts blazoned with soft-drink
logos, in brightly colored sport shirts. Older men in flowing
white four-pocket* guayaberas, *in linen suits. Girls and
women in thin dresses, in slacks and brightly colored
blouses, some with heads kerchiefed and their hair in roll-
ers. The* mulato-mestizo *crowd of a Latin city.*

*They fill the walks and spill into the gutters, closing the
greater portion of both lanes so that barely a yard is clear
along the center. They push and jostle for a better vantage.
They rise on tiptoe, peer up the street into the lifting sun.
The sun roars at them from a hazy sky.*

*Above, the balconies are packed, the windows gargoyled
with thrust torsos and craned faces. Everyone peers up
along the street, which is overhung with leaning balconies
and buildings, and widens toward a plaza higher up. Bolívar
Avenue! Ciudad Tinieblas!*

Four guardias *on motorcycles lead a patrol truck down
from Plaza Cervantes. Sirens on moan, bikes weaving in
slow* S *curves, they carve a channel through the crowd.
They ride straight-backed with elbows arced at shoulder
level, and their mirror-lensed glasses, their plastic casques,*

*their shiny carapaces of black leather, give them the aspect
of gigantic bugs.*

*The patrol truck follows with its head lamps blinking in
the morning glare, its dome light whirling hysterically. The
driver glances nervously into the tumult eddying beside his
fenders, but the major beside him stares straight ahead,
arms folded over camouflage jump suit, face copper-masked
in scorn, in contempt.*

*Someone trots behind the truck, on tether. Not someone!
Mandragon! Me!*

Howls of happy hatred from the crowd.

*Handcuffed by the right wrist to the tow hitch at the rear
of the patrol truck. Trots bent over, cupping the steel ball
with both hands. Blue cotton prison shirt flaps loosely.
Laceless prison slippers slap the street. Head hangs forward,
bobs between stretched arms.*

*Behind come three tall ten-wheelers, their engines grum-
bling sternly in low gear. Soldiers sit in rows along the truck
flanks, snake-faced assassins in camouflage jump suits and
berets. The blue-black barrels of their assault rifles poke
up between their thighs.*

*Objects are flying down from the balconies and windows.
An egg splats on Mandragon's shoulder. A corncob clips
my heel. A mango fizzes by Mandragon's ear and detonates
on the floor of the patrol truck, shrapneling slime onto the
boots of the three guardias inside, sending them scooting
toward the cab to put more roof between them and incoming refuse. An old woman leans from a balcony; stretches
out wizened neck the color of charred oak; smacks mandrill
lips and spits.*

*The troop carriers roll slowly down Bolívar Avenue, the
driver of the first keeping respectful distance between his
bumper and my bum. Mandragon trots bent over. The
patrol truck guides me between jeers and curses. The cyclists weave and sway, carving a path. Down into Plaza
Inchado. Across the square and on between the Alcaldía*

and the palace. Left between the palace and Parque Mocoso. Up to the porte-cochere, where all halt.

Mandragon stands head down and panting. My shoulders produce an equine shudder. Then, while the sergeant
and two privates jump down from the rear of the patrol
truck and brace facing the palace, while the troops swarm
down from their transports and form up in three ranks,
while the major steps down from the cab and adjusts his
beret, Mandragon sinks to knees, lays face on hands on the
steel ball of the patrol-truck tow hitch. Eyes closed. Face
smeared with terror and exertion. My powers have left me.

Parque Mocoso is cordoned off with presidential guards.
They wear dress uniforms, royal purple with yellow trim,
and stand at five-yard intervals with their machine pistols
at port arms. A band, also in purple, is phalanxed just inside the park near the lead cyclist. Simón Mocoso stands on
his pedestal, his left foot slightly forward, his left hand
thrust toward the palace, his right hand grasping a green-
tinged bronze replica of the Tinieblan Declaration of Inde-
pendence. Behind stands the old tree, leafless save at its top
branches, which (now that the early haze is burning off)
are drenched in sunlight. The rest of the tree, and all but
the top of the seawall well behind it, are in the shadow of the
palace.

A pulley has been rigged on the first branch, about
twenty feet up. A looped cable dangles from it. The cable
runs down and back from the pulley to a winch on the
front end of a Jeep parked to one side. In the Jeep sits a
guardia in olive-green fatigues and a black hood.

The seawall is crammed with spectators. Others, well-
dressed men and ladies, fill a grandstand set up near the
back of the Alcaldía. Beyond it is a panel truck with a
television camera tripodded on its roof, and beyond that
a police wagon with the first and last of Mandragon's followers. Five girls in prison smocks who clutch their fingers
in the wire caging.

Three officers stand at ease on the balcony above the porte-cochere, stand at ease in dress purples and high-peaked caps, in faces sculpted from dried dog shit. Two stories above them, at the roof of the palace, a large purple-green-and-yellow Tinieblan tricolor droops limply, flutters once in a light puff of breeze, then droops again.

Off beyond the seawall, pelicans wheel and swoop above the shimmering Pacific.

The major has got his beret set at a properly rakish, military jaunt. He steps round the patrol truck. Halts, comes to attention, and salutes. The officers on the balcony acknowledge. One of them turns back to the door and sticks his head inside. Draws his head out and nods it at his colleagues, who turn to face each other and salute while he, saluting, steps back and swings the door open. The major braces, bellows a command. Hands and weapons snap up in salute, bandmaster flourishes baton, musicians lift instruments. Loudspeakers crackle above the grandstand, hum and then blare forth:

"SEÑORAS Y SEÑORES! LA EXCELENTISIMA SEÑORA PRESIDENTA DE LA REPÚBLICA! DOÑA ANGELA DE SANCUDO!"

Fanfare of trumpets. All rise in the grandstand. All stand, looking toward the palace. All except Mandragon. Mandragon remains kneeling, face on hands.

A woman steps onto the balcony, a beautiful woman, more like an old-time queen or priestess than any modern head of state. Yellow hair and milk-white, chalk-white skin; pale eyes that seem much older than the rest of her. Her gait is graceful and her carriage stately. Black square-necked, long-sleeved dress; black fan. Stands at the parapet of the balcony. Opens her fan and holds it at her breast. Looks down at Mandragon. She smiles faintly, a smile both tender and derisive. Then, as the band takes up the Tinieblan anthem, she lifts her eyes toward the distant pelicans, and holds her gaze there through the solemn march.

When the last note of the anthem fades, the three officers drop their salute. One moves a chair front and center, and the woman sits. The major bellows again. Hands and weapons drop; musicians lower instruments; people in the grandstand sit. The major about-faces and shouts again. Assault troops to port arms, face right and left and split into two bodies, trot past the presidential guards and take stations opposite the grandstand and the seawall. They level rifles at the spectators and stare forward with the alert immobility of Dobermans.

The major marches to the rear of the patrol truck. Dips into the breast pocket of his jump suit. Plucks out a key. He tosses it to the sergeant, who catches it in both hands and turns to fit it in the cuff hooked to the tow hitch. He opens the cuff and hands the key back to the major. He draws the cuff, and my hand, behind my back. He seizes Mandragon's left forearm and pulls it back. He snaps the empty cuff on my left wrist. Then, holding the chain linking the two cuffs, he pulls me up. Mandragon offers no resistance. Stands, head down and shoulders slumped. Lick my lips as though in thirst. My powers have surely left me.

The two privates take Mandragon each by a bicep. They march me off into the park.

The major balls his fist and punches it twice into the air. Drivers scramble up into their cabs; cyclists leap onto their bikes and stomp their starters. The convoy pulls away, swings left behind the south wing of the palace. The major marches off into the park, followed at two paces by the sergeant.

The two privates have marched Mandragon to the tree, have turned me round so that I face the palace, so that the cable loop hangs just behind my back. The major arrives. He steps behind and drops the loop over Mandragon's head. He pulls the cable till the steel fits snugly. Then he and the sergeant step four paces to Mandragon's right front and come to attention. Major salutes.

All this while, Mandragon, that Mandragon over there under the tree, has stood with head bowed, blinking quickly, licking lips and rubbing them together, looking afraid. Now, as the major lifts his hand in salute, I look up. I bare my teeth, which are very white against my dark-brown face. I look directly at the woman on the balcony.

She flicks her fan closed. She holds it at arm's length and flicks it up. She draws it back and opens it against her breast, smiling faintly.

Slow roll of drums echoed by palace and Alcaldía. The major drops his salute and shouts a command. The Jeep starter whines. The motor catches and revs. The privates release Mandragon's biceps and step back. The crowd grows still. The girls in the police wagon begin keening. The gears of the Jeep grate. The motor races. The winch turns. Mandragon rises.

2

That's how I saw it, that's how it will be. My second sight was always twenty-twenty.

I will be handcuffed by my right wrist, not my left. The cob will clip my heel and not my ankle. My shoulders will produce an equine shudder. I'll stand with my head bowed, blinking quickly, licking dry lips, looking afraid. And Angela will give the signal with a little black fan. Not with her empty hand or just by nodding. She'll flick me to a mechanized strangling with her fan.

Spectators will gape at the gesture. Folks watching at home over TV will remark its aptness and originality. Flicking a bug off, you know. But I'll not be surprised. That's how I saw it, that's how it will be. Tomorrow morning.

I couldn't turn the visions on or off. I couldn't aim them. All I could do was suffer them when they came on me. But they were always clear and accurate. Twenty-twenty.

It's the precision that makes all the difference. There are all sorts of charlatans about who'll daub you a rough sketch of what's to come. Some use computers. Now and then one or another blunders near truth, fumbles out the gross outline, but that doesn't make him any less a charlatan. The mark of your true seer is that his visions are precise in every detail.

Futuretours really. Journeys forward. Mandragon would be snatched from the here and now, thrust to the there and then. To an embankment near Tokyo, for instance, where three weeks after I witnessed it two packed commuter trains performed a *Guinness Book of World Records* crash. To Madrid for the levitation of an admiral. Geyser of flame from the pavement, deafening blast. Limousine sailing upside down above the rooftops. Month or so later the event took place and made its hubbub, and I found out where I'd been and who I'd seen blown up. And to various capitals and hinterlands for what participants will call the end of the world. Which strictly speaking has begun already, though it's still in the foreplay stage. Mandragon has viewed aspects of the consummation.

Crops will cease growing in exhausted soil. Cities will explode and flame to cinder. Spectacular mutations will be spawned. I mean web-footed rats the size of collies, and babies like dolls, with no sex organs or excreting holes. Mandragon's seen them! I've watched one feed upon the other!

Billions will die. I've heard them shrieking. I've watched them trudge bewildered till they fall. Earth will be cleansed.

And one day I was flung here to Tinieblas, for a sneak preview of my execution.

Minus the finale, so I'm missing some details. Will I do an energetic dance? Will my gawps and twitches be properly comic? Will they last long enough to satisfy my public? Will the tongue poke from the left or right side of the mouth? No answers to such questions for a few hours, and I'll probably be too occupied to note them. I don't feel deprived, though. The gross outline's sufficient: strung up and strangled. I'd just as soon not know the fine points, and in any case, once the feet leave the ground, events are commonplace.

Miracles were once commonplace for Mandragon. Mandragon sweated marvels and crapped wonders. Mandragon pissed amazements. Then my powers left me, and the commonplace closed in. No miracles tomorrow morning. Mandragon's powers are gone, my gifts have left me.

3

Semireclined on a sea-green chaise longue, manacled hands clasped at my navel. Studying the far corner of the ceiling to give the closed-circuit cameras a three-quarter shot and a profile. Or insect-flipping over with my manacled hands crossed at my chest, fetusing my head in and my knees up to give the cameras blue cotton prison shirt and trousers, woolly crown, but of Mandragon's flesh only pink foot soles. I've had my trial, such as it was, and heard my sentence. I've had my supper, the little of it I touched. Nothing left except the hours until morning, fetusing my head in and my knees up, then flipping back over, semireclined.

They've put me in the prison V.I.P. suite, two rooms with bath, once the prison commandant's quarters, refurbished hastily eight years ago for Elena Delfi. A clique of Civil Guard majors deposed Alejo Sancudo a week after he took office, and arrested everybody, even his movie star daughter-in-law. Brought her up here and looted the stores for furnishings. Drapes to cover the barred windows. Queen-sized double bed and this chaise longue. Ornate armoire, possibly antique. Dressing table cretonned in pink toile, with stool upholstered in pink velvet. Two glossily lacquered Hong Kong night tables, red with black-and-gold dragons, and in the sitting room a blue silk brocade sofa, a bulbous imitation leather chair, and a teak table carved with Hindu gods. The only unifying theme is vulgarity, and when they released her and gave her passage to Miami, La Delfi accused the Guardia of torture by interior decoration. But questions of taste aside, these have to be the most luxurious prison accommodations in the hemisphere. Excessively air-conditioned. TV cameras mounted near the ceiling. Lights on day and night. And my hands are cuffed. But, on the whole, very soft confinement for Mandragon.

At Angela's suggestion, I assume—or at least that's how I had it in the daydream I invented yesterday. I've lost my gifts for managing the world, so now I daydream, like everybody else.

In its final, polished version my daydream opened with a fumbling of keys outside the door. Then two sharp raps, and it's flung open. Her military aide, a handsome captain whose wavy hair has been reprieved from clipping, takes one step in, clicks boot heels, and salutes.

"*La Excelentísima Señora,*" etc., etc.

Angela swishes by him, flicks him out.

After much experimental modeling I have dressed her in a dark jersey pants suit and gold sandals. Tinkle of gold bracelets on her left wrist; dime-sized gold hoop earrings; yellow hair bunned. Looks like the pampered second wife of a French doctor (or Swiss investment banker, or Swedish industrialist) arrived at a young actor's (or poet's, or radical agitator's) furnished room for a quick poke—the sort who'd say, "No, darling, I'll be on top this afternoon or I'll muss my hair." Imperious enough but much too glamorous for head of state in a republic. Impossible to believe she's the age she is. I *know*, but when I see her, even in daydream, I can't believe it, unless I look only at her pale-grey eyes.

She motions me not to get up and gives the following little speech:

"I'm sorry, darling, but I've signed the order. And I'm to give the signal. You mustn't take it personally. It hasn't anything to do with me. The colonels want you hanged, and they're in charge.

"Oh, they're letting me stay on, but only if I do what they tell me. If I refused, they'd simply toss me out and find somebody else. It wouldn't save you, and empty gestures are so immature. No use our both being ruined, is there? And as *presidenta* I can help a little." She waves her hand to indicate my lodgings. "This is so much nicer than a cell downstairs."

That's as far as I went with it. I didn't even do her exit. I'd spent a lot of time revising, and doing speeches of my own—all of which, in the end, I edited out—and when I'd got the polished work up to the part about her helping me, I stopped composing and amused myself reacting to her visit, as if it had actually taken place. Signed the order, but it wasn't personal! Doing what she can! Lucky Mandragon! So coddled, thanks to her, I'll scarcely feel the cable bite my throat!

But why assume that she's concerned at all, or that they put me here on her suggestion? Why flatter myself that much? And why be angry? Assume she sold me. Assume that she's gone over to the colonels. Assume, in short, that she looks after Angela—adroit and perfectly timed leaps to whoever's strongest, which she makes so gracefully (out of great talent and long practice) that it's absurd to let anger cloud their elegance. Enjoy the spectacle, join the applause. Always performs with verve, and so assume she demanded her presidential rights:

"*I'll* sign the order, thank you! And *I'll* give the signal!"

No need to make her change for that scene. The outfit I gave her yesterday will do smartly. Angela and Guadaña at the palace, in her state office. Sits on the high-backed, intricately carved, Spanish colonial chair that (for its thronishness) she ordered brought up from the dining room when she took office. Left hand in her lap; right thumb and index finger at her chin; legs crossed neatly, right leg over her left knee. Her right foot nods slowly, pretty toes peeking out from lamé sandal. Otherwise immobile. French window behind her. Afternoon sun flows in to bathe her hair.

Colonel Guadaña, whom she has not asked to take a chair, stands opposite her. In khakis, short-sleeved shirt and twill trousers—the uniform he will still be wearing eight hours later at Mandragon's trial. He has removed neither his cap nor thuggish sneer. His rooster chest is thrust forward arrogantly. His pockmarked cheeks are thinly glazed with sweat. His pupils float in semen-white puddles of lust.

"We've decided to execute your friend Mandragon."

Angela shrugs.

"In public. To put a stop to all this superstition."

"Probably the wisest course for you. But why tell me about it?'

"Well, you're the constitutional president."

"And you're not up to abolishing the constitution, not just now. You'd rather observe the forms, isn't that so?"

Guadaña nods. "It's easier that way."

"Then, Colonel, take your little hat off, use correct address, and pretend you have some class!"

Starts angrily, then smiles and nods. Takes cap from pig-bristly pate and, holding it tucked between his forearm and his flank, comes to an easy posture of attention. "At your orders, Excellency."

"Thank you. Now, what about this execution?"

"By hanging. Day after tomorrow in the park out front. The trial will take place sometime tonight, but I've already signed the order."

"*I'll* sign the order, thank you! And *I'll* give the signal!"

"Perfect! I mean, uh, very well, Your Excellency." Guadaña's smile is at once conspiratorial and lecherous. "We're treating Mandragon well, by the way."

"That's your affair."

"Well, we're going to do it in public. We want the prisoner fresh."

Right! Right! Going to trot me through town, so I'd best be fresh! Going to hang me without a drop, and if I'm fresh

I'll kick longer! Who'll watch the TV reruns if Mandragon simply droops there like a rag?

Oh, yes! Mandragon's going to do a lovely dance! They're keeping me fresh for it! Plenty of kicking! I can prophesy that much, though I've lost the gift of futuretouring, though it wasn't included in the vision I had last year!

4

I was living in New York, in a loft on Prince Street, with five white Anglo girls. I had renamed them Nightandmist, Todo Confort Moderno, Princess Paloma, Apple, and Full Moons. My tribe.

I let Nightandmist keep her job in a Park Avenue cosmetics salon, but as she was excessively vain of her clear skin and cameo features, had her mask her face each night with ashes from the potbellied stove. Made up this way, and with her boyish breasts (of which she was excessively ashamed) exposed, she also acolyted in the preparations for my journeys of descent.

Todo Confort was the daughter of a Cleveland surgeon. She wasn't ugly, just plain and plump and careless of her grooming. She wasn't spoiled, just self-indulgent and accustomed to material abundance. I took her out of college and sent her to work in a massage parlor, one of the plush kind that have their cubicles done up in fancy decor. The job paid no salary, but gave a girl many chances to earn tips. It pared the baby fat from Confort's spirit. It enabled her to contribute to the tribe's support.

Todo Confort was never to use money, not even for subway fare. She was never to question a client's request, or hesitate in the slightest to fulfill it, or quibble at the sum he offered her. She was not to think of herself as an employee, but as a slave on loan to each successive client. Not even as a slave, but as a docile beast. Not even as a beast, but as an instrument of physical convenience. She was not to feel pleasure or disgust. She was not to prefer one client to another. She was required, before leaving the loft, to pass inspection on her personal appearance. Upon returning, she was required to make a full confession of all her acts and sentiments while at work. Mandragon would assign her proper penance.

One night, while I was hearing Todo Confort's confession, a trance came on me. I saw a girl about fifteen walking in Bleecker Street. Barefoot. Wearing a raincoat, with nothing on underneath. She had been beaten, but she was singing. It lasted only a few seconds.

I interrupted Todo Confort in midsentence and sent her out. She returned in about ten minutes with the girl I'd seen, a soft girl, dovishly shy, gigglishly feebleminded from repeated beatings on the head. Her face was welted, and her hair matted in blood. I bathed her wounds and healed them with touches of my fingertips. I told her she was Princess Paloma, Eagle-King's youngest, dearest daughter. Hawk-Devil had stolen her in childhood, but now she was safe. I told my tribe to love her and protect her.

Princess Paloma had no duties, except to let herself be loved, and to accompany me on journeys of ascent.

Mandragon puts on a cap covered in black feathers. Struts about. Short and slight, yet muscular and agile. Piercing black eyes and skin the color and apparent texture of a highly polished black-walnut panel. Body suggestive of ferocity—a jungle cat, a leopard or tigrillo. *Physically imposing beyond its size.*

Mandragon hops onto the windowsill and perches. Blinking. Face jerking left and right.

The girls heat water on the stove. They bathe Princess Paloma in the large, gryphon-footed tub that stands, naked of plumbing, at the low end of the sloping plank floor. They brush her hair and plait it. They suck her breasts. They lave her thighs and stomach with their tongues.

Princess Paloma stands tranced in regal calm.

The girls dress Princess Paloma in a white brocade robe. They lead her to the center of the loft, under the skylight. They sit down about her in a circle.

Mandragon leaps from the windowsill into the circle. Dances about Paloma. Croaks and caws, flaps arms and hops in air. Paloma's eyes roll upward till only the whites show. Her head lolls to one side, she starts to fall. Mandragon's arms sweep upward, and as Paloma collapses backward, her legs rise. She floats in air, back arched and arms flung outward, as though floating in calm water. She rises slowly until her waist is level with Mandragon's head.

The tempo of Mandragon's dance increases. No longer hops but makes great leaps in air. With each leap rises higher, from each descends more slowly to the floor. Mandragon hangs in air, arms flapping slowly. Floats upward with Princess Paloma.

Mandragon stands in air below the skylight, face raised and arms extended. Paloma lies in air nearby. The top of the loft fills up with orange light. The girls lower their heads and shield their eyes.

Princess Paloma, wearing a prison smock, crouches on the floor of a Guardia Civil police wagon. Her face is pressed against the wire caging. Her hands, stretched high above her head, clutch at the caging. She stares out without blinking.

"We would go up into the sky," says Paloma softly. "There was a waterfall of light that we would dive through. There was a lake of light where we would float." She giggles. "Mandragon's spirit would make love to me."

Apple. She kneels beside Paloma, clutching the wire on either side of her face. She is weeping.

"I wanted to go too. We all wanted to be taken to the sky. We'll never go now. Never, never, never."

*   *   *

Apple was the eldest, twenty-four. She worked as a legal secretary. She came to Mandragon's tribe like this:

One evening, after she'd been working late, two men pulled Apple from a subway train into the station men's room. They raped her. They smeared her with filth. They kicked her unconscious.

Apple's boyfriend visited her in the hospital. He stood at the foot of her bed and pumped her for details of her ordeal. He visited only once. When she returned home, he didn't call.

Apple's mother worried that she'd been given a disease and nagged her to repeated examinations. Her father tried to be comforting but couldn't look her in the face. Apple felt permanently soiled.

Apple ate little, neglected her appearance, scarcely spoke. She went to and from her job by taxi, and made certain to be home well before sundown. Otherwise she stayed in. Once, when a young lawyer invited her to dinner, she slapped his face and then burst into tears.

Mandragon saw it all. Mandragon chose her.

One afternoon Apple found herself alone on an elevator with Mandragon. I got on at the floor beneath hers. I let the doors close behind me but stayed the car from moving. Apple and I stood face to face in the elevator, about three feet apart. I grinned at her.

Mandragon's teeth are small, sharp, very white. I have sixty-four teeth, arranged in double rows. The inner rows protrude slightly less than the outer. Extra teeth or bones are an unmistakable sign.

Apple began to tremble. She reached toward the control panel. I shook my head, and her arm froze. She thought: *I'm going to be raped!* I nodded. I held my palms forward toward her. I pressed them slowly down. Apple collapsed to the floor of the elevator.

Apple lies on the floor of the elevator, one arm flung out,

the other resting limply on her breast; one knee drawn up;
thighs parted. Breathes heavily through parted lips. Gazes
up at Mandragon.
   A deep glow flames about my head and shoulders. Man-
dragon's eyes glow darkly.
   Apple sighs, turns her face away, closes her eyes.

   Apple felt Mandragon enter her. Warm light flowed in
through all the openings of her body, soft light, soothingly
warm. Brilliant light poured into her, swelled scalding in her
till she cried out. Incandescent breakers tumbled through
Apple, flared in her till she cried out again, till her limbs
twitched and her shoulders writhed and her back teeth
ground together. A globe of white light exploded in her like
the sun and gushed out through her mouth in pulsing
screams. Then the light grew soft and tepid and drained
slowly from her. Apple felt perfectly new and clean.
   I felt her feelings as I stood above her.
   Apple opened her eyes. I held my hands out, palms up,
and lifted them. Apple got to her feet. I let the elevator resume its descent but had it drop directly to the lobby. I
kept my eyes on her flushed face and fluttering lids, but
when the doors opened, turned and strode away. Apple hurried after me.
   Mandragon was with her. Mandragon read her thoughts
and felt what she was feeling.
   She followed me for two hours. I glided along crowded
streets so that she had to trot to keep me in sight, then when
her side ached and she felt she could go on no longer, I'd
dawdle till she caught her breath. I'd turn a corner and then
disappear, leaving her glancing frantically left and right;
then I'd appear beside her, smirk, and take off in a new
direction. I led her along garbage-strewn side streets, past
wholesale markets where truck drivers leered at her. I
doubled back, then doubled back again until she lost all
sense of where she was. Then I drew her down into the
same subway station where they'd raped her, into the men's

room, though people on the platform gaped to see her follow me in there. And when the door swung shut behind her, Mandragon turned and smiled, a smile immensely tender, loving, gay.

Apple was astonished. She felt no terror of the place, no self-disgust. Then she understood: she was a new person.

Apple returned my smile. Her eyes teared in gratitude. Mandragon stuck his tongue out at her and darted past her out the door.

Apple fled after me, back along the platform, up the steps and through the streets again. I walked faster and faster. I loped along. Apple's side ached. Her feet were swollen in her high-heeled shoes. Mandragon gave her no chance now to catch her breath. Nightfall had come, and she was terrified she'd lose me in the shadows. She hurried on, weeping in anticipated loss.

Mandragon slips into the doorway of a dilapidated building. Apple follows. The hall is lit only by the glow of a streetlamp shining dimly through a window over the door. There is a long staircase, mounting to gloom. Mandragon bounds up it, taking six or eight steps at each bound. Apple watches, panting. Mandragon disappears. She follows.

The building is dark. Apple feels her way along. She tries the doors on each floor, but all are locked. She beats her fists against the doors and listens: scuttling of rats.

Apple feels her way up the stairs. Above the fifth floor a rotten step gives way beneath her and she wrenches her ankle. After that, she goes crawling.

At the top of the seventh flight she sees a doorway filled with light. Mandragon stands in it, smiling down at her. She crawls forward, sobbing. Mandragon bends and takes her ankle in both hands, drawing the pain out. Raises her and leads her into a large loft, bare except for a potbellied stove, some mattresses, and a large, old-fashioned bathtub. Four girls stand under the skylight, holding hands.

"This is Apple," Mandragon announces.

The girls smile and nod.

Apple knew then who she was, and that she mustn't think
of anything that had happened before she joined Mandragon. All that concerned another person, who had ceased
to exist. The next day I sent Full Moons with her to get her
things.

Full Moons had pranced pompom'd in vast stadiums, had
pouted by the doors of jet planes, had preened her honey
muff and custard bubbies across the double-fold of *Riggish.*
Her laugh had tinkled at Palm Springs poolsides. Her eyes
had flashed across after-ski dance floors at Vail. Now she
lived nunned in an attic, the housekeeper, Princess Paloma's
special servant. She was allowed out only to do the market-
ing, was forbidden to speak save in the entail of her tasks,
was required to kneel naked for long penance on the floor,
her full moons beaming at the skylight. Yet she was always
smiling. What Mandragon's tribe had in common, besides
their obedience, was their contentment. None had ever been
so happy, had ever hoped to be. They were reborn. They
were poured full of light. My tribe were all as though pregnant with light, and their contentment was that of women
who smile to themselves and clasp their hands over full-
swollen wombs.

*Full Moons, wearing a prison smock, sits at a scuffed,
cigarette-scarred table. Sunlight streams from a window at
her left, striping the tabletop with shadows of bars. She is
being interviewed by two gentlemen, the US Consul in
Ciudad Tinieblas and his young deputy, both in blue seer-
sucker suits. The younger man stares at a wall stain, roughly
the outline of Cuba, beyond Full Moons' head: the best
stratagem he has discovered to prevent himself from staring
at her hungrily. Even in a dirty smock, with her hair rumpled, she is delectable. The smock, in fact, which scarcely
hides the outline of her breasts, far from repelling serves to*

*stimulate the male protective instinct, makes Full Moons
look especially cuddly. In the same way, her hair calls out
to be smoothed, to be caressed.*

*"You don't understand." Full Moons is smiling as at chil-
dren, trying to get through to them "Mandragon was with
us. Is still with us. Will always be. Escape wasn't our problem. Our problem was making sure that we could stay."*

After Apple, I stopped taking girls. My needs were filled.
I was provisionally established. To take more girls would
have been empty flaunting of power. As for men, I would
take men later. I'd grown weary of men in El Olvido Prison
and had no need of any at the time.

The time of my emergence was approaching. I had no
inkling of what form it would occur in, or what it would
entail, but I knew it would come soon. I was impatient,
apprehensive, but I refused to let such feelings bother me.
Instead I luxuriated in a last interim of peace.

I tuned my powers, exercised my gifts. I practiced my
transformations. I rode the subways dipping in the minds of
strangers. I made this woman scratch and that man sneeze,
gladdened this weary straphanger with memory of an old delight, reddened that spinster's cheeks with shameful fancies.
I took patients of opportunity: the boy I found bad-trip-
ping in an alley off Thompson Street—neighing in terror, chewing bloody lips—whose mind I cleansed of demons
with a chant; the derelict whose scrofula I cured by laying
on hands. I ruled my tribe, watched over their restructured
spirits. Hearing Todo Confort's confession, I might, for no
fault at all, freeze my face into a glacial sternness, fire my
eyes until they scorched her brow, and then, while the poor
thing was blubbering, while the rest trembled at Mandragon's wrath, melt my frown to loving-kindness, cool my
gaze to blessing, so that all wept in thanks. I gave them
entertainments. Brought the kettle to a boil on the un-
kindled stove. Sent the tub skidding ponderously the whole

length of the loft, with the illusion that its gryphon feet were walking. Made Full Moons feel, and the four others see, a gladiolus sprout up from her bum and rise on a thick stalk until its blossoms wavered just below the skylight. I did appearances and disappearances, showed up on the ledge outside the window, gesticulating wildly, as though in peril; or shrank and scurried off into a rathole. I let them love me.

The girls are bathing Mandragon, who lies as though asleep, forearms draped limply on the tub sides. Nightandmist, her face masked in ashes, stands behind, cradling Mandragon's head. Todo Confort kneels on the left, her hands beneath Mandragon's lower back and upper thighs. Apple kneels on the right, soaping Mandragon's throat and chest.

Apple raises her hands. Full Moons, who stands beside her, moistens them with water from the kettle. Princess Paloma stands at the foot of the tub. She smiles vacantly at Mandragon, clasping her arms in the sleeves of her white robe.

Todo Confort raises Mandragon's loins out of the water. Hairless groin, penis the length and thickness of a child's thumb, foreskin gathered in a narrow point. Below, instead of testes, a young girl's cleft.

Apple soaps Mandragon's abdomen. Soaps groin and inner thighs. Rinses her hands, draws foreskin back, washes gently. Rolls the penis between lathered palms—no stiffening, and no engorgement. Dips her lathered hand into the cleft.

Mandragon's hands hang limply. Head floating calmly in Nightandmist's palms. But now Mandragon's eyes are open. Mandragon is smiling, a smile immensely tender, loving, gay.

I meditated, sat in a corner sponging my mind of word-thought. I made journeys of ascent and of descent, immersed myself now in light and now in gloom. I made journeys outward and journeys backward, witnessed events distant and events past. And when they came on me, I made journeys forward, presenced events to come.

One day I was flung here to Tinieblas, for a sneak preview of my execution.

It was early winter. I had gone into a cafeteria to get warm and sat at a sloppily swabbed table, watching a procession of overcoated tray-pushers shuffle toward the cashier. All at once I felt the anguished agitation, the pitiable weakness in my limbs, the sense of being prey to a cruel ravishment. My eyes unfocused in vertigo. My head fell forward to one side. Then I was on Bolívar Avenue, in Ciudad Tinieblas.

I stood back in the press with my back against the wall of a building. Later I was on a balcony near Plaza Inchado, then in the grandstand overlooking Parque Mocoso. I wore what I'd been wearing in New York, my fur cap and my parka, my field pants and fur-topped boots. No one remarked these oddities. No one noticed the Mandragon who was watching. The others and I watched the Mandragon who was performing in the morning's ritual.

I saw myself trot tethered to a patrol truck: I was handcuffed by my right wrist not my left. I saw myself pelted with garbage: a corncob clipped my heel and not my ankle. I saw the major drop the cable loop over my head. I saw Angela give the signal. I saw myself rise.

With that my vision faded. I found myself sprawled across a sloppily swabbed table in a cafeteria in New York City. But by then I'd seen enough. I didn't know Angela or the three colonels. I didn't know when my execution would take place. I didn't know why. But I knew how, precisely how. Mandragon would be hanged. With a steel cable, and a pulley, and a winch. On the big tree in Parque Mocoso where, in the old days, my countrymen hanged Feliciano Luna and many others.

Why did I return? Why didn't I stay put? Why didn't I run to the far side of the planet from Tinieblas?

Beloved, Mandragon knew another thing besides. I knew that no one stifles destiny, or alters, or escapes it. The best you can do is nurture it, and when it ripens take communion with it. The best you can do is seek it out and meet it gracefully. The best you can do is embrace it lovingly.

5

Mandragon would have told that to the colonels, but they didn't ask. I would have assured them I'll be as graceful as I can, though I can't answer for what happens once my feet leave the ground. Can't guarantee grace unless they furnish me a gallows and a drop, but I realize stringing up's an old tradition, and the tree an institution. Not that they're after grace. Grace wouldn't be commonplace, while their whole point is to assure folks that Mandragon was an ordinary fellow. Well, a bamboozler of talent, maybe, with an exceptional run of luck, but not an actual sorcerer. No powers —strangled when strung up, just like a dog. False messiah.

As for embracing my fate lovingly, I would, I would, but I'm used up. Empty. Depressed, as they say. I don't think I can manage a loving embrace. It's the best one can do, however, and I'd have told them so, had they asked.

Embrace it lovingly; it's what you're getting anyway. Seek it out, it's been prepared for you. Nurture it, and when it's ripe, take communion with it, because it is your portion. In short, chow down and lick your chops.

Alternatively, you can try pushing it aside; can balk, complain and grouse, demand a substitute; berate the chef and snivel that you should have been consulted; whine and hold your breath, howl if you care to; clench your teeth and kick your feet and struggle—and end up taking what's on your plate force-fed, or via enema.

The choice, just that much choice, is yours.

Or so, in any case, it was with me. The power of the universe chose Mandragon. The power that lived in me ruled my life. I tuned myself to it—or did until I forgot who I was. I went with what had been portioned to me.

Mandragon would have been honest with the colonels. I had no inkling what emergence might entail. I had no idea why I had been chosen. I had no preference. Having a preference would have been empty self-deception. Power had use for me, power had plans, and would let me know when knowledge was required. Returning to Tinieblas never entered Mandragon's head until the power in me booted me futureward. I didn't request that revelation either, any more than I'd asked for my other gifts. They were forced on me. Light was stuffed into me without my leave. My choice was to accept what I was stuck with, or to reject it and stay stuck with it anyway. I decided to trust my vision and perfect my gifts. So since Mandragon was going to Tinieblas, would end up there, Mandragon had best set out.

As for what I did after I arrived here, I acted from no plan of my own. Some people, it's true, think they can shape events. They deceive themselves. Mandragon knew better. I didn't dream the action up, or direct it. Oh, no! I only played the role I'd been cast in. Till I met Angela, that is, and went over to her and forgot who I was. Forgot my mission and my destiny, my obligations to the power that lived in me. Till then if I ad-libbed a phrase here and there, it was from enthusiasm, not from any false illusions about my ability to shape the scenes.

I would have told them this. Not in extenuation. Certainly not in any hope of clemency. No one can stifle destiny, or alter or escape it, but everyone's still responsible for what he does or doesn't do. I would have told them in the interests of truth. I would have made a full confession. But none was required, or even (under the circumstances) permitted.

The guard woke me by poking my throat with the point of his truncheon. I was stumbling along the hall before I realized I wasn't still asleep and dreaming. I swayed against the hand that gripped my bicep. I raised my manacled hands—in what must have seemed a prayerful attitude—to rub sleep from the corners of my eyes.

Colonel Atila Guadaña sat in a tall leather swivel chair behind the prison commandant's desk. The other two sat beside him on straight chairs. Colonel Lisandro Empulgueras. Colonel Fidel Acha. A major—the commandant? the duty officer?—slouched behind Colonel Acha. A balding gentleman in a dark suit sat at a low table set near the wall at a right angle to the desk. The only light was from two metal reading lamps, one on the desk, the other on the table. When the guard had guided me in and stopped me about three feet from the desk, Guadaña pushed the dish shade of his lamp so that the light bore on my face—from habit I guess, because I didn't get interrogated. I stood blinking into it, swaying slightly, my fingers dangling at my groin.

The gentleman in the dark suit asked my true name and, when I hesitated, looked in query at Guadaña. Who glanced left and right at his two colleagues, then shook his head.

"Skip all that crap. Read him the charges."

That took about a minute. The fellow mumbled. I was half-asleep. I recognized "treason" and "subversion," then "abuse of power," floating more or less submerged in a thick porridge of legal terms. There were others I couldn't make out clearly. When that was finished, Guadaña asked me if I had anything to say, and when I hesitated, collecting my thoughts, read me the sentence. ". . . to a public place . . . hanged until dead." Then he lifted his hands and flicked them toward the door. I was back in the corridor before I realized that I'd had my trial.

I thought there'd be more. True, I had the entire junta,

but in the middle of the night? Here in the prison? No witnesses or testimony? No questions or cross-questions? No scourging of any kind? It was all over before I was fully awake.

I'm not complaining. They didn't have to give me any trial at all. That's the whole point of government by junta. I'm sure they had things to do and couldn't take all night. I understand.

But I hope that they do also. Mandragon isn't recalcitrant. Worn out, yes. Depressed, as they say. But not rebellious, nowhere disrespectful of authority. Authority happens to consist of three festering dog turds, but that's not unusual in this or any other country. They serve their purpose, and soon earth will be cleansed.

Mandragon isn't even angry. Mandragon scarcely feels resentment. Mandragon doesn't mind being strung up. The animal minds of course, which is why I'll surely do a lovely dance, but Mandragon doesn't. There's no point now that my powers have left me. And I deserve to be punished. Not for any of those charges. For having lapsed from my assigned role. For having forgotten.

Had they cared to know more I would have told them. I would have cooperated. I would have made a full confession.

6

I couldn't have given them my true name, though. Or my birth date, or my birthplace. I couldn't have given them my sex, not in one word. Mandragon has parts standard on males, and other parts standard on females. Or, more accurately, I have substandard parts, some male, some female. Mandragon sits the gender seesaw at dead center, sometimes rocking this way or that. My sex can be described as "Neuter Wholeness."

I was probably born somewhere in Tinieblas, about thirty years ago. I suppose I had a father—though there's a story to the contrary—but I know nothing of him. My mother either died or got rid of me while I was still an infant. I know nothing of her either. So I can't give my true name.

As a child I was called Raro and Monstrito. Or Rara and La Monstrua. Also Aborto and Abortito. At times, to marveling third parties, Nuestro Fenómeno. In the circus, where weirdities abounded, I was billed as El Milagro Doble-Sexo. The Amazing Androgyne when we played Port-of-Spain. A British midget who was with the troupe called me Pronged Pussy. This was transposed, with variations, into Spanish—a familiar mode of reference and address. But when power chose me and I rose from freak to *mago*, I named myself Mandragon.

I might have divined my ancestry. That would have been within Mandragon's scope. I might have dredged up infant

memories, uterine memories, memories of when I swung
twixt my daddy's legs. I might have traced my line back
to the monkeys, but I never got round to it, it wasn't important. Mandragon begat and bore Mandragon. That was
enough. And now, of course, my powers have left me, so
I cannot give the facts of my origins.

There are myths though. Or rumors, gossip, tall tales.
The first members of my tribe had revelations. Or fantasies,
delusions, foolish dreams. Which, when I returned here to
Tinieblas, new members of my tribe heard and emended.
Five myths. I like them all, though I can't say what truth
there is to any of them.

In one, Mandragon's mother was a Bastidas dockhand's
daughter who spent a night with Alejo Sancudo during his
1948 campaign for president. He took a different woman
each afternoon and night, to calm his nerves, but none except Mandragon's mother ever got pregnant. His enemies
said he'd lost a testicle and become sterile, but that wasn't
it. He had a German astrologer with him in those days,
whom he trusted completely, even with the direction of his
campaign, and this stargazer foretold that if he ran for
president he'd win, but also father a child that would de-
stroy him. So he took care to make his couplings barren.

Except with Mandragon's mother. She was exceptional
besides in that of all the girls Sancudo had that year she
alone required coaxing. She was in the crowd that lined his
progress through Bastidas, a slim girl with clear beige skin
and cameo features. He spotted her, and stopped his motor-
cade, and sent his bodyguard to fetch her.

Sancudo's bodyguard was also German, a Nordic-hero
type, blond hair, broad shoulders. Mandragon's mother told
this German she'd go to bed with him if he felt like it, but
not with an old man. Which was unfair really. Alejo was
only forty-nine then, in the prime of life. The German
stood with his mouth hanging open while the girl turned
and stalked off through the crowd.

Alejandro Sancudo was accustomed to getting what he wanted. He sent his private secretary after her. He had an Italian private secretary, a former diplomat of Mussolini's, and this Italian followed the girl home and spoke to her parents. He held his hands toward them, as though weighing imaginary tennis balls, and told him that Engineer Sancudo would be pleased if their daughter visited him that night, and vexed if she chose not to do so. A car would come for her at midnight.

He didn't have to say that Sancudo would be president again in a few weeks. Everyone knew that. Everyone also knew that in his good moods Sancudo could be generous, but that it wasn't smart at all to make him vexed.

The parents yammered at the girl all evening, but she held out. A little before midnight a storm broke on the town. Rain hammered on the roofs, and lightning flashed. The lights failed. In the sudden darkness the girl said she'd go. Her mother reached to embrace her, but she pushed her mother back and went outside. Five minutes later Sancudo's chauffeur found her standing naked in the downpour.

Sancudo was staying in Judge Ernesto Paniagua's house. The occupants had been moved out, the pictures taken down, the walls hung with horoscopic charts. The place was lit, after the power failed, with jasmine-scented candles. Sancudo waited alone on the ground floor. When he heard the car, he went to meet his guest, candle in hand.

The chauffeur had offered her his coat; she had refused it. When Sancudo saw her, he staggered as from a blow, then held the candle at the level of her waist and studied her for about a minute. His gold front teeth shone dully in the uncertain light. An old scar at his throat glowed purple and gouted blood onto the velvet collar of his smoking jacket. She bore his gaze without flinching.

Sancudo put the candle down and reached for her.

When Alejandro Sancudo touched the girl's beige skin he forgot his triumphs and disasters, his destiny and his

astrologer's predictions. When she left the house the following morning, wearing one of Judge Paniagua's daughter's dresses, she was pregnant.

She never went home. She took a bus to the capital and
stayed there until after Sancudo's election and inauguration. Then she heard that he was searching for her and
fled from town to town. Sancudo's agents gave out that he
was wild for her and meant to keep her villa'd in luxury at
Medusa Beach. It may have been so. It may have been that
he recalled the prophecy and wanted to make sure she had
no child. In any case, she wanted nothing to do with him
and eluded pursuit.

Late that year she found herself in a remote village.
There she gave birth to a monster, a child with certain ex-
ternal organs of both sexes, who entered the world wrapped
in the caul, with eyes open and face serene and milk teeth
cut. A few days later she took sick and died.

Another story goes that Mandragon's mother worked in
a brothel, that Mandragon's father was an anonymous
client of the place, that Mandragon was conceived in the
normal course of business.

This was Lo Que el Viento se Llevó, the premier forni-
catorium of the continent, a sixty-room mansion, columned
and porticoed, built and owned by Don Horacio Ladilla
and set back from the airport road on a damp savanna. The
earth around it oozed odors of generation and decay. Beside it a huge fig tree bowed its roots into the air and
drooped its branches to the spongy soil. Torches flared
along the muddy drive, and the air throbbed with music
and rude laughter. And inside were women from all corners
of the hemisphere, most of them handpicked for wit and
beauty by Don Horacio himself.

But not Mandragon's mother. She was plain and plump
and placid. She was for drunk and rowdy clients, that girls
more in demand would shy away from. The grosser rioters

led her away like a tame heifer and returned sweetened. One of them left her pregnant.

Don Horacio raged like a madman when he noticed her condition. He'd built a whorehouse, not a lying-in home! A pregnant woman was a clear reminder of the sterner side of love, a side his house was designed to help men forget. But the girl pleaded so meekly that he said she could stay on, as a chambermaid, until her child was due.

This happened just after midnight, on the first day of the new year. A huge celebration was in progress on the ground floor, and the stairs groaned under a ceaseless parade of couples. Mandragon's mother wasn't the sort to trouble others with her problems, especially if they were busy with their own. When her pains came, she kept them to herself. But a friend looked in to give her New Year's greetings, and finding her in labor advised the madam. Who had a heart of mush. Already weepy with farewelling the old year and drunk with welcoming the new, she got up on the bandstand and wailed for silence. A million fucks, she said, had been performed under her roof, and all had come to nothing. Now one was at the point of bearing fruit. Couldn't one of the vagabonds out there be of some use?

Mandragon was delivered by the minister of health, and baptized by the bishop of the diocese. Both happened to be in the house that night, and both performed zealously. Their auspicious presence offset the shame of the birth.

Don Horacio wanted mother and child out at once.

"The only bastards here will be the clients! And any titnibbling will be done by them!"

For once, madam and girls stood up to him.

"If they go we all go. You can take the clients on yourself."

So Mandragon stayed on, the pampered pet of sixty of the most lovely and accomplished whores on earth, until the place was sacked and burned by soldiers from the US military base, and Don Horacio Ladilla judged that an age

had ended, and that its monuments ought not to be restored.

Another version, one popular with those inclined toward politics, makes Mandragon's mother a victim of imperialism, a symbol for her outraged country. It has her
working in a law firm in the capital, whose offices were on
Avenida Washington, opposite the US base, the Reservation. One night, after she'd been working late, two gringo
soldiers pulled her into a car and drove her to an isolated
sector of the encampment. They raped her, and beat her up.

A military police patrol found her at dawn. They scoffed
when she told them what had happened. Nobody raped
Tinieblan girls, they said. Nobody had to. Nobody beat
them up either, unless they tried to charge an unfair rate.
They took her to the gate and thrust her out. Whores
weren't allowed on base, they said, and she should be
grateful they didn't lock her up.

Her father went to her employer, a prominent attorney
who represented many foreign firms. He gave assurances
that justice would be done. The next day one of his assis-
tants called. They'd best forget the matter. The attorney
had spoken to the base commander. There'd been no rape,
and it was likely, were the matter pressed, the girl would
be arrested for soliciting. She needn't return to work. Her
services were no longer required.

Other lawyers said the same, but at length León Fuertes
took the case. He was just back from Europe then, had
just entered practice. He didn't care what gringo generals
said, he cared about justice. But when he interviewed the
girl, she said she'd gone straight home from work, had
seen no soldiers, hadn't set foot inside the base. And as for
rape, the question was insulting. She was a virgin.

She had forgotten the matter.

She ate little, neglected her appearance, scarcely spoke.
When it was obvious that she was pregnant, her parents

sent her to relatives in a small village. Still, she refused to admit a child was on its way. When she gave birth, she refused to nurse or even hold the baby. The first day she was up, she tried to smother Mandragon with a pillow. Then she ate roach powder and died.

A fourth account promotes León Fuertes from bit player to co-star and makes love, however brief and careless, the motive of Mandragon's bastardizing.

León Fuertes made a fortune at the law and became president of Tinieblas, but he spent part of his youth self-exiled. He served with the French in World War Two, rose to captain and won a tunicful of medals, then took a law degree at the Sorbonne, but he owed these years away from home to an unhappy love affair. A girl had killed herself over him, and it so scarred him that he fled the country. At the time of his return, he hadn't held a woman in his arms for ten years.

He disembarked at Bastidas and took a bus for the capital. Mandragon's mother was on it.

There's a wag's saying here that the Iberian colonists invented man's greatest boon: *la mulata.* Mandragon's mother might have inspired it. She was delectable, with laughing eyes and soft pouting lips and skin like mocha cake icing. When León saw her, his blood, frozen ten years, began to thaw. He sent her a look of longing that might have touched the cruelest woman, and she was neither cruel nor vain nor shallow. She had a great store of tender generosity for all those wounded by desire for her, especially when they were handsome, and had a presence of command. She smiled back.

The bus climbed half-empty into the premature twilight of rain showers, then dropped to darkness beyond the cordillera. The girl was dozing when she felt León's fingers touch her cheek. She let him lead her to a seat farther back. Rain drummed on the roof and pelted on the tarp stretched over the stacked luggage. Mist glazed the windows. Passengers sprawled sleeping, all but two.

Mandragon was engendered there in the humid stifle. The girl's hips synched with the humps and swayings of the bus as she knelt spraddled to León. Her lips nibbled his face. Her moons jounced in his palms like caramel custard. Then she pulled his face down and sighed and shuddered, and he flung himself up into her, home at last.

In the last story, Mandragon's mother was an orphan that a slum family kept as a slavey. They mistreated her, they beat her, but she was a good girl. No man had ever touched her.

The wind spoke to her. She could see the harbor from the tenement balcony, and when she went out there the wind bent to her and spoke into her ear. The wind told her to go out to Punta Amarga and bathe there at night, when the beach was empty. The wind gave her no peace, and so she went.

The wind swirled sand about her calves. It bent the palms and drove the breakers. But when she walked down to the line of spume and took off her dress and sandals, the wind dropped, and the sea grew calm and phosphorescent. She waded out.

A single wave rose and laved her. Then the wind whispered for her to go back onto the sand and kneel down facing the high ground.

The wind rose, sweeping a cloud across the moon. The wind pressed her shoulders, bending her forward so that her cheek lay against the sand. The wind struck her raised hindquarters and entered her. It filled her with a terrible disquiet.

She went from town to town. She begged for food. She slept in corners. Her belly swelled. The child in her took life. The wind no longer spoke to her, but she had no peace. Whenever she stopped, disquiet stung her onward.

One night the Civil Guard sergeant in a remote village heard what he thought was a sick calf moaning outside the guard post and one-cell jailhouse where he lived. He went out with a flashlight and found a pregnant girl huddled against the wall. He carried her in and put her on a straw mat in the cell.

She was no more than fifteen, ragged and filthy. Feeble-minded too. She couldn't say how or why she'd come there, and when the sergeant wondered out loud what kind of man would take advantage of a child, she said no man had ever touched her.

He nodded. "Sure!" Then he went to get the local midwife.

She saw the girl had been in labor for some time, and that her pelvis was too narrow to admit normal delivery.

"This one goes to the clinic. Whoever put the kid in her, only someone with a knife can get it out."

The road was deeply pitted by fall rains. The pickup pitched and staggered crazily. The midwife held on with one hand and cradled her patient with the other. The sergeant wadded his ears with newspaper against the screams. About an hour before dawn, when they were still twenty miles out, the girl stopped screaming.

The midwife beat on the cab roof till the sergeant braked. She told him to come back and bring his flashlight. When the girl stopped breathing, the midwife took the knife she kept for cutting navel cords and carved Mandragon from the virgin corpse.

Five myths. I can't say what truth there is to any of them, but I like them all, the last as much as any. Outsiders scorned it, but it was popular among my tribe. And there are precedents. At each celestial turning comes a sign.

It fits well, also, with my acts and powers. It fits my essence. Mandragon unites the opposites and reconciles them. Male and female, good and evil, strife and peace. Active and passive. End and beginning. Destruction and salvation. I gave my voice to none of these stories, but I denied none either. My tribe believed them all.

Night has fallen. A breeze out of the west has swept the rain clouds toward the cordillera. Starlit, the low hills of Otán roll gently like deep-ocean swells.

Mandragon's tribe are gathered in a pasture. They have prayed and sung. Later they will make love on the moist grass. Now they sit about a tall bonfire whose flames flare toward the vault of heaven, whose sparks fly up among the stars. Circles of hunch-shouldered figures ripple out into the gloom. They and Mandragon listen as a relay of tellers chant the myths of the birth.

Mandragon rises. Steps into the bonfire, climbing lightly up on its heaped logs. Flames leap about Mandragon toward the sky.

In the gloom beyond, youths and girls clutch each other's shoulders, rocking gently, moaning softly, as the teller's chant drones on.

7

Strange, this last.

One moment curled here, remembering stories and reflecting on them; the next I stood in air above the pasture, viewing the starlit hills, my tribe, myself. Mandragon had healed the land of drought, had cleansed it of tyranny, and we were gathered in Otán, preparing for the end and the beginning. But what I saw was not a recollection, no memories composed into a scene. I was there, six months backward in time, three hundred miles north of here. I witnessed the rite, observed my people. I watched myself, Mandragon, as another.

Strange, because my powers have left me. I'd say it was a journey out and back, except my gift is gone. Such transports were once commonplace for Mandragon, daily occurrences, though I only had one vision of myself, and that was future. But strange that one should come upon me now.

Of course, it wasn't any vision. Trick of my mind, particularly vivid memory. I don't have visions anymore.

And yet before, when I recalled the loft, something came on me. I was flung back there, then flung back again. Mandragon ascending. Mandragon adored. Mandragon and Apple on the day I took her. I was present, unnoticed, observing what took place in the third person. Or so it seemed.

Thrown forward also! Paloma in the police wagon near the park. Paloma and Apple. I saw and heard them, just before my hanging or just after, but future anyway, tomorrow morning. And I was present at Full Moons' interview. Yesterday perhaps, perhaps next week. That was no memory! I knew the young man craved to smooth her hair. It had the texture of an actual event, either past or future, which I, Mandragon, presenced, unseen yet there.

Hallucinations or true journeys? Have I that gift again? Might I, then, journey out from here now if I cared to, downstairs for instance to the cells and see my loyal ones?

Best not to think about it. Best not to look for pain and disappointment. What's over's over. I have moved objects without touching them. I have bathed in fire and not been singed. By the strong power living in me I have healed and punished. I have created and destroyed, murdered and saved. I have played in the minds of strangers, apportioned them emotions of my choosing, fashioned up their acts out of my whim. I have composed the world, and I have looked —clearly, unblinking—on what's to come. All this, and more, power has performed through me. But now power has left me. My gifts are gone. Best not to think about them.

Beyond these rooms there is a prison full of pain and disappointment. Thieves and brawlers beasted down on cement floors. Cramped with dysentery, bruised from the guards' truncheons. Trying to sleep, waiting for morning, for weak coffee and a trusty to hose out their cages. And downstairs, the politicals. My girls in a damp cell below ground level. Huddled together, comforting one another, mourning Mandragon.

A prison and a city. Women standing at screenless windows in ramshackle tenements. Plucking sticky cloth from sweaty flesh. Peering into alleys, hoping for breeze. Men strewn together in dimly lit cantinas—blared music, the rum-loud bray of their own throats. Tipped back against

the walls, hunched over tables. Swilling and swearing. Tonight and last night and tomorrow night.

The colonels scheming their own abuse of power. And
before the colonels it was Angela and Mandragon. And
before us it was Alejandro Sancudo. And before Alejo, it
was General Manduco. And before him it was the Mer-
cantile Club group. Before and before. Oligarchs, dema-
gogues, despots, opportunists, juntas. Around and around.

In the palace Angela lies naked between silk sheets.
Bites her lip between tiny, pointed teeth. Turns restlessly.
Doesn't enjoy being a figurehead, and even that's uncertain.
Scheming how to get the better of the colonels before they
toss her in here. Take all three of them to bed, I'd say.
One at a time, of course, and make them jealous of each
other. Let them get the better of themselves.

Or she gets up. Goes to the window and looks out into
the park. Grandstand set up. Pulley already rigged on the
big tree. They'll bring the Jeep in at dawn and rig the
cable, about the time they come to take me downstairs.
People already on the seawall. Cooler there, and they can
doze on the stone benches and be assured of a good view
tomorrow morning.

High tide now, or nearly high and rising. Slap of waves
against the ancient stones. Fish-salty breeze. Beyond, out
in the roadstead, the running lights of anchored freighters.
Voyaged in from every sort of country, each one as futile
as Tinieblas. A prison and a city and a world.

I shall curl here nuzzling soft fabric. Or perhaps flip
over and lie semireclined. Here at the center where there is
no movement. No pain of trying and no disappointment.
No powers and no gifts, no responsibilities to them. Pleasures of helplessness. Pampered confinement, reminiscent
of my early life.

8

I didn't speak till I was eight or nine years old.

My vocal cords were sound, so was my hearing. When people spoke to me, I understood—if understanding was convenient. But I used no words, not even in the privacy of my own mind.

It may be I had intuitions about language: a tool for chopping perceptions into handy bits: useful but dangerous. Words give you a firm grasp, and yet they work with only a small fraction of reality. As a child begins speaking, as he begins conversing with himself, he stops perceiving things language can't process. He puts a word membrane between him and the world. Marvels fade, or disappear entirely. The rest is broken up in labeled fragments, so unity fades too. A kind of bargain where you lose as much as gain. Maybe more.

It may be I intuited all this, and didn't want the cataracts and blinders words tend to fasten on their users. Or it may be the conditions of my life made words unnecessary, inappropriate.

I lived with a black woman, called simply La Negra. She dealt in love spells and the like. Her clients were mainly women whose husbands, legal or common-law, were unfaithful to them—had taken up with other, usually younger, women, or simply wallowed in loose fucking here and there. Since most men here fit one of those two categories, business was good.

It made no difference that La Negra was a fraud. Her clients came to her crammed with the desire to believe, and she gave them a convincing show.

La Negra was so ugly even the plainest, most decrepit woman began to feel attractive in her company. She was ancient, wizened, toothless; black as a telephone, bald as a brick: a proper witch, in looks at any rate. And like most successful frauds, she'd conned herself. She believed in her nonexistent arts, and thus exuded confidence and passed it on.

Her remedies were so disgusting they appeared infallible: nothing else could explain their being recommended. And most were so complicated they contained excuses for their failure. A woman whose man had no established concubine but sprayed his love hither and yon, everywhere save in its proper vessel, might, for example, recapture his affections by serving him hot, strong, richly sugared coffee laced with her menstrual blood and strained through the panties of a virgin—two cups at breakfast and two cups at noon, the panties to have been worn for three days running, the noon draught to be freshly brewed in a new pot. If, though, he monkeyed regularly with the same chippy, then it was likely that he was bewitched. The suffering spouse must bring La Negra some of her man's sperm and one of her rival's nightgowns, the sample to be pure, the shift unlaundered. A pomade mixed with these would, if applied strictly as directed, break the spell. A woman who had captured a man's love and wished to hold it should stuff a toad with scraps of his evening meal, sew up the toad's mouth and bunghole, and keep it in a pot under her bed. An unfaithful wife or girl friend—and we got some of these too—who wished to cheat without fear of detection should thread a needle with green silk, make the sign of the cross with it over the bobo's face while he was sleeping, then use it to sew up the eyes of an owl.

Besides all this, La Negra had her Fenómeno. She acquired me while I was still a baby—when, how, and from whom she never said. Most likely I was offered up in sale; most likely she bought gladly. A double-sexed monster! Human to boot! I was a valuable asset in her trade.

The mere presence in her house of my extraordinary groin greatly enhanced La Negra's prestige as an expert in love's mysteries. Clients were informed of my endowment, and encouraged to inspect it at their leisure. One glimpse brought admiration and respect, which were transferred to La Negra and her potions. And she would then point out that her monster's hair cured frigidity, and its nail parings kept a man from coming too soon. Her Abortito's sweat, daubed on a woman's throat, made her irresistible. Dump it in a man's drink and he'd keep humping the night long. Its excrement had an opposite effect, would make the randiest cocksman limp for hours, and turn the hottest sexpot dry as chalk. Just the thing to give your husband before he visited his chippy! Just the thing to feed the whore herself!

La Negra sold this stuff at flexible prices. She sold it well. To Domitila Braithwaite, laundress, whose fireman consort was useless when it came to quenching blazes in her loins. To Nuris Ciervo, doe-eyed file clerk at the National Registry. One day a gentleman both rich and famous, a man too prominent for her to name, had pulled her into a storeroom and wanked her bolt upright against the dusty shelves, and she longed for the favor to be repeated. To Señora Fulvia Punzón, whose wedded husband, Captain Franco Punzón, had no less than three official mistresses, each with a bungalow he paid the rent on and a brood of kids he'd recognized at law. To Doña Irene Manta de Hormiga. She had no need of La Negra's services herself. She was the reigning love goddess of the country, as everyone but her husband knew. She came to buy something for her forty-year-old virginal first cousin, and stayed to view La Monstrua's amazing crotch, and went away wishing she were equipped similarly. To housemaids and office girls. To housewives and professional women. To matrons of the ruling class. My hair hung in lockets on some of the best-pedigreed throats in Tinieblas. Some of the most important gullets downed my crap.

A valuable asset. I was treated accordingly. I was fed well and clothed very well, in dresses or short trousers as the day's whim fell. La Negra had a filthy temper, but she never raised hand or voice to Abortito. If I did anything untoward, she took it out on Nena, the mestiza woman who cleaned and cooked. And Nena took it out on her daughter, Vilma, my keeper and my slave. And Vilma cooed and crooned and stroked and fondled. Vilma was soft and brown and gentle. She fed me bathed me dressed me brushed me combed me. She sang and chattered to me. She waited on me by day and soothed me by night. I was pampered, in short, like a sacred ibis, like a rare egret, like a performing duck.

I was also guarded against loss or theft. From as early as I can remember, for as long as I stayed with La Negra, I wore a stout leather collar fitted with a padlock and a chain.

This bothered me less at the time than later on when I remembered it. Vilma cleaned under my collar, pushing it first up, then down. From time to time, as I grew, La Negra unlocked it and let it out a notch. But since it never left me till I left La Negra, I scarcely was aware of it till then.

My chain was twenty-odd feet long, of light steel figure-8-shaped links badly rusted by the soaked hair of rainy seasons. It was padlocked to the bedstead every night, and by day to the big bamboo sofa in the sala. Its weight was that of a natural appendage, its limit was my natural estate. Others weren't collared and chained, but I was different from others anyway. My chain and collar, like my private parts, were appropriate to me.

I didn't feel impoverished by captivity. The stimulations available to me within the limits of my chain were almost unbearably rich.

Dry-season morning at La Negra's. A brown child in a pink pinafore sits at the edge of the worn, manila-brown straw mat that covers all the center of the floor. A rusted chain droops from the collar on my neck and snakes off to the triple-dowel base of the sofa. Sunlight flows in through long chinks between the wall planks, across the floor and up into my lap, revealing galaxies of dust specks. They swing and gyre, making visual music my eyes hear. My shoulders tremble. My mouth twists in a rictus of delight. Each speck is a soloist. All sing in contrapuntal harmony. As the sun strengthens, as puffs of breeze grow rarer, the song crescendos and the rhythm slows toward a fortissimo of immobility—with which the sun lifts past the chinks, the dust-speck universes vanish, the music stills. La Monstrua rolls her eyes ceilingward and collapses, seized by joy.

The kitchen, in whose doorway I could squat without taking up all my chain's slack, poured out experience. I learned, for instance, that vegetables know their destiny and accept it, await it eagerly in fact, since to be eaten's not extinction but rebirth. I came to know the exultation of newly dug tubers, and the expectant serenity, like that of brides being adorned, of the tomatoes Nena peeled and sliced. Flesh, though, is ignorant and anguished. A cut of meat, the kitchen taught me, feels unlucky, as though the cow or pig it came from would have lived forever if there were no butchers. Flesh goes resentful to the pan and table.

Now and then a man would come through the barrio hawking lobsters. He carried them piled in a wire basket and passed between the houses, singing:

"Lan-GOHHHHHHHH-stas!
Vivas y sab-ROHHHHHHHHH-sas!"

Nena would consult La Negra and then, perhaps, call down. Presently the vendor and his lobsters would appear at the head of the kitchen stairs. None of the lobsters were contented in the basket, the way yucca or limes would be. They missed the sea and felt unlucky. They sulked in various ways. Those near the bottom were fearfully dispirited. They'd given up, and yet weren't resigned. Those in the middle took no comfort from not being farther down but struggled to climb over one another toward the top. And those on top worried about staying there. When the vendor filled Nena's order and took out two or three, the accidentally promoted lobsters just beneath them felt intense satisfaction, as from a victory achieved on their own merit, then instantly grew anxious about retaining their high rank. Those picked and dropped into the sink congratulated themselves. They were out of the basket and near a little moisture. Soon they would be home in the cool sea. So when Nena brought the pot to a boil and dumped them in, their disillusionment was greater than their pain. Their pain was hideous. It set me wailing and raised welts on my loins and stomach, though after one close-up attendance at a lobster boiling I always withdrew as far as my chain would let me from the kitchen. Their pain was terrible, but their disillusionment was worse.

The sala window, to which my chain reached easily, paid out bounties of emotion. I came to know the raindrop's anguish as it clung, with growing unsuccess, to a slick mango leaf, and the tree's maternal generosity toward birds that pecked its fruit. I came to know the tree's patience during the dry months, and its relief at the first rains. Or suppose a rich client arrived in her finned Melbourne at La Negra's, a wooden house set up on cement stilts in an outlying *barriada* of the capital. I felt the car's peevishness at having been guided onto unpaved streets, and its disgust at being parked there in the slop; its worry over whether, when it was started up again, its tires would find traction;

its fear of being trapped and left the night. And if another car passed it at speed, I knew the mud's glee at being splashed on its waxed fender.

I came to know the sleepless famine of the termite colony whose nest hung in the crotch of a ruined tree and whose collective mouth rose in a quivering tentacle along the wall to munch the joists under La Negra's eaves. I came to know the yoga trance of mantids. I came to know the restlessness of flies. And oh those children's voices raised beyond the frontier of my world! The shouts of children striving on an impromptu soccer field, the squeals of children dancing in the warm rain. The screams of children being whipped in nearby houses. The yelps of children taunting one another. I came to know human childhood through such noises.

Sometimes, as I stood at the window, a group of children would collect below, for the whole barrio knew La Negra kept a monster. They'd point and whisper, snicker, gasp disgust, and I would hop about in agitation, claw at the screening, make weird moans—"Come closer! Come and visit me!" Until La Negra's squawk would bring Nena and Vilma, the one to howl the kids off, the other to coo me calm. That never took long. I floated in contentment, not of infants but of household pets. Nothing ever muddled it for long.

But no amount of careful tending could keep weed humanity from sprouting in me. In time I began to resent being displayed.

For a long time I never minded. For a long time I found it nice to be the focus of attention, the object of La Negra's toutings, and of the clients' oohs and ahs. For a long time I took pleasure in being probed and stared at. But then I began to think of myself as too good for La Negra and her clientele.

I was soon to meet much less selective publics. I was to learn that all impresarios degrade the attractions they put

on display, collar and chain them, look down upon them
for the freaks they are; and that few are as generous as La
Negra, or as careful to restrain their native cruelty. But in
my ignorance I began to resent the touch of alien fingers,
the pull of fingers spreading me, the push of fingers peeling
me back, the timid waverings of lotioned pinkies, the pok-
ings of plump kitchen-coarsened thumbs. Sometimes no
fingers touched me, but I began to resent the palping of
thirsty eyes. Now and then the eyes merely brushed me,
then darted off, but I began to resent having to lie exposed
on the low table by the sofa, with my knees lifted and my
thighs spread and my butt propped on a cushion. I began
to resent La Negra's explanations and extolments, the
guided tours she offered of my loins. I began to resent the
mistress-of-ceremonies flourish with which she raised my
dress or pulled my trousers down, the soft tugs on my chain
by which she summoned me, the reverential whisper she
assumed when telling a new client what I was. I began to
resent the clothes she bought me and the treats that Nena
made me and the care than Vilma gave me night and day.
I became curdled with resentment.

All without cause! La Negra's was a paradise! At La
Negra's I was valued and well treated, coddled beyond
measure, gratified in every wordless whim—merely for being what I was. What princess gets more? Though she's
cameo perfect? Though her blood's pure through a hundred
quarterings? And I was the sort of thing that usually gets
stuffed in ash cans, or dumped in garbage chutes, or hacked
apart and flushed down toilets. A bastard monstrosity. A
failed abortion. One of nature's stupider confusions, sicker
jokes. The world owes nothing to any creature in it, but I
hadn't learned that. So in my ignorance I studied resentment.

I sulked. I squalled. I spat toothpaste in Vilma's face
and dribbled Nena's treats onto my clothing. I wailed when
clients came and bellowed while La Negra counseled them.

I stopped heeding her gentle tugs so that she had to drag me to the table. I squirmed when she undressed me. I wriggled when she placed me for display. I clamped my knees shut till she pried them open, glared in the clients' eyes, fouled their fingers with my precious piss. I bit the hand that fed me.

This was at the end of the dry season in 1957, when my resentment had been festering for some months. One afternoon a for-hire Beaufort from the Hotel El Opulento thumped slowly down our rutted street and trundled to La Negra's. The chauffeur leaped out and skipped around to open the rear door. A passenger emerged.

He was of middle height, though he looked shorter because of his roundness. He was a few years under forty, though he looked older because of his hair, which was entirely grey and thinning at the temples. I watched him from the window that day and spent the next thirteen years circling with his circus. Don Lorenzo Amichevole.

He wore a double-breasted, cream-color linen suit that covered his paunch sleekly, and tiny black-and-white pumps with tasseled laces. He told the driver to wait, took a large canvas zipper bag from the rear seat, and moved lightly toward the front stairs. Presently his knuckles rapped the front door.

By then I was crouched in a corner, so I didn't see his entrance. I had set up my customary howling, so I didn't hear his conversation with La Negra. Almost at once she hauled her Fenómeno to the sofa and tried to arrange me for display. I struggled, La Negra cursed, Don Lorenzo watched in amusement. After a time he touched La Negra politely on the shoulder, smiled broadly, and said in a courtly tone: "If you will permit me, madam." Then he seized the waist of my trousers and tore them open so that the buttons popped, so that the crotch seam ripped back to the seat. He snatched one of my ankles in each hand and, rising, jerked me in air. I hung limply, paralyzed by the violence of his attack.

Don Lorenzo held my legs apart and rested my bottom on his paunch. He studied my groin.

"Astonishing!" he murmured. "Astonishing!"

He set me on the sofa and turned to La Negra.

"Even if we cannot do business, madam, this has been worth my trouble and your fee—and, of course, the cost of the trousers. A true hermaphrodite! I am astonished."

He dipped a plump pink hand into his jacket pocket and pulled out a lime sourball. He peeled the cellophane and held the candy near my mouth. I bit him fiercely on the base of his thumb.

I was born with all my milk teeth cut. I cut my second teeth a few years later—two sets, sixty-four teeth arranged in double rows, an unmistakable sign. My teeth are small but very, very sharp. They sliced Don Lorenzo's flesh like lard. They grated on bone. Blood spurted, hot and salt, into my mouth.

"OOOGH!"

Don Lorenzo's eyes widened. He jerked his hand back, but my teeth held fast. Then he smiled, relaxed the hand I gnawed on, twined his free hand in my chain close to my collar. Slowly, apparently without effort, he raised me by the chain and held me out over the table so that my mouth, with his hand in it, was at the level of his eyes. I choked and spat his thumb out.

"Do you see, madam?" he said, still holding me aloft and taking care that his wound bled on the table not his suit. "The beast is vicious. And will become more dangerous as it grows larger. I counsel you to sell it whilst you may."

I hung from my collar, choking, kicking my feet.

"How much?" said La Negra.

That was the last I heard before I lost consciousness. That was the last I saw of her or Nena or Vilma. That was the last I had of the easy life.

9

"Our common denominator," said Angela, when I told her of my connection with Don Lorenzo. "He bought you, and he sold me."

In the same town, but not in the same season. Angela left Amichevole's Universal Circus almost eight years before I joined it, quit circusing for good about the time I began toddling, but I caught part of her act on ecstativision the first time I saw her. Truth coshed me into trance and flung me backward, and I watched her, bikinied in rhinestones, poise on the tabbed nub of a teeterboard, tuck her butt and point her spangled bubbies, until her salmon-tighted brother Pedro finished his handspring ramble across the sawdust and catapulted her off. Soaring back flip-and-a-half toward her brother Pablo, who stood facing away from her, reading a newspaper. Feather descent into a one-hand balance on his head. Entrechat flutter of naked feet aloft. Upside-down grin for applauders. Pretty toes curling in the warm bath of the spotlight, while a recomposed Pedro saluted with raised hands and Don Lorenzo skipped into the ring, beamed, and waved his top hat.

That's what it's supposed to mean when journalists refer to her as a former entertainer. In fact, though, she gave her most memorable performances outside the ring. For publics of one, and without Pedro and Pablo. Without a spotlight either, or even a costume. When Don Lorenzo had to deal with functionaries of the countries his troupe toured, he sent Angela in first to entertain them. They were so tractable afterward. Mouths open and tongues lolling, saliva dribbling slowly down their chins. Eyes glazed with bliss and faces wreathed in the beatific grins of idiots.

Caught that part too, but not in an involuntary trance. Reviewed her career in detail during the days and nights after I first saw her face to face. Ordered up dreams of her and reveled in them. Saw, heard, touched, and smelled. Tasted. Spectated and participated. Experienced it all both as Angela and the gentlemen she solaced.

Tribe thought I was meditating. Special reverence toward Mandragon—as if they weren't reverent before!—but it was no part of my mission, no means of preparing for the end and the beginning. Abuse of power. That charge is just, though not the way the colonels understand it. Not the power of the state, puny semblance of power; no power at all since it's fenced round by time and space. Abuse of the power of the universe that had chosen to live in me.

In the fall of '49 Amichevole brought his circus here and needed a permit to perform. So Angela performed for the mayor. Who praised her to the president of the republic, Alejo Sancudo. Who commanded a performance for himself. And the morning after Angela played the palace, Alejandro Sancudo bought her contract from Amichevole, gave him five hundred dollars, and twenty-four hours to get his circus out of the country.

Installed her in a villa at Medusa Beach, place built for my mother if that myth of the birth is true. Kept her two years, then sold her for five thousand to Mr. Dred Mandeville, the chairman and sole stockholder of Hirudo Oil. Who kept her almost two decades, then sold her back to Alejo for influence, worth easily five million except the payoff was delayed. Alex ran and got elected, even took office, but the Guardia deposed him eight days later. And General Manduco became dictator. And ran Tinieblas seven years.

Until Mandragon came and cleansed the country of him. And then Alejo returned and became president for the fifth (and last) time and made Angela his vice-president, and one of the first things she did was make a pilgrimage to Mandragon and tribe's retreat in Otán Province.

To pay the guru her respects. To thank the sorcerer. To choose the wizard for her lover, love of her life.

To bewitch the fool, La Negra would have said.

She walked up through the pasture from her car, her military aide stepping carefully behind her, carrying her shoes and trying to keep his own from getting too muddy. Barefoot on the wet ground. Print dress and wide, Chinese-style hat. Girlish, except for her grey eyes. Mandragon came down to greet her, followed by a group of youths and girls. As I neared her she smiled, ran her tongue along her tiny pointed teeth, and I toppled in trance.

I'd seen her and that smile before. Years earlier, in a man named Rebozo's nightmares.

Tongue-tied even when I came to. Mumbled a few words with my eyes lowered, then a few more when she invited me to visit her in the capital. Tribe thought I was simply showing deference to a representative of temporal authority, but I was already wandering in the fever-groves of her past.

Later on I was articulate enough, when I left my tribe and went to her. For a few days, I said, just a few days. I had plenty of words then, told her all sorts of things, including how I'd become connected with Amichevole. And she mentioned the common denominator I knew about already.

"He bought you and he sold me."

She didn't mention that she'd been the principal broker. In that and all the other transactions. When Angela is sold, she does the selling, though given the subsequent rise in her market value it was inevitable she should resent the low sum Don Lorenzo accepted.

"For five hundred dollars! Fah!"

As if he'd been trying to unload her. As if he wouldn't have held out for more had he held any leverage for haggling.

"I'm worth more than that, don't you think, darling?"

10

How much he paid for me he never said. A pittance probably, and yet probably more than I figured to be worth. He didn't know I'd be the vessel of power. My teeth were a sign, but Don Lorenzo couldn't read it. And while I was a freak of surpassing rarity, my monsterhood was difficult to market. And not really suitable for the kiddies.

Don Lorenzo's public line was that he cared nothing for money, that he was rich beyond the tally of accountants for his association with people of talent, and with examples of the wonder of God's world. He was lying of course, but not altogether. There was a strain of the collector in him that balked his merchant greed from time to time. Like most impresarios, he was an ordinary man, knew it, but didn't enjoy it—though to be ordinary is the summit of good fortune, as the disastrous lives of artists, saints, and other freaks attest. So he made himself marvelous by association. He loved possessing one-and-onlies, to the point where now and then he made himself the present of an unprofitable astonishment like me.

But your collector-impresario loathes while he loves. Talent reminds him that he hasn't any, strangeness that he's common. Denigrating artists and degrading freaks was Don Lorenzo's main out-of-the-ring employment. Fun, and good business too.

"Don't give yourself airs," he told Mohotty, Maestro del Fuego, when the Ceylonese—a holy man! a worker of great wonders!—asked for the chance to do some fire-walking in honor of his god, Kataragama. "Nobody comes to see you. They come to see the midgets and the geek. My geek's worth ten of you nigger pain freaks, with all your filthy heathen gods thrown in. If you think you're too good for the sideshow, get out of my circus. You take up more space than you're worth as is."

Mohotty got his fire-walk, but only after he'd groveled. After he'd begged and pleaded. After he'd agreed to perform gratis, and pay the costs of the pit and fuel. After he'd said he'd bathe in white-hot embers, and lash himself with torches, and drag a sledge across the coals from steel meat hooks stuck through his shoulder flesh. In the same way, Don Lorenzo admired my deformity enough to buy it and publish it, but he didn't hesitate to put me in my place.

The zipper bag, for instance. I came to wombed inside it, swinging back and forth. Began kicking and squealing, not that I could do much of either with my knees jammed under my chin, not that it did me any good.

"I've bought myself a baby tapir," I heard Don Lorenzo say, no doubt to his driver. "Best put it in the trunk. See? It bites."

That's how I went to the circus: crammed in a canvas bag, dumped in a taxi trunk.

Once there, I had my place as well. The bag and I were swung up and carried, swung up again and dropped.

"That's it, Zito. Open the zipper now so it can crawl out. Careful! Bites like a snake! That's it, now drop the door."

Heavy clank. I kicked my way out of the bag. Collar and chain were gone, and I felt strange without them, like newborns do, I guess, without caul and cord. But I had plenty other cause for feeling strange. They'd put me in the truck where Zito, Dominador de Bestias Salvajes, kept his animals.

Steel box barred widthwise into cages, twilit by seeping glimmers from slats at the top. Six doors on each side, two to a cage; heavy steel plates that could be raised from the outside. To put the animals in and take them out. To aim a hose through when the box was empty. As it was then, except for the stench and naked Rarito. Who squatted in a corner, clutching one handle of the overturned zipper bag. Hairless marmoset, shivering in terror, bobbing its brown face up and down, blinking its eyes compulsively.

The last show in Ciudad Tinieblas for that year was about to start, so the other beasts were working. Later on I was joined by a toothless lion, two gelded tigers, and a bear. The bear knew how to ride a tricycle. The cats knew how to sit on stools. I didn't know how to do anything, yet I received equal treatment, except that the others were fed. I fasted all the way to Chuchaganga, over the border in the Republic of Costaguana.

This is a pleasant enough ride for human beings. Even Bebe, Rebozo the clown's trained Pomeranian, seemed to enjoy it when she and I made it together in the front seat of Rebozo's Knauser van. In later years, I mean, when we were both performers. Southeast of Ciudad Tinieblas the highway slices across rolling *llanos*, where humpbacked cebu cattle mope and graze. Now and then a river and a bridge: box of rusting girders one lane wide. Now and then a town: gas station, store, cantina, cluster of dwellings. And always, off to the southeast, the jungled hills.

At the border, a bigger town; a wider river; a longer bridge. Beyond it the hills nudge in. They slouch up from the left and squat to slip beneath the highway, which now becomes a tunnel through the forest. Roof of leaf thatch oozing yolky gouts of sun. Walls of tree trunks writhed in arm-thick creepers. Lianas drooping snakily above. Flare of parrot feathers against a monkeyed umbra of twined branches.

Then the hills get up and lift the road out of the forest. They climb on one another and become the cordillera. Along whose crests one winds to Chuchaganga.

Humans (and favored pets) can freshen in the breezes from the wing vents, can poke their faces out the window if they wish. Feeling the miles whoosh by, watching the countryside change, they get the impression that they're going somewhere. Beasts in the animal truck, however, lie wrapped in their own stink, roasted on the steel floor, lapped by streams of piss that flow from cage to cage between the bars. They feel the truck's motion all right. When I made that trip, the bear was carsick at both ends all the way. But they know they're going nowhere. Very soon, even before the truck began moving, I entered the consciousness of my companions.

That was no problem for wordless Abortito. The problem was escaping from it. The consciousness of captive beasts is worse than hunger, worse even than the smell of baking bear mess. Caged beasts know that the world moves in a circle—from truck cage to show cage to truck cage, for example—and that there can't be any purpose to such movement. Exactly when I began using words is hard to say, but it was while I was caged in with Zito's animals. I needed something to put between myself and their truth.

"Hungry?"

Don Lorenzo pokes his head under the raised doorplate into the cage next to Monstruito's. Squints at the little monkey through the bars.

"I asked if you're hungry. Would you like something to eat?"

"Hunuuh!" Nods furiously.

Don Lorenzo puts a roll stuffed with yellow cheese on the floor of the truck. "Then ask me for it."

"Give! Give!"

"Excellent!" He pushes the roll to where Monstrua can reach it through the bars. "I knew you could speak. All a question of motive, isn't it?"

La Monstrua grabs and gobbles.

"Would you like to come out now?" The roll has disappeared.

"Yes!"

"Have you decided to stop being beastly?"

"Yes!"

"Will you behave?"

"Yes!"

"Do as you're told? No foolishness? No biting?"

"Yes!"

"Are you quite sure?"

"Yes! Yes! Yes!"

Don Lorenzo nods slowly. "Best sleep on it."

He draws his head back. The steel plate clanks down.

The next morning he lifted it again, hooked it up, and stuck in his pink cheeks and twinkly eyes.

"Still feel like coming out? Still feel like behaving?"

"Yes! Please yes!"

"I believe you. But first I must make certain that you comprehend your situation. Allow me to summarize it for you:

"You are alone. Small and weak. Utterly helpless. Unless someone cares for you, you will perish. But you are also deformed, a freak of nature. Most people do not welcome freaks. Most people are unwilling to care for them. Most would as soon they all died.

"Do you understand this? Do you grasp what I've said?"

"Yes."

"Of course you do. That's why you're so afraid."

He nodded very slowly, then he smiled. "Well, if you like, I shall help you. I shall let you belong to my circus. Have you seen a circus? Do you know what a circus is?"

"No."

"No matter. For the present, all you need know is that a circus is a sort of family, a tribe. It moves from place to place and sticks together. If you should become part of my circus, your deformity would cease at once to be a liability and become an asset. You will not be alone. Grown-ups will protect you. You will survive.

"Only one thing will be required of you: You must do exactly as I say!"

Don Lorenzo paused. Found his smile again. Clasped pink hands together on the truck floor. "There you are: the simplest of all choices: life or death. Perhaps you dream of returning to the black woman. Put it from your mind. No doubt you are angry with me. Control your anger. You have one chance. Best take it."

11

Amichevole's Universal Circus spiraled counterclockwise round the Caribbean. Southeast along the isthmus of Central America; east-northeast to Venezuela; north then west-northwest through the Antilles. I spiraled with it.

My hair was clipped short on the right, and on the left conked with hot irons and set in waves. My costume was on the right a short-sleeved shirt, on the left a pink blouse ruffled at the neck; a trouser leg and half a skirt; a boot and a satin slipper.

There was a poster of me in this getup. The artist aged me to puberty, gave me a budding left breast and a show-girl leg, a lotus flower for my left hand and a coiled snake for my right forearm. Above and below, in ornate script, "EL MILAGRO DOBLE-SEXO."

Placarded with the others beside the entrance to the sideshow tent, the Rotunda of Astounding Miracles. Open from noon till three, when the main show started; later from six till eight. Adults so many pesos or pizarros or whatever, the local equivalent of a dollar. Kids under twelve half-price. Infants in arms no charge. Come one, come all.

Pitch it in my mind, why not? why not? Raise the wide canvas firmament on its ash center tree and circumferential props. Strew the earth floor with sawdust. Horseshoe it with platforms on which we miracles display ourselves. Below us, signs with our circus titles; beside us, barkers. Behind us, curtains, and behind the curtains partitioned areas for special shows. Rim the horseshoe now with spectators, with gawks and gabbles, ganders and gapes. Bunch them before the platforms. Have them stare and sneer, laugh nervously or cackle to lewd cracks, buy tickets or drift off to other platforms. Pitch it and open it, fill it with rubes.

Opposite the entrance, at the horseshoe toe, were the midgets. Ruperto and Filomena, Gran Duque y Duquesa de Microlandia. Filomena wore a white gown and a paste tiara, Ruperto a scarlet hussar's uniform festooned in braid and starred with bogus orders, a gold-hilted saber fifteen inches long, and patent-leather boots. Ensconced upon tall thrones they reigned in freakdom.

His real name was Harry Cox, his wife's was Gwendolyn. They were from Cardiff. He had a fine lyric tenor, but there aren't any opera parts for midgets.

Behind the curtain, the platform was a miniature proscenium, arched with gilt rococo and set with a midget-scale grand piano. Their special show was a mock concert, she at the piano, he with his tiny fiddle. They began with the anthem of whatever country we were in, playing it straight, of course, and then did novelty numbers. Audience mostly kids, but Harry always sang them an aria, sang it for himself whether they liked it or not, and they usually didn't. Let them wriggle in heat and boredom on their foldable chairs while he shut his eyes and pretended he was in Covent Garden—full-grown, to be sure, towering beside Sutherland or Callas. Puccini or Verdi or *Pagliacci* or something else. Voice swelling up to bulge the canvas sky, drowning its tinkly accompaniment, too big to have come from his baby chest. Halfhearted patter of applause and maybe some catcalls, and she would plink out "The March of the Wooden Soldiers," and he would start fiddling. Stiff-legged strut back and forth across the stage front, snapping eyes left, eyes right at the audience with each about-face, bouncing his little bow across the strings. At the first ending he would tuck his instrument against his chest and do a somersault, come up fiddling, smiling his aged-baby smile. Strut on through waves of laughter and applause. Bounce his bow.

"Bleeding tone-deaf bumpkins!" from the side of his smile. "Filthy philistine swine!"

Elaborate bows and curtseys to the public. To each other. To the public again. Then they would withdraw in ducal dignity back through the curtain into the open part of the Rotunda, and their barker would lift them back onto their thrones.

To their left stood Titana, La Giganta Tatuada—eight feet tall, tattooed from throat to ankle. Years before, when she was fifteen and barely six foot ten, a Valparaiso tattooist had seduced her. Not for her charms, though she was a handsome freakess, but for the scope she offered to his art. He was weary of arrowed hearts and anchors, of scrolling "Mother" in all the languages of sailors, and when he saw Titana he knew he'd never find an ampler canvas.

Perhaps he loved her a little too, for he began with nude studies of her. Titana rose from her own navel like Botticelli's Venus, slept twined with her own twin under one breast, reclined across her abdomen in the pose of Goya's Maja. But then he turned elsewhere for subject matter. A seires of self-portraits descended her right flank: the artist as aviator with leather helmet and raised goggles; the artist as French tar with pompom'd bonnet; the artist as chess opponents, right and left profiles of himself examining a rook end-game; the artist as artist poised with his needle over a female haunch half-decorated with a tiny tattooist poised with his needle. And on her right buttock, the artist's face in life-size, smiling contentment, puffing a meerschaum pipe. On her left buttock was a still life. Across her shoulders, a panoramic seascape. And sweeping from her left flank across her back, "The Battle of Ayacucho," with Bolívar's guns on the high ground of her right dorsum and a confusion of mêlée along her spine. He wreathed her arms in curious arabesques, intertwining foliage, tendrils and quaint scrollwork, birds and fishes, reptiles and strange insects, bits of fantastic edifices and the calligraphy of unknown languages, but saved her legs for two religious visions. In "The Fall of the Rebel Angels" a stream of winged horrors cascaded along thigh and calf toward Titana's ankle. In "The Ascent of the Redeemed Prophets" a procession of Hebrew patriarchs mounted toward her cloud-wreathed crotch, led by the Christ triumphant!

None of this showed while greying, double-chinned Titana loomed on her platform draped in a high-necked, floor-length robe, but now and then, as her barker spieled of wonders to be viewed within, she lifted her sleeve to consult the gold Omega which her lover stenciled on her wrist the day the last usable patch of her was filled and he deserted her, stopping time once and for all as far as she cared, at twelve noon or midnight, the sixth of some month or another, whatever year it was.

Next to her was the geek in his wheeled cage. A sign, "CAVERNICULUS ASIATICUS—TERROR DE SUMATRA," was hung on the platform below him, and his barker (in pith helmet and safari jacket, jodhpur pants and boots) yacked volubly on the travail of bagging him, the danger and the expense, but in truth he was not especially exotic: a dipso Indian, spindly and terra-cotta brown, tremored with shrugs and twitches.

He looked fierce enough though. His hair stood straight out from his head like hedgehog quills. His nails were an inch long and bent like talons. He wore a loincloth made of imitation fur and a bone necklace that rattled with his tics. Just squatting in his cage he scared the children. And when the cage was rolled inside, he snarled and whinnied. And when the barker stuffed a chicken in, he squealed. He grabbed it, rent its wings, and popped its head—the snapping beak and all!—into his mouth and gnawed it off; then spat the head out through the bars into the audience, and (dribbling blood and feathers) tore the rest apart and

smeared the offal on his naked chest. He was the best geek
in the hemisphere, I'm sure!

They put him in his cage an hour before show time, and
made sure that he got no booze. Sometimes delirium seized
him while we miracles were waiting for the Rotunda to
open, and he hopped about howling, knocked his head
against the bars, flailed his hands across his thighs to sweep
away imaginary spiders—at which Gwendolyn would begin weeping, and Harry shake his little sword and shout,
"Give him a drink, for Jesus' sake! She can't bear that
racket," but there was no drink for the geek till the tent
closed.

Out of his cage he was meek as a kitten. He slept and
traveled with Imelda, La Centaura's Percherons, the wide-
rumped greys she rode around the big top, one foot on each.
He sang to them when he was drunk in a soft Andean
language no one else could understand. He never showed
anger, not even when the roustabouts teased him, promised him rum for chewing horseturds and then tossed him
an empty bottle. The only trouble he ever caused was in
Maracaibo once, when Imelda fainted from heatstroke, and
he snatched the rubbing alcohol that someone brought
and swigged it off. No matter how miserable the rest of
us were, no matter how low, the geek was always clearly
in worse shape, so all of us were glad to have him with
us. His name, or nickname, was Chancaca.

Next was the Seal Girl, La Foca Humana, whose hands
grew from her shoulders, whose feet hung where her thighs
ought to have been. Plenty of spectators came to her platform to gape and point, but all she could do for a special
show was tell her story, made up for her by Don Lorenzo,
about how her Eskimo father killed the sacred white seal,
and was cursed in all his offspring by the shaman. She told
it poorly, in a weak monotone, forgetting details, mixing
it all up, and people jeered—"An Eskimo from Barran-
quilla! If she's an Eskimo, then I'm a whale!"—and came

out yelling "Gyp!" and warned the others not to buy any tickets. She rarely gave more than one special show a day, sometimes only one per town, sometimes not even one, if people remembered her from the year before. That cost her money. Lesser freaks like her got only room and board and a cut of the specials gate, and the barkers cheated us out of most of that. But the worst was that Don Lorenzo posed her on an ice cake—for effect, of course—and no specials meant her bottom got no chance to thaw.

Mohotty was on her left, turbaned and loinclothed, lotused on his rollered spike board. From time to time he reached into the brazier in his lap and plucked up a live coal. Rubbed it on his chest like a bar of soap. Crushed it on his forehead so the sparks flew. Swallowed the glowing bits. And that was just an hors d'oeuvre. Behind the curtain he drove skewers through his arms, through his scrawny thighs, through both his cheeks. He poked a sword through his flank from back to front so that a foot of steel showed on each side—all without shedding one drop of blood! He held an iron rod out by the ends while his barker warmed the middle with a blowtorch, and when the middle part went white and soft, Mohotty bent the thing into a V, and hung it on his neck. Sat there like a statue, wearing a glowing bar of iron for a shawl!

They used a volunteer for the finale—and there was always someone, a welder maybe, or a body-shop worker, someone used to handling torches; a foreman, or an off-duty cop, someone who liked breaking people down. He got a chance to hose Mohotty with the blowtorch. Flame licked the bottoms of Mohotty's feet, lapped his crossed thighs. Blue flame tongued in Mohotty's ear, curled in his lips and eyes. Mohotty sat there on his spikes, palms and fingers pressed together, not even blinking.

Sometimes the torcher grew desperate, as though Mohotty's calm impeached his manhood. Drilled fire in Mohotty's armpit. Swept it along his spine. Stuffed it in his faintly smiling mouth. Once one of them swung the futile torch aside and struck Mohotty's turban with the fuel tank, knocked it off into the brazier. The cloth flared to ashes in a twinkling, but it wasn't even singed while Mohotty wore it.

Why did Mohotty leave Ceylon? Why did he work in sideshow? Some sort of penance maybe, for he took no money from Don Lorenzo, wouldn't touch money when it was tossed to him. Gili-Gili collected his salary and kept it all, gave Mohotty trailer space and his daily teacup of rice. Mohotty would take no more.

And I remember when Don Lorenzo was leading the latest rarity in his collection from Zito's beast truck to Rebozo's van. Gave me a blanket for my nakedness and pulled me by a corner of it. Mohotty came out of Gili-Gili's trailer, saw me and stepped in front of me, stopping me and Don Lorenzo. Studied me with his bright little black eyes. Gazed nodding at my teeth. Then pressed his palms and fingers together under his chin and dipped his head two inches.

"When you are ready I will teach you, if you wish."

It might have been better had I taken him for my master.

We had a pair of Siamese twins, Nico and Pico, Argentine Italians like Amichevole. Their place was between Mohotty and the entrance. But for their deformity they might have been movie stars, with their wavy hair and sparkling teeth, their long-lashed violet eyes. They wore a one-piece yellow satin coverall, and for their special show undressed in tandem, Nico feigning shyness, Pico taunting him on. Down to bikini briefs to show their juncture. Then they did a comedy routine based on their predicament: Pico the brash and Nico the tender, joined at the hip.

They played this bit off stage as well as on, though it was all pretense, a con worked for the composite freak's advantage, like the police trick where Brute berates a cringing suspect, snarls and threatens, punches him about, until Cute enters with a show of outrage, shoos the bully out, and offers apologies and a cigarette. Pico flirted scandalously with circus girls and customers alike, while Nico blushed and begged their pardon, told his brother not to be so gross, and in this fashion they got more women than any three men in the Americas. Night and morning their trailer throbbed with the love moans of women lifted past ecstasy by their duplicate attentions, and they played foursomes besides. With sisters, with sisters-in-law, with cousins or friends. With girls who, till the bedding, had been total strangers to each other. And in Havana once a woman who spent an hour with them between shows returned at midnight with her two teen-aged daughters, and called the turns in the quadrille that followed, and stretched the square into a pentagon.

Nico and Pico were in their twenties, had been in sideshow since their infancy. Their humporamic angst was fed by boredom. They were heartily sick of the Grand Duchy of Freakenbourg and longed to emigrate to the main tent, so they were always trying to put acts together. At length they hit on motorcycles—nothing original, just jumping over cars, but for them it meant two cycles side by side, precision teamwork. It might have been a good draw. Nico and Pico thought so. Don Lorenzo thought so too, could hear crowds roaring, could see crowds bustling to buy tickets, but he didn't let on. Told Nico and Pico not to give themselves airs. Said he'd not have freaks stinking up his big top. Followed, in short, his customary practice with attractions, his artist-freaks and freak-artists, keeping the twins in their place so that he'd get their act dirt cheap when it was ready.

It never was. One day in practice Pico left the ramp too soon. Or Nico lagged behind by a split second. In any case, they crashed. Not a scratch on Nico, but Pico landed on his chin and snapped his neck—as if he'd been hanged with a six-foot drop, declared the coroner. Dead as a stone before he stopped sliding, and Nico couldn't last long joined to a corpse.

"Go get a knife and cut this dumb stiff off me!"

And then: "Ahh, what's the use! It wouldn't work, and I'd rather stick with Pico."

And then: "Be nice to get laid again before it's over, but Pico always made the propositions."

On the other side of the Rotunda, half-circling round from the midgets' right, there was a strong man and a contortionist, a human reptile, a sleight-of-hand artist, and me.

The strong man was a gringo, but "Here and there" is all he'd say when asked where he was from. He called himself Bruno, but no one was sure about his last name. It sounded like some general's or some writer's. He wasn't tall, or very big of bone, but he had built himself up marvelously. His neck and biceps were a half a yard around. He had no picture build like Mr. This or That, but he could lift double his weight, nearly four hundred pounds, over his head. A large moustache drooped under his large nose. His smile was sad as any clown's.

Bruno wore a leopard skin in the Rotunda, and a wide belt, wider at the back than at the buckle, and leather wristbands. He had a show weight with bells like cannonballs, and from time to time he lifted it, grunting volcanically, to draw the spectators, but his real equipment was inside behind the curtain: an Olympic set, his prize possession: a two-meter bar with red cast-iron collars, and matched disks up to fifty kilos. He did the military press, the snatch, the clean-and-jerk, and when he squatted for a clean with the bar full, it bowed and flexed like a willow. He never put on the limit he could lift, not while performing, but he could break the national record of every country that the circus played, and from the grimaces he made, the groans he uttered, the way his face went red, it seemed that he was lifting all the world. For a stunt he lifted his barker, who knew how to keep his body rigid, then held him overhead in his right hand.

Bruno was a wrestler too, and had a standing offer on the poster of him outside the Rotunda: a hundred US dollars to any man who threw him off his feet, or lasted three minutes with him on the mat without getting his shoulders pinned. In all his time with the circus he never lost. He wanted to wrestle Zito's bear in an exhibition, and offered Zito half the gate, and pledged he'd take it easy on the beast, but Zito wouldn't go along, and no one blamed him. Bruno was gentle as a puppy sheep dog off the mat, but in San Juan, Puerto Rico, once a fellow he was wrestling bit his ear, and Bruno nearly killed him. Zito wouldn't have had much of an act without his bear.

Bruno slept fourteen hours a day and complained of insomnia. He always had a cold, or complained of one. He ate six soft-boiled eggs for breakfast, and for dinner a fish or lobster, then a whole chicken, then a steak and a few chops, then several scoops of ice cream. He drank only iced tea and never smoked. Between shows he played chess with Gili-Gili.

Magda, La Mujer Chicle, could poke her head and shoulders through her legs until her forehead touched her coccyx. She could wrap her legs around her neck and balance on her palms and walk around like a weird sort of bird. She could twist her neck until her face looked back over her shoulders, then clasp her arms over her spine so that her back looked like her front, so that her feet seemed to be pointed the wrong way. She could tuck her toes into her armpits and rock on her belly like a cradle, and tie herself into such knots no spectator knew which limb was which. And for her final stunt she did a handstand on a chair, and raised her head and put her chin up on the chair back, and dropped her feet and curled them round her chin, so that her face grinned out between her ankles, and her ankles seemed to support her severed head.

She was small and pretty, lean and supple as a weasel through the waist, but mangoed above with breasts that swung provocatively when she bowed to take applause. She was forever flashing her eyes at the men in the audience, even those who had wives and children with them. Huge black eyes, boldly outlined in kohl, and flicking her tongue across her rouged and pouted lips. She moved her hips sinuously before each trick and caressed her arms and shoulders. When contorted, she moaned ecstatically, and smiled out promises of bliss to every guy around. Men came out of Magda's special shows bent double, holding their sombreros over their groins.

Not a day passed when she didn't get three or four propositions, and if the fellow looked prosperous, she'd whisper for him to come to her trailer after the tent closed. And he would grin and blink and nod and hobble off, sperm backed up to his Adam's apple. She was no whore though. She had a husband, a gypsy like herself. Together they'd escaped from Hungary, and together they played the badger game. As soon as money had changed hands, when trousers were sloughed down around ankles, then enter Sandor, cursing like a fiend, waving his knife, to wilt the sucker's wand and send him skipping.

Don Lorenzo billed his human reptile as Ofideo, the Snake Man, but he looked more like an iguana really. His eyes were set wide apart, his neck was humped, his back was ridged with spines. His thumbs were on the outside of his hands, and his short arms could scarcely straighten out past a right angle. His skin was smooth and slick and slimy, fishy-cool to the touch, grey-brown in color, greyer indoors and browner out in the sunlight. When he was specially content, his skin turned a rich green. On all his body there was not one hair, not so much as an eyelash, and his translucent eyelids closed from the bottom up. He looked like something crept from a sick man's nightmare. And yet this monster put our whole troupe to shame. He knew four languages besides his Surinam Dutch, and read thick books in all of them. He knew the countries that the circus played better than most natives, and in his shows quipped cleverly about the local scene, drawing wave upon wave of laughter from the people, till he went green with joy, and unrolled his long vermilion tongue in flashing stabs, and joined in with a high-pitched hee-hee-hee. He gave the circus children lessons, even me, and there was no one abler when it came to arguing with Don Lorenzo. Performers took him for their advocate at contract time. They brought their personal disputes to him as well—that circus seethed with rivalries!—and would abide by his decisions. He was fair, and he attended every case in earnest, though not so earnestly as to lose his sense of humor. A human reptile, but fit to be president of any country that we toured. Pity he was freaked outside where everyone could see it, not in his heart like a legitimate politico!

He never whined or moped, though his disfigurement was the most hideous of all. Most freaks felt sorry for themselves, he said, because they had the idea normal folk are happy. Freaks ought to look more closely at the rubes.

Ofideo's love life was sparse, and that was a shame, but in Managua once a beautiful and wealthy woman took him for her lover, to teach her husband not to fool around. Ofideo stayed green as a palm for weeks.

Gili-Gili was an Egyptian, a round little man with eyes like ripe olives floating in their oil. His nose curved like a scimitar. His cheeks were so pouchy he could fit a string with all the flags of the United Nations on it into one of them, and not disturb his diction. For his finale he pulled the string out, drew out an end to his arm's length, then gave it to a spectator, and had him walk backward pulling it until the tiny flags were clotheslined from the stage to the tent wall. He wore tuxedo pants and a white dinner jacket and a fez, from which he took not rabbits but white rats. He pulled twelve or fourteen fat rats out of his fez and tossed them in the air above the audience and made them vanish. Or so it seemed to the squealing folks, though there was only one rat, and it never left his hand. He took a polished ebony cane a good yard long from the breast pocket of his dinner jacket and rapped it loudly on the platform. He poured a quart of motor oil into his side pocket, and not a drop soaked through or overflowed. He took a thimble from the nearest spectator's ear and turned it into a fishbowl, then with successive passes of a handkerchief caused the bowl to fill with water, and the water to have a goldfish swimming in it, and the whole concern— fish, water, and bowl—to disappear. Then fat white rats began creeping from his left sleeve, rat after rat, a new rat poking forth his snout as soon as the rat before it had gone sailing into nothingness above the public's heads. And with each trick and liquid stare and a low chuckle, an evil grin and a rumbled "Gili-Gili!" He was a first-rate journeyman illusionist.

But for tales of his triumphs there was no one like him. He had appeared, he said, in Paris and Berlin, at the Palladium in London, and at the Roxy in New York. He said he'd entertained Prince Constantine of Greece on his sixth birthday, and had a medal struck him by King Paul: a gold disk the size of a demitasse saucer which, alas! was stolen from his suite in Tehran when he performed before the Shah. He was, he said, Farouk's personal jester, and confidant, and friend, and when the Big Three met in Cairo in '43, Farouk (said Gili-Gili) took him to play for them. Churchill, he said, was hugely pleased, and Roosevelt offered him US citizenship, but Chiang demanded to know

how the tricks worked, then sulked when Gili-Gili refused
to tell him.

Gili-Gili smoked sixty Khedive brand cigarettes a day.
He held them between his ring finger and his pinky, and
made a fist, and drew the smoke in through his hand, because "A Muslim's lips must never touch tobacco." Besides chess, he liked young boys, and wished I were a fake
hermaphrodite.

The Double-Sexed Miracle stood on Gili-Gili's right. In
my boy-girl outfit. While my barker, who was dressed in
medical whites, spieled up a crowd:

"See nature mystified, the sexes in confusion. Science is
baffled by this case, ladies and gentlemen, but Professor
Tandprugel of Stockholm has agreed to attempt an operation, if we can raise sufficient funds to pay the passage.
Adults only! Absolutely no pregnant women will be admitted! We must take every precaution lest this frightful
deformity occur again."

When the barker had sold enough tickets to warrant a
show inside, the Miracle went back of the curtain and
disrobed, lay down in a barber chair at the bottom of a
small, steep amphitheater. Don Lorenzo had a parade girl
done up like a nurse to show me off. Hung my heels up in
gynecological stirrups and draped me with a sheet, and
when the audience was in and settled, drew the sheet up.
Folded it neatly on my chest, keeping the nursiest of
straight faces, then turned the chair while the "doctor"
directed attention to my amazements.

Which were now and then the target of cigar butts, or
chewing gum spat out from the front tier. Especially when
the sister of mercy reached down over me and spread my
thighs. She did that on the second slow revolution. Stops
the chair. Reaches down and pulls my thighs apart, though
with my heels up in the stirrups there was no way for me to
close them if I'd dared to. Holds my penis up with thumb
and forefinger. Lays it back on my pubis and spreads my

slit. Straightens and turns the chair another 45 degrees, so that Double-Sex was posed for about a minute before each eighth of the audience. Then another slow turn, and then another. And a fifth and a sixth, if the public wanted.

All very clinical, very scientific. The "nurse" cool and mechanical, the "doctor" spouting pseudo-medical blah and gesturing with his pointer. Most educational and proper, except of course for the cigar butts and the gum, the jeers and jokes, the squawks of "Do we get to fuck it?"

Around and around. Around the circle of tiered benches. Around the ring of leering faces. Around each little country. Around the Caribbean. Around and around.

12

And now I've spiraled back. Powerless; in the morning I go on display, exposed and degraded; for the general amusement of the populace. Then I'll stop spiraling for good, spun off the wheel.

Up at the window for a little. Tired of flipping over and flipping back, of regurgitating and restomaching lost time. Glass weeping condensed humidity, but I can see out. Pull the drape back, lay my forehead on the pane. Cup cuffed hands about my eyes to shield the lamplight. Here, where the driblets are sparsest, I can see out. The courtyard where they'll hook me to the patrol truck. The steel door they'll slide back to let us out. The wall, and beyond it a strip of street. The tenements, and above them a cloud-smudged sky.

Café on the corner to my left. L-shaped tile counter four steps from the gutter, metal stools plugged into the cement. Six, seven figures. *Guardias* from the *comandancia* between shifts. Whores between shifts at the cantinas dockside. Drinking coffee, scarfing rice and beans. Exchanging sneers and wisecracks, winks and banter. Wearing the warm night. Programmed from their loins, so that the puffed-chest swagger, sway-hipped strut, parade in their speech and faces even while they're sitting. Hormones ruling their lives as power ruled mine.

Or so I imagine. No steamy heat up here; too far to make out gestures or expressions. Figures seated at an L-shaped counter, washed by tears of condensed humidity in the hard, past-midnight glare of fluorescent tubes.

Place will be doing a good business before sunup, when the crowd collects to see them trot me out. Coffee and empanadas for brown-faced people in cheap cotton clothing, the *mulato-mestizo* crowd of a Latin town. They'll fill the walk and spill into the gutter, peer in toward the steel door. Good vantage really, better than Avenida Bolívar. Glim me close up while I'm fresh, and lots of time to settle round the TV screens before I start dancing. Mandragon's last gift to them, an interesting morning. Back in show business again, I've spiraled round.

No stars. Get rain before dawn, but the morning will be clear. Mandragon knows. Ought to have told Colonel Guadaña. That I've witnessed the event and can vouch that there'll be excellent weather. First public strangling here since General Luna's, ninety-odd years ago. Have to be concerned that it might rain. Empty spots in the stands and on the seawall. Angela hunkered under a butler-borne umbrella, stately composure mangled, loveliness masked. Band and presidential guards all sopping, creases soaked from their trousers, tunics soggy and stained. And the condemned shivering like a doused kitten. Lose half the effect if it rained, and I should have set the colonel's mind at ease.

Or at least tried to. He might not have believed I've toured tomorrow, but I should have made the effort. Cooperating with authority is consistent with my state. I cooperated with my "nurse" and "doctor." I did exactly as Don Lorenzo said. Until power chose me, anyway, and now I'm powerless again, I've spiraled round.

Round and around. Off shift, on shift, off shift. At the *comandancia* or the cantina, at the Rotunda of Astounding Miracles. Misery, mastery misery: all pointless. Be out of it in a few hours, spun off the wheel.

Mistake was taking Don Lorenzo's offer. Made the wrong choice. Best have said no. Best have stayed in Zito's truck. Turns out I never went anywhere, just round and around.

13

No pointless spiraling for Angela. Angela stayed put, on Dred Mandeville's estate in the Nezona mountains.

The revised standard version of her life denies this, but Mandragon knows better. The revised standard says she never lived with Mandeville, never set foot in his retreat, contends he merely gave her transport to the States, where she at once entered a convent and remained, doing anonymous good works as a lay sister, until Sancudo sent for her and married her. Vatican confirmation of this fiction cost Dred a bundle.

Staging Angela in his fantasies cost much more. Hollowed out a mountain and domed the cavern with an artificial sky. Created a garden out of artificial trees and vegetation, and stocked it with robot animals so cunningly devised no one could tell they weren't real. Angela walked among them, naked as Lilith.

Date palms bending near a well of living water. Fig trees heavy with leaf and fruit. Grape blossoms, beds of spices, orchard of pomegranates. And Angela walking beneath the cedars, stately as the stag that marched before her, graceful as the gazelle that paced at heel. High breasts and waist-length yellow hair. Lithe narrow tail in the cleft of her firm buttocks. I've seen her there! Mandragon knows!

From a control room banked in TV screens Dred could manipulate his robots. Speak from their mouths, see from their eyes through miniature cameras. He could direct the artificial sun in different courses, alter the phases of the artificial moon, compose the artificial stars into new zodiacs. He could make rain and toss down lightning, ripple and quake the artificial earth. He could scour the firmament with comets, project his face an acre wide across it, shake it with the thunder of his word. Or he could require some heavenly music, and as many hours as he wished of tranquil twilight, and descend in person, his gaunt and lofty frame robed in white linen, a diadem of gold on his broad brow. To bless his beasts that came to kneel before him, to chat and frolic with his demoness.

Outside, Dred had to suffer the existence of competing deities. Vachel Mundt, Thanatasis, Krapunkian. His garden was properly monotheistic.

When he bought Angela and made his garden Dred was still functioning in public. Visiting seats of government and finance. Chairing his boards. Touring his fields and his refineries, inspecting his factories and labs. But he returned more and more often to Nezona, and remained there for longer and longer stays. For the pleasure of the place, from the pain of being elsewhere. An unknown malady was gobbling his pigments. The handsome youth who'd built an empire around a single oil lease willed him by his father was now a prematurely aged albino, with skin like leprosy, and the blood-red eyes of a crazed bunny. As he piled billion upon billion, he was less and less able to bear sunlight, more and more revolting to human view. And so he moled into the mountain, and ruled his empire by phone, and played with Angela.

She didn't find his aspect loathsome. When Angela looked at Dred Mandeville, she saw money.

He coupled with her in his own person, and by proxy through his robot beasts. His ram and his bull covered her. She was feathered by his peacock and his swan. He built her an Adam that would heed her whistle, that she could operate by a keyboard on his back. This first Adam was a marvel of workmanship, but they grew weary of him after a time, and so Dred had another kidnapped, a handsome fellow in his early twenties, a perfect physical specimen but mentally retarded. The kidnappers told him his parents were sick of caring for him and had ordered him destroyed. Then they stood him against a wall and aimed a tommy gun filled with blanks at him, and as one fired, another shot him with a tranquilizing dart. When he came to, naked in Dred's garden, he thought he'd died and gone to heaven.

What else could he think when a great face in the sky proclaimed it? when the tiger that bounded up to him was tame, and capable of speech, and spoke his name? when an angel came to him and told him that God loved him, and took him in her arms and made love to him? What fun Dred and Angela had with that poor moron!

But like everything else he grew tiresome after a while. Dred had him drugged and shipped back to this world, set down at midnight on a corner near his home. No one believed his ravings about heaven.

Business too. Dred entertained statesmen from the countries where he had investments, or wanted concessions. And his interests benefited, oh yes, oh yes. I've watched the process. I've witnessed the effect. Felt it myself from a trance in Otán Province. Tasted. So docile, those powerful men, after Angela attended them. Tongues lolling. Eyes glazed with bliss. And other oil companies had the devil's time competing with Hirudo once Dred began receiving sheiks and emirs. For them he had his biosimulation lab run off a line of comely robots of both sexes. Angela was consulted in their programming, and Dred's guests agreed, potentate for potentate, that the immortal houris of the Prophet's Paradise could hardly be more pliant or beguiling, or show a more delightful blend of enterprise and servility. Each got a romp of virginal companions, whose plastic skin was lifelike and perpetually youthful, whose clever circuits held all the mysteries of love. His forever, to have and to hold back in Qatar or Oman, along with a technician paid by Hirudo Oil to keep them romping.

Dred's fellow gringos too, they weren't slighted. The estate had a baronial lodge and a championship golf course, kennels and stables, a hunting preserve. It had a heated swimming pool, a sauna, and a gym; a French chef and a vast wine cellar. Invitations were prized by senators and admirals, by chiefs of industry and molders of opinion. Dred never entertained them personally, but they weren't offended. They praised his delicacy. Shared his retreat, they said, with men he respected, but not from any wish for favors.

Early to rise, early to rest. Healthy relaxation in rustic luxury. But a gentleman might be lightly drugged at dinner. And zipped sleeping from his room into the garden. And there amused by Angela, as in a dream. Then he'd be drugged again, and bathed, and returned to his bed. So that he never knew for certain, till it was too late, if his joys were real. So that Nezona kept its Boy Scout image.

Dred watched the cavortings on video. He filmed them. Sometimes he lent an unseen hand. Angela knew, still knows, how to draw a man's secret yearnings from him, and Dred furnished props when they were needed. He had a wide-screen Technicolor film of the governor of Missibama being flogged and sprinkled by a black show girl. He had the commander of the Nuclear Annihilation Force indulging his taste for Asiatic lads. He had the Reverend Charlie Biscuit dorking a billy goat, whose horns were imprisoned in a bramble thicket, whose throat the preacher slit at the moment of truth. His guests included men still relatively young and unrewarded, who he thought might be destined for high office. Two of his movies were later screened by their stars in the White House.

And yet the world remained somewhat intractable. De-

spite his money, despite his garden, despite his films. It
didn't always dance to his baton. Sometimes money's voice
was laryngitic. Sometimes favors were forgotten. Sometimes a cooperative man died or retired suddenly, and was
replaced by a man Dred didn't know. Sometimes a man
refused to be blackmailed. Sometimes one couldn't be cor-
rupted, or another, who was willing enough, couldn't de-
liver. Not often, but Dred had never considered adapting
to the world, or bearing its stubbornness patiently. When
the world got out of step, Dred got annoyed. In the early
Fifties he got so annoyed with a certain prime minister he
spent a fortune, and a lot of time, having the man deposed
and put in prison. After that he prepared himself to deal
with annoyances on short notice. He turned part of his
Nezona retreat into an assassin factory.

Factory. First-rate assassins are fanatically loyal. Loyal
to the death, their victim's and their own. Such people
can't be hired on the market. Have to be made. Dred had
a file of likely prospects assembled, put people to work
on conditioning and control. Then he chose his instruments
and took them over, picked them and ruled them as power
once picked and ruled me. The infallible technique, a
device planted in the skull that gives direct access to the
instrument's brain, wasn't perfected for years. Meantime
Dred's doctors made do with reward and punishment,
pleasure and pain. And Angela, who melded art to science.
With Angela's help Dred's plant turned out a line of top-
flight murderers, who removed a score of annoyances
over the years. Most never got caught, the others were
lone madmen.

Angela's help was easy enough to get. That took only
money, and Dred had plenty. Money excites her. Physically.
A stack of ingots, the touch and smell of bundled bills,
and her breasts flush, and her juices begin flowing. Mandragon's watched it. I've felt it in my own hide. And
money keeps her young. Fifty-odd now, but you'd never

know it. Looked nineteen till she was thirty, and from then on she's looked twenty-five.

Dred's empire grew. His fields and refineries multiplied, his companies brought forth subsidiaries. Waylaid competitors and raped them. Kept them in harem. His money hawked round the world and taloned up resources; beaked in discoveries and crapped new businesses. Mandeville Biosynthetics. Mandeville Lethatronics. His bankers manipulated currencies, his brokers juggled stocks. His factors fiddled with supply, portioning out now dearth and now abundance. His advertising men finagled demand. His voice over the phone, his coded messages, brought peace or panic, misery or ease. His seclusion made him mysterious, confirmed his hold over subordinates, increased his status among the other gods. And yet his life remained uncertain. Infinite appetite, but not infinite power, so always in danger of reaching past his grasp. Then even Nezona wouldn't be safe for him.

For a time in 1963 it seemed he'd reached too far. Just for a time, and then the danger passed, but that year he began looking for an escape hatch.

And that year I fell ill, and power chose me.

14

Mid-April, 1963. Amichevole's Universal Circus lay outside the provincial capital of Huacho in northeastern Ticamala, in a fallow field beside the Pan-American Highway. I was about fourteen then, and sickly.

I had been sickly since I joined the circus. Nervous, asthmatic, subject to fits. But that year my health worsened. My heart fluttered, my digestion was disordered. I was morbidly sensitive to light and noise, had spells of vertigo and sudden weeping. And fearful headaches lasting days on end. Sustained explosions deep behind my eyes, and the sensation that my brain was fragmenting outward in tiny morsels. Always, too, a strange sense of foreboding. Something immense and terrible was rushing toward me, but if I fled it or resisted I would die.

I lived and traveled with Rebozo, a large, loose-jointed mulatto three or four shades lighter than me. With his Pomeranian, Bebe, he did a marvelous parody of Zito's cat-and-bear act, and that year he had begun training a pair of ducklings.

Rebozo was mute; that is, he didn't speak. He'd been, they said, a fine trapezist, and trainer of acrobats, but one of his protégés betrayed him so terribly he lost the confidence for flying, and stopped speaking, and took up training animals and clowning. Pain, which sometimes toughens, left him tender. He was too wary to form bonds with people, but he felt sympathy for those who suffered. When I came to the circus, he took me in. I was almost an animal anyway.

He too. We lived and traveled together like a cat and bear in Zito's truck. No emotion between us, a coexistence of solitudes.

One morning, about an hour before I was due in the Rotunda, I left Rebozo's van, left the field and walked into the forest. Walked past Rebozo and his ducklings, past Magda and Sandor's trailer, and out across the highway into the trees. Or so Magda and Sandor told me later on. I don't remember leaving the van. I don't . . . Wait!

Slight brown-faced figure on an empty highway. Hair clipped short on the right, and on the left conked and set in glossy waves. Boy or girl, depending on the profile. Me!

Gravel shifting under canvas shoes. Expanse of loose gravel about a yard above the field, like a low dike between it and the forest. Dark trees, and above them clouds gathering for the daily noon shower, but hazy glare around me. Specks of silicon glittering in the chopped rock. Oblong blotch of shadow to my left front. I walk as though drawn by an invisible cord joined to the waist of my cotton trousers. Cross the highway. Disappear into the trees.

I am walking in the forest. Trees thick around as pillars in a cathedral. Stand spaced apart, vaulting their branches high above me. Pale filtering of light stain the moss floor.

The invisible cord unhitches from my waist. I stop by a low bush. A bird appears and perches within reach of my hand, a pale-blue bird the size of a crow or raven, with a white beak. I reach my hand out, and the bird vanishes.

I look up and see flocks of red and yellow parrots. The forest nave is clustered with winged color, loud with fluttering and calls. Flocks of red and yellow parrots fly down toward me and disappear.

*   *   *

*I walk, tottering, back across the highway, toward the
big tents and parked circus vehicles. The sky has darkened.
The air is heavy with the expectation of rain. An odor of
decay and pulped annatto seeds emanates from my body.
I am mumbling unintelligible words. A sudden puff of
breeze makes me sway and wobble. I fall as though dead
and lie face down on the road.*

*Time passes. Fat raindrops daub the back of my cotton
shirt, splat on the gravel near me. I do not move.*

*The shower has lifted. Light wreaths of steam rise from
the damp gravel. Magda, made up and with a robe over her
Rotunda costume, bends over me.*

*I am in convulsion. I flip onto my side and crane my
head back. Tendons stand out like bass-viol strings against
the brown skin of my neck. Pink froth seeps bubbling from
the corners of my mouth. My limbs twitch spasmodically.*

Magda lifts her face and screams.

*I lie on a mattress in the back of Rebozo's van. Rebozo
sits nearby on a low stool. He has smeared off his makeup
but is still in costume, yellow ruff and polka-dot baggy
overalls. An oil lamp hangs beside his head.*

*My eyes are closed, my face is glazed with sweat. My
thin chest rises and falls rapidly under the khaki blanket.
Rebozo watches, bending now and then to sponge my face
with a damp cloth.*

*I sit up abruptly. I open my eyes and stare sightlessly
toward the rear doors of the van. I smile and begin singing
in an unknown language. I close my eyes abruptly and fall
back.*

*Rebozo draws the blanket up over my chest. Sits watch-
ing. Bends now and then to sponge my face with a damp
cloth.*

I am thrashing in my sleep. Rebozo nods, wakes, blinks,

*then leans forward to take hold of my shoulders. I thrash
against Rebozo's hands. At length I fall still.*

*My eyes open abruptly. I stare sightlessly up at the oil
lantern. My face contorts in horror. I shout rapidly in an
unknown language. My body arcs so that only my crown
and heels touch the mattress. I wail piteously. I shriek
twice, then collapse.*

*My eyes roll up so that only the whites are visible. There
is a gurgling in my throat, then my eyes close.*

*I lie on a mattress in the back of Rebozo the clown's van.
My chest is motionless under the khaki blanket. My forehead is dry. My face is tinged blue-purple. Rebozo sits by
me on a low stool, watching.*

What I remembered later on was flying. I flew above a
stony plain that stretched, empty and featureless, left and
right to the horizon. Ahead, in the far distance, mountains
rose.

The wind roared ceaselessly. It spread my mouth and
pulled my eyes to slits. An unseen force conveyed me at
great speed against the wind. Far below, my shadow,
gigantically enlarged, raced ahead of me across the plain.
The mountains rushed toward me.

I stood in air before a perpendicular face of grey rock.
A vertical fissure in it opened and shut rapidly. It opened
two feet or so with a rending creak, then crashed shut
dreadfully. I was terrified, but I had no choice: I must pass
through or die. I hurled myself forward into the open
fissure. I slipped through, and the rock crashed shut behind
me.

I was in a cavern filled with colored light. The walls,
the roof, the floor were set with crystals. Orange and
yellow, blue and green, violet and red. Crystalline light
fell over me and rose about me, pulsating slowly.

I was surrounded then by walking corpses, whose eyes

were reversed in their sockets. They seized me and killed me. They severed my head, and dismembered my body. One held my head and pulled my eyelids open with his fingers so that I had to watch while corpses chopped my corpse with crystal knives. They sawed my hands and feet off, hacked through my knees and elbows. They cut my legs off at the groin, my arms at the shoulder. They ripped my trunk from crotch to throat and tore out my heart, my lungs, my viscera. They pulled my innards out and tossed them aside—liver, kidneys, yard upon yard of gut. They scraped my flesh and dumped my naked bones into a caldron, a crystal pot that bubbled with dark liquid. They carved a circular hole in my forehead, and scooped my brains, and flung them on the pile of offal. Then they scraped my face away and tossed my skull into the bubbling vat.

My bones and skull floated round each other. Bobbing, sinking, rising. Cooking. And as they cooked, my bones gathered new flesh and grew together. The corpses raised me from the pot all in one piece.

They stuffed my head and trunk with crystals. They closed my wounds and disappeared. I lay in the cavern, and the same light that pulsed from its walls and roof and floor was within me.

Then I stood upon a high plateau, nothing above but an immense and brilliant sky. I felt stuffed with solidified light. A power which I did not know lived in me. I was the vessel and instrument of a knowledge that ordered the universe. Of a force whose lightest breath worked marvels. Of a truth for which the splendor of the sky was merely a mask. An unbearable duty had come on me without my leave, yet I felt lighthearted.

A voice spoke to me. In a language I did not know yet understood, in a monotone that was expressionless yet full of authority. The voice explained everything: Why I had been chosen. What had been done to me. What I must do.

When the voice finished, I went to the edge of the plateau.

The stony plain was miles below me. An invisible bridge led from the lip of the plateau into the sky. I stepped out onto it. I climbed along it. I felt no fear.

A vertical fissure opened in the sky, and I passed through it, into light.

15

Hard to believe now in the reality of my initiation, but nothing more real, nothing else real, though performed in dream. Out of myself, through the fissures between the worlds. Chosen by power as its vessel and instrument. Murdered and remade, poured full of light. A new person.

Hard to believe, impossible to deny. I'd deny it if I could, flush this sense of loss. But I was chosen and made over, filled full.

Abandoned now, teased with memories, visions. I journeyed backward just now, no doubt of that. Saw myself, Double-Sex, the freak. Crossing the highway, wandering in the forest. Thrashing in convulsion, lying inert. I smelled the odor of decay and crushed annatto seeds. I heard the unintelligible words. I witnessed.

Teased to dull fury. I journeyed once at will, outward and backward. Realm of the shadows, realm of the sky, descending and soaring. A luminous fire always in my brain. It swelled at times to dazzling illuminations. Always a high plateau, and now and then raised suddenly to immense height. Now only a few pale flickerings, an occasional puny lift from the chasm's bottom. Power slinking back only to tease me. Just enough to remind me of my loss.

Ought to be grateful, I suppose, for any favor. As for these comfy rooms. Bulbous white imitation-leather chair. Teak table carved with gods to put my feet up on. But best go back inside, the cameras will miss me. Guard will burst in to make certain I'm in good health. Need me fresh for the morning. For howls of happy hatred and a steel noose.

Another initiation? An end and a beginning? Murdered and remade, emptied and filled? Commonplace hopes of the condemned. Of course I'll be remade—as part of a grub. Or as part of crows and maggots if they leave me dangling. But not as Mandragon. Just as well, but animal flesh is stupid and resentful. Can't appreciate the rebirth in being eaten. Resents extinction and resists.

Almost extinguished there in Ticamala. Lay ill three days and nights, inert or in delirium. All but died, and when I woke I'd reverted to babyhood. Incapable of co-ordinated movement, of making any sounds save wails and gurgles. My mind was a blank tablet on which the buzz of flies, the play of light and shadow made indecipherable scrawlings. Rebozo cared for me, and tied me to the mattress when his act was on. And Ofideo, who figured fever had burned out my brain, waged a running fight with Don Lorenzo to keep me out of the Rotunda.

"I'll wait a month to see if it recuperates." That was Don Lorenzo's final position. "Counting from the first day that it missed. Then I'll exhibit it in whatever state it is. That's one freak I'll not coddle. I bought it. It's mine."

The circus played through Ticamala and crossed the border, played Otán and Angostura and Bastidas, went south for a matinee in Córdoba before its run in Ciudad Tinieblas. All the while I mewled and burbled. Then, a month to the day after I fell ill, I broke from my cocoon of infancy. It was as if I'd become deathly sick the better to gain health, stepped backward to leap into maturity. I didn't know why I was tied down, but my mind was clear and calm. My heart beat firmly. My body felt refreshed and full of energy. And my anxieties were gone. I undid the rope, got up and dressed, and left the van.

The circus was camped against the town in a large field

that had been cleared for houses and cut into blocks but not yet built on. I didn't know the place, but off to the left were the familiar tents, and the familiar racket of a march blared through loudspeakers. The main show was about to start, the Rotunda to close. The area where performers' vehicles were parked was deserted, except for a roustabout who was changing a wheel on Aristo the wire-walker's Andorra hardtop. I walked down and stood behind him.

Monkeyform squatting by the raised front end. Greasy undershirt and sweat-stained neck, blue baseball cap worn backward catcher-style. He flipped the X-shaped lug wrench to his right, pulled the flat off and flopped it to his left, turned round for the spare.

"Ah, ho! The Great Donged Twat in person! Stay out of my way, freak!"

He lifted the spare and hefted it onto the hub.

I stood behind him. Felt my mouth purse in a tight smile, felt my eyes glowing. I gazed down at the wrench, and after a moment it got up on point and did a pirouette. Took two little hops and pirouetted again. Circled and half-circled the car in linked leaping turns and sprang lightly up into the open trunk.

The roustabout put the last lug on its pin and reached for his wrench. Patted the ground. Looked down, got up, and stared about.

"Hey, no balls, you seen my wrench?"

"It's in the trunk."

"I tell you to put it there?"

"I haven't touched it."

Show of stained teeth. "Went by itself, uh?"

I nodded.

"Go get it, you little creep, don't fuck with me!"

I brought him the wrench, stepped back and watched as he spun it in his hands, then leaned his weight against it firming the lugs. Luminous fire in my brain, felt my eyes glowing. I looked down at the flat, and it ballooned with air, then flipped itself up on its tread and rolled away.

The roustabout saw it and grabbed for it, missed and pursued. The wheel picked up speed, stayed a yard or so in front, zigzagged provocatively as he trotted then sprinted after it. It bounced uphill and circled Rebozo's van with the ape behind it, then broke back toward the road. It widened its lead, began bounding. Three, five, ten feet in the air. Five, ten, twenty feet to a bound, till with a great leap it soared up and out and hung itself on the arm of a telephone pole. And my poor baboon was jumping up and down, rubbing his greasy hands against his cheeks.

"Uhahhh! Uhahhh!"

I stared up at the wheel. The fire in my brain receded. I felt the glow leave my eyes and a shy smile cross my face.

I went back to Rebozo's van and lay down inside it. I was trembling. I had willed nothing consciously, yet I had made the wrench and wheel perform. A power had been clowning through me.

I was awed and very frightened, but I found I could put fear off to one side, so that it was present but didn't bother me. This was a new ability for me and itself a little frightening, especially after such weird events. My trembling stopped, and I began remembering what had happened during my illness.

Everything returned to me with great clarity. My magic flight across the stony plain, my passage through the rock into the cavern, my dismemberment and my reconstitution. The high plateau. The expressionless voice. My passage through the sky and into light. Everything but what the voice had said. I remembered its tone and its authority, and that it had explained everything, but I couldn't recall the explanation.

I decided not to try to understand. I was changed, that was enough. I was a formerly sick person who had been cured, who had succeeded in curing myself. I was a formerly terrified person who had been shown, who had discovered for myself, how to control fear. I was a formerly weak, formerly helpless person, in whom tremendous power now resided, who had made myself worthy of it. During my April illness I'd been made over, had made myself over, into someone new.

16

From that afternoon, until my transformation was acknowledged, the circus was afflicted with pranking miracles. That night we went down to the capital and occupied the fairgrounds, eight unpaved acres where the old racetrack had been, on Via Venezuela near El Opulento. Next morning the Grand Duke of Microland, already in costume, climbed into the van, smirked at me, then spoke to Rebozo:

"The Chief Cheese says Prongo here goes to work today."

Scarcely were the words out when the midget rose as though snatched up by mighty hands, spun round and lay face down in the air, and then shot headlong out the door like a lump of flop off the end of a shovel. He bellied into the mud, slid forward and lay still an instant, then jumped up screaming abuse. At which his little sword flew from its sheath and jabbed him in the bottom, pricked him off, hopping and yelping, all the way to his trailer.

Two hours later, when the Rotunda was filling up, Chancaca the geek began to moan and flail imaginary spiders from his thighs, attracting a large number of spectators to his platform. But when his barker had sold about twenty tickets, a sliver flask popped from a gentleman's jacket and made a wavering progress through the air into the cage. The barker lunged for it, but it dipped under his hands and butterflied around him through the bars. Chancaca drained it—whisky, brandy, rum, whatever it was.

Didn't take the spout from his lips till the thing was empty, and slumped happily in a corner, singing in a soft Andean language, the tamest wild man in captivity.

The bunch near his platform began to hoot and howl for refunds, so Gili-Gili, seasoned trouper, stepped in to save the day. Shouted that he, the sultan of illusionists, would honor the tickets for his own show, which was worth ten Sumatran Terrors. To make his point he began pulling white rats from his fez and tossing them out over the center of the horseshoe, but the rats didn't disappear. They thudded squeaking to the sawdust, plopped onto ducked heads and cowering shoulders. Gili'd never had more than one rat, and he'd never really tossed it, but now his fez was full of them, and his hand was working uncontrollably, plucking them up, chucking them out.

People dashed this way and that, dodging the squeakers. Others stood paralyzed with fright, and the seventh rat sailed toward one of these. Señorita Grushenka Látigo, it turned out—twenty-year-old sister of Captain Dmitri Látigo of the Tinieblan Civil Guard. The rat plummeted head first into the scoop neck of her dress and lodged between her plump and heaving unchies, hind feet fluttering, tail swishing back and forth like a runaway metronome across her screaming mouth.

With that, Gili-Gili managed to grab his right hand with his left, clutched it so that it stopped plucking and chucking, but rat upon rat kept scrambling from his fez. Poised on the rim and took one look over its shoulder, then jumped, first to the platform then the ground, and scurried out among the panicked spectators. And when, in desperation, Gili-Gili hurled the fez back over the curtain, rats began swarming from his sleeves, streaming from both his sleeves and scampering out after their brethren.

The Rotunda emptied in short order, though a number of people were knocked off their feet and trampled. Only when the last of these had dragged himself out did the rat plague cease. Gili-Gili tottered about babbling insanely, jowls twitching and pudgy lips flecked with white froth. The rest, performers and barkers, were scarcely calmer. Except for Chancaca of course. Except for Mohotty. Except for me.

Yes, yes, what about Tasselsnatch? What about Quimdingus Weirdly, the two-way creep? Watched it all with peepers peeled and glowing. Part of it yet apart. Felt like a dynamo, some sort of transformer: energy surging in and pulsing out. Same as earlier, when smart-ass Harry Cox the midget got himself tossed out of the van and mudbathed, needled in the rump and terrified, though now it went on longer. Then it shut down, drained away, and I stood with my eyes half-closed and my head lifted, wrists crossed lightly over my chest. Exhausted but perfectly serene, so that my wretched, flimsy-cheap costume no doubt took on the dignity of what it symbolized: union of opposites.

I was learning not to be surprised at the power in me, not to be flustered at its being there working through me, or by the amazing things it did. Like a girl sixteen or so who'd always been ugly, and then loveliness flowers in her all at once. She learns to bottle up her wonder when men stare at her. Never even noticed her before, and now her presence in a room turns the men coltish, sets them peacocking, spaniels them around her. Learns to accept this, and not to be shocked when young men fight over her, when other girls glare at her in hate. A power has come into her. Without her leave and out of her control. Awed by it, couldn't be otherwise, but learns not to be startled by the miracles it works. Well, I was learning.

And learning to enjoy it too, though I'll admit that wasn't much of a problem. My confession, required or simply permitted, would have freely admitted that learning to like it was easy, since I was learning to stopper my wonder and not be distracted, since I'd learned to put fear off to one side. To begin with, the events were amusing in and of themselves. A pompous midget sliding in the mud. A rat shower in a crowded tent. But the real fun was in the terror that comes over people when the world stops functioning the way it's supposed to. Gili-Gili, for instance, a fat fraud with real magic on his hands, scared, quite literally, out of his wits. By something in me, something from outside me but working through me. It wasn't me that was warping reality, so I couldn't be blamed for unpleasant side effects. But whatever was doing it had picked me as its instrument. That made me feel powerful. The feeling was good.

Mohotty sat cross-legged on his spike box. Palms pressed together under his chin. Staring at me. Then he dropped his hands to the frame of his box, raised his body, swung off to one side. He stepped down from his platform and crossed the horseshoe, pressed palms under his chin and bowed.

"Now I will teach you if you wish."

I looked down at him, wrists crossed lightly at my chest. "I don't want to learn. I want to let it use me as it pleases."

"You think that then you are not responsible. You are wrong."

"I don't do anything. It uses me. I don't want to learn or understand."

Long gaze, then a faint smile. "As you wish."

Mohotty dipped his head, then walked away. It might have been better had I taken him as my master.

The Rotunda opened again that evening on schedule. Despite general consternation and without Gili-Gili. He was strapped down in the prison ward of San Bruno Hospital, a sacrifice Don Lorenzo made to keep his circus open. Grushenka Látigo told her brother about the outrage to her person and her honor, and Captain Dmitri showed up with troops and a blanket arrest order. Don Lorenzo gave him Gili-Gili, who was still raving and unlikely to be performing for some time.

"We've caught the culprit, sir, and you may have him. But surely you do not mean to deny the children of this cultured capital a spectacle at once delightful and educational. You must not judge us all by one Egyptian! Take him, my dear captain. Rid my troupe of him. You have my thanks. But let the show go on! As for the compensation due your esteemed sister, the rascal's trailer ought to fetch a proper sum."

It never crossed Don Lorenzo's mind that Gili-Gili might be innocent, not even when Mohotty told him so. It wouldn't have concerned him anyway. The blame fit Gili-Gili nicely: he was unable to defend himself: what more was needed? How he'd managed to pack four dozen rats into his fez and sleeves was his own business. Illusionist's trade secret. Why? was something the police could beat out of him if they wished. As for a mystic power working through a subhuman hermaphrodite, well, that was the sort of mumbo jumbo one might expect from a scrawny heathen nigger in a loincloth. Don Lorenzo wasn't in the market for it. One maniac a day was quite enough. He roared Mohotty out of the converted bus where he lived and had his office, and otherwise contented himself with kicking Chancaca soundly in the stomach, with docking his barker two weeks' pay and warning the rest of us that there would be, by God! no more foolishness. The show went on.

The evening news had broadcast that a mad necromancer had been arrested at Amichevole's circus. From the moment its flap opened the Rotunda was thronged with people expecting strange events. They weren't disappointed. When Bruno the strong man lifted his globed show weight, it continued rising till it pulled him off his feet. When he dropped off, it zoomed straight up and tore out through the tent roof. Three times during the evening the air above the crowd became abruptly full of red and yellow parrots that swooped down then disappeared, and Mohotty flew around the horseshoe, riding his spike box like a magic carpet.

Titana's tattoos were animated. The face on her rump blew smoke rings. The soldiers on her back fired their flintlocks, thrust their bayonets, throttled and clubbed each other, bled and died, while the Liberators' guns volleyed shot across her spine at the Spanish ranks. And the waves on her shoulders pitched so violently that half her audience was seasick.

As soon as the Seal Girl began telling her stupid story, those listening found themselves before an igloo on a frozen waste. Saw the action played in pantomime, by the light of a sun that hung on the horizon, no brighter or more warming than a lamp bulb. Left the partitioned area sneezing and shivering, their faces blue, their fingers stiff with frostbite. The Sumatran Terror sat placidly in his cage, reciting the Apocalypse in Latin, while his jodhpured barker tore chickens apart, and bit their heads off. And when the Double-Sexed Miracle was ensconced for display, the pimp with the pointer and the trull in the white smock floated up on either side of me. In my same spread, reclining attitude, and her uniform and his trousers split in tatters, flew off over the curtain, along with her blotched panties and his shorts. The two of them hung in the air a full ten minutes, revolving slowly, their parts on show for the jeering rubes.

Some people found the evening disturbing. Some fainted, some ran howling into the night. Some took to drink, and some swore off forever. But none complained that he'd been rooked. The general reaction was summed up by Lazarillo Agudo, writing the next morning in *La Patria*: he'd rather be dead than have missed it, and rather have three teeth pulled than go through it again. Another paper ran an eight-column photo of the Rotunda on its front page. "YES IT HAS MIRACLES AND YES THEY ARE ASTOUNDING." A popular disk jockey took calls all morning with opinions on how we'd worked the show. Super-thin black wires. Mass hypnotism. Smoke and mirrors. And the gringos in the Reservation put the circus off limits to military personnel. Small wonder more than a thousand people were waiting outside the Rotunda at noon next day. But the Rotunda wasn't going to open. It was bewitched, the performers and barkers said, and they were on strike.

Hard to blame them. They were more or less right. Spectators thought the craziness was part of the show, but the Rotunda people knew better. Demons and poltergeists, devils and imps. A few figured the source might be Chancaca. His chicken-chewing barker beat him unconscious, just in case. But the chief candidate was me. They would listen now to the roustabout's tale of the tire, and Ruperto's bit about getting a magical bum's rush from Rebozo's van. And reliable Ofideo had seen my half-naked barker take a swing at me and bloody his own nose. Ofideo wasn't sure what he believed himself, but he endorsed the strike and took demands to Don Lorenzo. An exorcist for me, and the archbishop to purify the tent with prayers and sprinklings.

Don Lorenzo was not sympathetic. He was beside himself with rage. He hadn't been in the Rotunda and didn't credit the reports of what had happened. Couldn't. Lacked the imagination. Some oddities had taken place, what of it? As far as he was concerned, nothing that drew a crowd could be disturbing, much less evil. The only deviltry, the sole incomprehensible event, was that a pack of imbeciles were breaking the circus code and costing him money. He told Ofideo he'd deal with them later, and put all his energy to getting those who'd come for the sideshow into the main tent.

The show went placidly through the parade, through the first acts. I didn't go over till after the halfway point. Found a seat high in the stands, and soon as I sat down I felt the surge, felt it and waited. Zito had got his cats up on their stools and was about to make his bear ride the tricycle, when a look of bewilderment crossed his face. He toured the cage apologizing to lion and tigers, then gave his whip to the bear and climbed on the trike. Pedaled briskly round and round inside the stools, head ducked and shoulders hunched, while the bear flicked lightly at him and the audience roared glee, while the bear held up its forepaws and bowed stiffly. Still pedaling as though his life depended on it when Don Lorenzo, face chalky with fear, ordered the cage wheeled from the ring and directed the spectators' attention to the spotlit perch above them, to the high wire and the Great Aristo.

In a white cutaway, white spats, and white silk hat. Picture of elegance and poise, but as he stepped out on the wire, his gravity began revolving. Trim and erect, but with every step his body swung to the right, till he was walking horizontal, till he was walking upside down! Then, at the center of the wire, directly above mutely shrieking Don Lorenzo, Aristo realized he was upside down and lost his balance. His gravity was reversed and so he "fell" upward. Thirty feet straight up to the tent roof, where he bounced as though on a net, and lay with his back against the canvas, staring horrified at the ground. Then he flipped over on his belly and scuttled upside down across the ceiling like a gigantic albino roach. He grabbed the nearest mast and clung there wailing, till a trapezist went up and tied a rope to his ankle, till three roustabouts hauled him down like a blimp. Would have tethered him to the grandstand, but then his gravity re-reversed, returned to normal, and he collapsed in their arms.

By then Don Lorenzo had called in Imelda, but after two circuits her horses developed the faculty of speech and began arguing over going clock- or counterclockwise. Stopped short, then turned in opposite directions, dumping Imelda to the sawdust. Went to opposite sides of the ring and took their cases to the public, flinging their heads back to bray obscenities at one another. And when Don Lorenzo shouted for the clowns, only whinnying came from his megaphone.

It was at that moment, as he stood pawing the sawdust, neighing through the cardboard cone, that he caught sight of me. Saw him spot me, then saw myself through his eyes: head and shoulders wreathed in an orange aura, and my eyes glowing like live coals. There was an explosion without concussion, like the immensely amplified crack of a high-powered rifle. Where Don Lorenzo had been standing was an airport limousine, with an Intercontinental Airlines flight crew. And then I glimpsed Don Lorenzo in my mind, megaphone still at his mouth, three blocks away outside the portico of El Opulento.

Later that afternoon he spoke with me. This was in the office part of his bus, while a tiny plastic fan beat petulantly at the soggy air, while a crowd of circus people waited outside in the tepid drizzle. His first impulse was to strangle me, but as he lunged his hands flew up to his own throat and squeezed till the impulse passed. Fell back into his chair, an aircraft pilot's seat bolted to the floor. Sprawled gasping till his throat cleared.

"Stop tormenting my circus!" Forty-nine percent command, 51 percent plea.

"It's not me." Slight figure in string-belted cotton trousers, shy brown face above rain-spotted T-shirt. "It's a power inside me."

"Tell *it* to stop!"

"I don't control it." Paused, then something came to me. "I think it doesn't like the way I'm treated. It's chosen me to live in, and I think that when I'm degraded it's degraded too."

"Degraded? Did I hear you say degraded? You are a freak of nature, a monstrosity, the lowest thing there is! How could *you* possibly be degraded?"

"I think it wants me to stop being a freak, I mean to stop having to show myself without my clothes on."

"Then *it* may be at ease! You may leave this instant, and take *it* with you! And should you, in your new dignity, feel any moral obligation for the shelter my circus and I have furnished, I hereby release you. Good-bye. Hail, and farewell!"

"I don't want to leave. I haven't anywhere to go, nothing to do. It's your fault that I'm here, not mine. It's you that have the obligation." Paused again, then something else came. Hadn't thought at all, till I heard myself say it. "I could have Gili-Gili's place, now that he's gone."

"Well, well, well. You could have Gili-Gili's place. Now that he's gone, of course. Well, well. Well, well. And that's why all these horrid things have happened."

"I don't know. I don't try to understand it. It's done what it's done, and Gili-Gili's gone."

"Don't understand? Well I do, you despicable little toad! If there is one thing in this world I understand, it is shabby jealousy among performers. I've seen enough of it, God knows, seen little else. You'd like to have his place, now that he's gone. How simple! But tell me, have you no tremor of remorse? Driving the poor man to lunacy! Getting him arrested! Putting my circus, your home, into this turmoil! Do you realize that Aristo may never be the same? That I myself . . . ? But I've a strong heart, and something of a constitution for bustling through the ways of freaks and so-called artists. No guilt at all, you disgusting reptile?"

"I haven't done anything. It's the power that's chosen me. I don't control it. It uses me."

"How marvelously convenient! And this power you claim is inside you; *it* will be happy, that is tranquil, if you have Gili-Gili's place?"

"I don't know. I think so. I think it made me mention Gili-Gili's place, so I think it wants that."

"And what, may I beg to ask, will my circus and I receive if I accede to this nauseating blackmail? Can you do anything? No! Wait!" He threw his hands up, palms forward. "I don't mean talking horses, or being whisked through space! Can you, or *it*, if you like, do any simple tricks such as might entertain normal folk without making lunatics out of my people?"

Dropped my head. Stood shifting left and right. Then it came on me, and I looked up smiling, reached forward and unscrewed the bulb from the lamp on his desk. I shifted the hot bulb from palm to palm, then grasped it by the bottom in my right hand. It lit, flared to an incandescence that filled the whole bus, and popped. Shards of grey glass fell softly down like snowflakes.

"Something like that?"

Don Lorenzo nodded slowly. He leaned back for a moment, then thrust himself up and stepped past me to the door. Paused there, then looked back at me.

"On the same terms you have now. One-fourth the receipts of your special shows."

"One-half." Didn't think of it till I heard myself say it.

Don Lorenzo gave me a look of total hatred. Which was at once prudently diluted with fear. And then a philosophic shrug: he'd still be making money.

"Very well. I am accustomed to dealing with vermin."

He turned and stuck his head out the door into the warm rain, called to the waiting people:

"We have reached a friendly understanding and a mutually rewarding settlement. There will be no more irregularities. The crisis is past.

"Don't stand there mooning at me! Get your costumes on! We play tonight on schedule!"

17

And play this morning on schedule, already in costume. For a quickstep parade and a hoisting, my prance and my dance. For a simper-bitch fanflick, the starter whines, grating of gears. For cablebite painhorror cannot-be-happening choke-anguish. For face levered down, ground dragged away from my toes. Falling, revolving, sway-rocking, into my . . . Bug-futile leg-thrashing jerk-shoulder worse-making agon-jounce, fish-stupid can'tstop, gaff-flounder flipflop, hip-twisting swivel-wrist yank-tightening strain-tendon tongue poking out from gaped carpmouth and troutbulging eyes brain ballooning on skullbone chest tugging heart thumppumping veins popping bowels voiding ultimate dreamterror helplessness chaosed to fact, stop it stop it now stop it, but not by knocking my head on the window or cameras will think I'm smashing a shard for my throat not a bad idea glass thick though rush in here too soon or I won't find a suitable sliver or, going to be hanged can't escape it or alter my second sight twenty-twenty so I'll stop it like this!

Knuckles pressed in my eyes. Excellent stellar-bright pain, present pain driving off future, I've got the thing stopped.

More to be safe, bring moth-flutter mind to rest. Now stroll to my sea-green chaise and recline sedately. Three-quarter shot and profile, never know the difference. Condemned spent a placid night.

Known as stage fright. Which all performers suffer, even veterans and headliners. Though in different strains. Present case like when I was still a freakling, if a bit more severe. Miserable during my shows and suffered their anguish beforehand, wished the whole thing was over.

Whereas El Mago Mandragon had jitters, but they always vanished once the show was on, so then I longed for the beginning not the end. Same when I learned I'd been cast for an interesting fate. Eager to get it onstage. But now I've spiraled round to dread again, wish it was over.

And making it worse. Animal fit provoked by human imaginings. Thing is to stay depressed. Imagination deadened, or at least dulled. Or cozened toward something less horrid. Or purged with a dose of pain, so that the animal doesn't start kicking four hours early, sick at both ends.

No aspiration to meet it gracefully. Going to be strung up and animaled. Hardly any more disgraceful if I went into my dance now for the closed-circuit cameras, if I'm already beshitted when the loop goes round my neck. Point is simply to keep the nightmare brief as possible. Four, five hours still before lift-off. Only two, three minutes of, let's call it bother, and then my act's over. Foolish to let imagination start it now. Stay depressed. Or put some word-thought between me and animal truth. Managed that naked in Zito's truck, can manage it now.

Not a flashy stunt. Not much beside even my lesser miracles. Modest attempt: get safely through a few hours into oblivion. But rather a challenge now that power's left me, that I'm helpless again, that I've circled back to dread. Worthy in its way of El Mago Mandragon.

Who was born on an evening at May's end, and the curse was lifted. The plague of wonders ceased. Events at Amichevole's Universal Circus observed a decent respect for commonplace reality.

For the most part, anyway. Fire still refused to burn Mohotty. And other supposed laws of nature were flouted

twice daily in the vicinity of the Rotunda's newest attraction. But gently, for the most part gently. So that people
whose sanity depended on reality's being commonplace and
law-abiding could look the other way, or pretend there was
a natural explanation, that there was a trick to what was
accomplished through me, something they'd understand if
they knew the secret.

Most of the circus people pretended I wasn't there. Mor-
tally frightened of me for a time—wasn't that tasty!—and
continued to avoid me even after memory of the May
Horrors had receded. Which was fine with Mandragon. My
audiences gave me plenty of human contact.

I continued with Rebozo. Our solitudes continued to
coexist. Contaminated by faint smears of human feeling,
but we ignored them, hoped they might fade. He'd nursed
me after all, some compassion involved there. But he
ignored it, as I ignored my feelings of gratitude. And, also,
I began dreaming his dreams.

Not on purpose. Later on, when I'd learned to direct the
power in me, I dreamed people's dreams whenever I had a
mind to, and read their thoughts, but in those days, with
Rebozo, it was involuntary. Found myself dreaming his
dreams, his nightmares of humiliation and betrayal. Always
dreamed of the same girl, a pale-golden girl with an acrobat's lithe body and a mocking smile. Way of running her
tongue over tiny pointed teeth. Saw it in what's called real
life many years later, in a field in Otán, in plenty of other
places. See it again in a few hours while I'm dancing, if the
cablebite doesn't unfocus my eyes. In his dreams Rebozo
loved her and suffered marvelously, and I began to feel
protective toward him. Worried almost paternally about
how he'd take Bebe's old age and death, about his painful
efforts to arrange a new act. But I gave the feeling no expression, I ignored it best as I could.

My solitude also coexisted with Bruno the strong man's.
He too lived folded in himself. Muttered complaints to him-

self, muttered chessboard comments. With Gili-Gili gone he had no one to play with, but chess was his only pastime so he played by himself. Set the board up on the edge of his platform same as ever and played games between his right hand and his left. Went from one side of the board to the other, muttering comments. One day I came by just as he finished setting up the pieces, as his right hand pushed the white king pawn forward. I glanced at the board, and the black king pawn hopped two squares out. Bruno grunted and looked up.

"I guess it wants to play."

He looked back at the board. Muttered, "It wants to play, so it wants to play, so we'll give it a beating." Slapped his king knight out. A black knight jumped out in answer.

"Wants to play, wants to play, but does it know how to play?" He whistled his bishop out to threaten black's knight, and the black queen pawn slid slowly one square forward.

"It wants to play Steinitz. Steinitz is what it wants to play. Then we'll eat its horse. We'll gobble its fat horse and give it check." Swept the bishop in and snatched the knight. "Check! "Check check check!" The black pawn charged diagonally forward into the bishop, knocking it up off the board and into the oblong piece box.

The game continued, Mandragon the *mago* standing two paces from the platform, Bruno the strong man banging his pieces and mumbling his patter, the black pieces moving, as it seemed, of their own will. Other performers and their barkers began conversing in unnaturally loud voices, glanced over nervously, tried not to watch. From then on chess was a ritual between Bruno and me.

Evenly matched, though different in style of play. Brawny Bruno played conservatively. Frail Mandragon—or, rather, the power that played through me—attacked boldly, flung pieces forward, made sacrifices, sometimes gave brilliant mates. But when these attacks failed, my pieces were liable to behave childishly. Captured men tried to sneak back onto the board. Pawns retreated to meet Bruno's counter-thrusts. Rooks attempted knight jumps, bishops impersonated rooks. To ambush Bruno's queen, or the king might leap from mate to a safe corner. At which Bruno would growl disgust. "Take your beating like a man, you little cheat!" And I'd protest innocence. "*I* didn't do that, Bruno; *I* wouldn't cheat."

Then I asked him to let me keep the set on my platform while the Rotunda was open. Chess became part of my act. I'd suggest that someone make an opening move, and the black pieces would answer. It drew people over, the sight of them moving without being touched, and for a small sum a spectator could play a blitz game with them. Funny, they always played at the strength of their opponent. Wood-pushers who barely knew the moves could give them trouble, could even win, yet in Caracas once they played a visiting grand master, and won a pawn from him, and made him sweat to get away with a drawn game. Playing more important than winning. Tried to cheat when Bruno had them beaten, but only playfully, to get him riled.

People who saw the show one day came back the next with their own sets, or sets bought for the purpose still sealed in their boxes, sets weighed in laboratories and examined by X ray, huge sets with pieces molded in metal and tiny sets whose pieces had to be unpegged then pegged in for every move. But any chessmen placed before Man-dragon would play without being touched, and always at the strength of their opponent.

I hadn't known the power in me would play chess. Never knew what it would do. I went to the Rotunda in the God-will-provide spirit of religious beggars, trusting the power in me would come through with something. And it did, it always did, it loved me then. I learned not to be surprised but remained in awe, was as delighted at a new stunt as any spectator. Never practiced, never rehearsed. Tried not to think of the shows when I was offstage. Oh, I had impulses, sudden ideals like putting the chess set on my platform. Came to me sometimes before the show and sometimes during, and I followed them blindly, without question or reflection. They always worked, but I never felt I was doing anything. A power was performing through me, I was its instrument.

Started with bulbs. A bulb would light when I held it in my hand, or in my mouth or in the crook of my elbow. Glowed or flickered, sometimes flared and popped, sometimes threw out all the colors of the rainbow. People always demanded to see the bulbs, know what the "trick" was, and I found if I said politely, "Pretend it will light for you," the bulb would like as not go on in a spectator's hand. Rarely failed to with children, and in my special shows behind the curtain I'd sometimes have as many kids as were there squealing with joy, waving glowing bulbs in their small hands.

In Cartagena once, early in my magoship, a bunch of Chilean naval cadets heckled me, yelled drunkenly I was a fake, and on impulse I tossed a bulb to one of the loudest. Began flashing in his hand the instant he caught it, and then his friends were laughing convulsively, flicking their fingers as if to shake them off their hands. The bulb, they said at last, was sending out insults in Morse, calling the fellow who held it smutty names, commenting on the love life of his sisters. Wanted to climb up and punch me, but they held him back, said he'd brought the ragging on himself, and when he shoved the bulb to one of the others it flashed insults at him too. They took it with them when they left, and one of them returned the next evening and told me it had continued blinking salty jibes into the night, but its light grew dimmer as they sobered up and refused to shine at all the next morning.

Even before that, impulses came to me during my shows. On my first night, here in Ciudad Tinieblas, I noticed a smirk-face young gringo standing back from my platform scribbling in a brown notebook. Spy from the army command in the Reservation, read that on him at once, sent over to investigate the circus and find out if it harbored any threat to the USA. From Moscow or Peking or outer space, and on impulse I waved him over and asked him to put his notebook and pencil on the platform. Soon as he did, the notebook flipped itself open to a clean page, the pencil got up and began writing. Very flattering account of my act, all in English, which the spy translated for us when he'd found his voice. After that I brought a pad to the Rotunda, and now and then it would come on me that such and such a spectator had, in pocket or purse, a pen or pencil with something to say, or a picture to draw. Then the miracle would be repeated.

Later on I bought a typewriter, an ancient Underwood, cobwebbed and rusted, that had sat ten years in a Veracruz pawnshop. Walking in the town, and on impulse I crossed the street and went into the shop, stood looking around till my glance struck that machine and I knew it was what I'd come in for. Its history too. Belonged to a novelist, Gamelial Garza. Brought it to Mexico with him when he was exiled from Costaguana, and then pawned it for next to nothing. Not because he was pesoless, though he was, but because it had failed to write a decent sentence in three months, not one imaginative phrase, not one apt word, so Garza figured it was empty. Pawned it and went out and borrowed money for a new one, but there was plenty of insight left in the old machine. It was weary of telling lies and inventing worlds, weary of being stared at angrily during interminable hunts for metaphors, of being pounded mercilessly when molten images threatened to congeal. It was weary to exhaustion of having cigarette smoke blown at it in long sighing expirations, but all it needed was a little rest. Got plenty too before Mandragon found it, before Mandragon put it back to work. I set it on the edge of the stage, inside, behind the curtain, and it held forth during my special shows. When someone from the audience laid hands along its sides, it typed out data—name, age, occupation. Then it gave advice.

It advised Ignacio Bustamante, twenty-two-year-old dry-cleaner's deliveryman of Guatemala City, to be more careful tossing humps to the young housewives on his route, especially with Purisima de Alas, whose husband had suspicions and a pistol. It advised Alma de Cañizales, widow, of Puerto Armuelles, Panama, to stop worrying about where next month's rent was coming from: if she played the last four digits of her cousin Primitivo's identity card number in Sunday's lottery she'd win first prize. It advised Isaias Levi, a merchant of Venusburgo, Ticamala, to curse God and die, because Mizrachi his partner was cheating him and Sara his wife put pork in the meatballs and Moisi his son was queer and Malca his daughter was four months pregnant by the black handyman and he himself had cancer. Then it advised him to disregard the previous advice, it was all a joke, only a joke, didn't he feel better? It advised Pablo Tocino, twelve, of Bucaramanga, Columbia, that playing with himself wouldn't drive him crazy but trying not to might, and it advised Juan Nulo, fourteen, who was from Garza's own village, Damonco in Costaguana, but who had run away to the capital and entered the famous pickpockets' school there, that the gentleman whose wallet he'd swiped earlier was just outside the curtain with a cop, and exactly what it advised Bonita Novilla, sixteen, of Maracay, Venezuela, doesn't matter, but it made her giggle and gasp and then turn red, made her tear the paper out and crumple it, made her whisper shyly to her boyfriend, so that both blushed and left the show at an urgent stroll, each with an arm about the other's waist. It might even have advised Mandragon, maybe saved me years of hardship, but I didn't want advice and never consulted it.

During some shows I'd go into trance and utter prophecies, or work marvels that startled even me. My trances were so theatrical they appeared faked, an impression strengthened by my costume. Don Lorenzo gave me a mandarin robe and a pillbox hat, both of the cheapest stuff available, a painted paper fan and vinyl slippers. Bogus in its own right, and its effect when joined with my un-Oriental features, my chocolate skin and Zuluy lower lip more or less announced me as a charlatan. So when my head flopped over to one side, when my eyeballs rolled up and I flung my arms out, when I lurched around the stage chewing my tongue, hecklers howled fake. Just as well. People who'd have lost bladder control had they been forced to know I was possessed by power could drain their tension off in hoots and giggles.

After maybe a minute I'd grow calm. Head still canted, eyeballs still rolled back, I'd start to speak. Not in my own voice though, in an expressionless, authoritative monotone. Sometimes this computer voice described lost objects and told where they were, an earring that had strayed into the kitchen and taken refuge in a teacup, a tax receipt that had sneaked between the pages of a book. Then someone in the audience would gasp, and maybe say, "Now I remember!" In Tegucigalpa once the voice announced the make, color, and plate number of a pickup parked outside, and said the keys to it had slipped from the driver's pocket and were now lying on the ground, under the green sedan with the cracked windshield next to it—at which a man in the fourth row jumped up and slapped his pockets and dashed out. Back in a few minutes waving a key ring, shouting, "*Fantastico!*" telling the now untranced Mandragon, "*Gracias!*"

Sometimes the voice gave details of unsolved or unsuspected crimes. The strangled streetwalker was done in by a well-dressed gentleman in his late thirties, who wore an amethyst ring and drove a white station wagon. The attorney who supposedly had died of ptomaine was in fact rat-poisoned by a woman with silver nail polish. Such in-

formation caused me trouble with the police. Best they could
do with it was try to make me the culprit. And sometimes
the voice predicted accidents or natural disasters, which,
when they happened, people blamed on me.

Anguished agitation, pitiable weakness in my limbs, sense
of being prey to a cruel ravishment. Then filled with mysterious light, luminous fire, that enabled me to look upon some
scene. Or in other trances I saw nothing, but instead grew
conscious of the worries of some spectator. And, with me
still in trance, the worries would be dramatically relieved.
In Curaçao once a spectator was worried about his camera,
an expensive Jap number with all sorts of attachments,
which he'd forgotten in a taxi, or on the counter of a ticket
office, or in a shop. There was an explosion without concussion, like the crack of a rifle, and the camera appeared
in air above me, then floated out over the audience and
hooped its strap and dropped to its owner's neck. And in
Santurce once I stumbled blindly down into the audience, to
a girl whose face was blotched with acne, and brushed my
fingertips across her cheeks, and the pustules healed. That
was the sort of stuff some people had fits over. People who
couldn't stand more than one reality, one stable ordinary
state of things, had a terrible time with stuff like that.

Bothered me too, though not in the same way. The trances
were unpleasant to begin with. The helplessness, sense of
being seized by an alien force. Bad enough when all they
brought were glimpses of misplaced objects. What about
murders, crashes, scenes of horror! What about other people's worry and woe! Relieving it left me drained, energy
pouring out like milk from an overturned pitcher, especially
when I was healing. And with this draining the fear that
everything would go, that life would piss out of me for
good into some stranger. Exhausted and terrified, but nothing to do, no way to hold back when the fit was on me.

Generous entertainer, El Mago Mandragon. Gave more
platform diversions than strictly needed to sell tickets. Pro-

longed my special shows past their set time feeding my public extra rations of amusement. Got me harsh looks from other performers and scoldings from Don Lorenzo, but it wasn't enough. Entertainment wasn't enough for the power that picked me. I didn't want to watch people being strangled, or ease their worry, or cure their ills, but as time passed the power that lived in me used me more and more this way. Flung me into trances. Drove me toward other people and their woe. Dragged me staggering from the show area once and out through the Rotunda, out into the parking lot just to heal a drunk who'd laid his head open in a fall. Clutched me in trance once while the Rotunda was closed, in the middle of a game with Bruno. Stuffed me with anguish from a woman in the main tent, knocked me cold with it. She'd let her children wander off and couldn't find them, and scarcely had I come to, sprawled in the sawdust, feeble as a crone, when a roustabout ran in shouting the world had gone crazy, that two kids had flown forty feet through the air, over the heads of people in the main tent, and landed lightly at their mother's side. More and more of it as time went on, outside the Rotunda and in it. People heard about my cures and came for that. Depressing to wake and find a line of cripples cringing near the van, or have my audiences mildewed at the fringe with deformed and dying. Useless too, since I didn't direct the power that lived in me, though now and then, just enough to keep sick people coming, the presence of suffering would pitch me to healing trance. And more and more visions of disorder, bloodshed and catastrophe, misery and ruin. More and more the power in me rubbed my face in other people's trouble.

Grew petulant too, took snide revenges on the skeptics. Afternoon in Kingston, five or six years after it chose me, when it set half a dozen kids, each with a glowing lamp bulb in his hand, floating around the show area like fireflies. Kids ecstatic, but a British tourist, from Porlock in

Somerset, there with his wife and another couple, couldn't stand it. "Unreal mockery!" he snorted. "Tricks and illusions!" The bulbs had batteries inside, the kids weren't flying. I was a fraud preying on superstitious wogs, and soft-minded morons who couldn't face practical reality. All but ruined my show with his raving and ranting. Well, it was the dry time of the year for Jamaica, but when he and his party left the Rotunda it began raining. Poured in torrents, but only on them, only in a circle three yards wide around the gentleman who liked practical reality. For the whole time he was on the island rain poured on him whenever he went out, and he got no sun and played no tennis, and his holiday was ruined. And there was the Mexican lady was refused to believe her eyes when Mandragon, with a touch of tranced fingers, magicked a disfiguring goiter from a girl's throat. Screamed that the girl was an accomplice, that the goiter was put on with putty. Said I ought to be locked up, since fakery gave foolish people, people with real ailments, vain hopes of a miracle cure. But then she broke off with a yelp of pain, jumped up and rubbed her bottom, squeaked that she'd been attacked, though no one had touched her. Wailed until a doctor came and examined her, but he found no damage, except for a large purple bruise, in the shape of a spread-fingered hand, on her right buttock.

With all of this I began to wonder what it was after, what the power that had picked me to live in wanted. Even considered asking Mohotty to teach me, thought about trying to understand. But the trances weren't crippling, and only came on me once or twice a week. And the visions were bearable, no worse than nightmares really. And only a few skeptics were punished, and none of them really hurt. Better stay passive, better not try to understand. Let it use me as it pleased and not be to blame for it. So the years passed, and I came back here again, for the seventh time as Mandragon the Mage.

18

Dred Mandeville was aimed for Tinieblas too, sharking the middle depths of the Brazil Basin.

No one knew, of course, no one but Angela, Alejo, and Mandragon. They wouldn't tell, and I didn't understand. Not till years later, when I'd met her face to face and dream-toured her life. I visioned Dred's whaleswim on our way south from Ticamala, but I didn't know who he was or what it meant. Tranced it from the front seat of Rebozo's van, but it meant nothing to me, while those who'd have understood hadn't an inkling.

The US government's best guess had him still holed up in the wilds of Nezona, but that theory was about to crumble. His lawyers were waging a rear guard against the prosecutors. Barrage of quibbles, smoke screen of specious motions. Clung to each technicality till they were pried off, then withdrew to new positions in higher courts. But few courts were left. Soon a marshal would set out, would board a plane for Draco, the state capital. Soon he'd guide his rented car into the hills, arrive at Dred's redoubt armed with court orders. To open the steel gates and leash the Dobermans, deactivate the laser beams and minefields, but he'd serve his papers on a cleverly wrought dummy, a dead ringer for Dred as last seen in public back in the Fifties. And the robot would accept them gracefully, would smile and say, "No one's above the law. Above the law, above the law, above the law," then thumb its nose and wrench its plastic head off, exposing a tangle of multicolored wires.

The former security officer of Mandeville Pathogenics, himself the quarry of an alphabet of government agencies, prowled the network airways with the tale that Dred was a captive at his hotel in Zeno, Arizada. Ol' Dred, the story went, had been gobbling pills so long his brain was like cornmeal mush. A bunch of young aides had taken over and were manipulating the senile freak on orders from the A-rabs and the Chinks. The ex-executive may even have believed his own twaddle—there was a dummy Dred in Zeno too—but he was no closer to Dred's whereabouts than the government. Guesses sped after Mandeville but never reached him. He was cruising two hundred fathoms down, beneath the long swells of the South Atlantic.

Mandragon knew. I saw it. USS *Scorpion*, lost with all hands, supposedly, off the Azores in 1968. Slid bullet-smooth through the deep-ocean gloom. Pale whisps of phosphorescence trailed her diving plane. Clung to her dorsal sail and whirled in vortex haloes round her screw. Inside no engine racket, no vibration. *Hiss-hum-whirr* of fans blowing scrubbed air through the compartments. Pop of circuit breakers, peptic gurgle of hydraulic lines, slow creak of hull. In the companionways the veinous twilight of red bulbs. In the control room the green glimmer of dials, the blush of a lone lamp at the chart table. Behind it, on a high stool, a man in pale-blue coveralls, the top of his rump against the lowered periscope, his head and shoulders bent over calipers. No way to tell he was a man and not a robot. Simply knew it, though more like a robot from his slack features and the socket implanted back of his left ear.

Another like him sat facing the portside panel, fingered the levers without moving them, studied the green dials. Two more reclined farther forward in bucket seats, behind airplane-style control columns. Hands in their laps, faces empty of expression. Stared up at a panel of sweep indicators: speed in knots and speed in engine capacity; stern plane and bow plane, rise and dive, gyro and rudder. The sweeps nudged right and left, down and up, as the control wheels inched clockwise and counterclockwise, forward and back, on autopilot. And opposite these two, on the starboard side of the boat, another robot-man sat peering into the sonar scope.

Forward of the control center was the radio room. Aft of the periscope was the guidance system, three gyrocompasses suspended from the ceiling in ash-can-like grey plastic cylinders, each independent yet interconnected, each checking itself constantly against the others, and all three linked to a computer that printed out continuous report of the boat's position. The gyros were oriented to the center of the earth. Earth's core, not anything in heaven, was the boat's lodestar.

One deck down a compartment stretched from the bulkhead forward of the radio room to the bulkhead aft of the guidance system. Forty form-fitting couches, twenty on each side, set perpendicular to the boat's keel. On each a supine man in pale-blue coveralls, at each man's head a cord running out from the wall and plugged into the socket back of his ear. Those on the starboard side lay with their eyes closed and their bodies motionless, breathing in the slow rhythm of deep slumber. Those on the portside couches stared blindly up at the red-tinged ceiling, their faces twisted in moronic grins, their bodies writhing slowly, their throats emitting low moans of delight. Hidden fans whirred sibilantly, pushing scrubbed air forward through the compartment.

The men on the portside couches grow suddenly calm. Grins fade, moans cease, limbs droop. Eyes close, they plummet to slumber. Those on the starboard couches wake. Unplug and let the cords wind to the wall. Rise and file forward through the oval door in the bulkhead.

They descend a ladder one deck and go aft to a com-

*munal lavatory. They strip their coveralls and drop them
in a hamper. In groups of five they use the showers, the
toilets and washbasins, the bank of electric razors. They
take towels from a stack and dry themselves. They take
clean coveralls from a stack and dress. They neither speak
nor look at one another. They neither smile nor frown.
They file aft along a short companionway into the galley.
They eat in silence, their hands and jaws working deliberately.*

*The fresh watch leave the galley and go off about the
boat. To the control room, to the reactor and engine rooms.
To the filtration plant, where the boat's air is scrubbed of
impurities and enriched with oxygen extracted from sea-
water. To other stations, relieving the men on duty. And
these scuttle, quickly and silently as rats, to the compartment on B Deck, and throw themselves down on the empty
couches, and snatch the cords from the wall and plug them
in. Fall back grinning moronically, writhing slowly, moaning in joy.*

Forward, at the round prow, Dred Mandeville was working. Gaunt frame draped in a contoured couch-chair, which
he could turn by a button on the armrest. Crimson eyes
staring up at a bank of TV screens, which he could program
from a calculator keyboard. Screens spangled with data on
his holdings, on the world's economy, and by a touch he
could summon any information he required. From time to
time he raised a microphone to his lips and dictated a memo,
then swung the couch toward another bank of screens.

Soon night would cloak the surface far above him. The
boat would swim up to a depth of a few fathoms. To gather
in coded bursts of signal, bounced off the sky from trans-
mitters on Mount Vervex, and freshen the data in the computer that fed the screens. In the darkest hour an antenna
mast would rise. Dred's memos would flash out to his empire. But neither periscope nor sail ever broke the waves.

No agency or court could touch Dred there. No light but the pallor of his screens could reach him. Yet his power, all he cared for, was undiminished. The long midsection of the boat was packed with stores. Spare cores for the reactor were aboard. The crew would go surely and silently about their tasks till death claimed them. Twice a day, as soon as he came off watch, each man got his pay: four hours of electronic tickling in the pleasure center of his brain. Nothing could match it, no joy on earth or in any prophet's heaven. No man who'd tasted it would give it up. Theirs for as long as they served loyally. Long ago they'd forgotten their homes and loved ones, the tepid rewards of human life. Slept without dreaming, worked the boat like robots. Dwelt in paradise four hours in every twelve, with bliss and glory plugged into their mortal brains. Dred might cruise on for years, invisible, invulnerable, potent.

Expected to be down only five months. Sent Angela to Alejo in November, and in January went on board his kidnapped sub. Dropped beneath the surface of the sea, and by then Alejo had returned to Tinieblas and was running for president. Elected by landslide. Took office on June 1, and in a week or so he'd be ready to receive Dred Mandeville, and give him an extradition-proof refuge.

So on June 8, when Amichevole's Universal Circus arrived in Ciudad Tinieblas, Dred Mandeville was headed this way too. In the Brazil Basin off Recife. Two hundred fathoms down. Sharking north-northwest toward the equator.

19

The circus wasn't much different from seven years before, when the power living in me made itself manifest. Gili-Gili was gone, of course. And so, in a sense, was Aristo the wire-walker. Never got over his terrifying "fall" to the tent roof, his upside-down roach-scramble across the ceiling. Took to the bottle, and in six months could scarcely walk solid ground, much less a swaying half-inch cable. Don Lorenzo let him stay on, gave him a paper-work job and overlooked the way he botched it, indulged his drinking. Not from any sudden attack of human decency or Christian love. Aristo was primed to slither into the geek cage when Chancaca died.

Which happened one pleasant evening in La Guira, about three years after I stopped freaking. Chancaca had just drained his after-show pint, was sprawled in Imelda's horse van. Bare, rachitic chest smeared with damp feathers, shoulders cushioned on a manure mound. When he felt death seize his lower body, knew the bottle he'd just emptied was his last. Tranced his epiphany myself, broke in on me while I was getting out of costume—deathtug, and he began gibbering in his Andean language. Too weak to pry the crabclaws from his loins, but then it seemed to him the muddy lot beyond the tailgate was a pool of shimmering celestial booze, limpid lagoon of solace glimmered in starlight. His heart, swollen with so much grief and joy, burst smilingly.

The whole circus was touched by his passing. Even Don Lorenzo, when he found out that despite all the priming, Aristo wasn't half the geek Chancaca had been.

On the other hand, Rebozo was twice the clown. Bebe was still alive, at the great age of sixteen, but had entered an honorable semiretirement. The ducks, trained patiently for years, could sing "The Beautiful Blue Danube."

(Rebozo—bedraggled frock coat, winged collar, gigantic wig—leads his artists gravely into the ring. Rolling breakers of applause and cheers. Turns, sweeping his arm, as they waddle past him and flutter up onto a round dais. Bows deeply—once, twice, thrice—to the audience: more applause, then faces the ducks and draws a baton from the breast of his coat. Flourishes it in air, right hand six inches northeast of his temple, left hand clasping his paunch; now sweeps it slowly in a reclining figure 8: left and over, right and over, left):

1st DUCK   Quaaaaaah; quaaaaaah; quaaaaaah; quaaa.

2nd DUCK   *(at Rebozo's cue, poked with a slightly bent left forefinger)* Qua qua, qua qua.

1st DUCK   *(as Rebozo's baton sways up-down-left, up-down-right)* Qua-quaaa quaaa quaaa quaaa.

2nd DUCK   *(cued by Rebozo's forefinger)* Qua qua, qua qua.

1st DUCK   Qua-quaaa quaaa quaaa quaaa.

2nd DUCK   Qua qua, qua qua.

1st DUCK   *(swaying its head, following the raised pinky on Rebozo's baton hand)* Qua-quaaa quaaa quaaa quaaa.

2nd DUCK   *(its bill nodding in recoil from the poked finger)* Qua qua, qua qua.

1st DUCK   *(as Rebozo's baton circles twice, then stabs roofward)* Qua-quaaa quaaa quaaa QUAAAAAAAA-AAAAACK!

2nd DUCK   *(with 1st duck holding its quack, baton aloft and vibrating, forefinger poking in cue)* Qua qua, qua qua.

1st DUCK (*as baton plunges, circles, stabs straight up and vibrates*) Qua-quaaa quaaa quaaa QUAAAAAAA-AAAAAACK!

2nd DUCK (*while 1st duck holds*) Qua qua, qua qua.

1st & 2nd DUCKS (*while Rebozo sweeps baton and empty hand in concert, first slowly, then accelerating into frenzy; while his head and shoulders sway with the ducks' singing, and with the lilting strains of an invisible hundred-and-twenty-piece symphony orchestra ranged on invisible platforms behind them; while he lifts his paste-caked face toward the tent roof, closed eyelids fluttering in esthetic bliss*) Quaaa, quaaa, quaaa, quaaa, QUAAA!
Qua-qua-QUAAAAA!
Qua-qua-QUA, qua-QUA, qua-QUAAAAAAAAAA-ACK!

(*Reboscanini brings both hands crashing down, snuffing the final note. Instant of silence, then stands motionless as applause cascades onto his shoulders and cheers foam up about his head. Straightens and slowly crosses his wrists over his breast so that the tip of his baton is six inches northwest of his left temple. Lifts his face and turns, spreads his arms slowly to embrace the shouts of "Bravo!" Finally he bows, so deeply that the mop-strands of his wig brush on the sawdust. Then he comes erect, half-turns, steps backward. Holds palms toward his artists and bows to them. They flap their wings in modest acknowledgment, briefly bob their bills. And ancient Bebe plods into the ring, bearing in her jaws a bouquet of gardenias, which she lays repectfully on the dais.*)

The ducks quack-quacked to the delight of crowds throughout Central America and the Caribbean, brought so much joy into the world even Rebozo was tainted with it. The integrity of his despair was blemished. Suffered intermittent mild attacks of happiness, was liable to break out in smiles from time to time. And his dreams, which I continued to visit, were often blotched and mottled with good cheer. With love even. Sometimes his dreams replayed the days when Angela pretended to love him, and then they were stained through with love. I first came to know love in Rebozo's dreams.

As for me, I wasn't happy, but I too surpassed myself entertaining people. My trances came with fearful frequency, so that I'd scarcely recovered from one when the next hit. Slept poorly, couldn't digest my food, was prey again to the strange sense of foreboding that possessed me before my initiation. But onstage the power in me poured out wonders. Shows so consistently spectacular that my partitioned area in the Rotunda couldn't hold my audiences. And Don Lorenzo resolved to put me in the main tent, make me a headliner.

Here in Ciudad Tinieblas. This was the spot for me to make my starring debut. Had never forgotten the miracles of '63. Most receptive stop on our whole tour, so Don Lorenzo expected to make a killing.

It began well enough. Alejo Sancudo had taken office one week before we opened here. Mood of hope and optimism in the city, sense of good times ahead that makes folks freer with their cash, eager to spend it on amusements. Capacity crowd, even at boosted prices. Delirious with glee at Rebozo and ducks. Gave them five minutes of applause and cheers, demanded encores, and laughter still rippling through the stands when Don Lorenzo announced El Mago Mandragon.

Who hadn't an inkling what my power would pull. Jittery, bubbles in my gut and my right cheek twitching, but had the God-will-provide spirit of religious beggars. Knew power lived in me and trusted it. Hard to believe now, but impossible to deny. And as I hesitated, there in the passageway between two sets of stands, it repaid my faith. Ex-

plosion without concussion, like a rifle crack: Don Lorenzo
vanished, and I, Mandragon, was where he'd been standing, at center ring.

Spectate it now in my imagination. Replay it, witness it
like one of the crowd. A lot healthier for my mind to chew
on than my show in the morning. The whole audience
breathed in, an audible wheeze. Don Lorenzo, translated
to the top of the stands beside the bandmaster, maybe had
time to wonder if there'd be talking animals or reversed
gravity or what. But even before Mandragon the Mage
could acknowledge the applause that rolled down in welcome, I reeled as though punched, then stood with head
to one side and arms flung outward, eyeballs swung up
in their sockets so only the whites showed. There was
silence in the tent about the space of half a minute. Then
Mandragon began to speak.

In a high monotone, empty of expression, full of authority. That reached clearly to the farthest spectator. And
with the first words, a pale-blue aura began to bloom from
Mandragon's forehead, swelled steadily in size and bril-
liance till it filled the whole tent, elliptical globe of frigid
flickering light. So unsettling, along with what the voice
said, that people wept in anguish, yet no one could rise
or close his eyes or look away, or lift his hands to press
them to his ears. The voice spoke, the aura glowed, for
about half an hour.

Began by prophesying the fall of Alejo. In itself not
surprising: he'd been flushed from office three times before.
But it went on to say the coup was set for that night, would
take place within minutes, had already begun. It named the
conspirators, a gang of obscure officers, whom many in the
tent had never heard of , and as it named them, their images
flickered in the aura that swelled from my forehead. It told
how troops would seize the palace and other buildings, the
assembly and the ministries, the TV and radio stations, the
newspapers and the phone exchange. As it spoke, pictures

of the event played in the globe. Soldiers hammering doors in with their rifle butts, herding people out into the street at bayonet point. The voice said who'd be arrested, and the aura showed them being taken. Some were in the tent, and would have liked to save themselves, or at least not to have to watch and listen, but none of them could move a muscle.

Terrifying in its strangeness. The trancing seer, the expressionless authoritative voice, the pale-blue globe with visions dancing in it. But these first prophecies didn't in themselves disturb many spectators. Tinieblans were used to abrupt shifts of government. Found them diverting, since they rarely brought much trouble, except to those tossed out of jobs. Alejo had never lasted a full term. Many who'd rejoiced the week before at his inauguration were, no doubt, glad at his being deposed. For the variety of it, though the conspirators might have waited a decent interval. But then the voice began to foretell what would come after. Things would be different this time; this time Tinieblas would be twisted inside out. Dictatorship. Calamity and upheaval. Cruelty and want, a binding ring of pain drawn round the country. The voice droned on, detailing horrors. And fearful scenes were imaged in the aura, flashed and dissolved into more fearful scenes, till the whole crowd wept in despair and terror. But before it could tell the end, the voice ceased. Broke off as if unplugged, and the aura faded. Mandragon collapsed onto the sawdust of the ring.

With that, the crowd was released. Burst from the tent and found everything as described in the first part of Mandragon's prophecy. Soldiers posted round El Opulento. Soldiers in the cable office opposite. Soldiers dragging citizens into patrol trucks. Alejo had been deposed while I was in trance. Civil Guard officers had taken power. Tinieblas was under martial law.

Not what the audience had expected when they bought their tickets. So shaken by the second part of my prophecy they forgot it at once, wiped it from their minds, though

later on, when an incident I'd predicted took place, some
had flashes of *déjà-vu*. But the first part had come true
even as power was using me to utter it: no way to sweep
that under a mental rug. Those who'd been in the tent
talked of nothing else. So inside an hour the new masters of
Tinieblas learned that a circus trickster had recited all the
details of their coup, plotted in total secrecy, while it was
taking place and even before. Busy tightening their grip on
the country or they'd have arrested me. Instead they gave
Don Lorenzo until sunup to get his circus over the border.
No killing in Tinieblas after all.

Enraged, of course, and at me. Out, he figured, thirty
or forty thousand. All my fault. As if I'd overthrown Alejo
myself. It wasn't my idea to make prophecies, I was only
an instrument, and even without them he'd have made no
money. Not that year. Not with martial law and a curfew
in effect. But Don Lorenzo didn't think like that. Couldn't
just accept adversity. Had to have someone to blame, and
the someone had to be vulnerable to vengeance. So he
blamed me. Let his resentment fester all the way to Chuchaganga and meanwhile ransacked his small but venom-
steeped mind for the cruelest way to hurt me.

And Mandragon? I lay twitching in Rebozo's van like a
galvanized corpse. Squeezed like a boardinghouse lime,
exhausted, and scared to boot. In my prophetic trance I'd
borne the pain of a whole country, years of tyranny and
suffering and woe. And I was through with that, oh I was
finished! I couldn't take the trances any more. I'd have to
ask Mohotty's help.

Never got the chance to. The profits Don Lorenzo had
dreamed of weren't coming, and he had losses to recoup,
all he'd spent advertising the show in Tinieblas. We set up
as soon as we arrived in Chuchaganga, opened as soon as
we were set up. Less than twenty-four hours after my collapse I was made up and in costume. Weak as an old
woman, jittery as a caged geek, but on the main-tent runway with Rebozo, waiting for our numbers to be called.

Imelda was into her finale when Don Lorenzo, who'd withdrawn to the mouth of the runway, turned his back on the ring and walked over to us. Not a shadow of resentment or discontent. Top hat set jauntily, smooth face beaming pinkly, rich red silk cravat blossoming prosperously from his white waistcoat, tuxedo jacket sleek about his robust trunk. Strutted over with bouncy little steps, gleaming boots clicking the planks lightly, thighs of his beige jodhpurs swishing softly. Stopped before Rebozo and smiled.

"Tonight you don't go on."

Rebozo spread his arms, each with a duck in it, and shrugged his shoulders—his way of asking, Why not?

Don Lorenzo's smile spread and glowed, lighthouse beam of kindness above the rock-strewn coast of human life. Thinking, as he raised his small pink hands to caress the ducks' heads, of how when I first came to the circus only Rebozo showed me kindness. Of how, when I was ill, Rebozo nursed me. Of how I'd come to love Rebozo. I didn't know I loved Rebozo, but Don Lorenzo did. Recognized love when he saw it, just as he recognized talent and beauty, though there was no beauty, talent, or love in his own life.

"Well, you see," he said, hands caressing the ducks' necks, eyes twinkling sweetly, "you've nothing to go on with."

Don Lorenzo's carefully manicured stubby pink fingers closed about the ducks' necks so quickly and tightly nary a quack escaped. Stepped back quickly, yanking the ducks from Rebozo's arms. Smiled his benign smile, and then he twirled them, right-hand duck clockwise, left-hand duck counterclockwise, like airplane propellers. Three quick twirls, more than enough, then held them out and dropped them on the planking. Two little lumps of feathers, without a particle of joy or music anymore.

"You see? Nothing to go on with, so you don't go on."

He swung the beam of his smile toward me and bathed

me with it for a moment. Turned and went back to the mouth of the runway. Took his megaphone from a rousta-bout and strutted out into the ring.

Don Lorenzo at center ring. Waves his top hat in air, raises his megaphone.

"SEÑORAS Y SEÑORES, NINOS DE TODAS LAS EDADES! AHORA, PARA SU ADMIRACION Y DI-VERSION, EL CIRCO UNIVERSAL AMICHEVOLE TIENE EL ORGULLO DE PRESENTAR . . ."

The runway: Rebozo kneeling beside his ducks. Gathers them in his arms. Rocks back and forth, letting out low howls.

Mandragon. Makes no move to comfort Rebozo. Stands perfectly erect and still, female-male features, male-female slight figure. Looks ringward. Eyes take on a piercing glow, orange light flames about head and shoulders. Listens to Don Lorenzo's echoing voice.

". . . DEL REMOTO TIBET, DONDE LOS SABIOS GUARDAN MISTERIOS OCULTOS, EL MAS ASOM-BROSO Y PODEROSO DE TODOS LOS MAGOS; SEÑORAS Y SEÑORES, EL MAGO MANDRAGON!"

Mandragon holds out a little paper fan and lifts it two inches.

Don Lorenzo. Turns, smiling, toward the runway, waves his hat. His silk tie flies up out of his waistcoat and points straight up in air beside his right cheek. The tie draws taut, pulls upward, drags Don Lorenzo off the ground.

"QUAAAAAA!"

The tie hauls upward, slowly and steadily. Don Lorenzo drops his hat and megaphone, clutches the taut silk with plump pink hands, chins himself up to take his weight off his throat. Rises till his toes are twelve feet off the ground, staring about wildly, trying to scream for help but only quacking.

Applause and laughter from the crowd, marvelous trick!

But *performers and roustabouts rush into the ring, gather beneath Don Lorenzo, gaping and shouting. The crowd grows still, then individual spectators start to scream in horror. Police break from their stations near the stands, run toward the ring.*

El Mago Mandragon steps from the runway. Wreathed in orange-red flame. Sweeps arms apart, and the police stop in their tracks, the roustabouts and performers draw aside.

Mandragon enters the ring and stands beneath Don Lorenzo. Face raised, arms spread. Turns slowly, as though receiving applause, while Don Lorenzo pulls himself up, hand over hand, until his fingers clutch the tip of his necktie.

"QUAAAAAAAAAAAACK!"

Weary fingers slipping from the silk, smooth silk sliding through clutched fingers. Full weight against his throat, noosebite and horrorpain. Choke-anguish, Don Lorenzo starts to dance. Armflail, legthrash, shouldertwist. Face beet red, eyes bulging. Tongue poked from gaping fishmouth, jitterbug dance. Jerking and straining above Mandragon, who raises both hands, directing the crowd's attention to the spectacle.

Bulged eyes clouding over. Last convulsive flipflops. Stench of corruption as the waste of an excellent lunch empties into the seat of Don Lorenzo's beige jodhpur trousers. Legs stop kicking. Arms droop limp. Body sways noosed in air, making slow quarter-turns.

Mandragon reaches out with the paper fan and slashes the air. Don Lorenzo's corpse blops heavily to the sawdust. Mandragon bows to it, then to the crowd. Flame fades, eyes lose their glow. Stands limply with head drooped as police and others rush ringward.

20

My last bow. Spectacular stunt, and I closed out my circus career. Early version, as it turns out, of my finale as prophet and savior.

Variations on a theme, first hangman then victim. Repeating myself, as artists are condemned to. Even the greatest have only a few themes, but sad to know one's done one's best work early. Circus version much superior, my masterpiece in the form, and not because I was hangman. Simply more original, imaginative. Don Lorenzo got a marvelous noosing, mystical-magical, miraculous. Like of it never seen, before or since, whereas mine will be merely mechanical, cable and winch, but I'd best not dwell on it.

I let the police lead me away. Utterly drained, empty, way I am now. Realized at last I was responsible for what the power in me did through me. Only an instrument, and yet responsible. Convenient that it happened in Costaguana. Can't say how things would have gone had we been elsewhere, but sorcery's a crime there, and they tried me. Guilty was what I was, and that's how I pleaded. Way out of it all, I thought, couldn't take any more, wished it was over.

Mandragon went to prison. Alejo went back into exile and married Angela. Dred Mandeville went gliding on through the deep-ocean gloom.

And here in Tinieblas, what I'd prophesied came to pass. The majors were only trying to preserve their status when they overthrew Alejo and took power. Not much prestige to a commission in the Guardia, but the only way a fellow with nothing—no wealth no family, no education; no courage, no brains, no talent; no inclination to hard work—could live in comfort. Alejo meant to purge the Guardia. The majors purged him instead. But as soon as they had power, they began to enjoy it and decided to get as much as they could of it and keep it. Promoted themselves colonels and formed a junta. Suspended the constitution, dissolved the assembly, outlawed politics for everyone but themselves and their friends. Stole the state and called their theft a revolution.

When the colonels had gathered up all the power in Tinieblas, they began trying to take it from one another. The junta came to resemble a basket of lobsters. Each colonel tried to climb on top of the rest. All were equally untalented, but one was more fearful and suspicious. This was Genghis Manduco. He became Crustacean in Chief. One by one he maneuvered his fellow thieves into exile. Then he promoted himself general and ruled alone.

General Manduco raised the pay of the Guardia and recruited new *guardias* and promoted veterans and gave them all exciting modern weapons. He enlarged the coastal service and equipped it with rakishly prowed cutters. He formed an air service and equipped it with helicopters and transports for dropping paratroopers. Then, when he was sure the troops loved him and could control any foolishness civilians might think up, he raised taxes.

Under General Manduco the tax on alcoholic drinks was doubled, and the tax on cigarettes was tripled, and the tax on gasoline was doubled and redoubled, and every other tax was raised—income taxes, property taxes, amusement taxes; withholding taxes and licensing fees—and tariffs were jacked up and duties hiked, and all kinds of new imposts, tolls, and tithes were levied. The general made his brother Mangu minister of finance, and Mangu had a genius for imposing taxes. Taxes copied from other countries, and taxes resurrected from past eras, and taxes never dreamed up before. A sales tax, and all sorts of excise taxes, and a use tax, and a transactions tax, and a value-added tax, and a Ceylonese expenditure tax, and a Tsarist Russian soul tax for concerns and households with employees, and a medieval poll tax, and an Imperial Roman octroi tax on goods moved across provincial boudaries. A personal effects tax on clothing and furniture, with everyone's home inventoried to collect it, and a surcharge eating tax on plates and silverware, and a surcharge sleeping-copulating tax— so much for beds, so much for hammocks, so much for straw mats—and a surcharge crapping tax on commodes and privies. Mangu declared air a state resource, and put a tax on breathing, and sent inspectors out to compute the volume of air consumed by each family and collect accordingly. Then he put a tax on mother's milk and a tax on coffins, so that Tinieblans were taxed for being born and taxed for dying, as well as everything that went on in between. Mangu thought these taxes up and then imposed them. That was that. Anyone who objected was put on the first plane out if he was lucky, and in prison if he wasn't, and those with no luck at all were put in the ground, or in the ocean, and objection ceased. Members of the government and the Guard were assessed no taxes and bought in special tax-free stores reserved for them, so they didn't mind enforcing Mangu's decrees, and since the exciting modern weapons—along with the cutters, transport planes, and helicopters, and a special helicopter for the general to zip him in comfort anywhere he pleased—came from gringo military aid, most of the new revenue from taxes was available to be stuffed in satchels and shipped out—to Panama, to Lebanon, to Switzerland—for deposit in numbered accounts.

All dictators can be depended on to build roads and make trains run on time, but Tinieblas had no trains, so

General Manduco concentrated on building roads. He made his brother Akbar minister of public works, and Akbar not only planned a huge program of road building but got a long-term, low-interest loan from the state bank, and went into the paving business, and built the roads himself. The general made his brother Kublai head of the state bank, and Kublai became famous for approving long-term, low-interest loans. Some, the ones he approved for himself, had no term or interest at all, and with them he bought up land and businesses from Tinieblans who happened to be in exile or in prison, and from the heirs of those in the ocean or the ground. The general made his brother Xerxes head of the gaming commission, and Xerxes raised the price of lottery tickets but not the payoffs, and the difference was stuffed in satchels and shipped out. Xerxes established casinos all over the capital, and put slot-machine centers in the poorer neighborhoods, and in his spare time devised an infallible system for roulette, which he practiced nightly after closing time at one casino or another. He'd been a compulsive gambler all his life and had never had a winning year till his brother became dictator, but now he never lost, not on one spin of the wheel. In his new system he waited till a number played, and then he put his bet down. The general offered his brother Timur several important posts, but Timur was content with minor office. He became head of the courier service of the foreign ministry, and after that the diplomatic bag for the UN mission bulged with strange parcels, and people in New York spoke of the Tinieblan Connection, and Timur grew rich. The general had seventeen brothers and sisters, and all held office in his government, and all prospered.

Still, there were certain discontents among the populace. Over things like the higher price of lottery tickets and brother Mangu's crazy taxes. Over the way men in uniform had taken to insulting citizens and knocking them about. Even over the circumstance that no one had asked the

Guardia and the Manduco family to run the country, much less loot it. News of these discontents reached the general and disturbed him. The people seemed lacking in moral fiber, in willingness to sacrifice. Disaffection toward the Guardia was treasonous. Resentment toward his family was worse.

He thought of his elder brother Kublai. Went to the capital and got a job in Don Felix Grillo's bank. Only a teller, though for shrewdness Kublai deserved to be the manager, and old Grillo was so jealous that a country boy could be so shrewd he pulled a surprise audit and fired Kublai, though his books were only a few thousand short. The same for all the others, jealousy and prejudice. He himself could have had a scholarship to study abroad, but his teachers were prejudiced against him. Sat him by himself during exams. Hovered over him like buzzards, so he got poor grades. Well, now he was dictator, and Kublai was head of the state bank, and the others had whatever posts they wanted. What was wrong with that? Why shouldn't they run the country and be prosperous? Didn't they deserve it after all that jealousy and prejudice?

Nonetheless, the general decided to become popular, to divert the people's discontents, and also to legitimize his rule. He declared the Tinieblan Revolution would go forward, and ordered elections for a constituent assembly.

This was at a great rally, paid for by the general's brother Sulimán, who was minister of health, with funds budgeted for buying medicines. Seven-story portrait of the general on the facade of the Hotel Excelsior. Huge reviewing stand set up before it in Bolívar Plaza, and the general stood there at salute. While elite units goose-stepped by in their camouflage jump suits. While the new helicopters clattered overhead. While schoolchildren sang a song called "Genghis Will Save Us" (composed, so the program said, by the general's sister Lucrezia, who was minister of education, but actually ghosted by two Cubans in Miami). Then the general spoke. In a voice graveled by the whisky he'd drunk to calm his nerves and further distorted by the pressure against his throat of the bulletproof vest he was wearing, but boomed to thunder by loudspeakers and flung to every crevice of the land by TV and radio and cheered at every pause by the multitude. By peasants dragooned from their fields and trucked in to the capital. By state employees mustered in their offices and marched in lockstep to the plaza. By children assembled at the schools and issued bouquets. All carefully instructed to cheer at each pause, and the general declared the Revolution would go forward!

No force on earth could stay the liberation of the Tinieblan people! They were equal to any sacrifice! Let the reactionaries beware!

Let the imperialists beware! (The general waved his left hand toward the Reservation, where all the exciting weapons were unloaded, where the Guardia drew ammunition for them, where the helicopters were serviced and repaired. He lifted his eyes toward Dewey Hill, from whence came his military aid.) He, Genghis Manduco, would liberate Tinieblas from imperialism!

(The general drank from his canteen, which was full of whisky.) If the imperialists resisted, he would crush them!

(The general put his hand on his heart, to make sure his bulletproof vest was in place.) If need be, he would take the first bullet in his own breast!

Let reactionaries and imperialists beware! The Tinieblan Revolution would go forward! And he, Genghis Manduco, would lead it, if the will of the people so ordained!

The people spoke their will later that month. All citizens were compelled to vote. All candidates were selected by the general. The winners ratified the constitution he presented to them. They elected him president for life. They delegated all legislative authority to a committee picked by him. Then they adjourned. The will of the people was clear, and so the general led the Revolution forward.

The general made his brother Caligula head of the legislative committee. It poured out a torrent of new codes. A rent code and a banking code and a labor code. An agricultural code, a commercial code, all sorts of codes. These took effect at once, though no one they concerned had been consulted. They were supposed to benefit the poor at the expense of the rich, and they hurt the rich very horribly, those who'd become prosperous before the Revolution. But the poor got no benefit. The codes were administered by the government, and the government was the general and his family and the high officers of the Guardia, and their only concern was filling the satchels.

Besides the codes, there was nationalization. Which meant confiscation by the Manduco family, or the Guardia general staff. Title passed to the Tinieblan state and people, but the wealth went into the satchels and the numbered accounts. Not wise to notice though. When *La Patria* was ordered nationalized, Lazarillo Agudo wrote that it was being "manduquized," and he was put in prison, and later into the Pacific Ocean, from an altitude of two thousand feet, out the door of one of the new helicopters.

All the newspapers were manduquized, and all the radio stations, and the three television stations. Profits stuffed into satchels, and their facilities used to tell the people how happy they were, what strides forward they were making under the general's inspired guidance. And also to remind them that if their happiness wasn't perfect, the reactionaries and the imperialists were to blame. The general made his sister Mesalina minister of information, and she had a gift for describing the people's happiness. And the vision to see progress where others saw decline. And appreciation for the general's virtues, his wisdom and selflessness, his patriotism, his courage and compassion and, despite all these, his modesty. And a knack for spotting reactionaries —anyone in Tinieblas with property worth manduquizing. And a talent for unmasking imperialists—anyone outside

Tinieblas who might be blamed for the country's problems. And limitless venom for denouncing their devilish crimes. But the imperialists didn't mind being denounced. On important matters the general was always obedient. They sent more helicopters and more exciting weapons, and also grants and loans, most of which ended up in the satchels.

Mesalina's work was a great comfort to the general, and to the rest of the family, and to the members of the government and the Guard. Gave them so much to be proud of, and someone to blame whenever things went wrong. But her venom filled people's daily lives with rancor, and curdled their dreams so that they went around scowling and snarling, though no one except those in power believed the newspapers, or the radio or television. Rumor became the only means of communication. Tinieblans inhaled and exhaled rumors day and night. A cloud of rumor hung from coast to coast, and a rumor breathed on the Costaguanan border reached the Ticamalan border in a matter of minutes. Not by telephone either. People were too smart to use the phone.

The telephone company was manduquized, along with the power company and the gas company, and all the rates were raised. The bus companies were manduquized, and the fares were raised, and a contract on new buses was let at the high bid to a manufacturer represented by the general's brother Nero, who was minister of transport. Many more companies were manduquized, and large sums were extorted from others under threat of manduquization.

After the Revolution had been striding forward for a while, the general took stock. His family was prospering, as were the other high officials of the government and the higher-ranking officers of the Guard. The troops were happy with their modern weapons and their tax-free stores, with insulting citizens and knocking them about. The people were happy, as anyone who glanced at a newspaper knew instantly. And he was beloved. His portrait was everywhere throughout the country. Children sang "Genghis Will Save Us" in all the schools. And yet, things weren't perfect. There were still problems, the problems Tinieblas always had. If anything, they'd grown worse, with so much being shipped out in the satchels. But the newspapers blamed them on the reactionaries and the imperialists, and promised that the Revolution would solve them, so that they didn't disturb the general very much. The real trouble was the lower-ranking members of the government, and the members of the government-sponsored unions and student groups. They believed the general's speeches and the newspapers. Mesalina's venom had them all worked up. They supported the general but wondered why he pampered the reactionaries—as if he could manduquize all their property, or even most of it, without cutting tax revenue and drying up the source of bribes and having less to stuff into the satchels. They wondered why he didn't drive the imperialists from the Reservation—as if he were actually valiant, as if he wanted a bullet in his breast. These people were restless and unsatisfied, but the general couldn't put them all in prison just for believing his speeches and his sister. He had to please them somehow—but not by interfering with the satchels! The satchels came first! So he stepped up his denunciations of the gringos, which pleased his supporters and took the people's minds off their real troubles. And the more he denounced the gringos, the more they gave him—since all he did was talk, since when it came to important matters he was still obedient. Besides that, the Reservation had outlived most of its usefulness, was costing too much money and should be scaled down. They could get rid of the useless portions and appear generous, and they proposed that sort of arrangement to the general. They didn't have to ask him to pretend it was his own idea. He convinced himself of that without any prompting and undertook to gain international support for his liberation struggle.

There were a number of countries ruled more or less like Tinieblas, by blustering thieves who'd stolen power and kept it by force. The general toured these countries. He was everywhere received by cheering multitudes. He was deeply touched. He might have remembered that whenever one of the other blustering thieves had visited Tinieblas, the general had arranged a touching reception—peasants dragooned from their fields; state employees mustered at their offices; children assembled in the schools and issued bouquets: the lot dispatched by truck and bus and lockstep, and anyone who didn't cheer was in bad trouble. The general forgot all that and took those welcomes for outpourings of love. The world, he judged, agreed with Mesalina. His speeches were always greeted by clamorous applause, although his translators, even members of his own party, had trouble making out his phrases. His voice was graveled by whisky, and further distorted by the pressure of his vest, but every time he paused, the crowds applauded. The trip did wonders for the general's spirits.

But on his return his elder brothers had distressing news. Not much was going in the satchels lately. Farms and businesses produced less once they'd been manduquized, and the nonmanduquized sector was floundering too. Caligula's codes had crippled industry, and maimed commerce, and left agriculture for dead. All sorts of concerns were going bankrupt. Their owners had stopped paying taxes and bribes. Many people were out of work and had stopped spending, even on slot machines and lottery tickets. Not much was going in the satchels.

The general wasn't sure the troops would continue to love him if their officers stopped prospering. He was for getting out while there was time. He was greedy only because he was fearful. He'd shipped plenty of money out, and he was for joining his money, before his nightmares caught up to him. Timur was greedy because he was greedy; he wanted more. Mangu pointed out that some of the

younger brothers and sisters, some of the cousins and in-
laws, hadn't got their fair share yet. He and Timur tried
to dissuade the general, but the general was resolute. Was
going to cut and run, but Kublai told him shut up, stop
being a baby. The cash was gone, but the country still had
credit. They all could keep prospering if the credit held.
The thing was not to lose confidence. They'd go to the foreign banks, and bankers liked confidence. Liked stability
too, and God knew the Tinieblan government was stable.
All the opposition was in exile or prison, if not in the
ocean or ground. The thing was not to lose nerve. The
thing was to keep a firm grip on the country.

With that, the general took heart. If Kublai said so,
things would be all right. Kublai was the shrewdest one in
the whole family.

The general embarked on a great program of public
works. Roads especially, superhighways through the jungle,
with bridges even where there were no rivers. And also
office buildings, a skyscraper for each ministry. And a
sports stadium for every town, and a new airport right beside the perfectly good old one. And a gigantic dam that
flooded half La Merced Province when it collapsed, and
a more gigantic one on the ruins of the first. All financed
by foreign banks at whatever rate they felt like charging.
No point, Kublai said, in haggling. Showed lack of confidence, and the thing was to get cash. Money poured into
Tinieblas, and prosperity was restored.

Prosperity raced on. Whenever it faltered, whenever it
slowed to a gallop, Kublai said the thing was to keep the
momentum, and devalued the currency. Prices rose, of
course, and people suffered, but Mesalina told them they
were happy. Those who still complained were put here and
there. But the satchels were full again, that was what
counted. The satchels were full and the numbered accounts
were groaning.

In this way the general and his fake revolution smashed

the productive sectors of Tinieblas, and ruined its currency, and wrecked its credit; sent thousands into exile or to prison; put hundreds in the ocean or the ground; taxed the people into penury and mortgaged the country to foreign banks to the fourth generation. Then came the drought.

But first the general had his agreement with the gringos. Under it they kept exactly what they wanted and relinquished what they had no use for. The general announced it as a great victory and held a huge rally to celebrate.

On the day the agreement took effect, thousands of Tinieblans entered the Reservation. Gates swinging open, no foreign soldiers demanding to see a pass, and people roamed about, picnicked on what had been the Fort Shafter parade grounds, strolled through the woods where my mother was raped (if that version of the birth is true, not just a dream of Apple's). People trampled the lawn of the Reservation Club, where for years there had been a sign: "NO DOGS OR TINIEBLANS." Went up on the porch and broke down the screen doors, swarmed inside and overturned the mahogany tables. They went out to the beach, where (461 years before) the shark-chewed head of the discoverer of Tinieblas had been washed up, and waded fully clothed into the surf. Or simply wandered about, speaking in hushed voices.

Amazement, then jubilation. More than five thousand collected in front of what had been the headquarters at Fort Shafter, around the flagpole where, for eight decades, a foreign flag had flown. Made and cheered impromptu orations on the greatness of the occasion. Perfectly orderly and democratic, but after a time the orators forgot themselves and began denouncing Mangu and his taxes. The cheers grew louder, and speakers began denouncing the general himself. Then two companies of *guardias* arrived and smashed a few hundred heads and hauled a hundred or so off to prison and truncheoned the others back into the city. Then they locked the gates and posted sentinels until the newly recovered property could be divided up among the general's family and friends.

Jubilation, then disillusionment. And almost as soon as the agreement went into effect, the drought began.

21

The rains quit right on schedule, the fourth week in December. They weren't necessarily scheduled to quit entirely. A few showers during the first months of a year are normal here. None came though, and no one really minded, but April, when the rains were scheduled to resume, was dry.

Schools reopened. Children sang "Genghis Will Save Us." The dummy assembly reconvened briefly to praise the Revolution and the general. Wind shifted too, for that matter, as it was scheduled to, and the Humboldt Current swung back out to sea. But no rain fell. It wasn't even cloudy.

All through May the sun sizzled in an empty sky. In June, at dawn on the sixth anniversary of the majors' coup, a light mist was seen on the Caribbean coast, but it burned off before midmorning. In July, a cloud the size of a lady's handkerchief appeared over Córdoba, hung there just long enough to be inspected by the general's brother Nebucodonosor, who was minister of agriculture, and Lieutenant Colonel Fidel Acha, chief of intelligence of the Guardia Civil. The general dispatched them to Córdoba by helicopter the instant news of the cloud reached him, and they inspected it and reported to a council of state. Acha said it was backed like a weasel. Nebucodonosor found it very like a whale. Dropped no rain, but the ministry of information squeezed a few lies from it. Announced that meteorological engineers, working under the immediate

direction of General Genghis Manduco, Life President of
the Blah-blah-blah and Blah of the Government, Commander in Chief of the Blah-blah-blah-blah and Blah-blah
of the Revolution, were conducting experiments in Salinas,
and that results were encouraging, and that the drought
would soon be broken. But August, September, and October
brought no relief.

From the air, the rice and cane fields of La Merced
looked boarded over. The banana groves of Tuquetá were
baked ocher. The hills of Otán, pastureland, sat crusted
in the sun like huge dog lumps, and in Selva Trópica the
jungle rivers shrank to trickles, then turned to empty
ditches of cracked mud. Tinieblas was drying up like an
old maid.

The worst was that Tinieblas had been singled out. The
rest of Central America had plenty of rain. In the south,
peasants gaped in fury at the thunderheads that billowed
beyond the Costaguanan border. North, across the Río
Agrio in Ticamala, rain fell in torrents, and the rice stood
shoulder high. At Tres Olmos, where the Pan-American
Highway crosses, where I crossed with my tribe the next
year, the Río Agrio is only fifty yards wide, yet there were
days when no one could see across it for the downpour.
Not a drop fell on the Tinieblan side though. The rain
stopped right at midstream, hung there like a curtain, and
a man could stand on the bridge, on the Tinieblan side
of the black stripe that marked the frontier, and reach his
hand across and get it drenched, while the rest of him
stayed dry as an oven.

Experts took atmospheric samples. Priests said special
masses. Congregations paraded saints through the fields.
The Indians in Remedios staged rain dances, and the Indians in Selva Trópica sacrificed iguanas, and then tapirs,
and then boys and girls. Witches like La Negra stopped
brewing love potions and cast rain spells, hired themselves
out to chant incantations. The West Indian community in

Bastidas imported a voodoo wizard from Jamaica, and a voodoo superwizard from Haiti. Don Julio Abeja, a devotee of Hermes Trismegistos, drew a pentagram in chalk on the pavement in front of the palace, and sat down inside it with a stack of ancient tomes, and spent three nights there conjuring in Greek and Latin. Nothing worked.

Relief aid poured in from all over. The general set up a committee, Timur and Sulimán and Nero, to distribute it. They organized a black market that kept the satchels passably full, but Tinieblan energies were mainly spent placing blame. Some blamed God for deciding to begin the end of the world in Tinieblas. Some blamed the government for calling down God's wrath. The government blamed the imperialists, that is, the CIA. The CIA had stationed special planes off the coasts, and was lassoing all the clouds that came near, and dragging them back out to sea so Tinieblas would wither. Those who managed, one way or another, to blame someone felt a bit better. Resentment canceled some of their despair. But the drought continued. On Discovery Day, a year after the Reservation agreement took effect, at what ought to have been the height of the rainy season, a few greasy gouts dribbled on the capital. But what did that count? Barely enough to dampen the pavements! No more than an insult and mockery! And December came and went without so much as a thick dew.

Through January and February and into March the country waited. Trembling like a prisoner between torture sessions. No rain, but rain wasn't scheduled for those months, but what about April? Would April be dry too? The terror was that it would be. The terror was that it had quit raining in Tinieblas once and for all.

Scaredest of all was Genghis Manduco, Blah-blah of the Republic and Head of the Blah, Blah-in-blah of the Guardia Civil and Maximum Leader of the Blah-blah-blah-blah. Supposed to be fearless, and that's how he looked in his portraits. On highway billboards and huge posters hung on the main buildings. Eyes wide-set and froggishly bulged, so he seemed eager to confront things straight on. Smooth brow, because no disciplined activity went on behnd it, so he looked serene. Firm jaw and uniform suggested soldierly confidence, and he was tall for a Tinieblan and broad-shouldered, beefy but not too much run to fat. An imposing figure, but for all that scared almost senseless, trembling in terror.

Poor Genghis. I've looked into your heart, seen it stewed in fear. All the Manducos were bullies, therefore cowards, but Genghis was the most craven of the lot. Afraid of going to bed and of getting out of it, and of everything in between on either side. Mandragon's seen it all, and pitied. That's all he ever wanted, only safety. Poor Genghis. There isn't any, not until you're dead.

Wangled a commission in the Guardia and rode the escalator up to major. Low-risk, low-prestige employment for low-caliber people. For parasites, for bullies and cowards. Scowled fiercely, spoke gruffly, swore foully. Sneered at softness. At love, that is, and religion and culture and art. Snorted and strutted, so no one suspected you were terrified all the time. All the time, though as safe as a person can get this side of a coffin. Decently salaried. Comfortably obscure. Best he could hope for, then the other majors ruined it. They took him for the brave fellow he pretended to be and invited him to join their conspiracy.

Poor Genghis. More afraid than ever, but he had to join. Suspected him of courage, but if he didn't join they'd suspect him of integrity, of loyalty to his oath. Unjustly, of course, but what did that matter? Slightest suspicion of integrity, and they'd do something unpleasant to him, to keep him from betraying their ·plot. So he joined it. Terrified it might fail and terrified when it succeeded. There he was, a member of a junta, basketed in with a bunch of ambitious scramblers. Fear sharper than ambition. Scrambled hardest, got to the top. But being on top didn't bring safety, did it?

Just made him more conspicuous, poor thing, just made him more threatened, like a roach when the kitchen light goes on.

Everything in fear, then as before. Afraid of the people, so he strengthened the Guardia. Afraid of the Guardia, so he pampered it, made it a privileged caste. Afraid of the future, so he stole all the money he could. Afraid of betrayal, so he put his family in office and let them steal too. Afraid of the anger this caused, of everyone who wasn't afraid, so he took repressive measures that made him enough enemies to scare someone brave. Afraid of being feared, so he invoked the spirit of revolution. Afraid of the risen spirit, so he ruled spasmodically, and got into fearsome situations. Afraid of the truth, so he wrapped himself in lies and made fearful blunders that damaged the country and made him less safe than ever. Poor Genghis. Look how he had to live.

Housed wife and children in the palace but spent little time there. Lived and worked in a fortified compound fifty miles from the capital. Walls topped by watchtowers and grounds patrolled. Rarely went out in public, and when he did wore a bulletproof vest and a curtain of bodyguards. Drank to calm his nerves, and since of all things most afraid of his own fear, invented, in collaboration with sister Mesalina, a fictional character, also named Genghis, and played at being him.

This imaginary Genghis felt deep compassion for the downtrodden, had pledged his life to the cause of social justice. Came forward at the people's call and led them to magnificent advances. A world figure, loved past all believing in Tinieblas, revered wherever liberty was prized. He was wise: his sayings were collected in a booklet and memorized in all the schools. Humble: he wore a simple fatigue uniform with no insignia. Above all, absolutely fearless, nothing less than every inch a man. Observe: he was a prodigious consumer of women.

Here was a Genghis! But, as usual in acting performances, the connection between the player and the role was mainly illusion. The flesh-and-bone Genghis had compassion only for himself: his cause was personal safety. No one had asked for him. His rule advanced nothing, except thievery and disorder. He was more slave of his own fears than leader of anything. A belch produced by the country's indigestion, a chancre not a spirochete. Tinieblans loathed him, and when safe from his spies reviled him and ridiculed him. Foreign leaders, once they'd met him, knew him for a poltroon and clown. The sayings where ghosted. The fatigues were for camouflage, so he could mingle with troops in case of attack. And he was always frightened. Basted in terror, marinated in dread, stewed in fear. At only one point did the real and fake Genghises meet: the appetite for female flesh wasn't an act.

The general's compound enclosed two bomb-proof bunkers. He lived in one and kept the other stocked with whores. Flew fresh ones in from Miami every week. Saw to it they earned their money. And when he toured the country and couldn't take whores along, his goons rustled local girls for his bed or hammock. Some would have gone freely— he was in power, after all—but he didn't want these. Liable to care for him, to enjoy themselves, and therefore unsatisfying. The whole point of women for the general was that polluting one who neither cared for nor enjoyed him made him feel brave. In that brief spasm he faced life with a high heart. Otherwise, he lived in fear.

And, since the drought, in abject trembling terror. Not for his country or the people in it. Cared only about himself and wouldn't change now. Not afraid of ruin either. He had his loot outside Tinieblas—a stock portfolio, and an Aegean isle, and a castle in Spain, and bulging accounts in Switzerland and Panama. Fields could go barren and cattle lank. Banks could fail and businesses go bust. Tinieblas could blow away, he'd live in plenty. But he had the common coward's fear of life and death, and the despot's

fear of comeuppance, and now he feared for the only relief
he got from either. Since the rains stopped, the general
hadn't had a spasm. It sprinkled throughout Tinieblas on that now wistfully
remembered Christmas Eve, and the general spritzed all
over his harlotorium. But neither he nor the Tinieblans
counted blessings. Christmas was rainless, but the rains
were scheduled to quit. And spritzless for the general, but
he was with his wife. Went with her to mass, though public
men had been murdered in cathedrals. Had himself photoed
with her on the steps, though the Alcaldía roof gave a
field of fire onto them, and snipers had been known to
elude police. Distributed Christmas baskets with her in
La Cuenca, though grenades had been thrown from tenements before. Sat opposite her at an eight-course Christmas
dinner, though she wouldn't let his mess sergeant cook it,
so all he could risk eating was the bread. Stood beside her
on the receiving line at an interminable reception, though
even a lightweight flak suit stifles and rubs. Spent a whole
night, not in the same bed with her, or even the same room,
but under the same roof, though the roof was hardly bomb-
proof. But when the ordeal was over and he could stop
acting; when, with every nerve screaming, he'd coptered
back to his compound; when he'd dashed to his quiffo-
drome, and torn his clothes off, and flung himself down
between two sides of US Prime; when he'd chosen the
juicier and plunged his gorged Genghishood in to the haft
—what then? Why, nothing. Nothing at all. He humped
and he pumped, but nothing happened.

Kept at it, didn't you, good soldier? Gave it your best.
On the satin sheets, among the plump pillows. Against
the mound of silk cushions, on the fluffy rug. Forty feet
underground, cased in concrete, while the air conditioner
hummed soothingly, and the phonograph moaned, and the
rose-colored lamps blushed softly. Remounted from a different angle. Nothing. Changed mounts. Still nothing. Dis-

mounted and let the professionals take charge. Nothing, nothing, nothing, nothing, nothing. Not all their skill could lure a twitch of solace, nor all their toil wring out one drop of ease.

Tried again that night. Failure. Canceled appointments and spent the next day at it. Zero. By then the trulls were rasped raw and couldn't continue, not even for bonuses, but it was all their fault anyway, wasn't it? Ordered your overseas pimps to send the new batch in early and, meanwhile, sampled a batch from your local pimps. The guards winked at each other in admiration for *mi general* when the *gringas* waddled out and eased their punished sterns into the staff car. They whistled in envy of *mi general* when the chopperful of replacements clattered in. But had they seen *mi general* a few hours later, they'd have cackled in scorn. Flaming horn and purple filberts. Whimpers of self-pity and defeat. You'd have cut your throat, wouldn't you have, *mi general*? If you hadn't been such a coward. And if you'd had my gift of futuretouring, you'd have cut it anyway, coward or no. *Mi general*'s martyrdom was only beginning.

As it slunk on, *mi general* expanded his pimpacy till it had branches in thirty cities on all five continents. Culled him the cream of the quimintern. Plucked the flower of strumpetry and shipped it to Tinieblas air express. Women so lovely a mere glimpse of one would drench the average man's trousers, so skilled that aged and desiccated gaffers, who'd given their loins up for dead, revived at their touch and performed prodigies. They arrived smiling and gay, confident of the huge bonus *mi general* offered to whoever brought in a gusher. And left dejected. All they pumped were salt tears. He had famous specialists flown in to examine him, and made secret visits to famous clinics, but the doctors were as helpless as the whores. So he consulted the best witches in Tinieblas, *brujos* and *santeros* and *curanderos*. In stealth, because he couldn't trust them to keep their mouths shut, and couldn't let it get out he was anything less than every inch a man. His bodyguards snatched them from their houses in the predawn hours, and whisked them to the compound in unmarked cars, and prisoned them there as long as their treatments lasted. And put them in the ocean when their treatments failed, from a good altitude, via helicopter. Would have done the same with any who succeeded, but since they all failed, *mi general* said he was doing the state a service, ridding it of quacks.

In this way, La Negra came to spend three weeks at the compound, and to leave it by air for a swim in the Pacific. She knew from the first *mi general* would never risk her gossiping about him, but she was very old now, and ready to die, and she extracted a harsh revenge in advance. Made him swill all sorts of excretions and secretions. Made him sleep with a live viper in a pot under his bed. Made him endure her own scabrous caresses—all in the name of curing him, of course. And when she judged his credulity had about run out, threw the hoax in his face.

"Your case is hopeless, you fool! I knew that the minute I saw you. You're bewitched by your own shittiness, and there's no cure for that!"

Then she turned back. Still faithful to her art, though she'd die that night and knew it. Still enthralled by love's mysteries, concerned by a baffling case. "Three women might have cured you. Alejo's Argentine whore, but you exiled him. Irene Hormiga, but she's been dead five years and wouldn't have touched you anyway. And I might have cured you too, if I hadn't sold my monster." Stuck her tongue out between empty gums. "But I wouldn't have! Not to save my life!"

Mi general was crying like a baby.

The drought worsened, and so did the general's martyrdom. The earth dried up and hardened, and his untapped gonads swelled to the size and consistency of billiard balls,

so that the least movement was painful for him. Fields
turned to dust, and the wind blew choking dust clouds from
border to border, and the general's unslaked dreads rattled
inside him, like loose stones. Thought only of himself
though, so time passed before he connected his suffering
with the country's. But when he did, he became totally
terrified, once and for all. He was Tinieblas's curse, and
Tinieblas was his. His drought and the country's were the
same ailment. He would never spritz again until it rained,
and it would never rain again until he spritzed.

Around and around.

Poor Genghis.

Mandragon will save you.

22

Mandragon came in the seventh year of the dictatorship, in the sixteenth month of the drought. As power's instrument and emissary, to accomplish its purpose and my fate. Saved and destroyed, brought harmony and strife, triumphed and fell; and now waits, wombed and coffin'd, for the next turning.

Pattern of all things on earth and out of it, each insect, tree, and star: emergence and flowering, splendor and withering, death and rebirth. Each nascent budlet doomed, each end always also a beginning. Spin off in a few hours, and also go round again, portioned to maggots.

Same when I went to prison in Costaguana: dismantled and recycled. Circus entertainer into harlot—not as pretty as Genghis's, but not as mercenary either, and my lovers weren't finicky about looks. Still giving delight, still bringing awe and wonder, but in a different fashion, through a different form of power.

My magoship died along wih Don Lorenzo, self-snuffed. I hadn't the strength to be power's toy any longer. For days I lay in a Chuchaganga lockup, my mind a static buzz, and when I rose to consciousness again, I was empty: the power that had lived in me was gone. Not for good, though I thought so then. And felt mixed anguish and relief as I do now. Abandoned and worthless, but free of responsibilities I'd never wanted and had pretended didn't exist, of obligations that I couldn't bear. Everything has its reward, even extinction.

Because it's not all that rosy trucking omnipotence around, having an alien force inside you, never knowing what monsters or miracles are up your sleeve. Oh, bearable enough, and even fun, when it's content with harmless pranking, amusing wonderlets, innocent monkeyings with commonplace reality, and if there are side effects, if it scares some poor bystander witness or drives him to drink, well, you can handle them. So long as you can pretend *you're* not to blame. But slaving for it, feeling it piss your precious strength into total strangers! drain your life away without even asking!—much less asking nicely! much less saying please! Having it toss you into trance whenever it cares to! sling you, willy-nilly, all over space-time! shove your face into messes you never made! Being its toy, its tool, its flunky, no! that's not so pleasant! No! that's not what you'd call a very good trip! And then, when it turns demonic! When it takes up murder! When it uses you to strangle people! When it makes *you* the instrument of its justice!—or its vengeance or horror-lust or taste for sick jokes! When it does that, and you know that you're responsible . . . Something inside you that isn't you and you can't control it, but you're still responsible for whatever it pulls! Nothing to do, but still, you should have done something! You ought to have tried! At least you ought to have been appalled! AT LEAST YOU SHOULDN'T HAVE ENJOYED WHAT IT WAS DOING! Oh, no, that's hideous, too hideous to bear.

There is a choice for those chosen by power. Step forward into the mystery. Put terror to one side, give yourself fearlessly. In respect and awe, but with your puny dignity about you; calm but also vigilant, unwavering. Then it may serve you even as you serve it. Or turn away, slink off, and hide your face from it. Then it may leave you as a thing unworthy. I chose the latter after Don Lorenzo died.

Not from contrition. Either one of Rebozo's ducks was worth a Hollywood of Don Lorenzos. The ducks had talent, they made people laugh. I chose from fear, the most disgusting of all motives. Fear of the power in me, of what it might do next, of the way it drained me, of being bound in its service. And also that special form of fear people call guilt, at the joy I felt when Don Lorenzo strangled, joy in his suffering and in having a part in it. I turned away and hid, and power left me, and, just as now, I felt anguish but also relief: no gift, no obligation. Yet even then I was about to take service with another form of power, for everything on earth and out of it is in the service of one form of power or another, knowingly or not, and all forms are part of the same network. I was about to take service with the power of love.

Already turning toward love there in the lockup where they held me till my trial. Cell to myself, a murderer's privilege, but now I was uneasy with solitude. Till then I'd felt complete in myself. I hadn't realized I cared for Rebozo till Don Lorenzo showed me. I'd know love only at second hand, in Rebozo's dreams, and years had to pass before I learned one must love everything, on earth and out of it, each insect, tree, and star. But in that lockup, empty and dispirited as I am now, I began turning.

Toward love, and carnal love is the first turn. For which one needs gender, and that was coming too. No luxuries in there, no brocade sofas, but I was softening already, rocking femaleward. It wasn't till later that my hips broadened and my breasts puffed, that my penis withered to the size of a child's fingertip and the cleft below it tuliped and swelled. The police medic gave me a glance and noted my donglet, foolishly X-ed me male, but I'd never been male and was femaling already, tipped toward that end of the seesaw by my craving for companionship and the presence all around me of lonely men. Plenty of males are tipped the same way in such conditions, but I went more easily. I hadn't any gender to give up.

I gave up my virginity in El Olvido. Which was different from this place, though all prisons are places of harshness and violence. But El Olvido was off in a desert place away from everything, as if the prison itself, not just us prisoners, had been discarded and forgotten. Harshness and violence all around as well as inside it; jagged escarpments, stony wastes, splintery-walled dusty pits where, chained in couples, we quarried rock for gravel. Strange venue for the flowering of love.

Wooden doors on the cells, like downstairs where they keep the politicals. And that's strange. . . . Never been down there yet I know the doors are wooden, not bars like the cages on this floor and upstairs. Can feel the texture of rough mold-stained wood against my cheek, though my cheek's pressed to the fabric of this chaise. Rough wood against my chest and palms, though I'm curled here. . . . *Confort stands with her breasts and palms and cheek pressed to the cell door, cheek wet with tears against the heavy wood.* I feel it through her! half down there already! I could go down and be with them! Power seeping back, filling me . . .

Trick of my mind, imagination. Or memory: I stood that way myself. Weeping against the cell door in El Olvido when Tulio Lobo, who was my lover, died. Not my only lover, not by a hundred, but I wept for him. Broke a guard's thighbone with a sledge trying to escape, and they buried him alive, head down in a pit up to his knees and made bets on how long his feet would keep kicking. I leaned against the cell door weeping for him, and that's what it was just now, a memory. Press my cheek against soft fabric and go back to El Olvido Prison.

Where the cells had wooden doors. And wooden bunks with sweat-blotched bug-rife mattresses. On a pile of which I gave up my virginity. A bandit from Hermosura, Aníbal Cuervo, dumped the mattresses onto the floor and pronged me there, while our two other cellmates waited turn.

No rape, I collaborated fully. Though when I depantsed and lay down, I was confused as to motive. Cuervo declared his intentions as soon as the door shut behind me. Partly political: establish power over me by using me, and over the other two by going first, and I thought, Yes, that's what I deserve. Full of guilt and eager to be punished, craving all the victimhood I could get from the moment Don Lorenzo's corpse dropped at my feet. Or that's what I thought in my confusion. I was about to take up service with love.

Depantsed and lay down. Opened to him before he could turn me over, and what surprise when he discovered I was female! Not female entirely, no one is, but female enough, more female than anything else in that prison, though plenty of the men there had been bent in that direction. Substandard parts, but I had them, and while gender doesn't depend on how you're equipped, they meant a lot to Cuervo. He hadn't seen female parts in fifteen years.

Howl of delight that put me off my thoughts of guilt and punishment. Turned me tender. Didn't feel victimized at all and no longer craved to, not that he puzzled long over his find or showed it much reverence. Pronged straight in. Stabbed and jabbed and flopped onto me croaking. Hurt me of course, I was all torn and bleeding, but also at peace. Seized, but the power working through him wasn't alien.

Now see me spraddled on the bedbugged ticking with a squirming thief nailed into me. Vitruvio Víbora, cellmate. Climbed on as Cuervo rolled off, speared me so quickly I hardly noticed the interruption, and it's a good exercise to give that scene a rerun, scan it in upside-down roachorama from the ceiling, or as if there'd been a mirror like the one over poor Genghis's divan. Help keep my mind off morning and my dance, off hope-fear that power might return to me. The light is from a loaf-sized crossbarred niche high up in the wall, afternoon rays bathing my riveter's rump as he wangles it clock- and counterclockwise. His hands grip my upper arms, his toes beetle for purchase on the stone. Bare knees planted on the edge of a mattress and trousers bunched at his ankles. Cuervo sits hunched on a bunk frame absorbed in the show, hands dangling between spread thighs, dork drooping tearfully, while Euclides Chova, number three, stands by at modified present arms, ready to take over, clutching his peeled wand with both fists as though he were afraid it might fly off him. My knees are raised. My brown calves reach to twine the waist above me. Getting the knack of it, and as the grip melts, as the loins untense and sag against me, my arms reach up to twine the shuddering shoulders, my smile floats up beside the tucked head, a smile immensely tender, loving, gay.

A natural. Born to it, or rather reborn. Doña Mandra ran her maiden heats like a thoroughbred. No careful breaking in, but she gave three jocks strong rides to the finish. Gave them and those who followed delight and wonder, and for herself took joy.

Joy in my lover's urgency, his need; or in his torpor if he needed urging. In taking and being taken: sea's joy engulfing, earth's joy being plowed. In being seized by power, swollen and stuffed, a power working through the man who tumored me, and also joy in conjuring that power—for I soon learned to summon and direct it—in using it to master men. Joy in submission, joy in tyranny, joy in giving ease and torment. Milking the violence from them, witching male arrogance to tameness, or remanning them when they'd been beaten tame. I had joy in all my lovers, though they were mostly animals of the worst sort, predators whose brains were circuited for cruelty and rapine, machines for broadcasting chaos and woe—and though El Olvido was designed to be joy-proof; not just the prison, that whole region of the earth.

In Aníbal Cuervo, whose eyes were kilned glass-hard by years of pillaging and prison, who took my virginity as roughly as he'd raped peasant girls and planters' daughters, but later cried his first tears since babyhood in my arms. In

Vitruvio Víbora, thief, who squirmed and serpented his couplings out as long as possible, and in Euclides Chova, bank robber, who was on and in and out and off like a jaybird. In Canuto Caimán, a bandit from the swamplands on the Tinieblan border opposite Selva Trópica, who was put in our cell after months in solitary—a huge man, thighs like mahogany logs, hung like a buffalo, and during *la rabia*, the ten-plus years when only violence ruled in Costaguana, he strewed the mangrove flats with corpses, men whose necks he'd snapped with his bare hands. But he was a gentle lover, and his pleasure came in a soft tremor along his spine, like the vibrations in a strip of rail when an unseen train's approaching.

In Nepomuceno Aspid, our cellmate for six months, small and slight like me and about my color, with whorls of blue-black hair from throat to ankles. He'd been sent in chains to El Olvido for passing checks on banks that weren't there, and stock in companies that hadn't been founded; for selling imaginary emerald mines and oil wells, and tracts of ranchland that turned out to be under the Pacific; for peddling shares in a project to make shirt cloth out of spider webs and patents on impossible inventions—a car that ran on ordinary rainwater, an ointment (perfect for secret agents) that turned whoever rubbed it on invisible—and he went crazy on the way. Bright-eyed cackling madness. Nonstop chatter about his brilliant cons, his intrepid talkings-his-way-out-of-trouble, his infallible escape schemes. He boasted that he could sell his own mother a sack of scorpions, but now he was as deluded as his victims, self-swindled into believing he'd fly to Panama on bird wings made from bunk frames and mattress cloth, or brew revolt among the guards and free us all. Sometimes he got the notion we were free already; that he'd amassed a fortune and controlled a hundred corporations; that the prison was the Hotel Maravilla in Cricamaña, a big resort, and our cell the presidential suite; that Cuervo was his executive assistant and Caimán his bodyguard and Víbora his lawyer and Chova his accountant; that I was a famous movie actress; that the guards were bellhops and waiters; that the rock pits were a golf course and our sledges woods and irons—and then he'd stop yapping and ball his fist and raise it to his cheek, and in it was an invisible telephone on which he took calls from God. As first he refused to make love with me—too busy on escape plans or financial matters—but at length he let me seduce him and gave me an invisible diamond collar in gratitude. In a way I enjoyed him more than my other lovers because he was a man of imagination, and I wept when they put him in solitary and he hanged himself.

In Tulio Lobo, whom I wept for too, standing with my breasts and palms and cheek pressed to the cell door, just as Confort stands this very minute, weeping for me. No fantasy, no mental trick, I'm down there, enough to feel the wood through Confort's cheek, to hear Paloma whimpering, her head in Apple's lap, to see Full Moons, her loveliness all grimed and tattered. Down there and here and back in El Olvido, brushing female fingers over Tulio Lobo's chest. He had a great scar next to his left nipple where a bullet had exited, for they'd never have taken him if he hadn't been shot, and he'd never have been shot except in the back. How he survived was a mystery—heart on the right side, I suppose—though Perfecto Buitre, who rode with him, claimed he had no heart, and we could ask people in the valleys where they raided if we wanted proof. Buitre was my lover too, and Procopio Grajo, who cooed like a pigeon when he made love, and Rigo Atahorma, and other bandits.

These followed Sergeant Cipriano Lechuza, the chief guard, who appreciated my charms enough to take me off quarry work and give me the job of taking food round to the cells, pushing a dolly with a caldron of black beans, from which I dipped servings with a wooden ladle. Run of the prison then, lovers at whim. Atahualpa Lince, who'd studied in Germany and had a bright career ahead of him, except that he enjoyed strangling young men. He had blond hair and golden eyes and a strong lithe body—a great conquest, not just for his beauty but because he preferred making love to men, though now, of course, he lacked the privacy to strangle them while he was at it. Longino Tintorera, who'd pirated in the Caribbean as though three centuries had never happened and buccaneers still roamed, and his cellmate Amadeo Crótalo, a thief and knife fighter, and Crótalo's prison wife, Ladi Topo. Topo was a sneak thief and pickpocket who'd gone to prison first when he was twelve and been bent female before male gender firmed in him. He flounced and fluttered like a debutante, languid and delicate, great violet eyes and arms like breadsticks, mouth in a pout and tongue all lispy, and yet one afternoon I manned him, had him on me like a boar in rut. And there were others too, just like him, that I tipped briefly maleward.

Sergeant Catulo Gimnoto was my lover, not that I'm proud of it now. Meanest of the guards, he'd been a criminal himself, an extortionist whose trick was burning people with a welding torch, and a prisoner there in El Olvido. During *la rabia* General Huevas, who was dictator in Costaguana then, though his rule was firm only in the cities, pardoned assassins and put them into uniform—just as the bandits who ravaged in the countryside enlisted the worst of the soldiers that they captured, for all that counted on both sides was spreading suffering, and those who were happy at it were the most adept. So Gimnoto tortured for the government instead of for his private account, and when the government fell, the police sanctuaried him at El Olvido as a guard. I don't think he would have changed his state for a fortune, since it gave him freedom for the practice of his art and plenty of material, garbaged men he could torment at will. He was small, squat, misshapen, dwarfed in his loins to boot, but I had joy in him, the whorish joy in being close to brute power, for men cringed at the mention of him. Each night he sent for me I preened, strumpeted down the dark corridor, while on either side of me prisoners beat their fists against the doors and howled they'd kill me. And would have, but for the thrall I had them in. In sight of me they melted, pardoned me anything for a touch or merely a smile, in the same way men melt before Angela. I had who I pleased and took joy in making men jealous, just as, often, I took joy in soothing them.

I drove Baco Escombro wild with jealousy. He was a pimp and prided himself on his appeal to females, so I made love with him once and after that refused him, meanwhile smearing affection on his cellmates. Abelardo Sierpe and Heraclito Raya and Virgilio Pitón, all murderers, but I pleasured them before Escombro's eyes, the three at once sometimes, while he knocked his forehead on the wall. But other men I saved, found them tombed in despair and called them forth. I was whore-queen-goddess of El Olvido for three years, at peace with myself and with the power I served. Then came another turning.

I grew weary of men. Gritty-dank sand crabs of weariness took to scuttling across my flesh when men caressed me. Wart-backed toads of weariness learned to materialize beneath my palms when I clasped the flanks of love-gorged straining men. A soft plump slug of weariness began to slither over me, trailing brown slime, whenever a man kissed my throat or body, and each time a man eased himself with me, he left a pus-white maggot-wriggle of weariness inside. Fat bottle-green flies of weariness buzzed in men's voices. Caterpillars of weariness squirmed in their eyes. The joy I had in men was consumed by weariness, munched up like a crop by locusts, and when I lost joy in men, I lost the magic to delight and master them.

Which didn't mean they left me alone. As I grew weary, I became aloof, and for a time men respected this, the spell held for a time—or the illusion of it, since its true force was broken. And for a time the men I did make love with found delight—by a trick of memory or imagination. But the day came when a lover—Otilio Halcón, a bandit and smuggler from Río Manso country—raised himself on his elbows and looked down at me and said I was no better than a papaya. The rural boys do that when they can't get women, take an overripe papaya and hole it with a knife and make love to it. Better than nothing but not very ardent, and all it took was for someone to grasp the truth and voice it. Everyone realized it then, and the last breath of magic faded. But they didn't leave me alone, oh, no, they used me. Joylessly, for want of anything better, but all the time. I was communal property, a slave on loan to any man in that prison. Not even a slave, a captive beast. Not even a beast, an instrument of physical convenience, and the pleasure men took using me was mainly in my weariness of them, my revulsion, and in the brutality with which they overcame it.

See me splayed on the stone floor of a cell, a man standing with his foot on my throat, a man squatting on each of my spread ankles, a man flopped on top of me, drilling away. Or kneeling, with a man twist-gripping my ears to guide my head. Or bent over a bunk, with a man levering my arm to make me wiggle. Vermin swarmed over me, and I lay howling. And after a time brutality wasn't even required, I let myself be used, but men used me violently for violence's sake. My gender was crushed, my body returned to neuter. My humanity went too, and I descended to a vegetable condition, inert as a fouled papaya, though now and then I rose to the condition of a whipped mutt, sullen and cringing, but capable of sudden viciousness. And in that mood I bit a guard, bit him very horribly in fact, for which I was most generously rewarded: beaten almost dead and put in solitary.

Planted under the prison. In a narrow hole with a steel lid clamped over me. Utterly dark. Silent too, although it pulsed with bugs. Buried, crypted in stone, coffin'd. But also wombed: each end is always also a beginning.

Power began seeping back into me. As it's doing now, no use denying that. As I remember who I am, I can feel it returning, stirring like a beast about to wake, budding like a tuber in spring soil. I forgot who I was, betrayed my mission, and power left me. For good, I thought, but it was only hibernating, waiting for the time of its renascence. And since I stopped remorsing and repining, as I research lost time and recall Mandragon, it quickens in me, just as it did before in El Olvido Prison. It chose me, possesses me till death, though it may leave me for a while or for a while lie dormant. But there's no need this time for hope or fear. Angela will flick me from its grasp before it wakes fully.

Last time, though, there was no one around to murder me. I'd have thought it a favor: buried already, after all, and I didn't want to be exhumed to please the rapists. I sat at the bottom of my grave—knees crammed under my chin, for it was only a couple of feet wide down there—wondering how Nepo Aspid had managed to hang himself. Tore his clothing into strips, I figured finally, and made a rope. Noosed it round his neck and worked the free end through the grates in the lid. Chimney'd up so there'd be no slack and tied it, and all he had to do then was relax. Not really a tough problem, though maybe he got the solution by phone from God. I suppose I wasn't so much wondering how as getting ready. Too dispirited for action, even suicide. And then, after I don't know how long, while I was still getting ready, I began flitting up out of that pit, brief journeys like those I went on last night and earlier this morning, like the one just now (still half in progress) to Confort's cell. Power was seeping back, stirring within me.

I went with it, I let it sprout. Not that I'd ever had a purchase on it, but I didn't deny it, didn't pretend its workings were tricks of my mind. Question of what was more horrid, being power's plaything or buried alive, and at that point I didn't care what it did with me. Certainly didn't mind being raised from that tomb, even when it made me witness

Mohotty's death. By fire. He'd left circusing and returned to Ceylon, was participating in Kataragama's annual rite. I heard the drums, I saw the temple doors swing open. The worshipers streamed out, straight to the firepit. Some strolled serenely across it in their white sarongs. Others danced to the center and jigged gaily. But Mohotty hesitated as he stepped onto the coals, his face twisted in fear. He'd lost faith in his god, his god had left him. A few slow steps, then he shrieked horribly. His sarong took fire. Wrapped in a leaf of flame he whirled and fell.

That journey was outward and backward. Mohotty had died a few months after Don Lorenzo. But quite soon after I'd viewed his cremation, he began to visit me. There was plenty of room. By then my hole had spread to a vast cavern, studded on its roof and walls and floor with crystalline light, and only when the lid was raised and my bread and water lowered to me did it shrink back to its original size. Sometimes the guard had to shout for my attention, for I was mostly in trance, and sometimes even shouting didn't work, but I would find my rags damp from the water he'd poured down on me, and the bread he'd tossed down lying against my knee.

Mohotty became my master, instructed me in the techniques of concentration. Oh, it was painful, but I didn't resist. Mohotty told me resistance was foolish, power had chosen me and that was that. My choice was to accept it or die, to learn control or meet disaster. The easy way, hard as it was, was forward. Mohotty came sometimes as himself, sometimes as an old woman. Sometimes, later on, he came as a winged tiger and took me through the crack between the worlds, to mountains where only old people lived, and villages where we saw only youths and maidens. Sometimes these people were turned into tigers. He taught me how to sponge my mind of word-thought, how to focus the eye behind my forehead, how to tune myself to power's network. His instruction went on for some years, two or three years. I'd lost track of time before they put me in solitary. Then Mohotty stopped visiting me, and I practiced by myself, or went alone through the crack between the worlds to visit him.

Then it came to me that my period of training was over. The second movement of my life was over. There would be an interim, and then the purpose I was chosen for would unfold. I had learned everything Mohotty had to teach me. I had surrendered to the power that lived in me, and therefore could direct it. I knew my obligations to and for it. I had paid for denying them, and for delaying to acquire knowledge. I knew why I had gone to prison, and that I did not require prison any longer.

As soon as these thoughts formed in my mind, there was an explosion without concussion, like the crack of a rifle. When the guards came and lifted the steel cover, they found my hole empty. And Nightandmist, waiting on line outside a movie theater on Third Avenue in New York City, saw Mandragon standing on the corner, and went up to me, and followed me through the warm night as I loped away.

I, Mandragon, controlled the power that lived in me. The power that had chosen me ruled my life.

23

Mandragon emerged at year's end, at the navel of the soon-to-fragment world. It looked like this:

Twenty or so minutes past noon on a chilly yet clear Friday a figure of considerable bizarrity, even for New York City, mounted the steps of the Presbyterian church on the northwest corner of Fifth Avenue and Fifty-fourth Street—by custom the impromptu showcase for Juilliard flute students, apprentice mimes, and other street-performing mendicants. This person had piercing black eyes and skin the color and apparent texture of a highly polished walnut panel; was small and slight, and yet suggestive of an animal ferocity; carried two gourd rattles and wore a rat-fur cap and homemade rat-fur boots, a quilted parka embroidered with outlandish symbols, and army-issue field pants, from the seat of which rose a long, thin, wire-stiffened, rodentine brown tail. A girl in ski clothes—a honey-blond, blue-eyed, retroussé-nosed marshmallow—followed as far as the first step and parked there, facing the street, smiling vacantly, holding an empty peach tin. The person on the top step sniffed the air; stared about; smirked, showing an array of gleaming snappers; then, rattling slowly, uttering little squeaks, began to hop-dance back and forth along the church front. Mandragon was emerging.

A client had coronaried the night before in the massage parlor where Todo Confort worked and everyone got busted. I viewed it all in the smogged skylight: the hazard flashers red on leering faces, the frost-breath'd intern and the stretchered stiff, the girls cop-hustled to meat-wagon places. I got on to Confort, telepathed her adrenal glands to quiet, calmed her terrored heart and soothed her mind. Then it came to me to go uptown and raise her bail.

I might have had Nightandmist or Apple raise it. I might have put it in the night court judge's mind to let her go. I might have had the cops neglect to book her, or simply snatched her from the wagon to the loft. Instead it came to me to go ministering in public, with Full Moons gathering in the contributions. I didn't think it over and decide. I saw myself at it and knew what I would do. I realized that my interim was over.

Sniffed the air and stared about. Squad car across the avenue in front of Gucci's, idling motor puffing out fumes, occupants pulsing out hate waves. *Weirdo boogie scumbag! Greaseball pimp!* Things scarcely better on the sidewalks, only a few nuggets of well-being. On the near corner, Mr. Amos Longstreet Lee, father of five, with his first paycheck in months nested safely in an inner pocket. Across Fifth, Mrs. Erica Salter, ash-blond beauty just turned twenty-six, northbound from Saks to the St. Regis for a nooner with a new acquaintance, Baltic eyes sparkling, cheeks rouged fetchingly by the nippy air and the anticipated thrills of careless love. And steaming past me, his pointed beard prowed forward, his breath pluming above, the tails of his Burberry billowing behind him, Mr. S. Heilanstalt, author, who'd just seen his latest book stacked in Rizzoli's window. Three moderately happy humans out of a hundred in my radar range, and for the rest the streets polluted with ill feeling, the symptoms of denatured life. Hostility. Worry and boredom. Tamped-down rage and papered-over terror. Along with twisted bowels and ulcerated stomachs, dysfunctional sex organs, crazed fifth-column cells. The eyes of captive beasts glanced up at me; a dozen cancers returned Mandragon's smirk.

Rat rite unquestionably apt. Hadn't thought about it. Seen myself at it, so I knew what I would do. But now, noting the troubles of my congregation, I realized the propriety of invoking the only beast, along with the roach of course, that actually thrives in centers of advanced culture. But first I worked a little one-on-one. Rattling slowly, uttering small squeaks, Mandragon hop-danced back and forth along the church front, drawing game.

Got the first inside a minute: Mr. Norman C. Baldeck, Esq., counselor at law. Large handsome chap in his late forties. Chesterfield coat, man-of-affairs bearing. Might have stepped from a Caddy ad, but had in fact just left his office for a business lunch at "21." I spotted him as he crossed Fifty-fourth Street headed south, spun him around midway over and hauled him back, speared him as he reached the curb. That is, I punched up FIRST LOVE in the computing instrument under Mr. Baldeck's homburg, so that he looked at Full Moons and saw a girl he'd dated thirty years before. Since then he'd led what's called an interesting life: Big Ten football, combat in Korea, deals that could have put him behind bars. He'd managed swindles, sweated out tax audits, but he'd never again lived with such intensity as when he loved that girl and was maneuvering her sackward. He'd won unwinnable cases, bested expert bargainers in delicate negotiations, married an heiress, and made gobs of money, but he'd never again known such joy and triumph as when that girl moaned "Normy!" and raised her rump so he could pull her panties down. He had obstructed justice, suborned perjury, committed fraud; betrayed his wife, his friends, and his associates; spoiled his children and neglected them to boot, but he'd never again felt such ecstasies of guilt as when he dumped that girl once she turned pregnant. When Mr. Baldeck looked at Full Moons and saw his own first love, all these sensations flooded back to him, pure as when he'd felt them first, so that for the first time in thirty years he was living fully.

Held him at that peak for thirty seconds—all he could safely take—then eased him down. The girl who'd moaned "Normy!" faded back to Full Moons, still smiling vacantly, cradling her peach tin. Norman C. Baldeck, Esq., began to sob. Forked his bill clip up into the tin. Let Full Moons blot his jowls with her mitten. Turned and shuffled off to his appointment, head bowed, heart full of wild regret and longing for the freshness of life that once was his. But also restored to it a little, just a bit cleansed and wakened, partially reminded of true value.

Netted my next contributor as Baldeck left. One Emil Vogler, Johannesburg export merchant, who was returning to his hotel (the Sherry Netherland) from the diamond center. He wore an astrakhan-style hat of Persian lamb, and a rich overcoat with matching collar. He had rings worth several thousands on his gloved hands. But he'd spent seven years in hell and left everyone he loved behind there: that was tattooed on his left forearm and his heart. So I recaptured time for him, made winter summer and Fifth Avenue the Tiergarten, restored his family. Vogler saw them strolling toward him across the meadow—Vatti in cream flannels, Mutti with little Heinie in her arms; his sister Lili, her auburn hair in ringlets; straw-hatted Onkel Max (who'd lost an arm and won a Knight's Cross at Verdun); Tanchen Mitzi, Cousin Willi, Cousin Fritz. They'd all been wafted up the Auschwitz chimneys; now Mr. Vogler had them back again, along with his cremated childhood. I let him keep all that for a full minute, held the vision while he wept and wheezed. Then I dissolved it, but its warmth remained, and he stuffed all his cash in Full Moons' tin.

I pulled in a few more, people who could pay well to have their lives enriched, and a few passersby stopped to watch me, though they couldn't see what my act had to make anyone come up with dough. Then I began the general service. My rattling swelled in volume, the tempo of my dance picked up. Tail swayed, nose crinkled, upper lip drew back.

Mouth opened and shut quickly, and the spectators—the more suggestible among them first—saw my ears bell, my face elongate, my cap spread peltlike down over my body. And then they understood my squeakings as this hymn:

> The wise rat of the sewers, the roach
> in the walls
> The rat who sees, the roach in the
> walls who senses
> I am above you all, I have every gift
> I am the one chosen by infinite power
> Come, then, O marvelous rat, and teach!
> Come, O clever roach, instruct them!

By the time I'd done half a dozen of the faster shuffles, everyone who'd paused to watch, everyone who merely looked up at the church front saw a huge brown Norway rat doing a dance there, and a giant upright honey-colored roach with a peach tin in its topmost pair of legs.

Not disconcerted in the slightest. Comforted. For all their size and strangeness, the rat and roach were benign. Everyone who so much as glanced their way, everyone around, walking or driving, stopped at once and watched them, captivated.

The roach smiled out contentment from its luminous, globular eyes; it waved peace and contentment with its feelers. The rat's tail swung in rhythmic, rapid arcs; its squeaks were an enchanting melody. Then all the onlookers were in an immense sewer, full of filth and every sort of vermin, but not a bit disturbed. At home. They had come to know the city as a sewer, and the knowledge brought great peace.

The squad-car cops squeaked, wriggled their glad haunches on the vinyl. Those in the street were dancing back and forth. They held their fingers bunched before their chests. Their noses crinkled, their upper lips drew back, their rumps moved with the rhythmic swaying of the long lithe tails they felt extending from them, and their mouths opened and shut compulsively, squeaking. They forgot their boredom and their worry, their rage and terror, their hostility and discontent. Mandragon had brought them life, Mandragon had freed them.

The cops and others got down from their cars. Passengers streamed down from buses and joined the dance. Shops emptied out. Windows filled with peering eyes, with crinkled noses, drawn-back upper lips, and where second-story windows could be opened people leaped from them, flew ratlike head-first down, and landed lightly on their palms and jumped up dancing. People formed wheel-like clusters with their imaginary tails entwined and spun along the avenue and crosswalks, rebounded from abandoned cars and buses, bowled dancers into one another, and others danced their way forward through the press and crammed their cash into the roach's tin. Avenue jumbled with rat-dancers. Cars backed up from Fifty-fifth to the park. But not all the honking or the wailing of cop sirens could bruise my congregation's newfound bliss.

Then the rat danced down from the steps and drew the roach out into the middle of the avenue and aimed it south. The giant roach stepped stately down Fifth Avenue, body upright, feelers erect, luminous eyes smiling. The rat weaved dancing circles around it. All the people danced behind—three blocks south to St. Paddy's, and as they progressed others were swept into the dance.

Opposite the cathedral the roach halted. The rat danced wildly round it, squeaking shrilly, and all formed clusters with their imaginary tails entwined. Spinning pinwheels squeaking in delight, whirling knots of joy. Round around, leaning out from the hubs of their twined tails, melded together.

Then the dancers noticed—those least capable of ecstasy among them first—that the rat and roach had vanished. The clusters slowed, then broke apart. People stood rubbing their flushed faces, twisting their necks, blinking at one another. Then they looked up toward the cathedral.

*Mandragon sits cross-legged in the air above the portal
of St. Patrick's. An orange glow flames all about me. My
teeth gleam in a smirk, my eyes sear down, piercing yet
kindly, on the staring multitude below.*
*Mandragon is entirely motionless. My lips do not move,
no sound comes from me. And yet my words are clear to
each member of the crowd.*
"Beloved, the universe is a network of power.
*"It is not a puzzle to be figured out. It is a network to
be tuned to.*
*"Reason is a technique for tuning out vast portions of
the network so that a petty scrap may be grasped. The bene-
fits of reason are illusory. Its comforts are false. Its ministry
is ending.*
*"Advanced cultures are mechanisms for jamming one's
reception of the network, for short-circuiting the network
itself. The time is near when these shall vanish. They will
explode and flame to cinder. They will crumble and be
blown away. Earth will be cleansed.*
*"Billions will perish. I've heard them howling. I've
watched them trudge bewildered till they fall. Earth will
be winnowed.*
*"A few will be saved. I will shelter them against the
holocaust. I will tune them to the network of the universe.
Earth will be renewed."*

My mission had come to me.

"RATMAN STUNS MIDTOWN"
"MASS HALLUCINATION ON 5TH AVE"
"MYSTERY GURU EMPTIES PRECINCT LOCKUP"

Mandragon emerged.

24

Mandragon moved south and west. Over high-crowned secondary roads head-lamped in loneliness, and highways rumbled with huge semis. Past sullen woods of bare-limbed brittle trees and fields patched with grey snow, down sudden gantlets of blared neon—ZIPPYFRY, FAST-O-SWILL, MAXIGAS, YUMMY-GULP, FLASHBURGER. Through wind-flailed country towns, along the outskirts of dinged cities. West and south onto the temperate waist of the continent, south and east toward its loins, pulled by merged revelations of mission and destiny.

Swelling my tribe en route. At the precinct I freed everyone along with Confort but took only three, Six String and Argo Who and Monorail. No bail, just drowsed the cops and slid the steel doors open, and we set out that night in an old school bus. Then I took novices from road and town, a remnant for the beginning.

Often I navigated by them, ordered new headings as knowledge of my salvagees came to me, homed in on them like beacons. Crossing New Guernsey our first night on the road I got an extrasensogram about No Puedo Más. That's what I named him: towheaded runaway sixteen years old, riding late through the wind and the rain in a fatherly old pervert's Hermes Malaga. I vectored us southeast on intercept, had us parked at a motel off the turnpike outside Fenville when they pulled in, plucked him from Dad's arms and we drove on. And next day sidetracked forty miles to

190

Clemency, West Jamesland, for Burundanga. I had a futureview of him in the sleet-streaked window, watched him wake up, hung over and strung out, beside a girl he couldn't recognize, then stumble round the room in Jockey shorts, hunting for his wallet. All his money, all his papers gone, and the next frame had him standing in the iced street beside the car he'd borrowed three days earlier in Swanee but forgotten to fill up with antifreeze. Joyride over, ripe for a new life, and so I detoured there and took him.

And swung across North Gloriana into Micherburg, to the laundromat Miss Nowhere worked in. All day I dreamed her dreams of being wanted, of being worth something; locked on them, rode them in, and let her join me. Then, leaving town, had Argo hang a left: kid brown as me and even thinner, pedaling along, delivering groceries. In chinos and a ragged warm-up jacket. Trying to whistle, but his teeth were chattering too hard. Mom dead and Pop run off, and Princess said that she was hungry, so I took the groceries and him, I named him Snowman.

Sometimes no change of course was needed. I'd get a glimpse into some place ahead, roadhouse or diner—kid staring at a row of empty beer cans, girl dancing by herself in an empty room—and tell who happened to be driving where to stop. They have him honk, and my new convert would come out, get on the bus or follow in car or pickup. And others came to join me at my stops.

No urgency to my progress. Used back roads more than highways, ambled on. Stopped when and where it moved me, for rest and rite. I'd feel the call of some deserted spot and guide us there, nudge in along dirt trackways dowsing for a hidden spring of power, and when I'd found it settle my people in and stop their minds and dance myself from my humanity. To stag or sparrow, weasel, hawk, or linx; to wasp or otter. Put on that knowledge and that power, passed alien being into my tribe's hearts. That gift too was mine.

Gone now. Drained from me. Feel power trickling back but not in time. Be transformed anyway in a few hours—fish if they put me in the ocean, worm if they put me in the ground, bird and insect if they leave me hanging. In those days, though, I danced my transformations, and when my ecstasy stepped from me I'd notice newcomers standing shyly beside their vehicles beyond the circle of communicants. Or I would wake to find them waiting. Or they would travel out to meet me on the road.

Often I felt or visioned them approaching. Sunlight and Nineveh leaving a lecture hall at Kennessippi State, hitching a ride out to the interstate past Ramses, waiting all day till I came by. Earthly Delights piloting her camper down through Arkalachee into Catchpole to hook on to my caravan. Or Perfume River. For days I had flashes of him. Watched him check out of the veterans' hospital at Manticore, where he'd lain for years, nonface to the wall and never speaking, where he'd coffin'd himself. I saw him draw his back pay at Fort Vermis, outfit himself in Salamandra. I felt him rocketing across the Utaho flats, steel hooks pinced on the handlebars, plastic knees gripping the tank—neuter as me, crotch napalmed smooth and dollish, but alive again, and he was waiting for me over the Texahoma line northwest of Deathwright.

Six String took him for a cop, and couldn't learn cops couldn't touch us. Eyes only twenty-twenty, and he'd been busted several times too often, so when he saw the bike parked on a rise above the road and the helmeted figure beside it, he came off the gas though we were doing only forty. I didn't have to look, I'd been expecting. I knew the bike was a Hakagawa not a Harley, the helmet had white wings and a football face guard, the wearer had no face. He mounted and kicked the starter as we went by, rolled down the bank and ran up on us slowly, weaving in and out among the vehicles I pulled in train, took station on our left front so that his head was just forward of Six String's, about a yard off and below. Then he looked round. One eye and two pink holes in a glaze of scar tissue, but they tried to smile when I raised my hand in welcome.

Still others joined after I crossed into Mexico, and on my counterclockwise progress south and east. I didn't summon them, didn't compel them in. Those who belonged with me knew where to find me. Brought me their wan lives to be refreshed, their aimless lives to be directed, their empty lives to be filled up with light. And I received them, named them, clasped them to me. More than sixty by the time I reached Ticamala. Nearly a dozen cars and trucks followed my bus into the fallow field outside Huacho, the spot where, twice seven years to the month before, power chose me.

And on that spot I paused for seven days. Fasted. Made journeys of ascent and of descent. Crossed the highway— which was paved now, the only difference—and wandered in the jungle, where flocks of red and yellow parrots flew down toward me then disappeared. Sat all one day under the sun and rain, sponging my mind of word-thought. Went through the windy crack between the worlds. Prepared my tribe.

The sun is down. An April canopy of clouds hangs close to the moist earth, masking the stars. Mandragon's tribe sit in a circle behind Apple and Nightandmist, Full Moons and Confort and Paloma, who kneel beneath tall torches spiked in the soil, marking the points of a pentagram. Within it Mandragon dances.

Framed in a pale, lime-colored aura; crowned with a single feather-horn. Arms lifted, face toward the dark sky, Mandragon dances. Leaps and turns, shivers the gourd rattles, sings shrilly in an unknown language.

The seated figures twist. Sway and bend forward. Clutch handfuls of earth. They moan and laugh as images form in them, as waves of feeling sweep them.

Above the darker line of jungle, lightning crackles.

* * *

Mandragon entered them, Mandragon joined them. Sang them from themselves in a wordless tongue they did not know yet understood. Danced them to a collective mind communing images and feelings. Then danced and sang the end and the beginning, the mutant monsters, flamed-to-cinder cities, the earth cleansed and renewed. The end was horrible, but they must long for it and love it as themselves. The beginning was lovely, but full of hardship. I danced the sea of water and the sea of air, the sea of stars beyond, and all the other forms that power takes so that my tribe might live respectfully beside them. I danced the force that moves each particle and sun. I tuned them to it —gave them the living ocean-swell of unity, not the dead fragments I can word-think now, not the autopsied and reasonable corpse chopped into morsels, into neat bits a conscious mind can suck on then spit out. I gave them participation in the universe.

Not once, many times. In Ticamala then, in Otán later, in other spots at other times. I melded them as one and made them one with power, gave them the experiences they required. They were to be the salvaged remnant.

Gone now. Dispersed. Fragmented in the wind. Mandragon betrayed them, forgot them and myself. Some jailed and some deported. Some murdered. Some will be in the streets at sunup when I trot by, jeering and throwing garbage. Why blame them? The news was true, but not the messenger.

I didn't know then I'd forget myself, my mission, and my fate. Then I was filled with light. Mandragon paused seven days, then led my tribe into Tinieblas.

Which was then in the last stages of dismantlement. Inhuman nature had about finished the job begun by foolish men. For miles, nearing the border, we moved through intermittent showers of blood—red soil, thirst-tortured to disintegration, raised and blown north and corpuscled in the warm rain. We moved too into a field of radiated suffering—a kind of deepening gloom or rising murmur of confusion, though not, of course, perceived via eye or ear—that even some of my tribe became vaguely aware of. Mandragon picked it up clearly. Mandragon raveled out its diverse strains: frustration of earth denied maternity; bewilderment of vegetation, for which the fire of the sun had now become a murderous instead of quickening element; the shame of shriveled rivers, the thirst and hunger pangs of beasts, the terror and despair of human beings. And, specially, their anguished loneliness, for drought had about finished the job (begun by dictatorship) of snapping all the jesses of community, so that the binding energy, chaotically released, carried each person whirling off along a solitary, wild trajectory. Ties between the classes had gone first, then ties of class and station, of friendship and neighborhood. Now even ties of blood were giving way. Parents couldn't afford to love bloat-bellied kids they couldn't feed. Brothers couldn't afford to feel sorry for bankrupt brothers they couldn't help. Each person hoarded what he had for his own use, including his reserves of sympathy. Each was a separate unstable system turning crazily around himself. Everyone was getting more and more like Genghis.

Whose pain I picked up too, but barely—as a kind of acid stench (though not, of course, perceived via the nose) discernible by noisomeness not strength. It flowed in the general wave, very much mingled, though to his view he was the only person suffering in the whole country, in the whole world.

We drove deeper into this belt of broadcast misery to the Agrio, to the Ticamalan frontier station, which was about sixty yards from the river but out of sight of it because the road curved and the land around was lushly overgrown with palm and bougainvillea and wild plantain: a zebra-striped barrier that closed the right-hand lane and a wooden booth set back from the right shoulder, with an identical arrangement farther on across the road for arriving travelers. There I did my stunt with the officials, had them take whatever my tribe showed them for valid documents. Pancake box tops, labels off tin cans. Newspapers, Kleenex, comic books. Became passports and tourist cards and auto titles. I loitered a respectful distance off under a tree, one arm on Snowman's giggle-convulsed shoulder, tinkering in the border officers' brains, rigging temporary circuits, rerouting signals—and also watching and enjoying the result.

The inspector, a round-faced little fellow, quite fair-skinned, sat primly on a stool behind the counter, his country's honor, post's importance, and personal dignity affirmed in that soggy heat by mohair jacket, long-sleeved shirt, and tightly knotted necktie. He treated each paper bag and flap of cardboard with solemnity: refused to touch it till it was on the counter; held it like a breviary in both hands; submitted it to reverent poring. Date of issue, date of expiration. Issuing authority, raised seal. Stamps and frankings—all the pompous bumf he loved and lived for. I made him fantasy that stuff and find it there, let him examine it to his content. Next, his regard fastened gravely on the traveler opposite, then yo-yoed slowly down and up, checking imaginary photo against face, dreamed data against protoplasm. Till, finally, a pursing of the lips; a series of slow nods; a careful placing of the papers on the counter. Then he slid them on to his assistant.

Now and then I hit him with a jolt. Made him see the square of toilet paper Argo Who put down before him first as a tourist card, then as a filthy picture—lewd cavortings between vulture-faced men and swine-haunched women! lesbian sphinxes and gay minotaurs! in motion and color! with a sound track of squeals and slurps!—then as a tourist card again, over and over. I turned Sunlight's paperback *I Ching* into the grandfather of all passports, with visas for every country in the UN, but kept altering its nationality and photograph. Each time he looked down, it was all changed; each time he looked up, so was Sunlight: now black, now white, now brown, now male, now female; now a statuesque Svenska with long, straw-colored braids; now one of those diminutive Japanese salesmen that scurry about all over Latin America, dark suits and plastic attaché cases, peddling everything from cameras to steel mills. But through it all he kept his reserved, proper-state-functionary demeanor.

The assistant was a swart, slovenly lout in a damp sport shirt, fingers all blue from fondling his ink pad, who lounged, tipped backward on his stool, against one of the posts that held up the tile roof, festered with boredom and sneering covertly at his chief's conscientiousness. But let a piece of paper slide his way! Then he roused, stretched like a cat, and pounced: swung forward, braking his fall with his right hand and, with his left, capturing the document— what I made him take for a document anyway, postcard or candy wrapper, magazine. Held it down with the heel of his hand, caressed it with his fingers. Took up his rubber stamp and inked it, thus: seven or eight affectionate light pats on the frayed pad. Raised the stamp, sat up, prepared to strike. Hovered it teasingly above the paper, prolonging anticipation, retarding release. Sly glance at the tourist, who had, as it were, surprised him *in flagrante*. Conspiratorial grin, display of teeth. Joyous nod, all the while keeping his victim pinned to the counter. Then he swung the stamp up behind his right ear and flung it down, FWAPP! onto the paper, with a violence that jostled the roof tiles and brought startled looks from everyone around—everyone except the inspector, who blinked and winced but pretended not to notice. And then his shoulders slumped, his mouth went slack. He sighed and flipped the stamp back toward the ink pad. Unpinned the ravished paper, left it sprawled there; half-closed his eyes, tipped back against the post.

Mandragon could have put them both to sleep, along

with the soldiers slouching by the barrier. I could have made my caravan invisible to them, and lifted the counter-weighted plank with a thought. But the inspector loved to scan documents. His assistant lusted to stamp them. My tribe enjoyed the break. I was in no hurry. We spent three hours there—a little longer than was necessary, but some wanted to go by the booth again, with plantain leaves or strips of palm frond. While others picked bougainvillea blossoms for their shirts or hair, splashed in the puddled potholes of the road. Like kids. Mandragon had returned them all to childhood. That was one of the best parts of joining me.

Every ten or fifteen minutes the sky opened and dropped cascades of rain. It swayed the trees and spouted from the booth tiles. It soaked my people's clothes and splatted ruddy on their upturned faces. Then the tap closed and sun burned through to steam up wraiths of mist, at the same time triggering a burst of plant growth that I felt like a commotion all around me, the bustle of a million small factories. Then clouds, the plants shut down, another torrent. Falling, rising, falling; round and round; ferris-wheeling into afternoon. At last, when everyone was satisfied, we crossed. Officials surfeited with scanning and stamping, my children eased from the long road-bound cooping-up, and we got in, turned motors over, rolled away. Past the raised barrier, along a corridor of rain-stooped palms. Around the elbow bend, onto the bridge. Out through the liquid veil that hung at midspan.

Into dry heat, and swirling dust, and ocher glare. On the right a sun-scorched barren field stretched back from the steep bank; billboarded in it the barren brow and wide-set, froggish eyes of Genghis Manduco. On the left, just even with the first girders of the bridge, stood the three big elms that gave the place its name—still more or less alive because they pushed roots down into the Agrio, but badly withered, giving little shade. Beyond the trees, the whitewashed stucco guard booths, each with a pole beside it on which a bleached Tinieblan tricolor jerked nervously in the uncertain wind. Beyond the booths, the town; beyond the town, the shit-brown barren hills.

A stout chain hung between the booths, closing the road. As the bus rolled off the bridge, double-clanking loudly, Sublieutenant Evaristo Tranca, chief of the Tres Olmos border station, stepped out into the road and put his slickly polished right boot up on the chain, placed right hand on raised knee and left hand on right wrist, peered bridgeward from under the cloth bill of his green kepi. Mandragon smiled at him, and the chain shivered. Every link broke at once, split in half-ovals which fell into the road. Sublieutenant Tranca lurched forward to hands and knees, sprawled on the blacktop, but then flew up and back and sideways to the shoulder, where he braced woodenly, his chin raised toward the left-hand booth, his right arm jerking stiffly up and down, a hundred salutes as Mandragon and tribe rolled by.

Perfume River first, my outrider, black face guard snouted out before pink holes, white wings feathered back across his helmet, stumps poked from shirt and shorts, plastic limbs glistening, and then the bus, with smiling faces at the lowered windows, and Earthly Delights' camper and Gashmaster's van and the grey Mastodon dump truck Porkospine hung behind me at a crossroads in Appalouri, with Nineveh beside him in the cab and in the bin (rainsopping, flower-spangled, baby-grinned) Albondiga and Rancio and Chancaca Segundo, deported fruit-pickers I took just after I crossed into Mexico, and twelve-year-old Sin Tetas I pulled from a whore-crib in Chiquimula, and Neverthink and Song and Spider Wantly, and then Koolisimo in his Scrambler pickup and the others—all gone now, all but five, my remnant scattered, but joined then at Mandragon's coming.

We rolled at moderate speed over the broken links of

chain, past Sublieutenant Tranca and the guard booths, past the Hirudo service station with its spitting-snake sign, past the town and on between parched fields.

A cloud of red dust followed us into the hills.

25

Patter of drops on the protruding cover of the air conditioner. Street seal-black-shiny in the glow of the café's fluorescent tubes. Small rain in the high hours of early morning, but dawn will be clear.

In two hours, maybe less, no way to tell. They'll come for me, an officer, two men. And walk me out, a fist gripping each elbow. Along the corridor and down the steps, into the yard. For a brief ceremony, salutes and exchange of cuff key, before the sergeant hooks me to the truck. Down there, below this window, among kidney-shaped puddles. In the cool time before sunup. In the still-misty dew-fresh tropic dawn, but Mandragon will be sweating.

Crowd-snarls beyond the wall. Sputter and *vroom* of motorcycle engines, patrol truck farting fumes past my right shin. They'll slide the steel door back, they'll trot me out. To howls of happy hatred. Through town for a mechanized AANGH! for some cablebite OUGHH! For the dreamterror helplessness AAGHH! going to . . .

Bathroom partially refurbished for Miss Delfi. Contoured pink plastic seat. Pert-cherubed pink plastic curtain for the shower. Camera installed later on though, I suppose: isn't the sort of set she'd care to perform on. Squints down at me from a mounting over the doorway, and I trust whoever's viewing approved my adroitness. In hitting the bowl with my supper, not splashing the seat. In getting trousers untied with manacled hands. Under harsh time pressure, in a state of profound distraction. Of gut-tossing, sphincter-dissolving fear to be exact: sick at both ends. My fingers beat my bowels in a photo finish, and I must ask leave for a squirt when they come to get me. Can assume, in fact, they'll allow that: in my vision my trousers were unsoiled.

Ungainly to wipe with your wrists cuffed. Hope it made good TV for whoever's on duty, and I'll tie these things loosely, don't want to get caught again.

Patter of drops. Snug sound it's nice to fall asleep to. Be nice to put the light out and spiral away. As at La Negra's before weed humanity sprouted, chained safely to the bedstead with Vilma beside me, and the small rain platting slow on the zinc roof. Or curled in Rebozo's Knauser before power chose me, my whimpers melding with the rain taps and his sighs. Or in the palace when I'd forgotten who I was: Angela asleep in my male arms, and plump drops slapping the balcony. Be nice to slide off into sleep for these two hours. Or spin off and not return, beat dawn to extinction. Or wake back in one of those havens and find this a dream.

Or wake up somewhere else, some other person. An ordinary person, properly sexed one way or the other, properly gifted with a filter on my consciousness for keeping miracles and monsters safely out. Except when dreaming, and I'll have dreamed all this, Mandragon and Tinieblas. Then wake and wonder for a moment at my dream while I slough sleep away, get up and go about some ordinary business and forget it.

Or someone whose work it is to package strangeness for the public's use, safe doses of the extraordinary so that ordinary lives needn't be too dull. A painter, say, doing big panels swarmed with miracles and monsters, an exotic landscape where outlandish fantasies take form and an emblematic figure who unites opposites. All made up, of course, but while composing I'll have gone off to that imaginary world, resided there till it seemed real. Then wake from that sort of dream and stand and wonder for a moment at my work; shrug and turn and leave it till tomorrow; go off to my husband or my wife, to my good dinner. Be nice.

But I know who I am. I know how power filled me once, where I am now, what's on my plate for later on this morning. No waking from this dream for a while yet. No placid drift into extinction. Not for Mandragon. For me a cable and a pulley and a winch, and, in the meantime, eyelid-twitching, stomach-twisting fear.

Of the same sort poor Genghis suffered. Fear and loneliness, self-pity and despair. He'd given up and yet wasn't resigned. In those days he flew out and back between his compound and the different regions of the country like a rubber paddle ball on an elastic string. Supposedly to inspect the drought's ravages but actually because he couldn't bear to be immobile. His thoughts were never at rest. His thoughts could never settle anywhere. Whatever they lighted on recalled his loneliness and fear, excited his despair and his self-pity, sent his thoughts flitting off at once, and so his body had to be in motion too. Like someone who knows what's destined but has unlearned how to accept it, who paces nervously around the room (bare feet taking no joy in the rich carpet), who lies uneasy on a silk chaise longue, flipping over and flipping back.

Poor Genghis couldn't bear to be immobile, not while his thoughts kept mothing here and there. And had the means at hand to rapid motion. So scarcely would he order a state meeting, scarcely had the thing got under way, when he'd leap up and go out to the pad and clatter off—to nowhere in particular, along whatever heading struck his whim first—with aides and officers strapped into jump seats, and the conference proceeding over the intercom, and his froggish gaze poked out the doorway, sweeping the defoliated landscape. Rapid motion soothed his fear a little. Distracted him from it, just as aides and officers somewhat calmed his loneliness. But scarcely would the pilot get on course when Genghis would order up another heading, scarcely had the conference got back on track when Genghis would interrupt it and order a radio hookup with the compound and demand a report from someone he'd left on the ground, and scarcely was that officer warmed up when Genghis would sign off and tell the pilot to set down. There! over there! beside that village! because although he'd given up, he wasn't resigned; although he despaired, he nourished crazy hopes; although he oozed self-pity from every pore, he was tormented by the fantasy that somewhere—sitting in a thatch hut mashing yucca meal with a smooth stone on a board table, or climbing up an arroyo from a shriveled river with a cracker tin of water on her head—there was a woman (girl or wife or crone) who could cure his dryness. Maybe she was down there in that village. So before the gear had settled he'd jump out, jocking his brick-hard gonads in both hands, and waddle off, with aides and officers in tow like ducklings, but scarcely had he entered the village, scarcely had he begun talking (about the drought, of course) with the men who stood around him holding their hats in both hands over their chests, scarcely had his frog gaze touched the women who peered at him from shadowy doorways, when he'd realize that his fantasy was barren—as barren as the condemned's fantasy of waking from the nightmare in a moment—and turn and waddle off and flap away. Back to his compound and throw himself down among his whores, but scarcely had he begun humping and pumping when he'd despair of it and roll off and soak in self-pity, when his stomach would twist in fear and his eyelid start twitching, his spirit implode in loneliness and shrink to a pinhead that weighed a billion tons, and he'd leap up and pull his clothes on and waddle out. Back to his conference room or (to save time) straight to his chopper, and rattle off into the sky again. So that his pilot found it simpler to keep engines running, so that his rotors never stopped spiraling round and round.

In those days he clutched at straws, then drew his hand away before he grasped them. He had brother Timur's couriers pouch him stacks of sex sheets and porno tabloids, all hot from New York—not for the pictures or the stories, for the ads. The little oblong quack ads in the back, and kept a Cuban whore from Miami to translate them to him, and fell for every one that promised, however remotely, to ease his plight. Sent off for pills, pomades and powders, for vibrators and vitamins, for hand-powered pumps and electric orgasmatrizers, for furred rubber contrivances to be strapped to the backs of chairs and then assaulted, for modified milking machines and facsimile joints. He ordered a dozen robot concubines from Mandeville Biosynthetics, each in the likeness of a famous gringa sex bomb—Gloria Monday, Carrie Ellison—that smiled and sobbed and sighed and squealed and sniggered, that murmured endearments and obscenities in any language one wished, that went into climax at the touch of a butt button and stayed there (unless switched off) till their batteries drained— and maybe if he'd had one in Angela's likeness he'd have been cured without Mandragon's intercession, but no robot Angela was on the market: only one was created, and it was on board *Scorpion* with Dred. Genghis answered the ads and waited in impatience for his merchandise, but scarcely had it arrived, scarcely had he got it unwrapped, when he'd despair of it and push it aside. Poured the potions down the toilet. Garbaged the contraptions. Gave the robot sex bombs to his guards. Nothing was going to work till the drought was broken. No spritzing till it rained, and so why bother?

He had aides standing by, all night all day, to brief him on the drought's developments, but the drought didn't develop, merely rasped on, and the aides had to scavenge ceaselessly for material. Not that they ever got to report much of it. Genghis would call them by radio from his helicopter, or grab them en route from helicopter to whores, or summon them to his insomnia in the high hours of early morning, but scarcely had they got an item out when he'd switch off or turn away or shoo them out, because the drought and any reference to it recalled his loneliness and fear, excited his despair and his self-pity, sent his thoughts fluttering. But they had to be prepared, and their material had to be current and, if possible, hopeful, so they scavenged up all sorts of scraps. In this way Genghis learned of a message from a maniac in Manizales and a letter from a lunatic in Luzon, along with other crankinform communications to brother Nebucodonosor, from crackpots in Krakow and nuts in Nutley, N.J., from madmen the world around who'd heard of the drought in Tinieblas and claimed they could end it. By boring holes in the sky with their laser-beam eyeballs or ringing up their twin brother Beelzebub. At which news Genghis would like as not zing off a telex to the appropriate consul and order the goofball in question conveyed to Tinieblas—by jet, front cabin, all expenses paid—because although he'd given up, he wasn't resigned. Some were in padded cells. Some were too zonked on Thorazine to travel. Some had forgotten all about Tinieblas, and some had new and pressing projects at hand—keeping the sun from going out or curing cancer—but a few showed. A burly blond young megalo, ordained minister in the Church of Jesus Christ, Surfboarder, accompanied by two keepers from the Fasholt Clinic in Los Angeles. An ancient Israeli schiz with a long white beard and blueprints for an ark—to be made of gopher wood, whatever that was, so many by so many cubits, and stocked with two of every species in Tinieblas, and then it would rain for forty days and nights. One or two others, but scarcely had they put shoe leather on the airport tarmac when Genghis would ship them out again. Because although he wasn't resigned, he'd given up. No one could end the drought, not while he suffered. No rain until he spritzed, so what was the use?

In this way too, in April of the seventh year of his dictatorship, he learned of odd happenings in the interior. Only tangentially related to the drought, but if his aides had to be prepared day in night out with fresh material, hopeful if possible, they couldn't be blamed for scavenging scraps. As, for example, that a band of outlanders had materialized in Otán. No one knew who they were or how they got there. All the foreigners in Tinieblas had been accounted for; no record of new ones at any port of entry. But up at Tres Olmos the border chief had gone wacky. Sublieutenant named Tranca, very steady man; up through the ranks, commended for touchy assignments, but he'd been found braced at attention saluting like mad, though there was no one around except for a couple of *guardias*, and they were out cold. It had taken six men to get Tranca into a straitjacket, and three days for the *guardias* to come to. And the chain had been broken, *mi general*, every link sliced through, around the same time this outlander band had materialized. In eastern Otán, *mi general*, where Otán meets Remedios, camped in what used to be a pasture. Sixty or seventy, gringos and Latins, boys and girls. All of them young, some hardly more than children, and what they did, *mi general*, was conduct orgies. At least one, *mi general*, to initiate some Tinieblans who'd joined up with them, young people from Angostura and other towns. They'd orgied all night right out in the open, stroking and poking, chowing and plowing, gnawing and pawing—all in a sprawl so you couldn't tell who was what. They had some kind of witch or sorcerer with them, who led them in some kind of mumbo jumbo, some kind of hocus-pocus besides the orgy. And yes! *mi general*, it might be a development, because that place had been the driest place in Tinieblas, dry as an oven, sir, and blowing away, but since those foreigners had appeared with their warlock or voodoo woman, since they'd started their abracadabra and open-air orgies, a spring had begun to flow. Out of the ground or out of a rock, no one knew for certain, but water, *mi general*, no doubt about that. And not just a trickle either, a regular gush!

Two hundred miles away in Otán, Mandragon could feel *mi general*'s scalp prickle. Here was something to clutch at, and not just a straw. And here was something to yank his hand away from. It was the combination, of course, that had him tizzied, spasms and spring together, since he'd finally connected his personal curse with the country's, and sensed they'd be lifted together or not at all. Most hopeful report his aides had ever delivered, though they didn't know it. They didn't know that Genghis was dry as the country. They thought he waddled from too much spritzing, not none at all. But also the scariest, because if this wasn't a real development, there'd never been one. Bad enough to be spasmless in a wasteland, groin gorged with cement and heart empty except for loose dreads; worse to take the risk of hoping and wind up disappointed. And for all that the combination of revels and gushing spring suggested relief, it also recalled his fear and loneliness, excited his self-pity and despair, so that his thoughts couldn't rest there, could only touch and then go mothing away. So he told his aides to investigate, then told them forget it. So he gave his pilot a course for Otán, then called a new heading. So he hung tremored in uncertainty three days, and Mandragon, two hundred miles off, could feel him quivering, clutching, and drawing back in the same motion.

At length he decided to clutch, summoned the secret policemen who'd kidnapped La Negra and colleagues and sent them to kidnap the sorcerer-witch from Otán. They set out at dusk—four ice-hearted thugs in an unmarked Piranha V-8—to make the snatch around midnight and be back by dawn, but at 1:23 A.M. poor Genghis, who'd whis-

kied himself to sleep down in his trull bunker, was jerked
from the relative peace of a nightmare by an eerie *whoosh*:
the car was in the room with him! Left fenders nudging his
divan, right fenders flush with the wall. High beams blaz-
ing, engine rumbling, whip antenna bent by the mirrored
ceiling. And occupants green with terror, sick at both ends,
but after a time all four began to speak—in unison, expressionless monotones full of a strange authority:

"Poor Genghis, Mandragon will save you. Go to Mandragon, poor Genghis, and be healed."

There was no way to shut them up, no way save gagging
them and putting them in straitjackets, and the car had to
be cut up with acetylene torches and hauled out piece by
piece. By then poor Genghis's thoughts were mothing less
crazily. He decided to draw his hand back once and for
all, summoned Lieutenant Colonel Lisandro Empulgueras,
chief of operations of the Tinieblan Civil Guard, and ordered him to get rid of *brujo* and band, put them out of
the country or into prison or in the ocean or ground.
Empulgueras assigned this mission to Major Bartolomeo
Chuzo and the 3rd Special Assault Group ("Wild Alligators"), and they set out at dawn—three hundred snake-
faced assassins in camouflage suits and berets—to strike
around midday and be back by dusk, but Mandragon sent
them home early. At 1:23 p.m. Genghis and staff, who had
convened in the work bunker conference room, were startled by a weird *whoosh* that blew the door open. Major
Chuzo came sailing in and landed on the table and spun
there like a pinwheel on his butt. At length he stopped
twirling and began to speak, in the neutral tone of a robot
or computer:

"Poor Genghis, Mandragon will save you. Go to Mandragon, and you and the land shall be healed."

At the same moment the Wild Alligators appeared outside, fell chuteless from the sky onto the compound parade
field, faces green and jump suits poo-pooed but unharmed,

except that they couldn't stop chanting the same message. Which Genghis might have heeded then and there and saved himself anguish. Sick to distraction and all the country with him, unable to clutch or draw back, and power's voice was offering relief, so obey it. Submit, beg help, be healed and saved. But obeying isn't so easy when you've been a despot for years, decreeing whatever comes into your head, and anyone who doesn't like it gets put someplace nasty. Submitting's a problem when you're Blahblah of the Blah-blah-blah-blah, with multitudes cheering and aides *mi-general*-ing and children singing that *you're* the savior. With your eyes frogging out from billboards all over the place and the newspapers calling you a great leader. And how do you beg for help when you're used to pretending you're an imaginary Genghis, nothing less than every inch a man? Demanding help, compelling it, that's not so bad. That doesn't wreck the act entirely. That way you're still in charge, you're still the master—though that way, of course, help never helps. Help helps when you plead for it, admit your need, but the greater the need the scarier to admit it. Admit, for example, that you were a miserable wretch to begin with, frying in fear, and that all your pretending has only made you more miserable. That the country was in poor shape when you stole it and your monkeying has just about finished it off. Admit that everything you are is sham and everything you do is minus. Poor Genghis wasn't quite ready for that. On his way but not quite ready, and off in Otán Mandragon felt his anguish, knew his confusion, smelled his pain, and watched his thoughts go mothing, round and round. Whirled and fluttered ceaselessly, beat futile wings, when all they had to do was stop striving. Then, mothlike, they'd fall upward into light. Mandragon ached with compassion for poor Genghis, but it wasn't Mandragon's part to make things easy, it wasn't Mandragon's part to go to him. A certain respect was due—not to Mandragon: to the power Mandragon served.

So whenever an aide reported, he was likely to halt in midsentence and stare stonily and then, ventriloquized, say, "Go to Mandragon." And whenever a whore tried to solace him, the same message was likely to emerge from whichever of her mouths happened to be unstoppered. When *mi general* dropped from the sky into famine-blasted villages, peasants snarled the message to him from gap-toothed gums, and when he turned away and waddled back toward his chopper, pariah dogs yapped the message at his heels. At midmonth he went down to the capital to receive Dr. Esclepio Varón, President of Costaguana, who had come on the petition of some Tinieblan exiles refuged in that country, and as they sat in the state office at the palace— Genghis hunkered behind his desk, fingers mashing his brow to keep this thoughts from fluttering; Dr. Varón staring past him out the French windows at the brazen sky— the distinguished humanitarian broke off his discourse on the rights of man to say, "Poor Genghis, poor miserable worthless Genghis, go to Mandragon and heal yourself and Tinieblas." At first light the next morning a red and yellow parrot flapped into the bedroom where Genghis had whiskied himself to the relative peace of nightmare and sailed along the rococo molding near the ceiling repeating, like a looped tape, "Go to Mandragon, poor Genghis, be healed and saved." And when the bird finally flapped out, Genghis was drawn after it onto the balcony that overlooked the Plaza Inchado, drawn out irresistibly though his bulletproof vest lay slung across a footstool, whereupon the twice-life-sized statue of Palmiro Inchado, Discoverer of Tinieblas, looked back over its shoulder at him and said, "Go to Mandragon, jackass, beg to be saved!"

His brothers Kublai, Mangu, and Timur came to the compound to urge him to seek extra drought relief—for the satchels were going lank now, meager as starving beeves —but not a word of this advice got uttered. Politic men, they told Genghis to come walking with them along the shore, where transistorized snoops were unlikely to be se-

creted, where the wind and breakers would roll their whis-
pers away, but when Kublai opened his mouth he recounted
his life of thievery. His voice droned flat and metallic, as
though a transistorized stoolie were secreted back of his
tonsils. His eyes bulged as if he couldn't believe what he
was saying, though it was all true. His hands waggled use-
lessly under his chin, unable to reach and seal his lips. And
when Mangu and Timur tried to interrupt, self-accusations
flowed from their throats too—greed and swindling, bri-
bery and fraud—till all three fell writhing to the sand, black
sand clustered with silica specks that glistened in the fur-
nace glow of the sun. They burrowed their jowls in the
sand at Genghis's feet, and as he gaped, a strange fish was
washed up from the sea beside them, big as a hog, pus-
grey, and bloated. A breaker flung it up onto the sand, and
it opened its toothless mouth as though for air and said,
"Go to Mandragon, moron! Let Mandragon heal you and
Tinieblas of these plagues."

By then he was almost ready, and that night his sister
Mesalina arrived with a film the ministry of information
had prepared for the seventh anniversary of the dictatorship, a three-hour documentary of the great strides forward
Tinieblas had made under *mi general*'s inspired guidance,
but when Genghis previewed it down in his bunker it came
out funny. When the narrator spoke of progress and prosperity, there were scenes of peasant children eating dirt
and ragged beggars squatting in city gutters. The narrator
spoke of honest, efficient government, and the film showed
mi general's brothers stuffing cash into satchels and highways to nowhere overgrown with ferns. "A National Government concerned for the human dignity of every citizen,"
and there were scenes of folks being chucked from helicopters, swung up by their wrists and ankles—*"Uno, dos,
tres, ya!"*—and garbaged out the door, wriggling and howling, tumbling down and down. "A Maximum Leader in the
forefront of the world's progressive magistrates," and there

was poor Genghis, humping and pumping futilely, sobbing in self-pity and despair. After each scene, the film cut to a choir of schoolchildren, but instead of singing "Genghis Will Save Us," they sang: "Parasite Genghis, go to Mandragon, be saved!" Before the film was half over, *mi general* jumped up and waddled out to his chopper and ordered his pilot to fly him to Otán.

Ready to seek help at last—and that was progress—but not really ready to receive it, not prepared. Still fungused with self-importance, mildewed with cravings for deference, so cruded with impiety he wasn't conscious of the disrespect implied in flitting to his salvation attended by flunkies in a clattering great metal bug. Off in Otán, Mandragon smelled these excrescences—all mold and fetor!—on Genghis's soul and thought to clean it up a little. When he spoke the order through the intercom—buckled snugly between a brace of bodyguards with triplet aides opposite eyeing him reverently—the turbojet above him wailed like a kicked hound and quit, the rotors slowed and stilled, the pilot's voice came back, "Don't be pretentious, pubic hair, go on foot!"

Mi general had the man arrested (though he claimed he hadn't known what he was saying) and summoned his driver, but when he gave the order to move out—escort assembled ahead on revving Harleys, and an armored car behind—the crankcase of his limo split in fragments, the oil poured out, the motor shrieked and seized up in a solid chunk. Then his driver turned and repeated, word for word, his pilot's message. It was the same with every car and driver in the compound, and when he called headquarters and ordered them to send him transport, he got the very same reply. By then he was whimpering. By then all he wanted was to go down to the bottom of his bunker and curl on his divan and snivel himself to sleep. Off in Otán, Mandragon accepted his surrender and sent him the desperation to go on.

At first light, then, General Genghis Manduco, Blahisimo of the Tinieblan Revolution and Commander-in-Chief of the Tinieblan Blah-blah-blah, set out for Otán. On foot, because all other means of locomotion were denied him. Alone, because everyone he ordered to accompany him said, "Go by yourself, asshole, you're the one who's cursed." Not disguised as a woman, because none of his whores' clothes would fit him—in a frayed sombrero and a tattered shirt and a ragged pair of trousers, all of which he begged plaintively from the compound's mestizo grounds keeper after a final attempt at command produced a sneer, a raised middle finger, and a burble of moist wind blown in his face. Waddled out through the chain-link gate in the cool time before sunup. Trudged off along the blacktop road that ran due east between sere fields toward the highway. Dipped his whimpering mug and teary bulgers as the sun popped up from behind the cordillera. Plodded on, hauling his grotesquely lengthened shadow.

Genghis Manduco was seven days between his bunkers and Mandragon's sanctuary—east to the highway, then northeast into Salinas Province, then northwest across La Merced into Otán; along the dusty shoulders of heat-blistered roads, beside scorched plains and roasted hillocks, past wracked and leafless trees. But before he had been walking seven minutes, he was aware of someone traveling with him, someone short and slight yet muscular and agile, with piercing black eyes and skin the color and apparent texture of a highly polished black-walnut panel, whose body, like a jungle cat's, suggested ferocity and was physically imposing beyond its size. This someone loped along ahead, looked back with taunting smirks, stuck out a long red tongue and bounded off into the distance; then appeared beside him smiling. Sometimes the smile would fester instantly into a mocking grimace. Sometimes it would guide Genghis's attention to things around him—a snake crossing the highway in graceful, rippling, sidelong eddies, or a

willowy vortex of swirled dust dancing on the plain—and
seed him with affection for the world (the first he'd ever
felt in his poor life), leaving him slaked and rested. At
night this companion shone with a pale, lime-colored aura
which beaconed Genghis on or spread back to bathe and
refresh him.

All that week clouds gathered over Tinieblas. The clouds
that billowed just beyond the coasts and borders pushed
wispy tentacles out over the land, filmy pseudopods of
vapor. They groped out, swelling and branching, thickening
and merging, till all the sky was loosely thatched, then
bulged and burgeoned, pinching out the gaps, so that by
the seventh morning, when Genghis crossed into Otán, the
whole country was swathed in cloud. No rain fell, but the
air was heavy, and dry winds no longer buffeted, and
Tinieblans gazed up, at once expectant and wary of rejoicing prematurely. Mesalina Manduco was likewise uncertain which way to jump. She prepared a communiqué
ascribing the clouds to the genius of Tinieblan scientists
inspired by the personal direction of Blahisimo himself, but
withheld it from publication lest they blow off without
dropping any rain. The problem was that the Blah-in-Blah
was missing from his compound. The place, his aides said,
had been bewitched, and no one could remember when
he'd left or why, so Mesalina prepared another release
accusing the imperialists of kidnapping him, and of strew-
ing the national airspace with fake clouds to torment the
Tinieblan people with empty hopes. But although the government took no stand one way or the other, people broke
from their normal activities and stood together in fields and
city streets and village plazas, gazing upward.

A large number headed for Otán, responding to rumors
that a sorcerer was newly settled in that region who meant
to bring rain and cleanse Tinieblas of the Manducos. The
road north from San Carlos was choked with pilgrims,
many in cars and trucks and many others on foot like

Genghis. The person traveling with him, whom no one else seemed to see, pointed out individuals among them. Rogelio Salmón from Salinas, whose father was in exile and whose patrimony had been mostly manduquized and the rest ruined by drought. A peasant woman named Delgado whose husband had been organizing other peasants, until the police came for him one night and put him in the ground under the barracks in Belém. Others. Genghis's companion told him their stories, without speaking, it seemed, and for the first time in his poor life Genghis was aware of other people and their troubles. The pilgrims never left off cursing him and the rest of the Manducos and praying that Tinieblas might be free of them forever, but none seemed to recognize him, and for the first time in his poor life his thoughts concerned things other than himself, so he moved calmly along in the stream of humanity.

Toward evening, though, the stream stopped flowing and pooled out from the road into the right-of-way and up the scrubby hill banks on each side. Cars and trucks were stalled in both lanes, pedestrians milled about, so that Genghis had to push his way through. His companion, suddenly, had disappeared. All the weariness and pain of his long journey came on him at once. Confusion and despair fell back into him. He stopped and stood with shoulders slumped and shaking, shoving mousy little glances left and right. Daylight was draining quickly from the narrow gap between the clouds and the dry earth, and to the east the hills were shrouded in gloom.

Then there was a commotion up ahead, honking and shouting. The sun, setting off to Genghis's left, flung its last light under the clouds, drenching the crowded road in a strange dawnlike glow. A path opened in the mob clogging the shoulder. Genghis's companion was approaching through it, seen now by everybody else.

Mandragon barefoot in an unbleached tunic embroidered

with childishly drawn animals—coyotes, alligators, buz-
zards—set at odd angles to each other. Stalks through the
crowd, eyes glaring, showing a spangle of white teeth. Peo-
ple skip out of Mandragon's way.

Comes to within five yards of Genghis. Catches sight of
him, halts, stares, then points. Grins and throws head back
in mocking laughter. Genghis inches forward plaintively.
Mandragon rocks, hee-hawing, claps in derisive merriment,
points again. High-pitched hee-hee-hee, and the crowd rec-
ognizes mi general. *Curses, insults, raised fists, but before*
they can mob him, Mandragon jumps forward and begins
a nose-thumbing, ear-waggling, tongue-showing hop-dance
around him.

Genghis begins to shuffle forward. Mandragon dances
round him, pointing and smirking, lip-farting moist wind
into his face. The crowd opens for them.

Insults and dry clods rain in on Genghis as, circled by
Mandragon, he moves slowly along the shoulder of the
road.

Poor Genghis didn't want to go forward. He wanted to
run off and hide. But he was drawn as though cuffed to a
moving vehicle, danced on through howls of happy hatred,
to where the road was blocked by a circling motorcycle
ridden by a fellow with no face, with plastic limbs and
metal hooks for hands, wearing a white-winged helmet.
Drawn there then to the left up a dirt track, *vroom*-ing
cycle weaving in front, clods and curses thumping on his
shoulders, till the track opened on a pasture thick with
young grass and the angry crowd was far behind him.
Ahead, between him and the day's last light, a group of
youths and girls stood smiling at him. And Mandragon
walked beside him smiling sweetly, a smile immensely
tender, loving, gay.

Beyond the crest there was a single huge old tree, and
at its base, between the bowing roots I'd struck with my

gourd rattles the night my tribe and I arrived there, a
spring gushed. Welled from the earth and pooled, flowed
down in rills, and there I had my newest converts bathe
him. Tinieblan girls, Promesa and No Toques, who hated
him more than he deserved. More chancre than spirochete,
but they hated him intensely, and it was good discipline to
have them peel the rags and lave His Loathsomeness with
their soft hands. Machoed him too, since while they went
about it dutifully and gently, contempt twisted their faces
and, along with their forced touches, turned him all randy.
Bathed and then dressed him, so that his tunic poked
jauntily forward, like a jib on a whisker pole, and led him
down to where my tribe was gathered and the beasts were
tethered and Mandragon tranced.

Torches spiked in the moist earth, tribe seated in a wide
half-circle, beasts tethered by their hooves to stakes sunk
in the loam. Mare from Otán and jenny from Salinas;
Remedios heifer, La Merced nanny, Tuquetá ewe; she-tapir
from Selva Trópica, and from Tinieblas a plump sow.
Seven she-ungulates from the seven provinces of the republic, standing tamely, bending placidly, cropping the
grass. Beyond them sat loinclothed Mandragon, arms and
legs crossed, spine against a man-high crackling bonfire.
The girls led Genghis—abluted, tunicked, wanged—through
the celebrants and stood him just inside the circle. Then I
went out of my body and took into it his dryness and the
country's.

*Nightandmist, breasts bare, face masked in ashes, rises
from the midpoint of the crescent holding an earthen bowl
of water in both hands. She walks out between the goat
and ewe toward Mandragon, runs the last few steps and
reaches the bowl out at her arm's length so as not to be
scorched. Mandragon takes the bowl, drinks but does not
swallow, sets it down.*

*Mandragon rises and walks counterclockwise round the
fire, left shin lapped by flame. Pauses at the four compass*

*points to turn outward and spit. Sits down again, spine to
the flames.*

*Mandragon's eyes roll upward. Mandragon's arms droop.
Mandragon's head falls forward.*

*Piercing noises, like the screech of steel, tear from the
air above the crescent, from beyond the fire, from the earth.
Yawning wails from different points beyond the onlookers,
hystercial coughs and heaves, plaintive lapwing cry and
falcon's crowing, interrupted by a woodcock's whistle. The
beasts strain at their tethers and buck crazily. The seated
figures clasp one another's shoulders. Mandragon twists
and writhes.*

*Sudden silence, save for the fire's pop and a faint hum
like a mosquito's. Two pale phosphorescent blobs push
from Mandragon's abdomen. Stumped tentacles of glow
push up and out. Wrist-thick pseudopods of bluish light
rise wavering from under Mandragon's navel and arc above
the beasts toward Genghis, pause near his closed eyes then
palp his brow.*

*Spurts of garish light pulse back along the arcs into
Mandragon. Mandragon shrieks, falls backward in convulsion. Tear-shaped green and purple globs pulse back along
the arcs and comet-plunge into Mandragon's body. Which
bows from crown to heels, vibrating rigidly.*

*The earth trembles. Thunder rumbles, and a shower of
small stones falls on the open semicircle. The glowing tentacles break from Genghis's brow and shrink quickly back.
Mandragon lies inert.*

*Mandragon rises slowly. Smiles wanly and steps back-
ward into the fire. Bares teeth, throws shoulders back, lifts
arms outspread. Mandragon stands chest-high in flame,
head back and arms outspread, smiling in triumph; then
floats upward with the sparks and disappears.*

*Thunder rumbles and a shower of small stones falls on
the circle.*

Mandragon in the embroidered tunic. Emerges from the

gloom beyond the crescent and steps primly through the seated tribe, minces coquettishly to Genghis. Mandragon begins to undulate before him, squirms and sighs, laps lips in a slow rhythm. Sways toward Genghis, mews, moves hands caressingly over his throat and chest, along his flanks, about the tentish bulging in his tunic, sweeping delicately, all but touching. Genghis twists and shivers.

Eyes fluttering in mock modesty, Mandragon lifts the tunic, gasps down in mock surprise and wonder. Gives Genghis the hem to hold, swirls hands around the gorged pork, all but touching it. Genghis grins, drooling a little, and rolls his hips. Rhythmic moaning rises from the crescent.

Undulating, swirling liquid fingers, Mandragon steps backward and draws Genghis toward the beasts. Genghis shuffles forward, holding the hem under his chin, grinning moronically. Out to the mare's broad stern, onto the mound of earth piled just behind it. Mandragon steps aside, raises the tail, wrist lifted, fingers bunched, arm's length in air. Sweeps left hand slowly through, wrist swaying, fingers fluting softly about Genghis's gilled truncheon. Flicks them up as Genghis sconces home.

Whinny from the mare and snort from Genghis. Horse haunch in each fist he bucks and rears. Hands aloft, Mandragon prances round them, but jouncing backward answering his thrusts—then sweeps hands downward and apart, and Genghis stumbles backward. Blinking confusion, panting frustration, throbbing disappointment.

Cruel, obscene smirks: Mandragon minces to him, resumes touchless caresses, draws him toward the ewe.

Beyond, rouged by the torchlight, the celebrants are rocking rhythmically, groping and fondling, moaning as though in pain.

I drew him on from one beast to another, coupled, uncoupled, coupled him again. Mare and ewe and goat, donkey and heifer; heifer and squealing tapir, tapir and sow. I animaled him, joined him to brute nature; I mated him to the fauna of the land. And when he knelt in the roiled grass glued to the sow's rump, clutching bristled flanks, deeply enswined, I raised my face and lifted my spread hands, I cackled and the sky and his loins opened. The seed pumped out of him like molten glass, and quickening rain drenched the dry earth.

The downpour doused the fire and the torches, broke like a wave, though Genghis and my people scarcely felt it. It slackened after a time but didn't stop. Soft rain was falling all across Tinieblas, even as it falls now outside this prison.

26

The rains continued seven months: small rain before dawn and showers at midmorning; afternoon torrents, evening cloudbursts, midnight cascades, so that when they quit the third week in December (exactly as they'd been scheduled to of old), all Tinieblas was green again and flowering. And for seven days Genghis Manduco took a fresh shot at being human.

He would have stayed animaled if I'd let him, took wonderfully to it. Rutted all night, baa'd and bleated along with his consorts. Pawed the mud during engagements and wallowed in it blissfully between, so that when I touched him in the rainbowed dawn, his heart creaked with nostalgia. Laid hands along his temples, raised him up; restored his speech and he stood sniveling in the warm drizzle, reluctantly rehumaned. With his first words he begged to join Mandragon.

Whose tribe were as little children; Genghis would settle for that. If he couldn't be a beast he'd be a baby. But Mandragon didn't want him.

I meant to make my people fully human, to nurse them through. To freedom and power and the responsibility called love. Infant them first and restructure them in balance, so head and heart and loins would music in trio. Hive them in a group soul, tune them to the universe. Ballast them with love, give them dominion. I meant to take what time there was and craft a remnant, to weather the end and welcome the beginning. That was Mandragon's mission, why I'd been picked. I didn't sift out specially gifted prospects. Anything on two legs has the potential. I took the ones I took as my whim struck. Even Genghis might have made it with my help. But I was sick of coddling him, didn't want him around. I'd watched him, lived inside him, worn his consciousness like a hyena skin. I'd sent him signs and portents, illuminations; stung him with insights, descummed his soul, taken on his pain. I'd cured his drought by dipping him in beasthood. I'd given him a good wallow, then raised him up. Saved him, in short—for the country's sake, not his, but what did that matter? He'd had more than his share of Mandragon's grace.

Mandragon sent General Manduco back to his compound, by teleport express just like his goons. Dumped him, slimed and wailing, near his ruined limo—no custom restructuring afforded, no interim of infancy allowed. Gave him a fresh shot to make or muff, and turned to more important matters.

But will give him a few more minutes now, to be rid of him before they come to get me.

Flip over on my back and draw my legs up, give one camera some teeth and the other a profile, and empty him from my mind, squirt the last of him out. Won't do to be soiled with thoughts of him at sunup.

Best purge is to Genghis myself again, squirm into his consciousness. In those days I had the power to live in others, the gift to fling myself into alien minds, and I can be him again—enough to recollect and unload the last of him. Power flowing back, enough for that, and my cable dance won't seem so degrading. Even Mandragon's fate is a step up from his.

Well then, Genghised—which is to have your mind a porridge of anxiety in which blurred blobs of thought float half-submerged. Wearing his consciousness, which is to see the world as menace or carrion meat. This is living, careful! That's dead and rotten, may be safely chowed. Except that Mandragon had descummed his soul a little, so he could see more now, fragments of the world's loveliness and majesty glimpsed vaguely as through a filth-stained, partially wiped pane, along with hints of other people's joy and trouble. Strong man, dictator, supreme chief: a disease, that is, pretending to be a doctor. Except that Mandragon had stung a few insights into him, had given his snout a few mashings in the mess he'd made. Goat-fragrant and blubbering, weary from his ordeal; nostalgic for the mud and yet revolted at having headlined an animal act; rejected by Mandragon, birthed rudely back into the world with a fresh shot at (and therefore the job of) being human.

But spasm-competent again, spritziferous. That thought bobbed up and briefly blurred all insights; it blobbed about, temporarily salving the stings. With humankind as well as quadrupeds, as he took instant trouble to assure himself, not pausing for so much as a wash. Scrambled up and scampered to his twatery, *mi-general*-ing guards snapping to before him, and speared the first strumpet he found as splendidly and mindlessly as he had Mandragon's porker.

"Phew!" the lady said when he uncorked, partly at the fumes that wreathed about him, mainly at the earnest of success that puddled after him onto the cushion, but when she presented her compliments and claimed her bonus, his grin of self-assurance froze and crumbled, his features twisted in pain. The stings Mandragon had lodged in him wouldn't stay ointmented. The remake of Mesalina's movie replayed in his memory, recursing him with recollected dryness, remarooning him in a desert of shame.

"Ya, *mi amor*, ya," the lady soothed. "It shouldn't hurt that much to pay my bonus. It's worth it, don't you think? After you waited so long and tried so hard? Ya! Ya!"

But Genghis's broad brow was already smooth. *Mi general* was grinning again.

"Mother cunt!" he chuckled, getting to his feet. "The

poor pubic hair tried everything, that's no lie. Busted his asshole, didn't he? even offered a bonus! And nothing worked! Ah, ho! Be sad, you know, if it weren't so fucking funny. But why bother me about it? It hasn't a donkey's prick to do with me."

And when she protested—Nothing to do with him? that was a good one!—when she called him a. tightwad and a welsher and a cheat, he told her to pack and be out of the place in an hour, to stop laughing at him (though she wasn't laughing at all), to stop that shitty laughing or he'd . . .

Mi general stamped out, hands clamped to his ears.

Mandragon had given him a fresh shot but no restructuring, had saved him but didn't feel like nursing him through. Mandragon stuck him with the job of being human, but gave him no instruction in the forms. Which amounted to destroying him, nothing less. People credit Mandragon with that, Mandragon accepts. His only model was an imaginary Genghis, the fearless, wise, compassionate, manly leader described in sister Mesalina's press releases. His only method was to pretend to be this figment. But Mandragon had flashed him some peeks at the Genghis he was—a cowardly, bungling, selfish, pitiful clown. The incongruity stung him very fiercely. He hadn't the courage to face it, much less the discipline to cherish the stings and learn. So he disconnected from what he'd been and done and treated his past as if it concerned someone else, a different person entirely, who hadn't a thing on earth to do with him. But Mandragon had damaged his machinery for pretense, had smashed a lot of those circuits in the process of goading him toward salvation. Whenever he unplugged, he heard a horrid laughter all around him.

Stamped out, hands over his ears, but the laughter rasped through them. Swept along the hall, squinting bewilderment. Why were the walls guffawing? What call did the doorknob to his private quarters have to cackle in that disrespectful manner? And the faucets in his bath: how dare they snigger? It occurred to him he must have done something foolish, but even so, to simper at him like that! Insubordination! Treasonous! He was Genghis Manduco, Blahisimo of the Blah! That thought blobbed up, muting the giggles. It bobbed about in his mind, muffling the hoots. The last titter had hushed and faded when, some twenty minutes later— booted, pistoled, kepi'd, combat-greened—he strode into the conference room of his work bunker for a breakfast consultation with his aides.

Who congratulated *mi general* on the end of the drought. As if he'd accomplished it! as if he'd been more than a tool! As if the brush deserves praise for the triptych, or the laboratory rat a prize for the cure! Mandragon worked the miracle, not Genghis. Mandragon brought the rain, and no one in the conference room knew that Genghis was even tangently involved. But that's the style with people in power: their sycophants miss no chance to stroke them. No matter how ridiculous the pretext, people in power receive congratulations, and accept them as their due as Genghis did, nodding curtly, giving his left hand a few sealish flaps, bending to slurp coffee. Then he leaned back, wiped his lips with his right index finger, wiped the finger on the front of his uniform, squared his beefy shoulders, fixed his bulgy eyes on Dr. Remo Lampazo Inmundo, his chief aide, and called for a full report on conditions in Tinieblas.

Which Dr. Lampazo didn't feel much like giving: conditions in Tinieblas weren't good. Tinieblas was in the last stages of dismantlement, bankrupt, mortgaged to the fourth generation, flying apart. Dr. Lampazo longed for the days of drought when all he'd needed on his clipboard was a wire from a weirdo in Winnetka or some similar twaddle, which like as not he never even had to read—not all the way through—before the Cheese-in-Cheese coptered off into the yonder, or slunk away for a quick boff. Today, it seemed, he meant business, and Dr. Lampazo didn't want to tell him about conditions, which were worse than they'd been the day before, for the government if not for the people. Drought relief was all that was filling the satchels; now it would end. The drought had absorbed much rage and hatred; now the dictatorship would have it all. But Dr. Lampazo had a young economist on his staff who was a genius for teaching figures to fandango and making data dance sarabands and gavottes, who could prove fourteen contradictory theses with the same statistics and had besides the most boring delivery conceivable, not simply dry but mumbled, halting, and confused. No disciplined thought went on behind *mi general*'s brow, so he'd scarcely keep track of all those nimble numbers. His attention span was at best but eye-blink brief, so he'd scarcely hear the economist through. There was every chance he'd doze off, or nip back across the way for a nick of nooky. Dr. Lampazo unleashed his data-dog and sicked him on the general— that is, he called the fellow forward (since secondary aides sat back from the table behind the principals) and gave him the floor.

Harumphs and rustling of papers. At length a stumbling mutter pitched just above the air conditioner's whirr:

"Analysis of information for the month of April—those figures, *mi general*, so far reported to the national government and subject to revision and supplementation—suggest that the per capita national indebtedness—the republic's obligations, *mi general*, divided by the best estimate of current population—has fallen, that is gone down, by point four two percent . . ."

(Not because the debt was any smaller, because lots of babies had been born, but he didn't say that.)

". . . whereas the rate of unemployment—the number of workers, *mi general*, divided by the number idle, that is, not working—declined also (a very encouraging sign) by point six two percent . . ."

(Not because anyone had found work, because a good many who'd been looking had starved to death or committed suicide, but he didn't mention that either.)

". . . while during the first quarter of the calendar year —January through March, that is, *mi general*—the rate of increase in inflation receded by nearly point eight percent . . ."

(As if that meant inflation was subsiding instead of getting worse a little less rapidly.)

". . . and the national money, the Tinieblan inchado, that is, entirely ceased declining on all financial markets . . ."

(Because it was totally worthless now, and no one bothered to quote it.)

". . . which, coupled with the fact that we project a point three six percentage of increase in revenue collection . . ."

The muttering ran on. Numbers thumped in it hypnotically, like devils' names in an incantation—always percentages of this or that, never a hint of flesh-and-bone suffering humans. Yet *mi general* wasn't lulled. *Mi general* was racked and moaning. Not with boredom either. The report had started a replay of a remake reflickering in *mi general's* mind's eye. His mind's snout was being remashed in the mess he'd made.

Rocking back and forth keening remorse. Beating his brow and gnawing his knuckles. Then, as the economist stuttered silent, Genghis unplugged. His shame was instantly replaced by righteous fury.

"*Hijo de la grandisima PUUUUUU-ta!* Kids are eating dirt, there are beggars all over, and you give me diddle about point what-the-fuck up and down! Say it, man, this country's in the shit up to the eyes! In the shit and sinking, you want to know why? Bungling, that's why, and liars trying to hide it! If I'd had anything to do with it, I'd hang myself!"

Snorted and stared grimly round the table. "Well, it's

over. For good, as of right now, I won't stand for it. I'm in charge now and my . . . Stop that laughing! There's nothing funny here, stop it, I say! I'll have no faggish laughing at my conferences! I won't stand for it! Bungling and lies!"

And he flung from the room—hands clamped over his ears—up snickering steps, through a doorway that screeched derision, out under a cloud-strewn sky that was belching ho-ho-ho's.

Nevertheless, he kept trying. For seven days he tried his pathetic best. No doubt he'd done something foolish (though for the life of him he couldn't think what), still the flagpole had no right to bray in mockery. He was chief of government! That thought blopped to the surface of his mind and deadened the laughter. It was barely audible by the time he reached his quarters and phoned the capital and ordered a cabinet meeting for the following morning. Then he slept, for to tell the truth he was weary. Threw himself down—not between two sides of prime, for with so many Tinieblans suffering it was unseemly for the head of government to revel. Went to bed totally tartless for the first time in years. No question, he was trying his pitiful best.

But at the sight of his brother Akbar, the minister of public works, alighting from the first of a convoy of limos, a replay of a remake began rescreening back of his brow. Fiery stings seared him, he wept and wailed. Then he began to harangue his assembled siblings, attacking the government. Thieves and vandals who stole whatever they could and wrecked the rest! Highways to nowhere and bridges without rivers! Criminal lunacy, which (thank heaven!) he'd had nothing to do with. He bellowed on, though a mid-morning shower descended precisely on schedule, until the raindrops began tittering and the puddles on the asphalt started to chuckle, and the sea (blue-grey, immense, and placid under the rain) sent basso peals of laughter rolling toward him. He screamed for silence and then clomped off, his hands pressed firmly over his ears.

The members of his cabinet glanced about at each other,

then hopped back into their cars and sped away, using the telephones with which ministerial limousines were equipped to alert their brothers and sisters, their spouses and children, their cousins and in-laws. Kublai phoned Intercontinental Airlines in Miami and chartered a jumbo. Mesalina phoned her ministry and issued a statement about a long-planned family excursion. That afternoon all the Manducos left Tinieblas. Flung clothing into valises, dumped jewels into handbags. Packed bankbooks into attaché cases, stuffed the last of the cash into satchels. Nero Manduco took a gunnysack round to the National Museum and collected the pre-Columbian gold figurines. Lucrezia Manduco made off with the presidential silver service. Each grabbed what he could and bolted. Limousine after limousine, sedan after sedan took the new toll road out to the new airport. Manduco after Manduco scurried up the ramp, took one look over his shoulder, and leaped aboard. By sundown Genghis was the only member of the family left in the country.

By then the thought had globbed up in his mind that he was head of state. By then he had called the assembly into special session. By then the laughter had stilled and he was going to give his country fearless, wise, compassionate, manly leadership—exactly what, he didn't know yet, but it would be the wonder of the world! The next morning he went down to Ciudad Tinieblas—bulletproof vestless! No question, he was trying—to steel the legislators for the hard task ahead.

And rewitnessed the remake, and suffered the stings. And bellowed righteous rage, and proclaimed his innocence. Crazy laws! Institutionalized confusion! He'd had nothing to do with it, his conscience was clear. And heard the horrid laughter. And rushed from the chamber, hands clapped to his ears.

For seven days Genghis spun in this spiral, toward the end making three or four circuits daily. Thought after thought glopped to the surface of his mind, pulling him from

one spin and flinging him into another. He was maximum
leader of the Revolution, so he coptered here and there to
hastily arrange village meetings, where like an old-time
feudal lord he heard peasants' complaints but where, inevit-
ably, he felt the stings of shame then disconnected, denounced the Revolution's blunders and, at the last, rushed
off tormented by mocking laughter. He was commandant
of the Civil Guard, so he collected the general staff to plan
new policy, but within minutes he was screaming accusa-
tions—seven years of terror! which, of course, he'd had
nothing to do with—and finished by begging the stone
portals of the headquarters not to gibe and cackle. He was
a world figure, so he called a press conference. Journalists
had flown in from all over to report the end of the drought
—leather-hearted cynics who'd seen everything, but *mi
general* soon had them blinking in amazement. He denounced the dictatorship in the third person, as if he'd just
come to power and was doing his best to correct abuses he'd
had nothing to do with, then shrieked for his audience to
stop laughing at him. He was president of the republic, so
he went about cutting ribbons and laying cornerstones, and
at every stop whirled through the cycle again: felt the stings
of shame and disconnected; denounced the government,
claimed he wasn't to blame, and fled away tormented by
rude jeers. Whip-snapped through it dizzily. Faster and
faster, on and on, round and round.

The end came on the seventh anniversary of the majors'
coup when purpled in a dress uniform (a general's gold
palm fronds at the lapels), draped with the presidential
sash, spangled with stars and crosses bestowed on him by
other blustering thieves, he descended to the roof of the
Excelsior. A reviewing platform seven stories high had been
set up at the hotel's facade. A great multitude thronged the
plaza—dragooned peasants, lockstep-marched public employees, schoolchildren singing "Genghis Will Save Us."
Elite units of the Civil Guard were formed up in adjacent

streets, ready to parade in his honor. But the instant he stepped from his chopper, his mind's eye was filled with horrors, his mind's snout was mashed in the mess he'd made, his mind's ears were rasped and pummeled with laughter. The end and the beginning fell together. Shame and scorn buffeted him at once. There wasn't an instant's relief from either.

At that moment Genghis Manduco gave up the struggle to be human. Then and there he renounced Mandragon's barbed grace. Hauled himself back into his helicopter. Had his pilot fly him to a manduquized farm in a remote sector of Remedios. Dismissed the aircraft, headed for the sty.

The celebration in the capital was held up, of course. A high-level search mission was organized. So it was that Colonels Atila Guadaña, Fidel Acha, and Lisandro Empulgueras found their commander-in-chief kneeling in mud and droppings grunting contentment, his dress trousers bunched at his ankles, his starred and spangled tunic smeared with slime, his genghishood porked deeply in a plump sow.

Bye-bye, Blahisimo.

Farewell, *mi general.*

Adios.

27

With the passing of the drought and the Manducos, Tinieblas began to revive. The ranking officers of the Civil Guard formed a new junta but didn't act like lobsters in a basket. None of them wanted to be on top of the others, not with so many problems to solve and nothing worth stealing left in the country. They didn't even want to stay in power, not with what had happened to Genghis fresh in their minds. Let civilians try to clean up the mess. Let politicians run the risk of getting swined. They set a date for new elections and meanwhile did their best to make amends.

Prisoners were freed and exiles welcomed home. Manduquized property was returned to rightful owners. Mangu's crazy taxes were rescinded. Caligula's mad fiats were repealed. Genghis himself was stowed in the Fasholt Clinic—at no expense to the state, since the doctors there were so eager to study him they agreed to board and treat him free. The junta even considered issuing a group apology for having associated with him, but in the end that wasn't necessary. The people weren't vindictive. All the people wanted was to forget the seven-year "*manducazo*"—like an obscene assault committed on them, like a loathsome disease they'd caught and then been cured of. The government had stopped preying on them, that was plenty. Rain had come at last, that was enough. No one wanted to tempt fate by seeking vengeance. With the parasites gone and the drought broken,

Tinieblans stepped from their long loneliness. Pseudopods of fellowship sprouted from them. Tendrils of love pushed out, touched gingerly, and merged. Bonds formed and energy was channeled. Bit by bit the country revived.

In Otán, Mandragon labored. Mandragon was refurbishing maimed spirits. Mandragon was restoring damaged lives. Mandragon was renovating people and rehearsing them for full humanity. I knew my business and worked carefully, taking infinite pains crafting my remnant so they'd be fit to survive the old and seed the new. I knew my destiny and I worked ceaselessly, so that no moment would be wasted. The time of my extinction was approaching, but I refused to let that trouble or distract me. I had my gifts about me, that was plenty. I was power's instrument, that was enough. I wore my fate as lightly as my skin, and went about my mission smiling gaily.

Recollecting now, reaching to recapture. Before, when they put me in here, I lay remorsing and repining, flogging the stale moments by. Last night I began remembering who I was, and bit by bit power revives in me. In those days, though, I knew, and power filled me. I was at my post, doing my duty, obeying undisobeyable orders I chose freely, and from acceptance flowed constant joy and ease. Revelation, that might have made life bitter, made it tasty. Responsibility, that might have been a burden, buoyed me up. Just as now, in pale reflection, recalling and reclaiming my identity releases me from heaviness and fear, refreshes this last hour.

Now everyone beyond these rooms is sleeping—thieves and brawlers in their cages, my girls downstairs: Apple and Nightandmist and Confort; Full Moons with Paloma in her arms. My keeper nods, eyes closed, before his monitors. Officers and guards doze at their stations. The sentinel leans drowsing at the gate. In the café the cook sleeps sprawled back in a chair, head flopped on his right shoulder, while at a counter stool a whore's asleep hunched forward, face pillowed on her forearms near the cool tiles. I do not have to leave this chaise to see them. Men sleep on the stone floors of rude cantinas. Women sleep beside screenless windows in tenement flats. And in the palace Angela sleeps naked in silk sheets—curled on her side, hands bunched between her thighs—just as, during imperishable nights, she slept beside me, her smooth rump softly spooned to my male loins. Soon all will be called back to guilt and error, but for this interim they're infanted in sleep. And, for this interim, Mandragon remembers.

Sunlight spilled into a forest clearing. Breeze and birdsong stilled for my mute word. Mandragon remembers. My tribe around me, repairing joyfully toward a new world. I was the father who curbs, the mother who nourishes. I was the mother who scolds, the father who shields. I was the gloom that shrouds a dying epoch. I was the light that guides and beckons to adventure. I was the path and the goal, the scourge and the unguent, readying them for the end and the beginning.

Without haste and without rest Mandragon labored, and each moment was fresh and precious.

Word of me spread. I had brought rain and cleansed the land of vermin. I took young people and presided at strange rites. I preached world's end and the earth purified. I promised both salvation and destruction. Word of me roused conflicting feelings—love-hate, hope-fear, desire and revulsion. Mandragon's presence was disturbing, for Mandragon's grace was barbed.

The ritual of communal love, for instance, raised yaps and squawks and rantings, secret yearnings, lewd and shameful dreams, in every crevice of Tinieblas, though my tribe celebrated it but once a month and, for the rest, went chaste. It was a means of lifting people from themselves, of dipping them into undifferentiated unity—distinctions vaporized, sexes confused, loneliness shattered. It was the vulgar image of my neuter wholeness, at the reach of new initiates, and so the rite was held at crescent moon. But from the stir it caused one would have thought that all we did was orgy, night and morning, all the year around, and Mandragon (they said) chomped and was romped by everyone, when in fact I stayed apart in trance. Not surprising, though, this intense interest, this fierce reaction, and sex can't account for all of it—no, not for half. Every effort to bridge opposites is both scary and seductive, for every human longs to escape himself, yet is afraid of losing his identity, of forgetting who he is. My tribe forgot themselves in me. I renamed them and created them new persons. That in itself was exciting and unsettling, orgies (which were just a means) apart. Infuriating too, for in their heart's heart many craved to join me, but fear overruled desire and transformed it to revulsion. Many of those howls of happy hatred will have been bred from thwarted love.

Word spread, outsiders came. In curiosity, in reverence, in need. In anger and impiety and envy. To scoff or to believe, to sneer or worship, and from the way Mandragon received them word spread farther and more came.

Mandragon received Gaspar Gaspacho and Melquior Melgacho and Baltasar Baldacho, the governors (respectively) of Salinas, La Merced, and Tuquetá. They came to salute the rainmaker and pay homage to the vermin-chaser, since their provinces had been savaged by the drought and their posts previously held by minor Manducos. But instead of receiving gifts from them, Mandragon gave. When the three governors returned to their cars, as they were driving off, there were three explosions without concussion like the timed-fire cracks of a high-powered semiautomatic rifle. An object appeared in air before each of them, hung spinning near the dome light of each car, then settled gently into each lap.

Gaspacho's gift was a gold fob watch with arrow-tipped hands and Roman numerals and *"Mens Sibi Conscia Recti"* engraved on the back. It was presented to Gaspacho's father

in 1927 by the Tinieblan Academy of History and Letters,
and bequeathed to Gaspacho's care in 1937 by that father's
dying breath, and plucked from Gaspacho's vest in 1947
on a street in Chuchaganga by an alumnus of that city's
famous pickpockets' school. The thief fenced it to a pawn-
broker who sold it to Gamelial Garza, who kept it ten
years then pawned it in a shop in Veracruz, Mexico—
not because he was pesoless (though he was) but because
he could not bear to measure the hours of his exile. There
it stayed ten years till it was bought by a British tourist and
carried home with him to Porlock in Somerset and buried
with him when he died. Mandragon's power traced it and
exhumed it and teleported it to Gaspacho.

Melgacho received a silver ring set with a tear-shaped
turquoise. He'd had it of his wife, Lea, while he was a
bachelor, and cherished it through their marriage and into
his widowerhood, but it was thieved from him by his eloping
daughter, along with many other things he could have sold
for more but valued less. Mandragon returned it to him.

For Baldacho, Mandragon produced a lead paperweight
topped with a globe and a three-sided obelisk. Dear little
Balti had lisped and mewed his parents into buying it for
him at the New York World's Fair in 1939, had marked
it with a deeply notched, top-heavy *B* and kept it on his
person, night and day, for the rest of their visit and on the
voyage home, until his sister, with unspeakable malice, pried
it from his six-year-old fingers and hurled it from the boat
deck of the *Moira* into the Atlantic off San Juan. When
Baldacho clutched that silly trinket—cleaned of barnacles
and sea slime by Mandragon, but still cold from the depths
of the Puerto Rico Trench—all the delight of childhood
flooded to him, fate was annulled, the drowned past was
revived, and plundered innocence was ransomed.

Mandragon received Felix Gato Montes, snarl-lipped,
amber-eyed storekeeper of Angostura in Remedios, who
came in a four-wheel-drive Pitman Dromedary with a

Spanish-made .45-caliber pistol and his brother Silvestre, the town magistrate, and a court order for "the immediate release from unlawful restraint and concubinary bondage" of his daughter Graciela. As if she'd been kidnapped! As if she were any concern of his! Mandragon had released her from restraint, had freed her from bondage. Mandragon was her mother-father now. Mandragon had picked her for the remnant and renamed her Promesa and transformed her, so that she now bore about the same relation to the girl Gato was hunting as a triumphantly empurpled moon moth does to the caterpillar that cocooned it. When he and his brother came roiling across the pasture—churning the turf up, gouging ruts in the young grass—when they stamped to where Mandragon sat by the bowed roots of the great tree, Mandragon told him—softly, smiling—that his daughter Graciela was dead.

(Mandragon's daughter Promesa was standing three feet back. Both Gato brothers looked directly at her but neither recognized her. How could they? She wasn't sniveling. She didn't cringe. She stood, hands clasped below her navel, smiling radiantly, pregnant with light.)

Felix Gato took his pistol from where he'd had it stuck in the waistband of his trousers under his flapping shirt. He cocked it, thumbed the safety forward, poked the muzzle toward Mandragon's forehead. He pulled the trigger. Mandragon smiled.

Mandragon's smile held back the hammer. Mandragon's smile eased the safety back with a soft click. Mandragon's smile depressed the button on the grip near Gato's thumb so that the magazine popped from the pistol to the ground. Mandragon's smile flung the receiver back so that the bullet was ejected from the chamber. Mandragon's smile lasered the pistol, fusing it into a solid chunk. Then Mandragon told Señor Gato to go home and mind his business, or Mandragon would take all his children, and his wife, and everything he had.

The Gato brothers ran to their truck, and started it and slewed it round, and sped away without looking back.

Mandragon received the ill and the afflicted, people who couldn't get ordinary care and people who'd been told their cases were hopeless. Healing wasn't part of Mandragon's mission. It drained Mandragon's energy and time. But power must be used, gifts can't be buried, so Mandragon healed, and the word spread, and more came, and the word spread farther. Then, on a day in August, Mandragon received a delegation from the Tinieblan College of Physicians, who came to observe the phenomenon or expose the quack, depending on the open-mindedness or prejudice they brought with them.

Forty-four strong, with attendant interns and technicians and a mobile diagnostic laboratory, a great hulking trailer full of heart machines, X-ray equipment, and the like. No way to get it up into the pasture, so Mandragon went down and saw patients near the road—after the medicos had checked them, naturally, which took no end of time and bother, but finally Mandragon got to work. Trailer and doctors' cars parked on the shoulder of the highway, bent queue of sufferers straggled up the path, Mandragon in the operating theater. Circled, that is, by craned-necked whispering practitioners, most of them in sport shirt for the outing, but a few wore the more formal *guayabera*. Dr. Alfonso Gusano de Sedas, their president, wore a white suit and a heraldic stethoscope, and a haughty sneer, while Mandragon shuffled barefoot in the drying mud, brown calves untrousered below a rude tunic, brown hands unrubber-gloved, woolly pate uncapped, snapper-flashing mouth un-gauze-masked.

Peeling cataracts off an old peasant's eyeballs, closing a child's pellagra sores by touch, taking the fever from a sick Indian. His two sons had carried him in on a litter from the mangrove marshes back of Huaunta and wouldn't let the interns sample his blood, so no one found out exactly what he had. Impressed by his fever, though. Passed around a thermometer they'd stuck in his armpit—hemming, raising their eyebrows, nodding gravely. I laid my left palm on his head and drew the fever out. Drew it into me, then spat it on the ground, and he got up and thanked me and walked away.

Spent about thirty seconds on each patient. Hurried a little because I'd started late, but I put on a decent show. Kid about five with a withered hand, and I laughed and said I could fix it without looking, that's how easy it was. Turned and closed my eyes and reached my left hand back to her. Told her to stretch her bad hand out and grab my finger. She did, and I felt the power flow out into her, and when I turned the hand was whole, just like the other. I didn't let her leave though. Next on line was a young woman with the shingles—a terrible case, her back all scaled and crusted. I guess half the doctors there had examined her and she was getting used to it, for she pulled her blouse off without the least show of embarrassment and stood placidly, her forearms crossed over her breasts, and I told the little girl I'd cured to cure her, to touch her back with the hand I'd healed. The power was still in it, and when she began I lifted her so she could reach the woman's shoulders, and power flowed out of me into her through the kid. Doctors all around, muttering, peering; shielding their eyes against the glare that fell about us out of a yolk-yellow sky, and where the little girl's hand touched, the skin went smooth. I set her down by her father and said, *"Mil gracias, señorita doctora,"* and turned to my next patient.

One after another, half a minute on each. All routine stuff till I faced a man who was dying. Taxi driver from the capital, no more than forty, and he seemed healthy enough, but a voice in my left ear told me where to look, and after that I saw what was wrong quite clearly. Laid my cheek against his chest just to make sure, then told him to take off his shirt.

Rising murmur from my audience. They knew his trouble, and not from their mobile lab either. He'd been turned away from San Bruno Hospital that week, been told to settle his affairs and come back when the pain hit. Then, when they came to visit me, the doctors brought him. "Nothing to do with this one," mumbled Dr. Gusano, and I put my hands together at the base of the man's neck and drew them sharply downward. The flesh of his chest opened and petaled back.

Gasp from the ringed onlookers. Dr. Gusano, face pale as his suit, jumps forward to seize Mandragon. Mandragon waves him back and glances quickly round the circle. The doctors rooted, motionless, tranced.

The patient's face: brow smooth, eyes all but closed, lips parted in a serene half-smile. His chest: flesh petaled open from the throat to below the breastbone. Carmine tissue lifts and settles slowly, but no blood flows. Mandragon repeats the downward hand-sweep, and the breastbone splits.

Mandragon: head bowed, eyes closed, temples clasped in a dark-brown right hand. Left hand pokes gingerly into the man's chest, inches into the left cavity. Mandragon stands motionless, left hand in the man's chest up to the wrist, left arm relaxed, right hand clasped to forehead.

Mandragon's head rocks slowly forward and back. Mandragon's left forearm tenses. The tendons stand out like strings on a bass viol. Slowly Mandragon's left hand reappears holding a lemon-shaped grey lump.

Mandragon turns, smiles weakly, holds the tumor out toward Dr. Gusano, drops it on the ground. Sweeps hands quickly apart. Repeats the movement toward the other half of the circle. Untranced, the doctors gasp and jabber.

Mandragon turns back to the patient. Sweeps hands together, and the split in the man's breastbone fuses. Repeats the movement, and the wound in the man's chest closes. A strip of pale scar tissue forms along it. The man blinks, shakes his head dazedly, turns away.

*   *   *

Tumor the size of a lemon in his heart. Malignant of course, and it was worse than being back in Don Lorenzo's circus. They wanted to know how: how I knew it was there, how I removed it. And the ones who didn't ask how refused to believe.

"Hypnotism!" squealed Dr. Alfonso Gusano.

I picked the tumor up and stuck it in his face. The whole business had drained me, and I wasn't myself, but then a voice spoke into my left ear, and I stopped glaring. I dropped the tumor in a metal dish one of the interns was holding and wiped my hands on my tunic. Then I spoke softly to Dr. Gusano.

"What about the nodules in your lungs? Would you like me to cure them? I won't have to open you, but you have to believe."

He stared at me. "How?"

"Sometimes I see, and sometimes a voice tells me, but I really don't know how. How doesn't matter. Your lungs are riddled with them, aren't they? Would you like me to cure them?"

"You can't!"

"I can't if you think I can't, I can if you do. Is denying me worth dying for?" I laid my left hand on his chest, over the top button of his suit, and closed my eyes. "Believe."

He stiffened, then relaxed. I felt the power flow out and him receive it. Then I turned to my next patient.

Dr. Gusano didn't go straight down to the trailer. He was too afraid, and I didn't blame him. He'd spent all his life believing in one reality, one his stethoscope and his machines could interpret, so he was afraid to admit now that there are others. Still, he'd known for several weeks that both his precious lungs were full of cancer, and though he bore it well, he was afraid of dying. Either way, the business was scary, so he waited another two and a half patients before he went down and had himself X-rayed.

After a while he came out of the trailer with the picture, blinking glazed eyes. He ran up waving it and pulled me from my patient and embraced me. Then he turned and began babbling to his colleagues.

"Spontaneous remission!" snorted one of them.

Mandragon received Mefisto Maroma, TV personality, who'd become (for a Tinieblan) rich and famous by scraping what he called news events off the bottom of his shoe and then smearing them in the viewers' faces each Sunday. He brought a film crew and a makeup man and a monster—a mongoloid boy about sixteen, mute and stunted, drool-lipped, bug-eyed, crazed, with a head like a partially deflated soccer ball, dented over the right eye, bulged over the left. Mandragon was supposed to cure the boy on camera—"Just even out his dome and make him talk"—but Mandragon refused. Why change him? He used no words, but neither had Mandragon for many years. He was a freak, but then so was Mandragon. All his sorrow and confusion came from being jeered at and abused, from having to grub his life from garbage cans. Simple kindness was the cure for that. Mandragon took him into the tribe and named him Perfecto, but told Señor Maroma to leave at once.

That Sunday Maroma told his viewers that Mandragon was a fraud who feared exposure and tried to infringe the public's right to know. He said he had exclusive films shot in the fake guru's hideaway before the people's eyes and ears were expelled from it. And, sure enough, there was Mandragon, frowning gravely, telling Maroma to clear out. And there was the mongoloid monster being led away by some of Mandragon's tribe. And there was Mandragon again, stalking off while Maroma's voice complained of disrespect for the press. But when the film cut back to him for his sign-off, for his trademark close-up smirk and his "This is Mefisto Maroma in Otán Province," there was Maroma (bug-eyed, drool-lipped, goof-grinned), shorts and trousers bunched around his ankles, playing energetically with himself.

What shame Maroma had from that prank! What fun he'll have covering Mandragon's dance!

Mandragon received weekend sightseers, tourist/pilgrims of the sort who went to Punta Huracán to see the Virgin of the Waves—a piece of driftwood vaguely like an effigy of the Madonna that fishermen had found and built a shrine to and said protected them at sea—or visited the village of Mandinga (where everyone was descended from African slaves) for what were called the "Congo Devil Dances." Doctora Matilde de Ardilla was the first of them. Her breasts had swelled earth-motherly above the lecterns of many international conferences; her sturdy neck had been togaed with many degrees. She'd fasted with Coptic mystics in Ethiopia, and meditated with lamas in Tibet. She believed in everything.

Doña Matilde believed in Jesus and Gautama and the Sufis, in Zen and Yoga and the Kabbala, in all sorts of things Mandragon had never heard of till she mentioned them. She believed in astral bodies and in transmigrating souls, in divination by tarot cards and yarrow sticks. She believed in shamans and sorcerers and witches, witches that formed covens and worshiped Satan and witches like La Negra, whom she'd consulted and bought potions from in the evil days when her husband took up with an usherette. She didn't merely keep an open mind. She believed—which was why, though she was past seventy, her eyes still sparkled and her heart was young. Doña Matilde spent an hour with Mandragon and the rest of the day with members of the tribe. She would have stayed longer, but that was neither possible nor necessary. No one stayed overnight except tribe members, and Doña Matilde was already in harmony with the universe.

She was the first, but many more came after her. From the capital mostly, one or two cars at first, later whole

convoys. Mandragon sent members of the tribe to meet
them, stationed people at the road to welcome them, to
sit with them and answer questions. Attending tourist/
pilgrims became part of the tribe's training. The mere
presence of Mandragon's followers was unsettling. They
were so contented, so serene; so drenched with love, so certain of the future; so puffed with the arrogance of humility
that visitors would wring their hands in envy, grind their
teeth in wrath. Few were as balanced and at peace as Doña
Matilde. Often they grew maudlin or abusive, sometimes
even violent. Putting up with them was good practice for
my tribe.

Some I received in person. I smiled at them and drained
their unwholesome emotions, spoke softly to them of the
things to come. I might have preached. I might have filled
my Otán pasture with frenzied multitudes at once terrified
of the end and exultant at the prospect of the beginning.
But that was not my mission. My mission was to rear a
remnant. I was not to re-create the mania I'd wrought in
New York. I did so only later, when I forgot myself. The
sightseers, the weekend tourist/pilgrims, came in curiosity
or boredom and went away amused or scoffing, perhaps with
an anecdote or two to tell at home.

Mandragon received these different sort of visitors,
and meanwhile months passed and elections approached.
There'd been no politics for seven years. No new figures
had come forward. Most of the old ones were dead or in
decay. There was talk of putting up this fellow or that, of
organizing this or that new party, but the only thing people
thought of seriously was bringing back Alejandro Sancudo.
He'd never been an ordinary politician. For Tinieblans he
had long since ceased to be an ordinary, flesh-and-bone
human being. He had become a myth, a ghost who haunted
the country's dreams, a perpetually returning incubus. The
people would have him back simply from habit, or from

a sense of fate, and he'd been out of power now so long those few who tried to judge rationally forgot he'd gone crazy whenever he was in and spoke instead of his experience. It was as if, after a rape and seven years' concubinary bondage, the country longed to give itself to an old love. No one even felt snubbed when Alejo refused to campaign. Tinieblans only yearned for him more ardently.

He issued a manifesto from his exile in Switzerland saying that he'd been elected in 1970, and that nothing since then in Tinieblas had been legal or real. As far as he was concerned, he was still president. He would return only in that capacity. He wouldn't compete for what was already his.

But General Manduco's constitution was still in effect. And there was a clause in it permitting a president to delegate titles, powers, duties, and authority to any citizen he chose. So when Gonzalo Garbanzo announced that he would run, people knew what was up and smiled contentedly.

Gonzalo Garbanzo had been in politics for forty-seven years without ever being elected to anything. All that time he'd hacked for Alejo Sancudo. He'd passed out propaganda leaflets when Alejo seized the palace in 1930. He'd stolen votes in the 1940 race. He'd been a river of hope and faith to *alejistas* during Alejo's first exile, and an island of sanity during Alejo's astrological campaign in 1948. He'd gone to jail whenever Alejo was deposed and rallied to him whenever he tried a comeback. There wasn't any question what was up. The people elected deputies pledged to Gonzalo, and the first thing Gonzalo did when they voted him president—right there in the chamber! as soon as they'd pinned the tricolor sash on his chest!—was to delegate his titles, powers, duties, and authority to Alejo Sancudo.

Who sent word that he'd accept on one condition: he'd have to have his wife as his vice-president. Which the deputies granted as soon as the word arrived: they elected her unanimously, though none of them had ever seen her. No, some of them may have seen her. One or two of them may have been in the tent that evening in the fall of 1949 when Amichevole's Universal Circus played the capital. One or two may have seen her (bikinied in rhinestones) handstanding on brother Pablo's head. But whether any had seen her or not, she was elected.

Alejo returned to Tinieblas with her, and they took office. Four months ago. In due course she went touring around the country. In due course she visited Otán.

Mandragon received the Most Excellent Lady, the Vice President of the Republic, Doña Angela de Sancudo. She was the last visitor Mandragon received.

28

Alejandro Sancudo received the presidential sash on November 28—the 462d anniversary of the discovery of Tinieblas and the forty-seventh of his own violent debut. His return to power was constitutionally valid. It reflected the people's will. But as he stood on the podium of the chamber pronouncing his inaugural address, many Tinieblans, both there and watching on television, repented their yearnings to have him back in office. His first lady vice-president sat below him on the dais, veiled and gloved, solemn in dress and expression, and yet so youthful as to seem only a girl, so lovely as to seem more-than-in-name angelic. In contrast Alejo looked aged and demonic— two golden eyes aglow in a disinterred skull; two skeletal hands wrapped in pale-ocher parchment; a hollow voice echoing from a wraith. People suddenly recalled his past, his howlings at the moon and rabid snappings. Crazy times would likely come again now.

These doubts about Alejo were unjust. Crazy times came, but he didn't provoke them. From the moment the national colors touched him, till the day two months later when they draped his hearse, he governed himself and the country with unexpected balance and restraint.

General Manduco's constitution was still in effect. Alejo had full dictatorial powers. He scarcely used, much less abused them. Or, rather, he used them so as to discourage abuse. The assembly's functions ended with his sashing. He could make the laws himself, or appoint a tame committee to make them. But his first act was to designate the deputies—those who'd voted for his stand-in and those who hadn't—as the legislative committee, thus giving the people's representatives the status proper to them in a free republic. Cabinet ministries, which Genghis had parceled out to his brothers and sisters, went to the most competent people in the country, but first Alejo assured himself that those he picked were independent enough in character and esteem to contradict him if and when they thought he was wrong. In choosing judges, he gave first preference to lawyers who'd been in prison during the dictatorship, provided prison hadn't turned them bitter. Every judge, he said, ought to know where he's sending people, and unjust punishment was the best school for defenders of the law, just as it was also the breeding ground for tyrants. And he amazed everyone, including the appointee, by making Carlos Gavilán president of the Supreme Court. Gavilán hadn't merely opposed General Manduco: he'd played a leading part, back in 1952, in deposing Alejo when he tried to subvert the state and become a dictator.

"*Señor Presidente,*" Gavilán told him, "I appreciate the appointment. But don't think that you can buy me with it. I'll show you no special favor, and I'll fight you if your ambition gets out of hand."

"Don't live in the past, young man," Alejo croaked back. (Gavilán was only sixty-three then.) "I have no more ambition. Except to die in peace, and that can wait. If it were a question of ambition, I wouldn't be here. But when you and León Fuertes removed me from office, the stars decreed I would be president once more, and that week in 1970 wasn't sufficient. I had ambition once, that time is over. Now I have a destiny to complete."

Destiny or sentence. Whether or not he was president by starry decree, he seemed condemned to unlive his life in the last months of it. All his life he'd been a man of mystery, who never did what he said or said what he did. He'd been the most arbitrary leader in the hemisphere, launching abrupt maneuvers, making wild pronouncements—often, it's true, to the people's great delight, but never with any by-your-leave or warning. He'd been haughty, distant, stern, answerable to no one. He'd communed with his private lunacies, then imposed his will. But now he acted with profound deliberation—openly, consulting everyone. Now he made every aspect of national policy the subject of consideration—by ministers, by deputies, by functionaries, by people outside the government entirely, those who might be affected and those who simply seemed experienced enough to have a sound opinion. Now he was almost humble. He could still be curt in private conversation. The stars hadn't chosen him for nothing, after all. But in public matters now he merely proposed, and did so in an unassuming manner: *"I seek the cabinet's counsel on this question." "I crave the assembly's wisdom on this bill."* Where once his customary mode of operation had been a series of dramatic leaps from the wings, of swoopings from the rafters on invisible wires, of poppings-up from trapdoors in puffs of smoke, now he moved like a figure in a ritual procession, calmly and reverently.

And unpopularly, though no one in the country would admit why, not even to himself. No crazy times came, and (suddenly!) none were likely to—not with all those wise appointments, those measured steps. Secret resentment festered in people's hearts. Alejo was no longer entertaining.

Some said the change in him was due to Angela. Elder Tinieblans recalled the midyears of his second term, when he'd kept her in a villa at Medusa Beach. Guarded by four eunuchs, or maybe they were only homosexuals, but all to himself: his was the only villa there in those days. How calm he'd been! Benign, in fact, like now. Things were so tranquil in Tinieblas it was as though he were in exile, not in power, and people joked that the gringos had kidnapped him and substituted an imposter. At first he'd been as crazy as ever. Proposed a horoscope law that couples couldn't get married unless their stars matched. Brought a witch doctor from Haiti to make voodoo against Harry Truman. Then he found Angela and went abruptly sane. Later on she left him, or he threw her out, and right away he turned wilder than before. Stirred up a war between the classes. Abolished the constitution, or at least tried to, so that he had to be deposed. Well, now he'd found Angela again, and married her, and made her the first lady and vice-president. All those years she'd spent, praying in a convent, waiting for him to do the decent thing. Well, look! Now he was sane. It had to be due to Angela's influence.

The truth was somewhat different. Alejo's mind had been a den of dragons. He'd been tormented by mad dreams and visions, driven by ungovernable lusts. By temperament he'd been a saint or an artist, but he believed in nothing but his personal stars, and his only talent was for politics. Only political power gave him the means to act his nightmares into life and so find ease. But power's possibilities were infinite and intoxicating. At the first taste his head swam, and he went reeling, howling off. Till Angela calmed him. That part was true. She had the gift of transformation. Still has it! Mandragon knows! She could flesh his fantasies, as later she did Dred's. She made him forget himself, as later she did Mandragon. For two years she milked Alejo's venom—a handy knack! She lulled the owls and panthers in his brain so that he didn't have to dose himself with power. Then she betrayed him with his son for money, and Alejo sold her to Dred Mandeville, and right away got power-drunk again.

Years later, Dred sold her back—for a consideration, not for money. Living with her seven years in exile (or growing old, or both) cured Alejo for good. His lusts burned out, his dreams cracked into shards. The monsters in his mind shriveled and died. When at last he returned to power, its possibilities no longer dizzied him. He wasn't even conscious of them. He noticed only power's obligations. He made Angela vice-president because he'd promised to, but she had no dominant influence on him anymore.

Which was why Dred Mandeville kept sailing, kept tunneling on through the deep-ocean gloom.

Alejo was scarcely settled at his desk in the palace when Angela raised the matter of Dred's safe haven. She'd tried to raise it in the limousine that carried them down Bolívar Avenue from the chamber, but he finger-waggled her to silence.

"I want to try to enjoy this," he said after a moment.

It was raining, yet crowds lined the sidewalks, peering for a glimpse of him and Angela. She smiled and waved at them from time to time through the drop-spattered glass, but Alejo sat motionless as a stone, staring straight ahead over the driver's shoulder.

"This drive," he went on after a bit. "It's the best part of a presidential term."

And then: "I used to enjoy these little drives."

She tried again when they arrived, when Alejo halted in the palace patio before the mosaic pool with its bronze-faun fountain and its pudgy goldfish. He hand-flapped her to silence and gazed down at the fish.

"When Epifanio Mojón was president," he said finally, "a hundred-some-odd years ago, he kept piranhas in this pool and fed them live puppy dogs."

And then: "We'll have the diplomats along in a few minutes. Please see that everything's in order."

And then, though she'd gone: "I used to like this spot."

She tried a third time in the ballroom. They stood, flanked by their military aides, waiting for the first guests to be shown in, and Angela tried to raise the matter of Dred's haven, but Alejo shook his head the moment she spoke.

He opened his bloodless lips and then said nothing, only gazed across the polished floor into a full-length, rococo-framed mirror on the wall opposite them. Forty-seven years had passed since he'd first looked into that mirror. He'd admired his reflection in it—his slim waist and carefully trimmed moustache, his seal-black hair and delicate widow's peak—and then wandered out of President Abúndio Moral's Discovery Day reception to find an empty room and unlock the windows, so that he and his men could sneak in when all was quiet, and kill the guards and seize the palace and power. Now the mirror gave back a group portrait: "Lady and Officers with Resurrected Corpse." The corpse wore the same purple-green-and-yellow sash Abúndio Moral had been draped with, and a suit cut in the current fashion, but it seemed just raised from a long sojourn in its crypt.

When the reception was over, though, and the last dignitaries had departed, when Angela and Alejo had climbed the double staircase (down which, seven years before, he'd hustled in fury when he learned the majors had seized the capital) and walked past the Salón Amarillo (in which, twenty-five years before, he'd sat down in front of radio microphones and proclaimed himself absolute ruler of Tinieblas for life) and entered the state office (into which, thirty-five years before, Lieutenant Colonel Domingo Azote had come, under a flag of truce, to advise him that the Civil Guard was deposing him); as soon as Alejo was settled behind the mahogany desk (from the top drawer of which he'd taken the pistol he shot Azote dead with), she raised the matter:

"Would you like to send the cable, or shall I?"

Alejo swiveled round so that his back was to her. He gazed past the French doors (through which he'd lugged Azote's bleeding cadaver) and past the balcony (off which he'd dumped it) toward the running lights of ships out in the roadstead.

"What cable?"

"The cable to Mount Vervex, darling. That we're in power, that *Scorpion* can come in."

He swiveled back and stared up at her with his strangely youthful, golden eyes. He smiled.

"That little cable," he said at last. "We'll leave it a while."

Nor would he elaborate—not then, not later that night, not the next morning; not at the light lunch they took together between the auditions he held for posts in the cabinet; not at tea before the foreign bankers came in; not over the herb infusion he sipped, long after midnight, in his bedroom; not on any of the occasions during the next few weeks when she raised the matter again—to say how long the "while" would last or why he imposed it. A stare, a smile, a hollow croak:

"*Aquel cablecito. Lo dejaremos un rato.*"

In the dead calm of the siesta hour, for example, in his private study—a small room tucked between the office and the Salón Amarillo—when he sneaked in for a surprise attack on some overdue paper work and found Angela waiting in ambush:

"He must know by now, you realize."

"Know what?" (Alejo didn't have to ask who "he" was.)

"That we're in power, darling, it's not a secret. Mount Vervex relays him the news reports."

"I assumed you'd advised him by now yourself."

"I have. He must be getting just a bit impatient."

"I assumed he'd told you as much himself by this time."

"He has. Then what about the signal, to bring *Scorpion* in?"

Stare. Smile. Croak: "*Aquel cablecito. Lo dejaremos un rato.*"

Or late at night, in the tiny former maid's room, high up at the back of the building, where he slept alone (since no outsider was going to catch him sleeping in the presidential bedroom as he had poor Abúndio Moral); he in a nightcap

and flannel pajamas despite the humid heat, Angela in a
negligee (since he refused to let her promenade around
the palace naked as she'd done at Medusa Beach and in
Dred's cavern):

"His offer stands, the same as in 1970."

"I don't doubt it."

"He's prepared to invest millions, a hundred million.
Aside from what will go to us."

"That was the arrangement."

"I want that money, darling."

"I don't doubt it."

"Send the signal then. Or let me send it."

"*Lo dejaremos un rato.*"

Or at any hour, day or night, in any part of the palace
where she found him alone:

"You promised him citizenship and residence."

"That was the arrangement."

"In return for things of value, some of which he has
already delivered."

"Correct."

"It's wrong to break a promise, darling."

A glowing stare.

"It's foolish to break a promise to him."

A smile.

"Keep your promise, darling."

"*Un rato.*"

Meanwhile he moved, deliberately and solemnly, like a
figure in a ritual procession, to form his government and
deal with the shambles bequeathed by Genghis. And meanwhile Dred Mandeville kept sailing.

Scorpion slid through the darkness, shrouded by ghostly
whisps of phosphorescence. Always at dead slow or half-
speed now, in the bowels of remote and unfrequented seas.
At depth the hull groaned like voices in a nightmare, creaked
and cracked like the joints of a person in seizure. The fans
wheezed, the red bulbs blinked and flickered. Mold clung

in dark tufts at the corners of bulkheads. It spotted the walls of the companionways. It blotched the flesh of members of the crew.

They were going grey now—from age, not human sorrow, for the sockets at their napes still functioned. The pleasure centers of their brains required higher intensities of stimulation though, for longer periods, so that they scarcely slept and went about their duties weak and listless. They had barely energy to work the boat, to keep equipment operating, to make the constant necessary repairs. Their bodies were paunchy soft, their eyes were bloodshot. Their flesh was chalky-white and blotched with mold. Their teeth were stained, their cheeks were stubbled. Their uniforms hung in faded tatters. They rose from their couches sighing and shuffled through their watches bent and trembling. Then they threw themselves down and plugged glory back into their brains.

Forward, Dred lay among his consoles in a kind of living mummification. His mind still burned with a cold incandescence. His appetite still craved. His will still ranged the globe, portioning out peace and misery, plenty and dearth. But his tall body, once firm and athletic, was all wasted— lank skin and toneless sinew, wizened arms he could clasp between a bony forefinger and thumb, shriveled legs that wouldn't bear his weight, slight though it was. For a time he'd had stewards help him to and from the toilet, but even brain-gadgeted zombies with sockets behind their ears were too human for him. Their touch revolted him, so now he crawled. His ulcerated flesh couldn't bear fabric. He no longer had the strength to groom himself. He lay naked on the rotting vinyl, his white beard scraggled down across his chest, gazing at the flickering monitors.

Sometimes he dozed and dreamed of a fresh breeze brushing his face, a breeze thick with the fragrance of wild jasmine. Sometimes he dreamed of grass beneath his feet. Sometimes he merely dreamed of being carried aft to the

control room and of peering through the periscope at the
night sky scattered with stars.

Alejo kept putting off Dred's havening. He had no in-
tention of allowing it. He noticed only power's obligations
and had decided that granting Dred citizenship and residence would be bad for Tinieblas. So Dred kept sailing,
kept rounding and rerounding the promontory of receding
hope. Then, early in the new year, Angela went touring
round the country, and visited Mandragon in Otán.

To meet the famous guru/healer/prophet.

To pay her respects to the rain-bringer/tyrant-ridder.

To bewitch the fool.

29

Shame-crimped face wraithed in the night-dark glass. Shame-curled toes burrowing the carpet. Mandragon was unworthy.

Whored from my mission, slutted my children's trust. Drabbed my destiny, mocked my election. Poured my gifts down a cesspool, sowed my powers in a swamp. Bewitched myself, made love to my own snaring, rather not recall it.

Rain's stopped, or too thin to see. Dark courtyard puddled with ink blots. Morning's first customers across the street. Gaffer in his seventies or eighties, bald as a doorknob, spooning up a bowl of something (oatmeal?), and a couplet of young goons in undershirts and nylon-stocking skullcaps. Twisting their shoulders, slapping palms on the tile, in time (I guess) to the radio perched there between them. Cook slides coffee mugs along the counter; they bend to slurp. Tart lifts her head three inches, eyes them yawning. Drops her head again and dozes on, but soon the city will be stirring.

Sitting up and blinking, rubbing eyes. Padding off to empty the night's staleness. Arrange the day's mask, prepare for this morning's ritual. I, Mandragon, could go out and witness.

Could, for example, watch Angela rise, stretch pale-gold arms, lift hair with lacquered fingers. Watch her pad off and then return to bed, settle back against plump, lace-

trimmed pillows. Watch her stare gravely and unthink-
ingly into a nowhere of lamp-yellowed brocade drapes—
child's sleep-creased forehead, ancient storm-grey eyes—
as she sips chocolate from a pansied teacup. Watch her
small, avid, pointed teeth morsel a cone of honey-beaded
croissant, just as, so many times, I watched, resting beside
her, my male thighs swathed in tumbled sheets. Or I could
watch the bandsmen shine their flutes and trumpets, the
presidential guards polish their boots, the colonels' orderlies lay out dress uniforms, scanning for lint. Or visit the
assault troops where they'll stand at ease outside Monteseguro Barracks, waiting in predawn twilight for the trucks,
snarling filthy cracks and smacking ape lips, fondling the
barrels of their guns. Or join the happy haters on the seawall, and watch my conscientious hangman test his winch.

The city and the prison, stirring soon. Brawlers in their
cages, my girls downstairs. Huddled in the vermin-scam-
pered darkness, curled in the night-chill damp of chain-hung
metal slabs. All five asleep now, I can feel their measured
breathing. Each dreams her special version of the birth.
Each nourishes power's instrument with her flesh. But soon
they'll stir. Boot-bustle in the rain-pooled yard above them
will chide them back from truth to wake and mourn. I
could go down and comfort them, be comforted. Ask and
receive pardon, soothe my shame. I could go down and
sweeten this last hour.

Best decline it.

Best decline that and every other diversion. Best be stern.
Best drag my shame-crimped face back from the window.
Best turn away. Best couch myself, withdraw, close eyes,
peer inward. While I have time (enough, I think) to recall
the rest. Remember who I am, recapture the last of it.
Reclaim Mandragon.

Who recognized Doña Angela de Sancudo as the presiding spirit of Rebozo's dreams, the presiding figure of my
execution, the portioner of love and death. Who toppled

into trance and was flung backward to catch part of her circus tumbling act. Who did not at first accept her invitation to visit her in the capital, but who straightway visited her past. Who conjured the demoness, who summoned her into his visions, who bewitched himself.

Himself. Already sexing when I toppled. Dragged off the poise of neuter wholeness by a tongue tip, tugged maleward by a smile. Once out of balance I swung further over. Angela's pull strengthened. The weight of gender grew. But when I toured her past, I lived in her as well as in her lovers. I wore her skin as well as theirs. I minced in her slim haunches at her first conquest, as well as flushed and panted with Don Serafino Salma, circus proprietor, promoter of attractions, her mother's uncle and her father's boss.

His study: framed glossies of performers on the walls, nimbus of cigar smoke above the buff-and-white cowhide chair. Nine-year-old Angela minces in. Nimbles to his lap, twines his fat neck. "Give me some money, Tío Fino."

"Hmph! Money? For what?"

Lays her cheek on his lapel and, very softly, jounces her young nates. "For ice cream. For something."

"Bandit! Well, then. We'll see."

Twists her head under his palm and jounces softly.

Then, one day, with a pert wiggle, "What's that, Tío Fino?"

"Nothing!"

"Don't fib," *jiggling and giggling.* "You've something down there, Tío Fino, I can feel it."

"Nada!"

Then, finally, one day: "Tu tienes algo, Tío, algo duro."

An anguished croak: "Toque la, pues. Mete la mano dentro."

Giggling and groping: "Y me des mas plata. Me des un montón."

I shivered his shiver at the scurry of mouse-foot fingers. I sighed his sigh as they fumbled Jack round and let him spring out of the box. I gasped his gasps and squirmed his squirms, I tremored his tremor. I blushed his blush. But I also knew her peso-stuffed fistlet's triumph, and her other hand's scorn for the pale pearls of Don Fino's bliss.

As adolescent Pedro and Pablo I gave myself up to seizures of delight—in hidden corners of Don Serafino's theater, in the gym where they practiced tumbling, even at home—while Angela's soft palms and agile fingers did what their own had used to. As Angela I smirked and collected their pin money and played each against the other. As Rebozo I nurtured her and worshiped her and suffered for her. As Angela I toyed with him and tortured him and leeched away his manhood. I ordered up dreams and visions. I flung myself about her past. I lived in her and in her lovers. All the while, though, I tipped further maleward, so more and more I found myself in them.

In the beefed back and hairy arms of the Bremen ship's oiler who had first plowings—for about forty marks' worth of pesos, in a twenty-minute room above a dance hall, beside the Buenos Aires waterfront. Hooked from a circus matinee by a grey-eyed twelve-year-old, who propositioned him as forthrightly as any veteran street whore. He took her to a place beside the docks. And I, Mandragon, lived those moments in him. I knew the trembling of his knees as he climbed the stairs with her, his heart's leap when she put her foot up on the chair and bent to roll her sock down. Cane-backed chair scarred at the seat rim with cigarette burns. Calf-length white sock. Changing with the gesture into a girl he'd ached for long ago in Germany, then into his sister. I knew the desperation of his groin as it bludgeoned into her, its wild rejoicing, its crestfallen regret when she squidged it out. I knew his throat's clutched wonder as she mashed the bank notes to her stained thighs, arching her neck back, nether lip between her teeth. I knew his nape hairs' bristling awe at her cat squeals in the tango-throbbing dusk.

In the book-crammed skull and chalk-smudged, bony fingers of Américo Paz, her tenth-grade Spanish teacher, whom she bedeviled for six months with lisps and flouncings and then finally pleasured (for cash, not better marks), becoming when he touched her a succession of sweet nymphs and willful queens out of old tales, so that (till she shriveled him) he thought himself a god or conqueror. In the puffed pigeon-chest of Dr. Raúl Mallea, who succumbed on his own examining table with his mind's arms full of the cadavers he'd dismembered while a student. In the thin lips and pallid brow of Padre Pío Sibauste. Him she set writhing simply by confessing her sins—in a low murmur, with a luxury of detail, and accounts of their effects on the men involved—until he went to the booth all goatish and in mortal terror for his precious soul, until the day she said she'd done a sin she couldn't tell in words, she'd have to show him. He gave up then. They did that sin together in the vestry, along with others she had managed to describe. And under Padre Pío's lips (flushed now and fevered) Angela turned into one after another holy saint, spicing his fall with blasphemy and desecration.

In the pink, hairless, and cologne-doused flab of Lorenzo Amichevole as he knelt behind her on the carpet of the hotel suite he took for the purpose—her buttocks nuzzling his loins, her slender tail bent sideways against his abdomen, her smooth back bowed beneath his chest, her hand enfolding the contract he'd just given her. Threading her deeply, clutching a golden breast in each pink fist. Chewing her neck and striving to hold motionless, as she became the ten-year-old son of a hated business competitor, then the competitor himself. Who squeezed and wriggled till Don

Lorenzo couldn't keep from plunging, and Angela whispered, "Now," and husked him dry.

In the men he sent her to—for pay, of course; she wouldn't have gone otherwise—men in authority in places they played. In the bull neck and narow eyes of Colonel Dionisio Huevas Pandilla, the future dictator of Costaguana, when he was chief of the Michagrande military district. In the limp shanks of Heliodoro Marañon, mayor of Ciudad Tinieblas. In the talcumed thighs of Don Cipriano Vargas, governor of Zacapetl or Tehuantezuma or Xibalba, who enjoyed her ministrations seated on his balcony while, in the patio below, a twenty-piece mariachi played "La Golondrina." In the zombie-streeled brain of Dr. Dubonet, the Haitian despot, since nothing, not even a circus, happened in his tormented country without his say-so. And in the men she chose herself, for she vamped more monied spectators than Magda ever dreamed of, and gave them fair return, very fair return. Crepitating waves of ecstasy, tongue-lolling satiation, mine-shaft glimpses into their hearts' cores that tinged the drabbest physical sensation with all the heady hues of guilt and horror. She manned them and unmanned them, roused them to perform prodigies and drained them, blissed them to infancy and wrung their souls, eased them and left them filled with longing.

Mandragon lived it all. In Angela, in the racked flesh and boiling minds of Angela's lovers. For days and nights Mandragon sat immobile, under a great Indian laurel tree. Its trunk, melded from dozens of thick intertwining stems, pillared stoutly behind me. Its branches wombed me from the sun and rain. Its fragrance sweetened my departures. Its cool breath freshened my returns. No muscle moved, yet Angela's life raged in me. I journeyed to it over and again, immersed my spirit in that caldron of unholy loves. With each plunge, gender burgeoned in me

Not physically. It wasn't till later that I got the outward badges. Male gender came first as a restless yearning to expand myself, to press out on the world and make it notice me, a yearning I had never felt before. As a performer I gave my spectators delight and wonder, but I never cared how many came or whether they applauded. As power's instrument, I did its bidding, with no concern for public recognition. Now I wanted all the world to acknowledge Mandragon, and even as this strange craving came upon me, the world narrowed into Angela, Angela crescented till she encompassed all the world. I came to know it first through her old lovers, this longing to enter and reenter Angela's ambit, to plumb her depths and swell within her, make her notice and acknowledge. It drove me ceaselessly back to her past—and grew more frustrate with each pilgrimage, for I was more and more trapped in their minds and bodies, less and less aware of what she felt. This hunger drove me to repeated gorgings, and panged more savagely with every taste.

Mandragon spiraled downward into maleness, and gendering fell back to carnal love. The love I'd learned for all things on earth and out of it bent in a narrowing focus on one object. Angela filled up Mandragon's spirit, and emptied it of everything besides. So when I'd summoned up her past and wallowed in it, proved every crevice, seen, heard, tasted, smelled; when I'd enjoyed her in the flesh of all her lovers, and toyed with them in hers, reveled and writhed; when I had wrenched my gifts to that unworthy purpose and worked them to the fullest, I was implacably bewitched, more captive than I'd been in El Olvido, or in Zito's beast truck, or with La Negra's collar round my throat.

I didn't know that then, I know it now. Then I felt free, freer than ever in my life. As power's instrument I'd worn true freedom, dancing to the rhythm of the universe. I know that now. But then I was bewitched and thus bemused. Of a sudden and like too many other fools, I conceived freedom as the independent exercise of individual will, and thought that's what I was doing. When I completed my journeys of exploration through Angela's past and realized I was going to visit her present, I thought I'd had a choice and made a decision—to further my mission on my own initiative by cultivating the first lady of Tinieblas, and through her the temporal powers in the land. That's the sort of twaddle I told myself. That's what Mandragon honestly believed. But free choice had no more to do with my leaving Otán than it will with my strangling. My butt will drag my throat against the cable, in an hour or so, when the winch takes up the slack. Free choice began and ended for me when I summoned Angela into my visions and fouled my spirit swining in her life. Once I did that, I was dragged to her relentlessly by the brute gravity of gender and mortal love.

On the way I stopped to preach in Aguascalientes. I went on foot, alone, and with every step the pull of Angela strengthened, the weight of gender grew. At the time, of course, I construed these forces differently—as the bright allure of independent action, as the ballasting poise of new responsibility. I wasn't yet entirely out of touch though. Now and then I received illuminations, mine-shaft glimpses into my true state. I was in thrall to a false power. I was on the way to forgetting who I was. I didn't credit these insights much, still they disturbed me, so when I passed the baseball field at Aguascalientes, which lies outside the town against the highway, and saw a thousand or so people watching a game, I thought to stop and prophesy to them, as if to my tribe, in a reminder and affirmation of myself and my mission. That, anyway, was the twaddle I told myself. That's what Mandragon honestly believed. But everything in Mandragon was warping by then. I was forgetting who I was: power's instrument. I was losing the sense of my mission: to rear a remnant. What I was after that day in Aguascalientes—and from then on till Angela released

me—was to expand myself in the world and make it acknowledge me, to make Angela notice Mandragon.

*The field at Aguascalientes. Bright sun and heat waves
shimmering the turf, light breeze ruffling the pennants on
the backstop. Brown-faced people in open stands along the
foul lines—short-sleeved shirts and floppy straw sombreros
—the mestizo crowd of a Latin countryside. Yelping en-
couragement at the Salinas hitters, catcalling the Remedios
pitcher, enjoying the game. Smack and thwop of horsehide
on wood and leather. Cheers and groans.*

*Off on the shoulder of the highway, beyond the chain-
link fence in right-center field, a solitary walker stops and
turns. Stares in toward the diamond, then looks upward.
Lifts his arms.*

*The sky darkens. The breeze stiffens, swells to a rising
wind. Rumble of thunder.*

*A sudden hush falls on the stands. The players stop their
game. The fielders trot, then run, toward their dugout.*

A bolt of lightning cleaves the chain-link fence.

I dimmed the sun, I shrouded the day over. I called a
wind out of the east and roiled it in with thunder. By the
strong power living in me I convulsed the heavens—and
could do so now! for power rises in me as I remember. I
sent the players scampering but held the spectators trans-
fixed, plucked down a thunderbolt and strode into the field
with lightning crackling about my brows. I drew a tempest
with me so that all would know the coming of Mandragon.

*Mandragon halts on the infield, storm clouds above him,
lightning crackling about his brows. His face is scowling,
his aspect is fierce, his voice is harsh. His periods are scored
by peals of thunder.*

"This age is doomed, it will explode and crumble!

*"I am Mandragon! I have seen it flame to cinder. I, Man-
dragon, have watched it seethe and die."*

The clouds above Mandragon vomit flame.

"Billions will perish. I have heard them howling. Earth will be cleansed!"

The air above Mandragon is rent with screams.

"The end will begin here in Tinieblas, at the periphery of the soon-to-fragment world. I, Mandragon, both announce and bring it. My coming will be marked by days of turmoil. Take heed, the time is short!"

A dusty whirlwind stalks across the field and wraps itself about Mandragon. Fat ruddy raindrops spatter in the dirt. Mandragon stands erect, funneled in wind. The spectators are moaning terror.

A woman's yellow scarf blows from the stands and wraps itself about Mandragon's wrist. He takes it, tosses it in air, holds his hand aloft, fingers spread wide. The silk floats upward, spreading as it rises, until it hangs pavilioned forty feet in air and covers all the infield and both grandstands. The tempest breaks.

Sheets of rain fall on the outspread silk. Streams of water pour down from its edges. Thunderclaps peal.

Mandragon lowers his hand slowly. The thunder fades. The rain lessens. The wind drops. Mandragon's voice is sweet, his face is smiling, a smile immensely tender, loving, gay.

"The universe is not a machine to operate. It is not a gadget to tinker with, or a problem to solve. The universe is a song to be in tune with, a ceaseless rhythm. Each end is always also a beginning.

"The new age will begin here in Tinieblas, at the center of the soon-to-be-born world. I, Mandragon, both announce and bring it. Some of those who follow me shall see it. Of those who acknowledge Mandragon, some shall be saved.

"The beginning will be born here in Tinieblas. A new age will march from here on a cleansed earth. I, Mandragon, will lead it. Those who follow me shall be its kings."

The soft rain stops. The covering shrinks to its former size and falls at Mandragon's feet, a soggy square of yellow

*silk. A great radiance glows about Mandragon, so that the
spectators shield their eyes and drop their heads. When they
can look again, the field is empty.*

Then I went down to Ciudad Tinieblas and delivered
myself up to Angela.

30

Once more from "I went," but quietly, without excessive melodrama:

I went to Angela in Ciudad Tinieblas, and put my gifts and powers at her service.

That was on the night of my arrival, three days after my ball-field prophecies. The sky was clear and starry, crescent-mooned. A salt breeze off the bay cut the heat a little. People strolled along the wide seawall. In Parque Mocoso old men were playing *damas*, bending around a board set up on a folding chair under a streetlamp. Lit by floodlights on the porte-cochere, its second-story windows glowing warmly, the palace was a friendly, stately presence—as though it had at last had its fill of turbulence and was reminding itself and passers-by that the aim of government is concord and decorum.

The officer of the guard told me to come back in the morning. Good of him, I guess, to say that much to a barefoot peasant in a scruffy tunic. I tossed my consciousness up into the building and saw Alejo and Angela and some dozen or sixteen others seated on heavy, high-backed, intricately carved chairs at formal dinner in a brilliantly lighted hall. I thought of making a dramatic entrance—the glaring prophet and the startled guests—then put the thought aside. It pleased me more to wait like a humble suppliant. I liked the irony of that: the bringer of the end and the beginning cooling heels. Oh, I was very conscious of my own importance, having all but forgotten that I was merely power's servant—so taken with myself that despite my choice to wear a fake humility I couldn't resist giving the officer a small display, a chill in my voice that made his shoulders tremble.

"When the guests have gone, send in to Doña Angela. Tell her the person from Otán is here."

"*Sí, señor!*"

I waited a long while. On the grass inside the park, about where the band will be setting up soon. It would have pleased me to wait all night. I was weary from my journey yet alert, full of anticipation yet in repose. I sat with my back to the palace to lessen any temptation to intrude. I cleaned my mind of word-thought and watched the seawall strollers, listened to the old men's squabbly patter—until the last strollers drifted off and the old men folded up their game. Then I watched the moon rise and listened to the tide slap at the stones. At length the officer called me and said word had come for me to wait inside. A soldier took me into the patio, to a stone bench facing the goldfish pool. I sat, he stood nearby in silence. Then Angela's military aide appeared and took me to her. It must have been midnight by then.

Angela received me in a small sitting room on the third floor of the palace, a room so feminine in decor she might have guessed just where I sat the gender seesaw and chosen surroundings that would advance my maleward swoop. Frail silk-upholstered chairs, récamier sofa; an inlaid writing table with an oval mirror; and, on the mantel, pert porcelain shepherdesses all ablush. In the filmy haze from three candelabra fixtures, each with three soft lamps, each lamp demurely shaded in beige gauze. I was the only remotely masculine thing around.

Angela wore her hair loose on her shoulders, and an ankle-length housedress, very rich and simple, open at the throat. She sat half-turned toward the door I was shown in through, her right arm against the chair back, her hands in her lap. The aide withdrew and shut the door behind me. Angela smiled. Truth plucked me from myself and flung me forward, for a fifteen-second peek at our lovemaking: coming attraction.

Staged on the sofa, posed conventionally, shot from middle distance at keyhole height. My double sprawled on Angela's white breast, his hips astrive between her lifted thighs. She cupped his woolly crown and walnut bum, fluttered her eyelids at three-quarter closed, grinned serenely past his cheek.

By the time this preview faded, I was hers entirely. Angela knew. She rose and came to me. She took my hand and pressed it to her throat.

"You'll kill Alejo for me, won't you, darling?"

Mandragon nodded. When Mandragon's hand touched Angela's cool flesh, he forgot his mission and his tribe, his election as power's instrument and vessel, the myths of his birth, and his destiny's revelation. He agreed without hesitation to the fee she proposed. Then he performed dutifully and with vigor as she led him to and through the scene he'd just glimpsed.

Took to it like a natural in fact, as though I'd been born male and bred for stud. No fears, no trepidations. Howl of delight as her dress sloughed to the carpet that put her off her thoughts of exploitation, that turned her tender for a moment, and as I entered her with the pitiful equipment I had for such work then, my spirit entered her as well in a flow of power that she experienced as an incandescent flaring. It took her mind off my substandard parts. Not that I really reached her that first bout. That came later. But I enjoyed her avidly and touched her briefly, actually made her forget herself for a moment, something only money had ever accomplished before.

Too busy gorging to notice. Later on she confessed she'd felt my spirit flare in her that night, breathed it to me grammared in caresses, along with many other lovely things, on nights when darkness closed around us like a bulwark, when I was her consort, not merely her dupe and tool. But at the time I had no inkling. I was totally absorbed in my own sensations. It seemed that I was piercing the whole world, exercising my private will upon it. Soon enough, that is, she remembered what she was about, and grinning serenely jellied me in pleasure. When she squibbed me out, I looked like all the others: mouth open and tongue lolling, eyes glazed with bliss, face moron'd in contentment. Which lasted only moments; then I craved more.

Still, not a poor debut. I'd only lately reacquired gender —a new one at that, one I scarcely knew how to wear—yet I acquitted myself no worse than most of her lovers. I put myself in her power, abandoned myself. Took pleasure, I mean, and that's a part of love. I gave Angela no joy and no glimpse of herself, but she wanted neither, and no one can say I was entirely selfish. I was keeping my part of the bargain, I was paying her fee. The moment I mounted her, President Alejandro Sancudo woke from his brittle, old-man's sleep convulsing, and filled the stuffy maid's room with strangled yelps. His bed had been transformed to a nest of scorpions. They gouged their fiery stings into his back.

Wait. Play it through with Angela's reactions. I let her watch, I gave her that amusement. Best remember everything while I have time.

She pinched me out and slid from underneath me, slouched to the writing table and sat down there—wrongway-round, legs spread, arms on the chair back, making bored faces in the oval mirror, switching her little rodent tail left and right. When my idiot contentment faded, I called her to me. She smirked her smirk and laughed her tinkling laugh.

"When are you going to do *my* favor, darling?"

I was still Mandragon. I had forgotten everything that truly mattered, but my powers were intact about me. I was her captive, but I wasn't tame. I choked her laugh with a frown. I smeared her smirk into a mask of terror. That's when Angela learned she was onto something different. She'd reasoned as much when she chose me as her weapon, but when she laughed at me, she learned it in her flesh. Nearly wet the chair she straddled before love-longing melted me and I smiled.

I gestured toward the mirror: "See for yourself."

When she looked round, she saw Alejo's room.

View from the window opposite the night-light, Alejo in his brittle, old-man's sleep. Convulses, fills the room with strangled yelps. His bed has been transformed to a nest of scorpions.

Angela (leaning forward, peering in the glass): "Ay, sí! Qué bien! Qué bien!"

Alejo heaves himself to a sitting position. The pain subsides. He breathes, shakes off his nightmare, re-reclines. Whips of fire flail his back again. Flops over, and they lash his chest and midsection. Leaps up, and the pain dissolves.

Angela (without removing her gaze from the pictured scene): "It's good. I like it. But what exactly are you doing to him?"

Mandragon explains.

Alejo walks about, sits down again, leans gingerly. The instant his shoulders touch the headboard, burning needles. He jumps up and switches on the overhead light, peels his pajama top and examines himself minutely via the bureau glass and a hand mirror. Not a mark. His parchment-dry old skin shows no welts or redness. Bewildered frown.

"Oooh!" *squeals Angela, like a five-year-old at a puppet show.* "The old fool doesn't know, he can't imagine!"

She collapses forward against the chair back, giggling, and Mandragon experiences, for the first time in male gender, the essential happiness of love, which comes when one administers delight.

* * *

And how she enjoyed Alejo's subsequent experiments! his gingerly attempts at lying down (intermezzoed with catchings of his breath and mirror-scannings, with strippings of the bedclothes, pressings of the mattress, searches for a concealed electric grid), each finale-ing in outlandish fish-flips, eel-writhings, roach-scrambles:

"*Ay, sí! qué, sí! qué, sí! qué maravilla!*"

Only a few were necessary to persuade him that lying down was out, that putting any weight on his chest or shoulders, on his midsection or back, produced agony.

And then (chuckling), as Alejo settled for the night, sitting on the bed with his shoulders hunched forward: "That's it, don't kill him too quickly. Punish him first for not keeping his promise."

And then (still watching and still pleased, but remembering Dred Mandeville's restless cruising): "Not too long, though. Not too long."

And finally (rising and stepping backward, eyes still on the glass; then turning, smiling, slinking toward the sofa): "But not too quickly either. Take your time."

I took three weeks. That was the limit, I calculated, to which I should postpone climax. Angela's mirth at Alejo's suffering was nicely balanced by her impatience to get Dred to port. Wise and considerate lover, I didn't want her pleasure to pall or cloy. I tuned myself to her. I made her happiness my guide and master. I drew it out. I modulated her excitement upward. And at the last moment, just before impatience outweighed delight, I gave her his death. A thoughtful and a loving act of love.

I can't claim, though, that I planned all this beforehand. I was entirely unaware when I began. My awareness was absorbed in the delicious business of climbing between Angela's raised thighs, and while a part of me was honest and unselfish enough to get down to less pleasant business one story above us, no word of that transaction got through to my twat-reeling, musk-woozy brain. Her fee was Alejo's murder; I agreed without quibble—and paid (or at least began to) as I enpronged. Unconsciously, however, and I hadn't the resources to pay in full. Not right then: my energy was ninety-nine hundredths invested elsewhere. Had it not been, I'd have dispatched him at first swipe—a certainty that made me shiver later, for it would have cost me many smiles, many low chuckles, many ecstatic squeals. Many displays, that is, of Angela's delight, and many proofs that she noticed Mandragon. But when my idiot contentment faded, when she laughed at me and implied I couldn't pay —as whores will do, I've been a whore myself—I was immediately aware that the powers in me were at work on him. And showed her their handiwork. And discovered she'd like it to go on awhile. Which required only a little concentration, and I would have done anything to please her.

So poor Alejo got what rest he could. And lucky Mandragon got another gallop on Angela. Preambled by some delicate caresses (and some admiring phrases when her sweet mouth wasn't full); sequeled by a snooze on her soft breast. Then she woke me gently and showed me to a guest room, kissed me good night and wished me pleasant dreams —kept me folded, that is, in imbecile serenity so I'd be fresh the next day to get on with the business of murder.

At dawn, of course, Alejo summoned his doctor, and had himself examined top to toe. The man found nothing, but that didn't mean Alejo was in health. Hardly. When asked to sit back while the medico checked blood pressure, he balked, then made a cautious essay, then bounded forward snarling. Knives of flame stabbed in his upper back. He was then persuaded to cancel his appointments—they included lunch with tyrant-purger Mandragon, an honored guest—and go to San Bruno Hospital for a full-scale probe. He made the trip perched on a limo jump seat, clutching the strap to keep from leaning back, and was received by no less august a practitioner than Dr. Alfonso Gusano de Sedas. Who peered and palped, took blood and urine samples, X-rayed abundantly and would have graphed heart and brain had Alejo been able to lie down or at least sit comfortably. All to no conclusion, so he convened a dozen of his fellows, the cream of Tinieblan medicine, and murmured with them earnestly for half an hour while poor Alejo got what rest he could, balanced on the edge of an examining table. Gusano emerged from this conclave with the opinion that the problem was psychosomatic.

"You're not the first Tinieblan who's called me crazy, Doctor. I've learned to ignore it."

"Oh, no, Mr. President, nothing of the sort. It's that we cannot find organic defect, and your symptoms are bizarre. You say you have pain only when you try to rest."

"Haven't you noticed? You spent all morning poking me, that didn't hurt. But when I lie down or sit back . . ."

"Then I concur with my psychiatric colleague. Please let me call him."

And the psychiatrist explained, in cascades of mumbo jumbo about imaginary parts of Alejo's mind, that while no exact diagnosis could be made without extensive interviewing, it was clear that Alejo's pain was mental in origin, and likely the result of an obsessive concern for the duties of his office. A part of his mind resented his body's normal, human need for rest, and sent the pain to keep him on the job.

"What you need, Mr. President, is to relax."

"*Bravisimo!* I knew that when I came in here. The question, *doctorcito*, is how. I can't even sit decently."

"I would first of all counsel you to relinquish your duties."

"Are you proposing a treatment or attempting a *coup d'état?*"

"For a time only, Mr. President, until therapy removes the symptoms."

"I haven't enough time. The little time I have you're wasting. Just do something about the pain."

"For that, sir, there are drugs. That's very simple."

But it wasn't. Not all the drugs in the ministry of health's warehouse could give Alejo any sweet repose. Still, the doctors' efforts weren't entirely wasted. Angela enjoyed watching them.

They tried tranquilizers first, grading up in chemistry and dosage, but as they intensified, so did Mandragon. On the fourth night of Alejo's martyrdom Dr. Gusano hypoed him enough Thorazine to stun an elephant, put him virtually in coma, yet as soon as his shoulders touched the bed, he bolted upright howling. And as they sought fruitlessly to administer relief, I administered delight to Angela. I put permanent coverage of Alejo's torment on her little mother-of-pearl-backed mirror, and piped a sound track through its silver handle. That way she could follow while we were cuddling, in whatever part of the palace we chose to defile.

They switched to outright anesthetics next, pumped Alejo's dorsum full of Carbocaine and sat him in a comfy reclining chair; I stuck the flaming pringles in his chest and kept them jabbing till he heaved himself up. They Pontocained him front and back; I grilled his shanks and armpits till he was standing. Xylocaine, Nupercaine, Nesacaine, Metycaine, tetracaine; ditto, with amusing variations: needles in his nostrils, thorns in his tongue. And when they generaled him unconscious with Surital, Mandragon was ready. Mandragon waited till the effects wore off, then sizzled him all over, even while he was standing, an hour's agony for each hour he'd spent zonked. So where was the gain, Mr. President? What good were the doctors? Mandragon taught him he was better off without them. No pain so long as he didn't lie down or sit back, and after a week he accepted these conditions, dismissed Gusano and the others, got what rest he could sitting hunched forward, canceled his social engagements, and attended his presidential duties sconced on a stool. Attended them diligently, in fact, though he was nearly convinced the psychiatrist was right. But when the fellow made a final plea, Alejo was adamant.

"Go home, *doctorcito.* I haven't time for a vacation. I have a destiny to complete."

I gave him a day after he'd accepted the conditions, and one more night of sitting abed hunched over. Then I sent the pain across his butt and thighbacks, and fixed him so he couldn't sit at all.

And ministered to him also, beginning the same afternoon—so that he'd last, so that he wouldn't be suspicious of Mandragon, so that Angela would have that irony to chuckle at. I asked an audience—supposedly to take my leave and thank him for his hospitality—and expressed concern about his health. He stood perfectly erect, as if he'd chosen, for formality, to receive me standing, but he was obviously very weary and admitted that he was afflicted with a strange disorder that virtually prevented him from resting and that no medicine could ease. At which healer Mandragon offered his services.

"Maybe I can help you. I have a gift."

I went to him and touched the fingertips of my left hand to his forehead, dry and creased like an old document. "Sit down."

"I . . ."

"There will be no pain. Believe."

He lowered himself very carefully into his swivel chair and very carefully leaned back.

"Ahhhh!" He smiled in gratitude and closed his eyes.

Without taking my fingertips from his forehead I walked round to the back of the chair. "Sleep."

And Alejo dropped like a sack of feed into the first decent sleep he'd had since my arrival.

It was a mockery, of course, of my gift for healing. All I did was stop tormenting him. As soon as he was sleeping, I took my fingertips from his forehead and went out, went back upstairs and played a bout with Angela. I stayed with her two hours, then returned, took up my station at the back of his chair, fingers on his forehead, and brought him awake gently. He was both grateful and ashamed.

"You've been here all this while!"

"You would have paid if I removed my fingers."

He stood up quickly, drawing away from my touch. "Forgive me for imposing on you."

There followed assurances from saintly, kind Mandragon that no imposition had occurred, that one who had a gift was obliged to use it, that I was sorry to find my power so inadequate (unable, in this case, to cure completely, or even bring relief save by actual touch), but happy to help my president and host any way I could, to the limit of my poor capacities. Mandragon smiled a kind and saintly smile, and tossed his consciousness one flight upstairs, into the sitting room where Angela was watching, to savor her delighted whoops and squeals.

"I cannot ask you to spend all day and night with me."

"You may ask anything, anything at all."

The final compromise he struck between his physical well-being and his pride was that I would stay on at the palace and attend him, but that he would only call me at times of special need.

"At any time at all, *Señor Presidente*. Day or night. I am at your service."

I was back upstairs by the time he tried (as I knew he would) to sit without my comfort.

"Watch this," I said to Angela, and, as he settled, I spangled him with pain from crown to toenails, so that he twitched all over, then went blue and rigid, then flew up out of the chair with a yelping wail.

"*Ay, sí! Qué maravilla!*"

I was the pain and the relief. Mandragon was the solace and the torment. I played him delicately. I made him suffer, and I made him thank me.

I hadn't anything against him. I'd forgotten the birth myth in which he ill-used Mandragon's mother. I couldn't say he'd ever injured me. He was unfailingly polite, showed me every courtesy, extolled me to his ministers and aides, and would have honored my services to the republic with a medal had he thought I cared for that sort of recompense. He called me only when he was in extreme need, always apologized for imposing on me, never complained when I took my time arriving (though I did so often, to please Angela), and gave so little show of what he suffered that far from bearing him malice, I admired and felt sorry for him. But admiration didn't hold me back. Pity didn't make me reconsider. Love gave me the strength to rise above personal feelings. Killing him was what Angela was charging; torturing him brought Angela delight. She especially enjoyed the method he devised for resting after I fixed him so he couldn't sit. He put two cushions on the floor and knelt on one of them, then laid his arms on the other and his head on his arms.

"*Qué bien! Perfecto!* He looks like he's praying!"

Mandragon paid, and Angela delivered. He administered intellectual (or perhaps it was moral) delight; she basted him with somewhat grosser pleasures. In the sitting room, which as the site of our first embraces was sentimental Mandragon's favorite trysting nook—on the sofa, for the nostalgia of it, or on a chair before the writing table, with Angela astraddle, rolling her hips, squinting past my head to admire Alejo's discomfort in the mirror. On the narrow, swaybacked, gaily squeaking bed in the room assigned to me, and in other guest rooms till we'd left our spoor in them all. On the broad, firm, silk-rustly bed of her boudoir, in an artfully contrived T-cross conjunction where Angela lay supine and motionless with her knees raised and her calves on Mandragon's right flank and thigh (admiring Alejo's discomfort in her hand mirror), while Mandragon lay perpendicular on his left side and winkled his no-longer-quite-so-substandardness inside her.

In the Salón Amarillo (this amusing review could make a condemned person jolly), with Angela's shoulders pressed to the canary silk *fleur-de-lis*'d wall covering and Mandragon cramming against her, squeezing her pink silk bottom in his fists. On the polished hardwood floor of the state ballroom—Mandragon reclining, Angela perched finchlike on him facing his feet—while on the frescoed ceiling rosy-plump cherubs smiled down from cottony clouds. On the sturdy table in the state dining room, with Angela's squab positioned at the edge of it and Mandragon standing to address it, crooking a slim leg in each brown elbow.

In the Cabinet Room (jollier and jollier!), where they took turns, one sprawling in the presidential armchair, the other acrouch beneath the conference table to nip and nibble. In the presidential office while Alejo tried to siesta two floors above, and copycat Angela assumed his resting attitude, and Mandragon lifted her tail and mounted hound-style. At midnight in the Salón Redondo, while a sextet of early presidents of the republic glowered at them from heat-warped canvases in burnished frames. At midmorning on the settee near the head of the stairway, while a women's rights group Angela had just finished receiving were still chattering in the foyer one flight down. At midafternoon on the terrace outside her bedroom, where Mandragon lay face down in a hammock, his parts adangle through a surgered hole, and Angela squatted at his waist like a milk-maid, then went on all fours and nuzzled like a calf—where his moanings mingled with the cries of seabirds, and the sun stared down unblinking at them both.

In whatever part of the palace we chose to defile, since my appetite for her was boundless, while when she was bored or otherwise reluctant, I had only to tune Alejo in on her little mirror and hit him with a decent twinge of pain. That always perked her up and made her feel grateful, or at least reminded her I was paying well.

I don't know if anyone saw us at it. I assume business continued more or less as usual—no social functions, but the usual bustling in and out of politicos, and the come-and-go of servants keeping the place clean—but I noticed only Angela. Angela was the world, and I its only denizen and master. I roamed in her sweet valleys, swam in the solitude of her calm and uncharted seas, and if a shocked chambermaid had squeaked at us, if an irate aide had shouted, and then come up and seized me by the throat, I doubt I'd have noticed; I certainly wouldn't have cared.

As for Alejo, he noticed only power's obligations, and was preoccupied with handling his suffering so he could carry them out. Or he couldn't notice me wanking the first lady because he couldn't imagine Mandragon the comforter as Mandragon defiler. Or he noticed and simply didn't care. Or he noticed and was grateful—taking note that I remained in the palace and eased his pain, that she had stopped nagging him about Dred Mandeville, and putting these favors down to love's attractions and distractions. I spent no time inside his mind. I spent little in Angela's. I concentrated on my own sensations and troweled away.

All the while plummeting further into maleness, to the point where I received full badges of my gender. My penis grew till it was nearly normal size. The cleft below it closed and pursed and baggied. Hair sprouted at the corners of my mouth, so that by month's end I had a passably fine moustache, of the limp and whispy-black, drooping-to-the-chin sort that late-show viewers might associate with Tartar conquerors and mixed-breed pirates and other merchants of disorder and sorrow. By then, of course, I'd killed Alejo and was engaged on a new project for Angela.

After ten days or so she no longer much delighted in the kowtow he assumed while trying to rest, or in the similarly reverent pose he took while telephoning, kneeling by his desk with his forehead against it, or in the discomfort he endured keeping appointments, leaning forward with his thighs pressed to the edge of the conference table, with his palms braced on the top and his chin slung wearily onto his chest or (if obliged to make eye contact with his visitors) hoisted bulldoggishly. After a week she no longer sniggered much at his fury (shivered in his shoulders, glared in his eyes) when a minister or assemblyman missed the point, or answered irrelevantly, or lapsed into small talk, or otherwise prolonged the meeting unnecessarily— understandably fury, perfectly excusable (since Alejo now was always near exhaustion, and longed to rest, yet couldn't very well kneel with subordinates present), but Angela enjoyed it, it made her snigger, though not much after ten days or so. Accordingly, Mandragon amplified. I twiddled the torment knob another notch. No more kneeling, no more leaning either, no more putting weight anywhere except on the soles of his feet. Or he got pin stabs in his eyeballs, wasp stings in his ears, hot wire-jabbings under his fingernails. I monkeyed in his cortex tripping synapses until he learned to stay on his feet.

Except, of course, when Mandragon the good, Mandragon the selfless and saintly, was tending him. How he thanked me! All the old curtness gone now, all the haughtiness sanded down by pain. Praised and repraised me to the people round him, extolled me to his ministers, had me attend informal meetings, my hands on his forehead, so he could get through them sitting down—all of which later contributed to my acceptance as Angela's prime minister. I gave him 1 part comfort to 10 parts pain, though for Angela's amusement I let him use his hands for balance, and to take a little weight off his old feet. Aside from when he received my fake ministrations, Alejo got what rest he could swaying in an upstairs closet doorway, holding onto a chinning bar installed there in the early Sixties by one of President León Fuertes' sons.

"*Estupendo!* He looks like one of Lorenzo's second-rate trapezists!"

And, in his fatigue, he was liable to forget his lessons, and collapse onto a chair or bed or couch, onto the floor. Then there were poisoned-rat fits, wounded-lizard slitherings, sprayed-bug twists and flailings of the limbs—and much delight, of course, for Angela—before he hauled himself onto his feet again. I did it all for her. I made her happiness my guide and master. I modulated her excitement upward. And when impatience was at the point of overtaking delight, I gave her his death.

A few minutes before sunset, on an absolutely splendid afternoon.

A breeze off the Humboldt Current had blown all day, so that even when it dropped the air was cool. The tide was full, a little past the flood, and lay against the seawall winypurple, carpet-flat, sleep-soft. Far out, beyond the bay, a curtain of rain cloud hung at altitude. Beneath it, exactly centered between its lower fringe and the horizon, the huge sun floated, casting its red rays across the water into the palace windows.

In the Cabinet Room on the second floor, President Alejandro Sancudo stood speaking to his ministers, his trunk canted slightly forward, his knuckles resting on the conference table. One story up, in precisely the same attitude, the vice-president stood naked at the writing table in her sitting room, gazing into the mirror while Mandragon wanked away at her silk-smooth stern. A slackness in her shoulders revealed petulance. I thought to sting him with some pain and perk her up. Then it came to me I'd postponed climax long enough. I monkeyed quickly in Alejo's brainstem, firing synapses, paralyzing his diaphragm and (as a backup) shutting the throat valve on his windpipe. President Sancudo began to strangle.

"That's it! That's it! Don't stop."

I'd given him a good siesta earlier, and he was relatively rested. He'd learned his lessons so well that even while choking he took care not to sit down. He merely bent a little far-

ther forward and put more weight on his hands, precisely as
Angela was doing one floor above. His parchment-yellow
face began to purple. Her pale-gold throat and breasts began to flush. His eyes bulged, his lips fluttered, his tongue
poked out. Her lips drew back, her tongue flicked, her eyes
narrowed. Ministers scrambled from their seats and leaped
to Alejo. An aide jumped up and dashed out of the room.
Mandragon squeezed Angela's haunches and quickened
tempo.

In the forty seconds before mind chaosed to garble, as his
ministers swatted his shoulders and slapped his cheeks, then
hauled and hoisted him up on the table and began rhythmic
pressings on his lower back, Alejandro Sancudo remembered his gains and losses, his years in power and his years
in exile, the mad cravings that had driven him, the fearful
joy he took when he assuaged them, the peace that came
when they at last burned out. He remembered his astrologer's predictions, and a tempest-wracked midnight in Bastidas, and a beige-skinned girl—things I could make no
sense of, since I'd forgotten all the myths of Mandragon's
birth. And in the last instant human thought remained to
him, he knew that Mandragon was the torment as well as
the solace, redeemer and destroyer, love and woe. Then his
brain processes descended the catalog of animal forms, re-
sembling those of a choked dog, a drowning rat, a strangled
duck (just as mine will do in about an hour), and he went
into a horizontal dance, flopping his head, wriggling his
shoulders, kicking his legs.

Meanwhile a delicious warmth (which was also an
orange-red light) began to swell in Angela's calves. It
mounted through her thighs. It tossed fat swelling bubbles
up into her loins. She bent forward till her face was only a
few inches from the mirror (whose Alejo-imaged surface her
gaze never left) and went into a dance of her own, swivel-
ing her hips and rocking her shoulders. And a crimson
glow (which was also a hot lava) began to flow along my

spine and press deliciously (but also painfully urgently) into my now-not-the-very-least-substandard parts, and I bucked ferociously at Angela's sweet rump in a very old and yet still stylish dance and found it increasingly difficult to concentrate on Alejo, to continue monkeying in his throbbing brainstem so that his diaphragm stayed immobile and his windpipe shut. But I knew that my monkeying in his head (not my wanking at her tail) was what made Angela twist and twitch in pleasure, and love gave me the strength to carry on. That, then, was the situation—the three of us dancing toward climax, Angela and I more and more fiercely, Alejo more and more feebly—when there came a pounding on the sitting-room door and Alejo's aide screamed for Doña Angela and Mandragon.

"We're coming!" I managed to squawk.

Which got a strangled giggle from Angela.

The pounding continued. Alejo's legs went rigid, his arms shot straight out from his body, his head craned back. The warm light billowed into Angela's loins. The lava began to force its way into mine. Then Alejo's head dropped, and his arms drooped, and his legs untensed, and his jaws relaxed, and his bleeding tongue flopped free, and his eyes rolled back, and his throat gurgled, and the warmth burst through Angela's body in brilliant globes, and the lava spurted from mine.

Angela fell forward onto the table.

I fell across her back.

The sun fell into the Pacific.

31

And rises now, lifts out of the Caribbean to gild the eastern beaches of Tinieblas.

All's dark here still, roofs shrouded up in darkness, but off Bastidas the horizon's flame-bulged. Red dawn billows toward the paling stars. I could go watch.

As on the morning when we went to meet Dred Mandeville: could stand on the ruined wharf at Punta Amarga and see the sun reborn from the warm sea. Awash with fire, hymning might and order; gilding the waves, the sand, the jungled hills. I could perpetuate that ritual.

But soon red rays will crest the cordillera. A phone will ring, a summons will go forth. Boots will clatter in the corridor. A key will turn, these rooms fill up with guards. Who'll take me down and cuff me to the tow hitch.

No time for recollections after that. Best get back to them.

To Angela's investiture for example, which was performed in the Salón Amarillo about twenty minutes after Alejo croaked. Chief Justice Gavilán handled the swearing. On hand were the cabinet, the archbishop, the commandants of the Guardia, Alejo's middle-aged elder son Alfonso (my half-brother in that version of the birth), and a few representatives of the press. They stood in a ragged semicircle scowling grief and worry at the incoming president. Who played the scene to perfection, in the very dress she'll put on in a few minutes. Minus the fan but plus a black mantilla, as elegant as she'll be at Mandragon's hanging.

She'd managed some excellent dry sobs over Alejo's body, drawing on the aftershocks of orgasm to give her head and trunk the proper shudders. She'd stared about bewildered and nodded distractedly when told she'd be sworn in as soon as the judge arrived. She'd let herself be led away upstairs by Alejo's secretary, then had the devil's time getting rid of the woman, who was in genuine hysterics of the affectionate, blubbering, poor-dear-how-you-must-be-suffering sort. Which left her very few minutes before going back onstage, but she used them to good effect. Got into mourning, put on just enough makeup, dabbed cologne near her eyes to teary them up authentically. Tried on expressions in her dressing-table mirror and carefully built up a composite mask: a base of nunnish spiritual serenity overlaid (successively) with heartbreak, with physical pain, with determination to bear her new obligations. Built it, put it on, wore it downstairs.

There she stood with her shoulders a bit too straight, her chin a bit too high (like an acrobat poised on the nub of a teeterboard), to show the effort of will required (and so courageously achieved) to keep from weeping. Held pose and expression while Gavilán intoned and she repeated, while flashbulbs flared and popped. Thanked Gavilán softly, asked the ministers to remain in office, hoped they would serve her as loyally as they had her husband, and on the word "husband" broke down—magnificently, like a slow-motion film of a monument being demolished. Dropped her face, that is, and quivered her shoulders, drew her mantilla's folds about her face, half-turned, and crumbled—onto the broad chest of Alfonso Sancudo, whom she'd corner-eye glimpsed moving toward her in concern.

She mascaraed Sancudo's lapel for a long thirty seconds. She let him pat her shuddering shoulder blades. She nuzzled his grey goatee with her laced crown. Then painstakingly, at great expense of will, to the amazement of all present, she

put the smithered monument back together—not completely, to the point of having it stand a noble ruin. Hoisted
her forehead from Sancudo's shoulders. Drew back and
clasped his hand in her gloved hands. Nodded her gratitude,
flickered a valiant smile, squared her shoulders again, and
turned back to the others.

"Forgive me, gentlemen, we've much to do. But I . . .

"The cabinet will meet in half an hour. But not in the—!
Will meet in my state office. Post officers to guard, to guard
my husband. The diplomatic corps . . . Our consulates
. . . Each of you knows his field of competence. Please
carry on till I am more myself.

"Monsignor, please attend me.

"Alfonso, dear, please let me have your arm."

And leaning on Sancudo's proffered forearm, followed by
the purple-cassocked prelate, she made her halting way out
of the room.

Bravisima, Angela! If I dance half as well as you acted,
Mandragon's strangling will be a smash!

Mandragon, by the way, didn't watch in person. I was
outside in the street with the gathering crowd, moping at the
rear of the Alcaldía, about where they're laying TV cables
now. I had to toss my consciousness through the wall of the
palace, or I'd have missed Angela's performance. Angela
had kissed Mandragon off.

I'd had to hang around Alejo's cadaver, give some bogus
opinions as to what had killed him, utter a certain few bogus
laments. By the time I got back upstairs, Angela was fully
made-up and mourninged, modeling expressions for her
mask. I put my hand on her shoulder, she flicked it off.

"I'm busy, darling, surely you can see that."

Then: "You shouldn't be up here. I'm a stricken widow
and must be alone with my grief."

Then: "You shouldn't even be in the palace, or here in
the capital. You might put in an appearance at the funeral,
but after that you'd best go straight back to Otán."

"Otán?"

I'd forgotten that I'd ever been there. All I knew was that I wanted to stay with Angela. She saw that in my face in her vanity mirror, and that love made me entirely harmless to her.

"Don't be a bore, please, darling. It was marvelous, now don't be a bore and spoil it."

I hung there mooning over her. She sighed and swung her legs around, looked up at me.

"All right. Since you oblige me to, I'll spell it out:

"I wanted something from you, I asked a favor. To get it I made you very, very happy. Dozens of times, over and over again. You gave me what I wanted. You were perfectly marvelous, and it was lovely. But it's done now, and you've nothing more I want.

"Now I'm very busy, and you can't stay here."

She turned back to modeling expressions.

I stood there for a moment, then slunk away. Parts beginning to shrivel back toward substandard. Feeling totally empty, the way I did when they first put me in here. The latter was partly the drain of murdering Alejo. Murder's a very enervating business, even when done in the heat, as they say, of passion, to someone you despise (as with Don Lorenzo), and I'd murdered Alejo as a favor to Angela, in perfectly cold blood, without a drop of malice toward him. It was partly sudden loss of status, from master of the world to dismissed servant. I wasn't at all prepared for it. I'd been expecting a hero's and lover's welcome. And curtain calls too, every artist expects them: applause for my elegant plan and faultless execution, the three of us expiring at once! But my emptiness was mainly lack of purpose. I'd forgotten my true mission. I'd put my gifts and powers at Angela's service. Now, suddenly, she didn't need or want them. I hadn't any function on the planet, no use or worth.

I moped about outside in the gathering crowd. Who no doubt assumed I was grieving for Alejo. When actually I was grieving for myself. I tossed my consciousness into the palace, caught Angela's swearing-in act, watched her at prayer. I monitored a few minutes of her first cabinet meeting, enough to note that she was totally in charge. The ministers had evidently decided among themselves that they would run the country and she be a figurehead. That arrangement endured about twenty seconds from the time she sat down. Called the session to order and began serving carefully aimed questions to particular ministers. Judged their responses and stroked back firm decisions—exactly as if she'd been running the country for years. I passed up the rest of the meeting and whatever followed it and replayed our most extravagant copulations, the first and the last and a number of in-betweens. Thus engaged, I erred about the city in an ecstasy of worthlessness and self-pity such as I hadn't known since I was a double-sexed miracle, since I lay in a revolving barber chair with my freakdom on show to a squabble of gawking rubes. My gifts were perfectly intact, but it never occurred to me I might use them to master Angela. I loved her and had put myself in her power and was far too happy suffering over her.

I vagabonded through the city, which was as deeply in mourning as I was, though for better cause—everyone's countenance at half-staff and the very buildings sweating praise for Alejo, as if he'd never been feared and despised in his life. This general grief nourished my private rapture. I'd murdered a great man for a faithless woman. How wonderfully sorry for myself and useless I felt!

All night, all day. I passed up the cathedral and the cemetery, didn't toss my consciousness to either spot, took no real heed where I was or where I was going, but at sunset found myself at the Guardia control point west of the capital, trudging the highway with a band of silent peasants who'd come in the night before to pay their respects. Or, rather, Angela's all-points bulletin found me there. I was halted, questioned, then saluted—and presently installed on the front seat of a patrol truck, speeding toward the palace with two cyclists out front. Mandragon was back in favor.

On my first night in the palace, as soon as I slept, Angela phoned a code word to Mount Vervex; a complex operation got under way. *Scorpion* set course for Tinieblan waters. A team of communication experts assembled in Miami. A jet plane full of equipment stood by. Between prayers with the archbishop and putting the cabinet ministers in their place, Angela cabled the good news—that Alejo Sancudo was dead, that she was in power, that Dred might come ashore in a few days. *Scorpion* was by then lying off Bastidas, at forty fathoms, just south of the shipping lanes. The jet took off. A guest at El Opulento Hotel asked to see the manager. But at midnight, after *Scorpion* had come up to communicating depth, Angela got an urgent signal from Mount Vervex: Dred was taken ill, was very far gone; further delay might be disastrous. So his havening was put forward as early as possible, to dawn on the morning after Alejo's funeral (which was held, of course, the day after he died, for it's traditional here in the tropics to get the departed underground straightaway). A ward was cordoned off at San Bruno Hospital, even as the top floor of El Opulento was being cleared. A cutter and a helicopter were put on alert. And the Guardia was ordered to find Mandragon. Angela respected my gift for healing, and was taking no chances lest Dred croak before paying off.

"I'm sorry about yesterday evening, for what I said."

Of course! Of course!

We were in the sitting room. Its aphrodisiac effect was melting my rancor. But not entirely, at least not all at once.

"I was under tremendous pressure, darling, you understand. I didn't really mean to send you away."

Of course not! You were filled with gratitude and admiration!

I dipped into her mind, something love had restrained me from doing up to then. Not out of respect for her privacy:

passionate love doesn't understand that sort of thing. I'd been concentrating on my own sensations and didn't care to be distracted by Angela's thoughts. Which weren't really on Mandragon now. Her mind was clotted with concern for Dred—for the money, that is, he represented to her, and which he had to be in some sort of health to pay off.

"I've had the whole Guardia out searching for you."

"I've something you want."

Tinkling cascade of laughter, she rose from her chair. Lynxed to me, licking her tongue across tiny sharp teeth. Reached down and fondled the badges of my new gender.

"Oh, darling, you do, you certainly do! I just didn't realize how much, or how badly. I was so foolish, you forgive me, don't you?"

And then: "We have to leave in a little, but I think there's time."

So much for the joys of worthlessness and self-pity. So much for rancor at having been cast as a tool and a dupe. So much, in fact, for the power to read people's thoughts. In less than a minute I was wanking away again.

We didn't leave, it turned out, till nearly midnight. After consummating Mandragon's return to favor, Angela conferred with some Guardia officers, worked out final arrangements, relayed them to Vervex—who relayed them to *Scorpion* and sent confirmation back. During the which Mandragon took his merited ease, and communed with his own sensations, and concluded that while it was exquisitely pleasant to suffer over Angela, it was even more fun to enjoy her.

We went by limousine. Angela didn't care to fly at night. North-northeast to Córdoba, then east-northeast over the cordillera. Along the narrow highway to Bastidas, the same stretch of road where Mandragon was engendered, if that version of the birth is true. Our head beams carved the buggy gloom before us, pressed at the leathered backs of the lead cyclists, flowed round and were sponged up by buggy gloom. Behind came Colonel Lisandro Empulgueras and four Jeeps full of soldiers. The helicopter dragonflied above, its rotor-slap reduced to a dull thumping by thick upholstery and bulletproof glass.

Angela's military aide sat up front beside our driver, his kepi crinkled on the glass partition. From time to time he took the intercom to answer Angela's requests for reports on our progress. She sat far over on the right, legs crossed, her left hand clasping her right elbow, her right fist pressed against her cheek. Or holding the intercom phone while she asked for reports on our progress. Or holding the radiophone while she spoke with Guardia headquarters, with the cutter cruising off Bastidas, with the doctor in the helicopter above. Twice she asked to be put through to Mount Vervex, and for Vervex to put her through to Dred. Mandragon could have spared her the trouble. Mandragon knew poor Dred was too weak to speak. Mandragon's consciousness was on board *Scorpion*. I lounged on the rich fabric as though dozing, and flung my consciousness out through the gloom. Across the jungled ridges, over the marshes. Down through the tepid sea and the steel hull. Dred lay immobile on the slimy vinyl, no more substantial than a wraith. His pale-pink eyes were wide with horror.

I could have spared Angela the trouble of trying to reach him, but I preferred to spare her the knowledge of his state.

Predawn glaze, the wharf at Punta Amarga. Weather-ravaged planks, decaying timbers, stumpy pilings shambling out to sea.

Cutter alongside, stern toward the beach—diesels throbbing, deck lifting and falling lightly, gunwales rasping on the creaky wood.

The captain came down and touched his cap to Angela, helped her on board. But gave no order to cast off.

"Why don't we wait out there?" She gestured seaward. "It would save time."

"*Perdoname, Señora Presidenta.* I don't want that submarine coming up under me."

Off to the right and back of us the helicopter knelt in the soft sand, coughing regularly, blinking red. Quite near the spot where Mandragon was engendered, if that version of the birth is true. Beyond, invisible against the darkling palms, a company of troops from the Bastidas barracks mounted guard along the fringes of the beach.

Smells of salt water, of diesel oil, of tar—of Angela's perfume. Moist breath of breeze, sea calm and phosphorescent. The horizon grows distinct, bulges with flames. Red dawn flows up about the paling stars.

The sun and *Scorpion* came up together.

"*Allí está!*"

Voices barked, screws churned, lines fell away. We swung off and stood out into the sunrise.

The crimson sky, the wine-red placid sea. The sub's thin sail and spreading planes scar a dark cross against the sun's fiery globe.

The open bridge, Angela beside the captain. Stares seaward, squinting, over lifted bows. Her yellow hair flows free. Her lower lip is pinced between her teeth. Her knuckles on the rail are livid.

When we were fifty yards out, the cutter dropped her bows and glided broadside, lay wallowing in her own wash. *Scorpion* was dead in the water, like a reef from which the tide had ebbed. Her sail, her planes, her deck, and her humped hull were encrusted with barnacles, carbuncled with coral, bearded with sea anemones. Whose tendrils quivered in the breeze and swayed with the soft swells. There was no sign of human life aboard her.

We swung a boat away—three seamen and the doctor

from the chopper. It sputtered in, we circled. Forward of the
sail a hatch swung open. A man emerged. In ragged, faded
blues, with unkempt hair. Another followed. They stood on
the crusted deck and blinked at us.

Another man came up holding a line. The three stood at
the hatch and hauled away. And presently drew up a basket
stretcher. In which a human form was strapped.

Angela gasped.

A fourth man came up after the stretcher. Each grasping
a corner in one hand they carried it forward to where the
deck sloped away and waded out with it along the hull,
ankle- then calf-deep, to the cutter's boat and got Dred
Mandeville aboard it. The boat bore him toward us. The
doctor's bent back covered him from our view.

The four men on *Scorpion* returned to the hatch and entered it. The last stood with his head and trunk above deck,
looked for a moment at us, then lifted the hatch cover and
drew it closed. *Scorpion* began to settle. Her deck went
awash, swells lapped about her sail. Nudging forward, her
planes and masts went under. The turbulence of her screw
ruffled the surface. Which calmed again. Submerged, she
turned back out to sea, for her orders were to continue sailing. Nor did anyone on board complain. In a few minutes
the four men who'd been above decks had forgotten all
about the cutter, had forgotten the red-gold dawn and the
strange green shore. They lay writhing in pleasure, with
bliss and glory plugged into their brains.

As the boat swung up, we got back under way. Angela
stood beside the davit, her right hand over her mouth, her
left hand clinging to the rail as the cutter raised her bows
and then heeled over. Four seamen drew the stretcher from
the boat and set it on the deck. The doctor scrambled down
beside it. Dred Mandeville lay naked except for a pair of
frayed undershorts. His white beard scragged down across
his chest. His chalk-white skin was cankered with open
sores. His limbs and trunk were wasted. His finger- and toe-

nails curved away like talons. His gaunt frame looked seven feet long.

Angela gaped down at him, her right hand over her mouth. Tiny beads of spray glistened in her hair. Her face was pale, and her grey eyes looked very ancient.

Dred's eyelids fluttered. His right arm, which the doctor had just unstrapped, flung up and flopped across his face.

"The light! Please, someone, take away the light!"

Then his whole body convulsed against the straps. His arm flailed up and flopped away. His throat gurgled. His pink eyes stared up past us at the sky, then rolled back in their sockets.

The doctor crouched and put his stethoscope to Dred's chest. He smashed Dred's chest with his fist, pounded three or four times, listened again. He looked up at Angela.

"*Señora Presidenta*, this man is dead."

Angela howled. She glared at the doctor, then at Dred's corpse as if she were going to kick it. She looked beseechingly at Mandragon. Mandragon smiled.

"He isn't dead, only unconscious."

Dead as a stone, of course, and Angela knew it, but I didn't want to confuse things with the doctor present. He began to protest, but I shook my finger at him. I bent and touched my fingertips to Dred's forehead.

"Listen again, but listen carefully. The engine noise, you know, and the vibration."

He crouched and listened, then looked up contritely. "I was wrong. Forgive me, señora. I was absolutely certain."

"Don't concern yourself about it, Doctor. It was an understandable mistake. Concern yourself with your patient."

She stepped aft, past Dred and the doctor. I followed.

Angela and Mandragon on the fantail. Shuddering deck, below the sea churns by. She stops and turns, leans back against the rail, forearms spread along it. Stares at him in gratitude and triumph.

"You are magnificent!"

Sea spray on her cheek, her hair blows back. To her left the fluttering Tinieblan pennant. Behind her the sun is rising above the frothed wake.

"I need him talking, and if possible walking, as soon as possible. For a month, for at least two weeks. Can you do it?"

Mandragon smiles.

"Anything! You may have anything at all!"

32

". . . your confession."

Moon-faced type about my age and color, in Guardia fatigues and shiny jump boots, captain's bars and inch-high silver cross. Must have slipped in while I was on the cutter's fantail. Stands in the sitting-room doorway with the turnkey and two guards behind him, eyes olive-ripe with compassion while the other three pairs are merely curious.

I blink and shake my head.

Could say I've been confessing and he's interrupting, but I don't want to start a conversation. And confession isn't it exactly. Recalling who I am, redeeming Mandragon, but it's not the same. Don't need him, for instance.

"These men will wait outside."

I shake my head.

Gives a little swing to his little satchel. Containing prayer book, Testament, and shawl. Unguent, crucifix, and holy water. Hosts. Props of his act, Mandragon didn't use any. A Guardia chaplain, because with a condemned of Mandragon's importance you don't take chances. Hold Mandragon incommunicado. If there has to be a priest, get one who's under military discipline. And yet his concern seems as sincere as the guards' curiosity.

"Are you sure?"

I nod.

"There's very little time, less than an hour."

"I know, and I don't want to waste it—Captain." He'd

have liked "Father" better, but he's wearing the wrong togs. "Leave me alone."

Eyes brim up with hurt, he looks away. "I'm sorry I can't be of help."

Something odd. Looks back at me, biting his lip, then turns, takes three quick steps, and kneels before me.

"—?"

"I . . . I saw you once. I mean . . . Aguascalientes, I . . ."

Blinks at me, inarticulate. No matter. I see his mind. That gift returning also. Thoughts all atangle, webbed, but I can picture them as from above. Reverence for me that compelled him forward, made him kneel down: there's the main thread. Entwined with concepts out of his religion, and vivid recollections of that day. Was what he witnessed real or an illusion? I could say: both. Is kneeling here a blasphemy? there's another strand. Who inspires this reverence, God or the devil? Could tell him Mandragon served both, but that wouldn't relieve him. His mind functions by separating, works by either/or. Mandragon united opposites. Contraries were joined in me.

The chaplain blinks unease. I tell him softly:

"I was the instrument of power."

As if to mark my phrase, make it exclamation, the prison shudders. Floor and walls shake, the window rattles loudly. Guards flinch and groan, the chaplain stares wide-eyed. For about fifteen seconds, then it stops. Quite common here: earth tremors.

Mandragon sits up. Folds legs, raises cuffed hands Mohotty-fashion. Fingertips at the chin, nods serenely. The chaplain sighs.

Mandragon smirks, pops fingers open, flops back against the fabric, grinning broadly. The chaplain blinks, then gives a sad, shy smile, gets to his feet.

"I'm sorry, I don't know what . . ."

"Thank you for coming, but I need this time alone. If

you want to help, they've got my girls downstairs. Please
go and . . ."

My head swims, my eyes unfocus, I leave my body.

*Their cell. Gloom and dampness, light from the corridor
trickling beneath the door. Paloma wailing, clutched in Full
Moons' arms, Apple stroking her hair. Terrified by the
tremor. Confort fetused on a chain-hung metal slab, whimpering. Nightandmist sitting opposite, unkempt head slung
forward, hands drooped beside her thighs. Fear and deso-
lation.*

Paloma quiets. Full Moons looks up.

"Can't you feel it? Mandragon's here with us!"

"Yes! Yes!"

"I feel it too!"

*A pale-green radiance glows beside the door. Swells,
fills up the cell, then slowly fades.*

"Here with us! Mandragon was here!"

"Are you all right?" The chaplain bends beside me.

I nod. "They've got my girls downstairs. Please go and
see them."

"I'll try. I'll see if it's authorized. But, are you
sure . . . ?"

"Please, leave!"

Turns and goes out with the guards. The door locks behind them.

33

Impulsive fellow, kneeling to me like that. Broke discipline to Church and Guardia, risked angering both sets of bosses, and all because he heard me preach once. Imagine if he knew what I pulled with Dred!

Mandragon raised Dred Mandeville's cadaver, and kept it on the job for seven weeks.

Without dramatics. I could have had that corpse up on the deck of the cutter doing a barefoot, talon-toed buck-and-wing. Or waited till it was duly boxed and crypted, then had it claw free and slink out of the tomb. Or arranged a thrilling public entertainment—made it pop up out of the coffin during the eulogy, gape, and streel down shrieking off the bier. Instead I merely touched it and gave it a pulse —respiration, brain waves, the life functions—then brought "recovery" along in careful stages. Discreetly, to avoid suspicion. Yet briskly, because my darling thirsted for pelf. Almost too brisk for the doctor and his colleagues. They judged Dred's mending just short of miraculous, and had to be prodded to congratulate themselves. Miraculous and more! my masterpiece! but Mandragon wasn't seeking public recognition. The only public I cared to please was Angela.

Pleasing her was why, I don't know how. Power working through me, as in healing. I've never understood and never tried to. Energy flowed from me into Dred's corpse, all in a great rush that left me feeble. A fearful amount just to get it ticking over. Against strong resistance, like dragging a sledge uphill. The living want to stay alive, corpses want to stay corpses, and but for Angela I'd have been afraid to spend the force required. Love vaporized all sense of danger: a longing to administer delight; a need to have her notice and applaud me. I still could reach her only through third parties, murdering Alejo, raising Dred. In neither instance did I hesitate.

Mandragon hauled Dred Mandeville back to life. Or, rather, yanked him undead. I zombied him into my darling's service. I kept him on the job for seven weeks. More convincing than an animated dummy. More compliant than a roboted sailorman.

Cutter to chopper, chopper to hospital. Bundled in blankets, oxygen-masked at the snout. Serums and vitamins pumped into scrawny buttocks. Dextrose and plasma adrip into breadstick arms. None of which was actually required, though it kept the doctor employed, made him feel useful. Mandragon rode with the newly returned departed. Angela's smile applauded Mandragon's art.

We followed the dawn across the cordillera, thudded southwest above pastureland and cane. En route I lifted him to slumber. His eyelids fluttered, he moaned against the mask, twitched his legs weakly. I brushed his brow and calmed him to sweet slumber, having brought "recovery" along another stage.

At the hospital a badly needed sponge bath, a clipping of finger- and toenails, a shearing of beard. Plus regarmenting in a clean white linen bed gown, not unlike that he'd worn of old in his mountain cavern, though now of course his role was entirely reversed. Through all of this our reborn slumbered sweetly. The name on his chart was Dagoberto Manrique. Best not to unsettle the nurses with a celebrity.

Angela remained on the helicopter. Best not to attract unnecessary attention. It lifted away and returned her to the palace, where she received the minister of justice, the president of the chamber, and the local counsel for Hirudo Oil. As soon as she had that meeting running smoothly, she had it moved to another room and received the foreign minister, then the minister of finance, then Gonzalo Garbanzo. And when they were prepared to tackle the matters she assigned them, she received a gringo gentleman who was staying at the El Opulento, a greying gringo gentleman with granolith eyes who had taken over the whole top floor of the building and moved in communications equipment and had thick velvet blackout curtains hung, a grim-faced gringo in a sharkskin suit—steel-grey like his hair, with knife-sharp trouser creases—whose icy stare didn't thaw when she informed him that their mutual friend was still under the weather, but the gravity of his case had been grossly overplayed: he'd be up and about in no time, perhaps by tomorrow, perfectly prepared to resume control.

"When do I see him?"

"When *he* wants to see *you*. The proper form of address, by the way, is 'Madame President' or 'Your Excellency.' I prefer the latter."

"How do I reach him by phone?"

"You don't. He doesn't want to be disturbed. This audience will end if the proper form of address isn't used."

"Doesn't want to be, Your Excellency, or can't be? The word from *Scorpion* is he's very sick. I got the idea that he might be dying."

"I've already told you those reports were exaggerated. But have any idea you please, it's the same to me."

"Is it? That's odd. Your Excellency, Madame President, whatever. I understood that part of your, uh, compensation is to be in the form of options. I was instructed to bring the relevant papers."

"So?"

"So we're talking about a very important man. He's been out of sight, but his hand's been on the tiller. Very firmly.

And very obviously to people concerned with these things. The way he moves, his style, shows he's in control. If that control ceased or were significantly interrupted, or even if people got the idea it had or might be, you'd see, shall we say, significant downward movement in a number of securities. On every major exchange. Worldwide. So it's not the same to you, not if you're expecting to hold options."

"Are you threatening to leak false information?"

"Your Excellency, I'm not threatening anything. I'm trying to tell you my idea of his health is important, that I'd better find out pretty soon just what's going on. Other people had access to those messages. Very few, but one is enough. We're talking about very inside information. The possibilities for profit are enormous, and therefore very tempting. And why do people resist temptation? Fear, that's why. In this case fear of a particular man. But at last report that man was deathly ill. All right, they've seen the messages, I'm on the spot. Thirty-six hours have gone by. If word doesn't come from me soon that the man's all right— and I can't send it till I've seen him or at least heard his voice—someone's going to be tempted to take short positions—through intermediaries, of course, it can be done —then leak the information from the sub. Someone may have been tempted already."

"You've gone short yourself, haven't you? Or are you still only thinking about it?"

"The question in my mind, Your Excellency, is whether you have. It would be a way of clearing something on this venture. If he's not all right, I mean, and you can't expect to receive the agreed compensation."

"Anyone who goes short will be wiped out! He'll be up and about by tomorrow, ready to resume control, from an open and secure base of operations, something he hasn't had for years. And then you'll see significant *upward* movement!"

"Oh, I hope so, Madame President. He's my principal.

But what if there is a leak, can you produce him? What if he's just a little sicker than you think, or takes a little longer to get back on his feet? Or assume he hasn't even got a head cold, can you get him to parade for the reporters? What about that, Your Excellency? He never went for publicity, never gave one interview, not even in the boy-wonder days. Suppose the news gets on the wire, that the last his people know he was deathly ill, 'in coma, on the high seas. It won't work just to deny it. Or have him talk by phone, that could be a fake. If it isn't clearly refuted, right away, in person, those stocks won't just go down, there'll be wholesale dumping. Severe disruption in the markets, suspensions of trading. You can't turn that sort of thing around in a hurry. It might be months before present levels are regained. Meanwhile, you never know, he might have a relapse. I'd really like to speak with him."

"I'll tell him of your concern. Perhaps he'll call you."

"I'd really like to speak with him by this evening."

"Before the *Times* and the *Journal* go to bed."

"Let's say by eight."

"I'll tell him. He knows where you are."

"So, I'm afraid, do the press, that's another problem. They track me everywhere. Your Excellency."

"How flattering! And how convenient! In case you have any juicy tidbits to leak."

"Annoying, actually, Your Excellency. The price of being his chief executive agent. It won't be long before they know he's here. They don't even have to know, they'll report it anyway. Now that they've tracked me down. As soon as they see what's going on at the hotel. Which is why I've called a conference for this evening."

"For eight o'clock?"

"That's right, Your Excellency, eight o'clock. Now, assuming I speak to him by then . . ."

"You will!"

"I'll release the information that he's in this country. They'll ask for how long, I'll say indefinitely. But tomorrow we'll have to deal with the federal government. He's under several serious indictments."

"None of which has a shred of validity here. This is an independent, sovereign republic."

"With an extradition treaty with the US."

"To which Tinieblan citizens are immune. His application will be filed today. A bill waiving the term-of-residence requirement will be offered tomorrow. Sponsored by the government, of which I am the head. Endorsed by the majority party, of which I am the leader. Supported by deputies from every region of the country, of which I am the constitutional president. As long as he enjoys my hospitality, he'll be more secure than he's ever been in his life."

"Well, Your Excellency, I hope to hear from him. With a hostess like you, he may not need a jailer."

"You do yourself no service by impertinence. Your principal and I are in perfect accord. Return to the hotel, you'll be contacted. This audience is over."

So the next person she received was Mandragon. Sent a limousine, cyclists with sirens, the lot. Whisked me over from Señor Manrique's bedside.

"How is he?"

"Asleep."

We were in the state office, which she'd found time (perhaps on the day of the funeral) to rearrange. Alejo's desk and chair put into storage. A thronish article brought up from the dining room. All other furniture against the walls away from it, except for a footstool and an end table with phones. Sat slumped against the carving, hands clasped behind her neck, legs stretched, bare feet plumped on the stool. No sleep for thirty hours and not much before, so that she looked nearly two-thirds her age. Half-eaten plate of food on the table beside her. Damask napkin chucked down on the intercom phone.

"Can you have him talking by eight o'clock this evening? One phone call, but it might go on awhile."

Mandragon smiled.

Sighed deeply, let her chin drop. "Good!"

Brought her hands around to knead her temples. Then dropped them to the chair arms and sat up quickly, ancient eyes gleaming.

"Can you have him out of bed, standing up, walking?"

"I can have him doing handsprings, like your brother Pedro."

"Things he doesn't want to do? Things he's never done?"

"Like to see him bite the heads off a few live chickens?"

"Lovely! But later. Tonight I want him to hold a press conference."

And then: "I'm terribly tired, darling, you must be too. Let's continue this in bed."

Mandragon had no objection.

Becoming her consort, her confidant, companion, confederate. The siesta enlarged his comprehension, as well as his self-esteem and other parts. He learned what a stock option was and what was a short sale, that truth was whatever the news media reported, things he'd lived in ignorance of before. He heard an account of her chat with the gringo gentleman, and the plan she'd hit on to teach him some respect—"Just make him squirm a little; you'll help, won't you, darling?" He snoozed while she used the phone, then got up and helped.

By then the hospital grounds were vultured with journalists—jeaned or seersuckered gringos hovering and circling; a flapping gabble of Tinieblan stringers. Who accosted every passing nurse and doctor, demanding to know about "the mystery patient," the one flown in by chopper early that day. At dusk a TV film crew joined them, straight from the airport, down from Miami, all hot. In time to shoot the hearse sliding in on a side street, convoyed by dozens of cops, no common event. They shot the sheeted stiff on the wheeled table, Mandragon and orderlies stoking it gently inside. They shot the sullen-faced hospital spokesman as he mumbled, "No comment," then had a name pried from his lips.

"Dagoberto Manrique?"

"Catch those initials, dummy? It's got to be him!"

The hearse slid away. Police closed the street behind it. Disrespect for the dead, they warned, was a crime in Tinieblas. Those who tried to follow would be arrested. No matter, they had plenty. The flock swept off.

And found that cable, telex, and international telephone service was suspended, that Monteseguro Airport was shut down, that Tinieblas was cut off from the rest of the planet.

The subject of their unfiled scoop slumbered sweetly. On a slab in a funeral parlor, but only moderately stiff. He slumbered while a barber trimmed and combed him, while Angela herself dabbed his cheeks with rouge. He slumbered while we dressed him, just as he'd done that afternoon while a haberdasher took his measurements. Silk underwear, broadcloth shirt, calf-length stockings. Cream-colored flannel trousers, snowy buckskin shoes. A double-breasted blazer with brass buttons. No tie, he never wore ties, a sea-blue ascot—the very shade to set off his bunny-pink eyes. Then Mandragon lifted him awake.

Like dragging a rock up from the bottom of a quarry. Didn't want to be alive, much less awake. Such marvelous peace when his infinite will stopped goading, when his senses dimmed and flickered and then went out. Bad enough to be yanked from that peace into unconsciousness. Bad enough being hoisted to slumber (though I'd let him dream about grass between his toes). Hideous to be awake, all senses flaring. No solace that his will no longer goaded. Mandragon's did.

I zombied Dred into my darling's service. I ran him with my will for seven weeks.

Whined about the light, we gave him dark glasses. (Made him take them off later for flashbulbs and TV floods.) Begged to go back to sleep, but he'd had enough coddling. No sleep for Dred, it was time he got on the job. Angela briefed him on what to tell the reporters, catechized and rehearsed him until he had it straight. When he whined and tried to malinger, Mandragon's will goaded.

At El Opulento the journalists fumed and cursed, the chief executive agent bubbled with fury. At eight o'clock he mingled his rage with theirs, howled bodysnatch and swindle, while they screamed about the public's right to know. Mutual lamentations for the future. What hope was there when the forces of civilization—corporate empire and the free press—could have their sacred functions thwarted in a banana republic? We let them stew together thirty minutes. Then we gave them Dred.

At eight-thirty that evening the nattily attired, undead corpse of Dred Mandeville climbed out of a palace limousine at El Opulento. He looked neither left nor right, marched slowly forward, legs stiff and arms held stiffly at his sides, invisible tin key revolving between his shoulder blades. Through the lobby, up the stairs, into the ballroom. Across the polished floor to the microphone. Bumping against the shoulders of gawping journalists. Chesting his gape-mouthed executive out of his way. Then turned, reached stiffly up, removed dark glasses. Held bunny-pink eyes unblinking for flashbulbs and floods. Spoke—in the tone of a recorded announcement, of a voice giving weather data over the phone:

"Good evening. My name, as you know, is Dred R. Mandeville. I am, as you see, alive and well. I shall reside from now on in this country. I have applied for Tinieblan nationality. I expect it to be granted in a few days. I shall continue to manage my business interests. Good evening."

Mandragon's will goosed him before the speech replayed.

The bunny-eyed undead corpse stepped stiffly forward, chesting the mike aside. He did not look down as it leaned and tottered floorward. He marched slowly out through exploding clusters of journalists. He did not flinch as their questions flew in at his cheeks.

"How much did you pay for asylum?"

"What about the indictments?"

"Where have you been hiding all these years?"

The questions thwopped against Dred's pale, rouged cheeks, fell harmlessly to the polished floor of the ballroom, and were at once forgotten, may still be lying there, abandoned and trampled, for as Dred marched out, turned left, stepped onto the elevator, the hotel manager entered, announcing that communication service had been restored.

34

Alive and well in Ciudad Tinieblas!

The tune went tooting gaily round the planet, was blared at full volume, day and night, for weeks. Every outlet featured it. Every analyst warbled a background backup. Every pundit cut his own arrangement. It was bigger than Negresco's waltz, bigger than the theme from the Coward Cooze story. It was Dred's greatest hit.

Angela sang it over a nationwide hookup in her first presidential address. In her version Dred was the victim of political oppression. Granting him refuge was the course of compassion and honor. The assembly voted to waive all obstacles. The ministry of justice pronounced him a Tinieblan. The Supreme Court rejected an extradition writ. The chief executive agent flew back to Arizada, declaring the new base of operations secure. Mandeville issues reached new highs on all the exchanges.

And Dred? Dred lurked behind thick velvet blackout curtains, undead and zombied at El Opulento.

The top floor of the hotel was sealed by private guards flown in from Draco. A staff flown in from Zeno took up residence, manned their desks and phones, worked the rooms full of communications equipment. The northwest quadrant was sealed off for Dred. Only the guard that took his food in entered. He never left. He lurked behind the velvet curtains, among the flickering data display screens. They were fed directly from the transmitter on Mount

Vervex, through a huge antenna set up on the hotel roof. Dred prowled among them peering, now and then picked up a phone to dictate a memo, or to speak with one of his satraps around the world. He managed his business interests, he ran his empire—with the same verve, the autograph style he'd always shown. But the will that drove him was Mandragon's.

Mandragon's will kept his bored organs working, kept his blood slewing wearily round and round. Mandragon's will kept him breathing, though air tasted rancid and death-musty, though his lungs resented every breath. Mandragon's will kept him feeding regularly, though he had no appetite, though all food was repulsive to him, though he chewed it in the sullen rhythm of a convict breaking stones in a deep quarry. Mandragon's will sent his frail body tottering among the screens, forced his burning eyes to focus, goaded his reluctant mind. Dred's mind knew what to do, it was long-practiced. It culled up ordinary scraps of data and formed them to intricate, unlikely patterns, made them dance elegant capers along the ancient theme of human greed. Reluctantly. All the joy was gone now from these creations. But his mind performed as masterfully as ever when sternly goaded. I lodged part of my will in Dred like a poisoned splinter, stuck it in and left it like a scorpion's sting. It seared and prodded. It kept him on the job.

More convincing than an animated dummy. His moves and stunts were authentic. His voice on the phone was instantly obeyed. More compliant than a roboted sailor. He multiplied his holdings in Tinieblas, and poured in funds for development, and gave Angela power of attorney. He issued her new stock options. He transferred dizzying sums to her secret accounts.

She grew more lovely and more youthful. The options rosed her flesh, toned her firm thighs. The power of attorney smoothed the nascent wrinkles from about her eyes. The cablegrammed confirmations of deposits swelled her breasts and turned her riggish. And, specially, Mandragon's light was with her. It made her more stately when she was in public. It warmed her to soft languor when we were alone. Mandragon's power touched her.

From the evening of Dred's press conference, which we watched on mirrorvision in her bedroom. We returned there directly from the funeral parlor, while Dred was on his way to the hotel. Angela collapsed on the bed, exhausted. I put the ballroom on her full-length mirror. We watched Dred's entrance, his presentation, his brusque exit. We watched the journalists mobbing out to file. We caught Dred stepping off the elevator on the top floor, followed his silent march to the flickering gloom of his sanctum. He threw himself down at once and at once heaved upright, tottered to a phone, began calling his satraps, sang them his new tune, alive and well. After a bit he took a call from his chief executive, who'd come up and was hovering nervously in the staff room. Dred scolded him very horribly —which pleased my darling, as I'd thought it would. Then I had another idea.

"If there's something you'd like him to do, just think of it. Make a wish."

She closed her eyes tightly for a moment. When she opened them, Dred interrupted himself in midsentence to order a sum transferred to Switzerland. He named a bank, gave an account number. The other repeated the instructions, assured Dred they'd be carried out at once.

Angela stared into the mirror. Her face shone with happiness. I let the scene fade.

Angela shifted the pillows and lay back. Gazed up at me, lips parted. Lifted her arms.

Mandragon took possession of her.

My body entered her body. My mind entered her mind. My light filled her. I felt her pleasure as the warm radiance spread within her, her helplessness and terror as it flared and burst. Then she forgot herself. She stopped struggling and abandoned herself to Mandragon. She let herself be swept off like a swimmer borne out to sea in an undertow.

Later she said imperishable things, phrases grammared softly in caresses. That evening, other evenings, when darkness thickened round us like a bulwark. In her bed or on the balcony beyond it, tumbled in the hammock under the stars. She fashioned the most charming adorations, and performed them shyly, all at once unsure of her power to please—offered herself up to Mandragon with artless lavishness, then glanced from trembling lids to see if Mandragon smiled upon her devotions. She knelt in anthem to me: "You are magnificent!" She prostrated herself before me and called for the most abject mortifications: "Anything! You may have anything at all!" She revered and felt herself unworthy.

Best not dwell on it, recalling it's enough. Not really much to triumph or take pride in. I gave a whore experience of love. The power in me touched her. It scourged her from herself, made her feel love.

Will she remember when I'm dangling?

Best not dwell on it. Abuse of power.

35

"Take it."

The kitchen trusty, imp-faced, hog-round, squat. Nose and cheeks blossomed with pustules, narrow eyes like crab holes in soft sand. Pudgy feet overflowing ruptured slippers, sausage forearms bulging from prison shirt sleeves, paunch portholing prison trousers below the tie. He holds the metal mug out to me. "Don't you want it?"

Shake my head. Tepid coffee dolloped with canned milk, paste of unstirred sugar at the bottom. Be squirting at the first swallow.

"Afraid it's poisoned? Afraid it'll hurt your tummy and spoil your day? It's not poisoned. Look." Has a good slurp of it, licks his lips and hums. "It's good. Take it!"

I shake my head.

The guard takes another step into the sitting room.

"Just leave it on the table, what do you care?"

"Wait a moment. This isn't correct. This isn't the way. Hardly touched his supper last night, no coffee this morning. Special food and special service, but nothing's good enough for Assholiness here!"

"Come on."

Plops the mug on the night table but then turns back to me, goes on haranguing. Window paling to grey. Hardly time to finish my recollections, though they're almost complete. Let the imp run down, run out of venom.

". . . still think you're the Sainted Pigeon, the Big Pod!"

"Come on!"

"You'll see, in a little while! *No eres nada!*"

Softly, to myself really: "I was the instrument of power."

And at that word the prison quakes again.

Stronger than before, longer too. Guard and imp terrified, I should be too. Animal doesn't want to be buried alive any more than be gallowsed, but the tremor brings me an odd calm.

Chaplain soothing Nightandmist, mumbling broken English.

Angela's face contorted in her hand mirror, lipstick smeared along her cheek.

Cable noose swinging softly from the force of the tremor.

The mug has scuttered off the night table to the floor. Imp stares at the spreading stain. Guard murmurs, *"Carajo! Hijo de la gran puta!"* Then collects himself and shouts, *"Vámanos ya!"*

He turns, goes out. Imp scampers after him. The door locks behind them.

36

Earth going brittle underneath this country. Elsewhere likewise; weary, wearing out. Under all the vain and stupid prancing; empty clamor, turmoil, cruelty, waste. Fatigued to brittleness, and who can blame it?

Or simply nauseated. Earth heaves and shudders, longing to be cleansed.

Of vain and stupid people, of the vain and vicious rulers they have and deserve. Such as Angela de Sancudo and her consort Mandragon.

Mandragon was Angela's consort seven weeks, as vain and vicious as your usual ruler.

And rule I did, Mandragon ran the country. Possessing Angela enlarged my head wonderfully, more than enjoying her enlarged my parts, so that it throbbed mightily for public deference. Angela's love squeals stabbed up at the ceiling. Her body heaved and shuddered, then lay still. Mandragon unquiffed and rolled off her, gentled his tumescent head onto the pillow, and at once began to muse on his magnificence and consider what posts and honors might become it.

Only the highest, of course. Tinieblas itself seemed a pitifully small and dingy setting for a jewel of my splendor. The whole world ought to acknowledge and pay homage. Angela turned to Mandragon, murmuring sweetly. He visioned multitudes applauding, kneeling, groveling. Sweet murmurs, soft caresses, Mandragon mused on.

A spanking new Mandragon, my last transformation. I'd never cared about applause as a performer, or exulted in the adulation of my tribe. None of that was really for me personally. I was power's instrument and servant. Then I forgot the power that lived in me, abandoned it, served Angela instead, but at least I had a guide point and some ballast. Now I served only myself. Now I worshiped only my Mandragonhood. Nothing grounding it, nothing above it. Hollow, puffed with importance, swollen yet light. My Mandragonhood ballooned away on the pointless vagaries of auto-adoration, while I tried to fill it up with public deference.

Angela made no objection when I mentioned my hunger for high office. Much the reverse: she was enchanted. I'd proved a loyal and capable accomplice. Passing me her burdens of state would let her concentrate on squeezing the maximum pelf out of Zombito. But she would have been enchanted by any request. She was experiencing love. She welcomed any chance to please me. And the mechanism existed whereby she might. General Manduco's constitution was still in effect. It gave her dictatorial powers, and the right to transfer them to anyone she wished. So in her first address as president—delivered at 7 P.M. the following evening, over a nationwide TV and radio hookup, from her thronish perch in the state office—after she'd thanked the Tinieblan people for accepting her, and the cabinet for its support and the Guard for its loyalty, and the functionaries of the three branches for their devotion; after she'd promised to revere her beloved husband's memory (sniffling softly, producing two pearl-perfect tears) by adopting his principles, the foremost of which were honor and compassion, and proceeded from that to touch on the Mandeville question (denouncing oppression, urging asylum for Dred); after she'd vowed to govern as wisely and vigorously as God's grace and her own strength permitted (clasping her fingers, bowing her saintly head), she confessed that her strength was, femininely, frail. She intended, therefore, to invoke constitutional privilege (waving the document, citing the pertinent text), to shift some of her burdens to sturdier shoulders, to cede her powers and responsibilities as head of government to a first minister, retaining only those of head of state. For the new office she had looked beyond the realm of politics to one dependent on no party or faction, one who had already done the nation service in a dark hour, and who (besides) had been a friend to her husband, their great leader, easing his pain and comforting his last days. Then she named me.

In the nick of time too, though I doubt she'd admit it now. She wouldn't have lasted long without Mandragon. She had no following and no known qualifications. (All reference to her genius for gonadal management had been snipped from the authorized version of her life.) As the shock of Alejo's death faded, the Tinieblan people began to doubt she should stay in charge. The ministers had already decided she shouldn't, and as the shock of her first cabinet meeting faded, they began to cabal, intrigue, scheme, conspire, and plot. So did the Civil Guard officers. So did the functionaries of the three branches. The Tinieblan government looked like a basket of lobsters, and Angela wouldn't have stayed on top for long. Not long enough, maybe, to swing Zombisimo's citizenship, or give him a proper squeezing, or avoid being shaken down herself. Too many pretenders, that was the problem. Not even Angela could have humped and gagaed them all.

Not in time, that is. In theory she could have managed, but practical politics imposes stern time pressure. The lobsters keep clawing and scrambling. They don't wait while you manage them one by one. Much easier for her now, thanks to Mandragon. Mandragon's regime provoked a coup by the colonels—successful because my power abandoned me. They suppress all other rivals, and there's only three of them to hump and gaga. Angela can stay on and rule Tinieblas if she chooses, or decamp and live in luxury on her squeezings. Another story entirely eight weeks ago. Angela would have fallen; Mandragon prevailed.

Mandragon was (simply) better qualified, supremely gifted. To head the Tinieblan (or any other) government. He was (first of all) free of extraneous motives, high or low, honorable or dis-. He was not encumbered by principle or patriotism, by concern (imagined or real) for the people's welfare, by worries about his eventual place in history, by cruelty, greed, or any of the other curbs and urges that sometimes distract practitioners from the essential payoff of political activity. All Mandragon craved was public deference, to be the one that people stroked and fawned on, the Sainted Pigeon, the Divine Heron, the Big Pod. He didn't have to engage opponents singly—and sooner or later everyone here's an opponent; elsewhere likewise, each lobster for himself. Mass bedazzlement was one of his specialties. Nor was he obliged to maneuver via sentiment or self-interest, or (like Angela) to establish a beachhead on the enemy's groin and then slog brainward—an effective tactic but relatively slow. Mandragon could seize the cortical high ground in a blitz, as he proved during his very first minutes in office with the commandants of the Guardia Civil.

Colonel Atila Guadaña, Colonel Lisandro Empulgueras, Colonel Fidel Acha: Mandragon's regime began and ended with them. Since they were the sharpest-clawed crustaceans in the basket, he dealt with them first, immediately after Angela's address (which they were present in the palace to witness) in the high-ceilinged, richly mirrored first-floor ballroom, henceforth for seven weeks the prime minister's lair. They entered with the arrogance appropriate to military men in an area of the world where the sole enemy is likely to be a cringing and defenseless populace—confident stalk across the polished floor boards with chests puffed out and sneers firmly in place—though as they approached, their haughtiness was tempered a bit by memories of what had happened to Genghis. The spacious hall was empty of attendants, and of furniture, but ablaze from half a dozen chandeliers. At the extreme end Mandragon sat cross-legged on a large cushion, barefoot, in peasant garb, hands in his lap. He halted them ten yards off by raising a finger. He and his cushion rose abruptly until his head was just below the ceiling, provoking a powerful compulsion to prostrate themselves which he allowed them to control, though only barely. Then he punched up GUILT in the computing instruments under their grotesquely high-peaked kepis: the colonels looked up at Mandragon and saw their victims.

In the more or less normal course of their careers the three colonels had inflicted a good deal of pain and indignity on more or less defenseless members of the populace, without ever feeling the slightest twinge of guilt. But when they saw the citizens whom they had (variously) brow-beaten, terrorized, degraded, tortured, or murdered assembled in the air above them—no longer cringing but glaring down at them in awful judgment—when they stood arraigned before this ghastly throng, all the appropriate guilt hit them at once. They quaked with fear of merited retribution.

Needlessly really. Mandragon wasn't concerned with doing justice. No such extraneous motive distracted him. He had no wish to punish the colonels, or remove them, or even to make them mend their ways—so long as they paid him proper deference. And there they were beneath him, groveling. Mandragon held them in the absolute pit of guilt for thirty seconds (which was all they could safely take), and meanwhile rewired their cortices so that a vague vision of their victim-judges would remain with them constantly, properly associated with Mandragon. Then he stopped monkeying and dismissed them with a flick of his finger.

The three colonels backed slowly from Mandragon's presence, heads bent, eyes lowered, all the length of the brilliantly lighted ballroom. Once out the door, they turned and left the palace, first at an ordinary pace, then faster and faster, till they ran in a frantic, panicky stampede—through the patio and past the fish pool, bowling into visitors and guards. Hours later they were still green with terror, and their hands shook, and their teeth chattered, and their knees trembled. For as long as the vision persisted they showed Mandragon perfect deference, fawned on him in fact like triplet poodles, did his bidding, all but licked his hand.

How they will enjoy Mandragon's noosing!

The ministers were even more fun and less trouble: they all resigned. Mandragon received them after the colonels departed—in the Cabinet Room and without any mystifications, no rising to the ceiling or other display, since they had only modest stores of arrogance, which they hid very cleverly, even from themselves. All decent men in fact till three days before, but Alejo's demise had lobstered them severely. Each suddenly discontented with his spot; all scrambling frantically but trying not to show it.

They entered smiling, full of congratulations. Pledges of support and helpful suggestions (deviously contrived, cunningly veiled) as to how the new head of government should proceed. To promote the national welfare, of course, of course, though each was only after his own advantage. Mandragon let them mill and churn about him, grinning and nodding like a perfect moron, while white-jacketed waiters passed them drinks and tidbits. Then he begged them to take their places at the table, confessed his ignorance of the exact state of the nation, and hoped they might inform him, one by one, each on the area of his responsibility. First was Don Ignacio Hormiga, the minister of finance. As he opened his mouth, Mandragon punched up SHAME. Don Ignacio at once resigned and began confessing.

His cabals, intrigues, schemes, conspirings, plots; his dis-

loyalties to the former governments he'd served in; the
minor accommodations he'd made with the late dictatorship; the swindles he'd swung during his days as a banker
—the sort of compromises and corner-cuttings that few men
of affairs live very long without making, none of which had
bothered him much before but which now made him writhe
with shame and feel unworthy. He even confessed that his
wife, his lovely Irene (God rest her soul!), had been out-
rageously unfaithful to him, a new lover every month for
twenty-five years—not much of a revelation in itself since
everyone at the table had been to bed with her (excepting,
of course, Your Worship, Mr. Prime Minister), since all
the world knew of Irene's flagrant fuglings, but (the point
was) Don Ignacio had known also, had looked the other
way, had put up with them, in a manner scarcely befitting
a Tinieblan, much less a minister of state. He would have
confessed even more, but Dr. Armando Loza, the minister
of planning and development, interrupted to tender his own
resignation and confess his own shame. (Don Ignacio did
in fact continue, but in a low stammer drowned by Dr.
Loza's wails, and then, since he'd resigned and no one was
listening, got up and left the room and, still confessing,
wandered out among the journalists in the hallway, clutching them by the lapels of their jackets, spilling the rest of
his shame into their notebooks.)

Dr. Loza confessed his schemes against Doña Angela,
and the intrigues he'd begun concocting against Your Worship, and went on ungarbaging his heart without restraint.
Of fantasies mainly. Armando Loza was an intellectual,
and what he'd done (padded the bibliography of his thesis,
for instance) was small compared to what he'd daydreamed
of doing. Turning Tinieblas into the ideal state, for example, which naturally involved murdering half the populace and enslaving the other half for generations. He had
shameful daydreams aplenty and could have gone on all
night confessing them, but licentiate Edgardo Luciérnaga

interrupted him. He gaveled Loza's bleatings to a murmur by leaning forward and bashing his smooth, shiny forehead three, four, five times on the smooth, shiny surface of the table. Then he resigned and spewed out his own shame, even bed-wettings that plagued his adolescence, while Loza, still murmuring, got up and wandered out.

One by one the ministers resigned. Minister after minister made his confession. As much as he could there at the conference table, the rest to the reporters waiting outside. All the while Mandragon grinned and nodded. Later he collected the reporters—against their will really, since all had juicy stories to write and file—and announced that he would appoint a new cabinet, but only after due consideration, and for the present would handle all the portfolios himself.

At ten the next morning he received the deputies, the fifty-three honorable members of the chamber. Who were more than ever aware of their own importance, or (as they put it to themselves and to each other) of the grave responsibilities to the republic it was their sad lot to bear in these troubled times. With a president suddenly dead at the start of his term. With his successor handing control to some kind of mystic. With the cabinet resigning en masse in an orgy of breast-beating. They were the only stability left in the country. The Tinieblan people were singularly fortunate to have elected level-headed representatives.

Who'd put things back in place, no doubt of that. Who'd settle things down and govern—after all someone had to. By calm, considered steps, no hasty action.

The deputies bustled about harumphing at each other till they were shown into Mandragon's presence.

Mandragon chose not to overawe them by rising ceilingward. He received them already levitated, cushion and all. He spoke no welcome, made no introduction, but at once began describing the new Tinieblas that his regime would midwife into being—a land without want or conflict, a land of ease and frolic, where every man was a prince, every woman a queen. As he spoke a dawny aura rosed the ballroom. A carpet of fleecy cloud billowed the floor. It fluffed soothingly about the deputies' ankles, then took body and lifted them, till they all sat in the air at Mandragon's level. The deputies smiled like little children.

It was all, Mandragon told them, perfectly simple. They themselves could bring it to pass. They had only to vote Dred Mandeville a refuge. Then the billions would come pouring in. No Tinieblan need work unless he cared to. Ticamalans and Costaguanans would be imported to do the bothersome, degrading jobs. Dred's billions would be invested in Tinieblas, and every citizen would have a share.

At these words each deputy was instantly convinced that the best shares would go to the people he represented, or into his own pocket if he happened (like some) to be the greedy sort. They looked at Mandragon and saw the new Tinieblas. Each fashioned it according to his whim, and each believed in it completely.

Mandragon gentled them down and then dismissed them. The deputies rushed from the palace, rushed to the chamber, and unanimously voted Dred Mandeville citizenship. Then they threw themselves into a celebration that lasted until dawn the next day.

It was just as well they enjoyed themselves while they could. Money poured in all right, but not a cent was actually invested. Every drop of those squeezings went to Angela. For the moment, though, everyone was happy. That evening Mandragon went on a nationwide hookup and told everyone about the new Tinieblas. As he spoke, images of peace and plenty played in each listener's and viewer's mind. Everyone visioned the future he most longed for, and everyone believed it was on the way. Level-headed skeptics jubilated. Gristled cynics beamed and wept for joy. Then Mandragon made a progress round Tinieblas, to glut his hollowness on the people's praise.

For almost a year now since the lifting of the drought

and the fall of Genghis, rumors about Mandragon had been circulating. His isolation had fostered them to legend. Actual deeds (which were marvelous enough) had been refashioned in the public mind into prodigies even more marvelous, and more in line with people's yearnings, which tended mainly toward material wealth. Mandragon, they said, had multiplied the herds of Otán ranchers, had given Remedios planters three harvests a year. Mandragon had fed an entire tribe of Selva Trópica Indians from one 10-pound sack of beans. It sat on the porch of the chief's house, and everyone went and scooped out all the beans he wanted. Six months had passed, and the sack still wasn't empty. Mandragon had added five zeros to the bank balance of a widow in Bastidas, and when the honest woman pointed out the change, said it must be an error, the manager assured her that the funds had been duly transferred from Lebanon and were on hand in her name. Others had been millionaired in the same manner. Mandragon had tapped the Manducos' secret hoards and redistributed their thievings to those who'd suffered most under their rule. And more tales in this vein, so when Mandragon emerged from his Otán isolation (and from his three hothouse weeks with Angela in the palace), prime minister of the nation, head of the government, with the paradise blueprint of the new Tinieblas—the whole land to be suddenly greasy with unworked-for wealth—the people ascribed the coming blessings to him and abandoned whatever they were doing and flocked to pay their benefactor homage.

Down from the jungled hills, up from the *llanos*. On foot, in buses, horseback, muleback, burroback. To every town along Mandragon's route. In Córdoba, La Merced, and Belém people slept in the streets because the houses and patios couldn't contain the flood. On the night before Mandragon arrived in Puerto Ospino the *alameda* there was carpeted with sleeping pilgrims so that one might have walked from one end to the other without stepping on ground, and in Angostura, where it downpoured, the

Guardia commander had to open his jail in response to public outcry so that some of the little children could sleep in the cells. The population of Bastidas quintupled. All the adjacent hinterland emptied out. Indians, peasants, peons; cane-choppers, copra-choppers, banana-choppers; ancients, adults, toddlers, infants in arms.

More remarkable even than the crowds was the spirit that attended Mandragon's progress, that traveled two or three days ahead of him and hit whatever spot he meant to reach next. All business stopped and everybody feasted. Townspeople feasted each other and invited in the pilgrims from the countryside. Huge quantities of foodstuffs were prepared, much more than could be consumed despite the influx. Every house had a permanent feast in progress, and almost-full platters were dumped and the food thrown out so that new servings could be heaped upon them. People gave away personal possessions, pressed heirlooms on casual acquaintances and strangers. Merchants gave away their trade stocks, cantinas served free drink, ranchers butchered their herds and held mass barbeques. Why not? Everyone was soon going to be rich. Everyone tried to get rid of as much as he could on the unconscious conviction that the more he got rid of now the richer he'd be. As quickly as possible. The sooner everything was gotten rid of, the sooner the new Tinieblas would arrive.

Besides food and drink, love also was in abundance. Sexual restraints dissolved in a way not seen even during carnival, and suddenly every man had plenty of women, every woman had plenty of men. People made love at whim with whoever they felt like—out in the open if that was where the urge struck them; under the table while other people ate No man begrudged another his wife or his daughter. Nc woman felt the slightest twinge of jealousy if one of her gossips pleasured her husband or her son. It was as if everyone had decided that the more love was made the sooner the new Tinieblas would be born.

Yet along with this exuberance went austerity. When

people weren't feasting, they fasted. When they weren't making love, they put on sackcloth. Smeared their brows with ashes, raked their fingernails across their cheeks. To mortify the flesh and cleanse the spirit. To make themselves worthy to behold the new Tinieblas. Wherever Mandragon stopped, the throngs that greeted him displayed this strange blend of penitence and rejoicing, and without any prompting, from one frontier of the republic to the other, people took up a new reckoning of time, counting this as the Year One and beginning the calendar with the day of Mandragon's nationwide address, with the revelation of the new Tinieblas.

Mandragon went by car (in the huge, open-topped, Hochgesäss Kaiserwagen despotmobile that General Manduco had ordered and then never ridden in for fear of being snipered), with swarms of Guardia cyclists fore and aft but at the slowest snail-crawl they could manage without tipping over. At every town, however small, he stopped and got down, glutting on the people's adulation. He mingled with the homagers, let them cheer him; let them hold babies up to see him, and reach in to touch his garments, and kneel down to slobber kisses on his bare feet. At Mandragon's approach people dropped in spontaneous seizure and began prophesying the new Tinieblas, each according to his personal vision but always along the theme of unworked-for wealth. Some fell to the ground at the sound of his escort's sirens and lay as though dead, without pulse or movement, while strange voices spoke from their open, immobile lips. Of silken hammocks on ivory verandas. Of bejeweled wondercars juggernauting down golden freeways. Children shrieked about ice-cream glaciers. Indians who scarcely knew Spanish articulated words that they themselves didn't understand. Mandragon's presence brought mass hysteria.

Which, in turn, drugged him to illuminate ecstasies. He built mirages of the new Tinieblas on the horizon: mile-high pink marble skyscrapers with silver domes; golden freeways flashed with jeweled wondercars. He projected full-color visions across the sky. And these acts intensified the frenzy vortexed about him.

Sometimes, though, the throng would abruptly fall silent, would draw back from Mandragon in deferential awe. Mandragon would proceed then at stately paces, head high, face somber and severe. Pace by pace down the gap that opened before him, the sky grown suddenly dark and crackled with lightning. Through the death-silent town, back to his car. And then drive slowly off. The mournful wail of his escort floated behind him. All his progress round Tinieblas was touched with this strange blend of wild license and solemn dignity.

In this way the Tinieblan people received Mandragon, and hailed him as their savior, and paid him homage. And Mandragon glutted on it and stayed hollow. But in every part of the country there were minorities (always small, sometimes three people in a whole town) who didn't accept the dream of the new Tinieblas, who didn't believe. For the most part these people stayed home and kept their mouths shut, but believers nonetheless grew aware of them, noticed they didn't feast or make love in public, or give away their prize possessions, or share their wives. Believers missed these people at the orgies of praise and deference that greeted Mandragon—or, rather, later on they thought of Doña Fulana and old Mengano and realized they hadn't been there. Then they'd go and smoke the heretics out. A certain number didn't have to be questioned but went around telling folks they were crazy. The whole thing was an idiot delusion. Nobody gets anything for nothing. The world just doesn't work that way. The first reaction was almost always amazement: What was wrong with Mengano, why couldn't he see? But this gave way very quickly to anger and hatred, as if the coming of the new Tinieblas (on which believers would serenely stake their lives) was somehow threatened, might even be ruined, if someone doubted. So that unbelievers were insulted and abused.

Some were beaten up, some were driven out. Some were murdered. And those who weren't injured were sneered at and lorded over and terrorized.

A person here and there, sometimes a family. Sometimes a tough old matriarch and all her kin. Sometimes a priest and a fragment of his congregation—though most of the priests were quick to accept Mandragon and find ways to square Scripture's revelation with his. (With the revelation he was peddling to the country. He didn't believe it—except during brief terms of illuminate ecstasy, when his worshipers' hysteria got to him. He knew that all the squeezings would go to Angela, that no one was going to be a prince or a queen.) The only large concentration of unbelievers was Mandragon's tribe. Not that they'd renounced him: much the reverse. They doubted the coming of the new Tinieblas because they clung to Mandragon's original prophecies.

Mandragon stayed two nights in Ciudad Otán, the provincial capital. While he was there, the chief of the military district, Major Bartolomeo Chuzo, asked an audience and spoke to him about his tribe.

"About your people, *señor Primer Ministro*. We're doing our best to protect them, but it's not easy. A few of them got roughed up the other night."

"What people?"

"Your people, Your Worship. The ones you brought in last year."

"Major, I don't know what you're talking about."

"Your bunch of kids, *señor Primer Ministro*. In the pasture over by the Remedios line. They say there's not going to be any new Tinieblas, and that makes folks angry. We're doing our best, but some of your people got hurt."

"My people are the people of Tinieblas. I have no others, Major."

"Do you mean, *señor Primer Ministro*, that you've given up that bunch?"

"Major, I still don't know who you're talking about."

"Very good, sir! I understand, sir! I read Your Worship's meaning loud and clear! And if Your Worship will pardon me a private opinion, I think you've done the patriotic thing. I take it, then, sir, that Your Worship does not wish us to make any special effort on that bunch's behalf."

"You serve the Tinieblan state and people, Major. All are equal here before the law. No one has any right to special treatment, certainly not those who doubt this country's future."

"*Sí, señor! Entendido!*"

Major Chuzo saluted and withdrew. Mandragon's tribe was scattered on the wind. Their error was in keeping faith. Mandragon had fogotten all about them.

Mandragon drew his progress out four weeks. He inched around the country, pushing mass hysteria before him. He glutted on the people's adulation. He approved their rage of penitence and license, let it infect him, intensified it by his acts. The new Tinieblas was coming, was on its way. The frenzy spread before him from province to province, until only the capital remained calm. People there heard reports from the interior and wondered at them, but went about their ordinary business in a mood of slightly puzzled optimism. They too knew that the new Tinieblas was coming, but the fever of it hadn't struck them yet.

The government idled along. The Guardia commandants shared their terror with their subordinates, passed as much of it as they could along to them, so that all the plots and intrigues ceased immediately. For the rest, they kept order in the normal fashion. At the ministries officials continued standing policy and put off consideration of new matters until the head of government's return, chastened by the example of their former chiefs to curb their ambitions and tend to official business. As for the deputies, they had voted a recess, had returned to their districts, were feasting and fasting along with everyone else.

At El Opulento the undead corpse of Dred Mandeville

tottered among the flickering data screens, spoke by phone, sent messages by telex, ran his empire. And responded readily to Angela's squeezes. Issued stock options to her, transferred funds, and (for the big wads, for the super-swindles) set up huge Tinieblan investment trusts with the president of the republic as their executor. So that his satraps didn't get suspicious but admired and respected him all the more. The old creep was clearly in charge down there in Spickburg, getting himself naturalized overnight and now evidently swinging all sorts of sweet deals in cahoots with the president. And picking up lots of PR bennies too by developing an underdeveloped nation. That's what you call it these days when you take advantage of cheap boogie labor. Getting some decent press for once in his life. Mandeville money flooded into Tinieblan banks. And drained out just as fast, went sluicing through, on its way to Angela's secret accounts, but she said it was going to purchase heavy industry and would soon flow back in the form of a steel mill from Japan, a Canadian shipyard, an oil refinery from Texas. An entire automobile plant was coming from Germany—to use the steel from the Japanese mill, of course. In sixty-seven oceangoing freighters. Machinery was being loaded in Hamburg right now. Angela squeezed pelf from her pet zombie, and waited expectantly for Mandragon's return.

Mandragon spiraled back to Ciudad Tinieblas, came snail-crawling down from Bastidas hamlet by hamlet, across swampy lowlands, over the cordillera. Pushing frenzy ahead of him. Three days before his return it hit the capital. Pilgrims streamed in from all the surrounding countryside, and the engorged city gave itself up to revelry, to mass paroxysms of generosity, consumption, and waste, to indiscriminate frigging, firking, and futtering. And also to fasting and other mortifications. Bands of sackclothed flagellants roamed the streets, stumbled about among the coupled futterers, flailed themselves with brambles, raked their cheeks. The population (swollen now to nearly a million) swung back and forth to extremes of joy and contrition, caroming temporarily to hatred whenever an unbeliever was exposed.

At Mandragon's approach the mania passed all bounds. Thousands fell in fits of prophesying. Feasts flowed from house to house about the barrios. The squares were packed with dancing, singing mobs, with lovemakers, with penitents in chains and crowns of bramble. Alfonso Sancudo, a confirmed hedonist all his life, stripped himself to a loincloth and gashed his thighs and crawled the length of Via Venezuela, dragging a heavy oaken cross behind him. Don Hunfredo Ladilla, a notable skinflint, filled a gunnysack with rose-red hundred-inchado bank notes and took it up on the roof of the Hotel Excelsior and strewed cash on the revelers in Plaza Bolívar, all the while grinning blissfully, shouting *"Viva el nuevo Tinieblas!"* An unbeliever was torn apart in the streets of La Cuenca. Raging women seized him and fell upon him, pulled him limb from limb, then beaked up morsels of his flesh and chewed them. And when Mandragon entered the city, he was at once infected. A crimson aura burned about him. He levitated himself above the throngs and marched in air at an altitude of several meters, down Avenida Washington, into Plaza Bolívar, on to Plaza Cervantes and Parque Mocoso, whipping his homagers to new ecstasies with this performance and pausing every few blocks to cast mirage visions of the new Tinieblas across the sky, at which all fell to their knees and cried out in wonder. In this fashion he proceeded to the palace.

(Mandragon will take that route again in a few minutes, on solid pavement this time, trotting tethered to a truck.)

Then Mandragon came out on the balcony with Doña Angela and appointed his cabinet. In his gyre round the country he had collected a number of personal retainers, especially fervent believers who had tagged on behind him at one stop or another and whom he suffered to follow and attend him. Mandragon chose his cabinet from among these. A druggist from Belém named Anselmo Tostado, whose duty it was to carry Mandragon's toothbrush and bring it to him each morning and each night, became minister of justice. Doña Alma de Gorgojo, one of the richest women in Remedios Province, had followed Mandragon when he left Angostura and since then had prepared his coffee. Mandragon named her minister of foreign relations. A cane-cutter's daughter, Prudencia Zorrilla, whose office had been to fluff Mandragon's pillow, was appointed minister of public works. And so forth, while the multitude hurrahed, until all the ministries had been distributed. Then Mandragon uttered a new revelation, that within three years Tinieblas would be rich enough to expand and bring its blessings to less favored peoples. He declared the coming of the Tinieblan Empire and began distributing kingdoms.

Ticamala and Costaguana would be incorporated first. Mandragon appointed kings to rule them. Their reigns would begin at the appropriate moment, but they might use their titles at once. In recognition of Alfonso Sancudo's unprecedented fervor of belief, Mandragon named him King of Mexico, with New Mexico tossed into his realm by way of a bonus. He named a Tuquetá Indian woman who'd cooked for him during his tour Queen of California. He created a King of New Orleans and a King of New York. And so on, until some forty dependencies of the Tinieblan Empire-to-be had been disposed of, the mob in each case cheering Mandragon's choice. Then he urged them to keep on displaying their faith in the future (as if urging were necessary!) and declared a national fiesta (as if it needed declaring, as if it weren't already zinging along!) and withdrew into the palace with Doña Angela.

To tour the provinces of her mind and body, swilling up deference all along the way. Angela received him and paid homage. Fugled and bugled, that is, to an accompaniment of transformations.

Mandragon changed into a leopard, and Angela changed

to a gazelle—timid flesh for clawing, pawing, and mawing. Then he changed himself to an otter, she to a trout. He turned into a falcon, she into a dove. Then Mandragon became a sacred ibex, preening and strutting, and Angela became its attendant priestess, adored it and worshiped it, soothed its plumage with soft fingers, laved its person clean with respectful tongue. He became a rare egret, she its custodian. He became a performing duck and she the audience that applauded its antic flappings.

Angela changed herself into a rose (isn't this review charming?), and Mandragon became a slug and trailed slime across it. She made herself into a wheat field and he into a cloud of despoiling locusts. She changed into a garden; he changed into a hog and rooted it up. Angela changed herself into a rich carpet and spread herself before him. Mandragon became an army of filthy boots. She turned into a pool of clear water. He turned into a scaly caiman and slithered in and thrashed it foul and muddy.

All this by way of enhancing their plucking and shucking, she savoring love, he gobbling up deference. Mandragon became an ax; Angela became a flowering medlar. He turned himself into an iron plow (this lovely parade of changes could go on all day, but soon the door will open, the guards will come), she changed herself at once to a yielding plain. Mandragon became a spit, and Angela a shoat and impaled herself on it. He became a dagger, she turned into a wound. He changed himself to fire, she became kindling. He changed himself into an ocean breaker, and she turned into an unprotected shore. Mandragon transformed himself into a cyclone; Angela became a supple, bending palm.

In every part of the palace, in every style and posture of connection that confirmed his mastery and her deference. Mandragon despoted, Angela serfed. Happily too, though she wouldn't admit it these days. Couldn't debase herself enough, since that was what administered him delight. He gorged and still stayed hollow.

For two weeks, their appetites kept fresh by their transformations, while all around them the country raged and
reveled. All government business had stopped, but Mandragon held court for an hour or two each morning, repaired to his mirrored lair and received homagers while the
ministers and commandants waited on him. Angela used the
time for squeezing Zombito, called him up and had him stuff
funds in her secret accounts, since there was no way to set
up new investment trusts, not with all the banks and courts
and law offices closed, not with all the clerks out feasting
or doing penance. Each afternoon she accompanied Mandragon on an hour or two's perambulation through the city
—she and his train of personal attendants, the cabinet and
commandants, the kings of this realm or that. He walked
among the people, sopped up their deference, witnessed new
proofs of belief, appointed grand dukes and crown princes,
whipped the frenzy on with visions in the sky and other displays. After a time he decided walking was beneath him,
even strutting along in the air at an altitude of several meters. He had a pair of portable thrones constructed—arm-
chairs from the state dining room with horizontal poles
clamped to their legs. He and Angela were carried through
town on these. By ministers and kings and princes regent.
They vied for the honor of being bearers, and the commandants marched alongside in their dress uniforms, and whenever the procession stopped, presented themselves. Colonel
Guadaña bent his back and braced his hands on his knees,
and Colonel Empulgueras got down on all fours, and Colonel Acha lay prostrate, and Mandragon used them as steps
for his descent.

Until one day at the end of the sixth week of his regime
when his procession met another. The Guardia Civil had
captured five foreign girls wandering in Otán without proper
papers and brought them to the capital for deportation, and
when the truck they rode in reached the outskirts, someone
recognized them as members of an unbeliever band. A mob
surrounded the truck and convoyed it on toward Bondadosa

Prison, jeering and howling insults, tossing fruit and refuse, while the girls cowered behind the wire screening like beasts in a cage. The two processions met at an intersection in La Cuenca.

Mandragon got down from his throne, stepping on the backs of the three commandants, and went to inspect the captives. As soon as they saw him, they began laughing and weeping and crying out for joy and lamenting, pleading with him in English and saying they loved him, while Mandragon stood blinking in amazement. Then one of them, a lovely girl (though her honey-blond hair was all rumpled, though her blue eyes were all puffed and inflamed from weeping), quieted the others and began to dance. She danced bent over in the rear of the patrol truck, moving slowly, miming birds and insects, humming and squeaking. A look of horror passed Mandragon's face.

Mandragon backed slowly away from the truck. Then he turned and set off on foot back to the palace, first at an ordinary pace, then faster and faster, till he ran in a frantic, panicky stampede, and his hands shook, and his teeth chattered, and his knees trembled, while Doña Angela and his train tried to keep up, and all the citizens gaped and babbled in wonder. He screamed for his attendants to leave him alone and shut himself up in the palace with Doña Angela.

A week later Mandragon fell. Happy hatred howled from border to border.

37

Grey dawn at the window, boots in the courtyard below. They'll come for me soon. To give me a mechanized strangling, but no matter. Almost done recalling and reclaiming, a process begun on a street a few blocks from here.

Full Moons had reminded me who I was.

Too hideous to bear, I'd betrayed everything. For three days I lay on the polished floor of the ballroom, my mind a static buzz. When I rose to consciousness again, I was empty: the power that had lived in me was gone. Mixed anguish and relief: worthless and abandoned, but free of all responsibility.

Angela's anguish unmixed; fun to recall it. Her glorious lover out of commission in coma (she had doctors discreetly in, but they couldn't help). Her prime minister out of action with the country in chaos (she issued statements in my name, but they went unheeded). And her zombie was out of business permanently. Dred's undead corpse collapsed the moment that I did, dropped like a felled pine among the TV sets and began stinking so powerfully the security guards straightway broke in the door. Dry bones and putrid flesh was all that was left of him. His passing filled poor Angela with grief. She'd given him a perfectly marvelous squeezing, but she grieved over all the pelf she'd failed to wring out. While worrying about being able to enjoy what she had with her lover/protector/prime minister out of service.

How relieved she was when I returned to consciousness! Laughed and wept for joy, soaked me in caresses. That passed soon enough. I cared nothing for her, hated her in fact—or, rather, I showed her some of the hatred I felt for myself, blamed her for bewitching me, though of course I'd done it all myself. And she realized almost at once that my power had left me. No use to her anymore, but a memory of love may have remained with her. Or she may have thought my power might return. In any case, she didn't send for the colonels. She simply left me. In a few days I swung back to neuter, parts substandard, facial hair gone, just as before. She stayed in her suite of rooms, I moped about the lower floors of the palace, both of us waiting to see what would happen.

The moment I collapsed, everyone in the country stopped believing in the new Tinieblas and the Tinieblan Empire-to-be. No one admitted it for some time, however, not even to himself, much less to others. The gulling people had taken was just too painful. Two or three days went by, for instance, before Alfonso Sancudo burned the plumed-serpent visiting cards he'd had made up with the legend "ALFONSO I, REY DE LOS MÉJICOS," while another day or so passed before he told his cook to stop calling him *Majestad*. But the feasting and fasting piddled out in short order. People stayed home, then began straggling back to work.

The victim-vision I'd keyed into the colonels' cortices faded the instant I started my own panicky stampede, but it took them a full week to get over their terror. One morning, at their regular meeting in the *comandancia*, all three of them realized at once that they were their old selves again. No twinge of guilt would ever again afflict them. All three at once proposed overthrowing me.

It took them three hours to collect sufficient troops—the Wild Alligators, the Mountain Tapirs, all their assassins. Not to intimidate the populace: no more welcome military coup has ever been celebrated on this continent. Out of sincere respect for Mandragon's powers, but I went docilely as a lambkin. My powers had left me.

Returning now, recalled, reclaimed, no matter. I'll go docilely this morning too. Best be out of it. No more welcome execution will ever . . .

Here they are.

38

Fumbling at the lock, the door swings open. Officer, two guards, more out in the corridor. Best meet them standing.

But can't! Anguished agitation, limbs gone weak! Eyes unfocusing, head lolling! Not fear, felt this before, a cruel ravishment! Seized and flung, snatched from my body, whirling . . .

A grandstand filled with well-dressed men and women. Line of assault troops with their rifles trained. Angela and the colonels on the palace balcony. Cordon of presidential guards in dress uniform. Parque Mocoso, Mandragon's execution.

Two privates have marched me up to the big tree. Have turned me round, they stand gripping my biceps. My shoulders are trembling. The major marches up, he steps behind me. Drops the loop on my shoulders, pulls it snug. Cablenibble.

Mandragon stands head bowed, blinking quickly. Lick my lips, rub them together, very afraid. Of cablebite painhorror. Choke-anguish agon-jounce . . .

Strange! Fear draining from me, gone! Power, peace, and order flooding to me! Singing in me, filling me again!

Mandragon looks up, bares teeth, stares toward the balcony. The major is saluting. Angela holds her fan out at arm's length. She flicks it up.

Slow roll of drums. The crowd goes still, Mandragon's

girls start keening. Angela draws her fan back, opens it at her breast. Angela smiles faintly at Mandragon.

The major drops his salute and shouts a command. The starter whines, the motor catches and revs. The privates release Mandragon and step back. Gears grate, the motor races, the winch turns. Mandragon rises.

But rises independently of the noose! Cable slack above it, no strain on the winch! Body motionless, head lifted, face serene! Mandragon rises like an acrobat filmed in slow motion, soars as if from a springboard or trampoline. Rises majestically, until the noose is just below the pulley.

The Jeep engine coughs and stalls: Mandragon has stopped it. Mandragon stands in air. A pale-green aura floats about Mandragon.

Moans and shouts in the grandstand, along the seawall. The keening turns to high-pitched wails of joy. Angela snaps her fan closed, flicks it frantically. The major bellows, the starter whines and whines. Mandragon stands in air, features serene. Throat in the noose, the cable slack above it. The drum roll wavers, stops. The crowd falls silent.

Mandragon lifts knees and calves, raises and tucks them. Swings manacled hands under butt and tucked-in toes. Brings hands forward, holds them toward the balcony. Lets legs extend.

Mandragon stands in air, opens outstretched hands. The chain that joins the handcuffs shivers. Every link breaks at once and falls to the ground. Mandragon spreads arms wide, holds them outspread. The handcuffs split apart and fall to the ground. Moans of fear and wonder from the on-lookers.

Mandragon bunches fingers, flings them open. The padlock on the wire-mesh door of the police wagon breaks and falls. The door swings open. Mandragon draws palms inward. The girls get down from the police wagon. They walk in single file toward the great tree, weeping faces radiant and uplifted. They kneel in pentagram beneath

Mandragon, faces lifted, hands clasped at their breasts.

Mandragon is smiling. Mandragon speaks:

"Beloved, the universe is not an adversary. It is not an enemy to be subdued or destroyed. It is a rhythm to accept and dance to."

Mandragon is dancing. Mandragon dances in air, eyes closed, face smiling—a dance immensely solemn, immensely gay. Floats dancing, left and right, backward and forward. Above, the cable dances with Mandragon. The onlookers moan and sway to Mandragon's rhythm.

Shout of command from the balcony. The major salutes and shouts commands. The assault troops at the grandstand come to attention. They turn about and trot into the park, weapons at high port. They halt below Mandragon ten or twelve yards off. They form two ranks of eight facing Mandragon. They stare fixedly ahead at the big tree. Their bodies pulse out tension and ferocity, like dogs on leash, like snakes about to strike.

Mandragon opens eyes, smiles down at the soldiers, a smile immensely tender, loving, gay. Dances on, spreads arms as to embrace them.

The major shouts: "PREPARENSE!"

The soldiers in the second rank take half a step to the right so that each stands behind a gap in the first rank.

Mandragon is singing. In an unknown language somehow full of meaning. Mandragon's dance and song say this:

"Beloved, the end will begin here in Tinieblas, at the periphery of the soon-to-fragment world. All of you will perish, I have heard you howling. Earth will be cleansed."

"APUNTEN!"

The soldiers raise their rifles to their shoulders, slapping the stocks with their palms as they bring them up. They aim at Mandragon.

"Embrace it lovingly, beloved. The end is always also a beginning."

"A FUEGO AUTOMÁTICO . . ."

The soldiers thumb the small levers beside the receivers and push them forward.

"Earth will be renewed."

"FUEGO!"

Barrel flashes, thunder roll of fire. Spent cartridges fly up from shuddering weapons. Mandragon's arms embrace the ascending hail.

Reverberate thunder from the palace and Alcaldía. The park is silent. The screams and keening, cries and moans. Mandragon's body, chewed apart by gunfire, hangs by a thread of flesh from the woundless head. Blood bursts forth, soaks the tatters of shirt and trousers. The thread of flesh gives way, the body falls. Mandragon's head remains, swings back and forth, gripped beneath the chin by the noosed cable. The head continues singing, it smiles as before.

No one moves. The soldiers with their rifles raised and pointed. The major, braced at attention, chin lifted, fists clenched. The two privates, flinched forward with their hands over their ears, flanking the bullet-chewed, blood-sopping body. The girls, kneeling in pentagram about it, their weeping faces raised toward the singing head. The spectators on the seawall and in the grandstand. The cameraman on the roof of the panel truck. Angela, half-risen from her chair, her hands braced on the parapet of the balcony. Colonel Guadaña beside her, Colonels Acha and Empulgueras standing behind. While the sun lifts from behind the palace, stripping the palace shadow from the park.

The old tree flowers into leaf, branch by branch to the branch Mandragon's head swings from. Then the earth begins to heave and shudder.

The palace shakes so that the tricolor above it flaps and billows in the breezeless air. The facade collapses inward, pitching the balcony and its occupants backward under a cascade of rubble. The Alcaldía topples toward the grand-

stand. The seawall cracks and crumbles to loose stone. People are howling.

The earth beneath Tinieblas heaves and shudders. Great fissures open, new hills are thrust up, graves and monuments tumble in ruin. The sea draws back from the shore, the bay drains empty. Vast expanse of mud, flotsamed with gasping fish, with careeened shrimp boats.

The top of Dewey Hill begins to rise. A section forty yards high, a quarter-mile in diameter, separates from the base and lifts away, then smithers to dust in a thunderous explosion. The sides of the hill split outward, streaming lava. Flaming cinders spew across the sky.

The sea returns. A wall of ocean walking in across the mud flats. Rolls up over the land to meet the lava. Great seething hiss. Billowing clouds of steam.

The ocean recedes, flows back, carrying smashed bodies and smashed objects with it. The earth is still. The bay is calm. The ruins of Tinieblas lie under a cloud of ashes. Here and there people trudge about bewildered.

Mandragon's head is floating on the water. Floats out to sea. Mandragon's head sings in an unknown language. Mandragon's face is smiling, a smile immensely tender, loving, gay.

January, 1975–September, 1978

R. M. KOSTER, originally from Brooklyn, New York, has lived in Panama since the early 1960s. His academic appointments have included ones at the Universidad Nacional de Panama, Instituto Mexicano-Norteamericano, and Florida State University—Panama Canal Branch. A writer of fiction and essays, he has been published in the *New Republic, Harper's, Quest,* and *Connoisseur,* among others. He is a very active member of the Democratic Party and is on the Democratic National Committee.